MW01089316

Through the Years and Far Away

Through the Years and Far Away

by Qi Jinnian

translated by Moying Li

Jorge Pinto Books Inc.
New York

Contents

Chapter I

At moments when life was hanging by a thread, I knew all I could return for the thousand natural shocks was but toleration and love.

Love is a tragedy that can only be parsed with death.

You are a truly joyous lady. Your grail shall not remain empty for my sake.

Jian Zhen, "Rending Silk in April"

1

The winter—in her memory—was the time when the only attire of the land was snow. On the boundless frozen horizon, the scattered black tents on the snowy highland gave shelter for herdsmen and animals. Inside the tents the remnants of flames glimmered in the dark. Butter tea was boiled on the fire, giving off a rich aroma, the plainest temptation and consolation of food. Outside it was deadly cold; the black tents were buried so deep in the snow that the felt flaps could not even be pulled open.

Kazan. Grandpa lay on the blanket, calling her name gently.

In her childhood, she could see snow in all seasons. Even in June, a cold snap would sweep the land with the gale, scattering thin snowflakes everywhere. During the cold winter, the whole world would don silver apparel after every heavy snow. The storms and blizzards that raged in the dark reminded one of the glacier period in the primeval times. The frozen earth on the grassland became frigid soon, and icy steam rose from beneath the clefts.

Within seconds in a heavy snow, the gale began to wreak havoc on the land and the temperature dropped abruptly. Shepherds had to drive their sheep home in deep worry. They were virtually helpless with the bleating lambs, which huddled closely together with their eyes shut, trembling at the mercy of the whistling gale. Like a drop of mercury that flowed sluggishly on the flat ground, the lambs twisted and turned in the gale and would hardly move a step forward despite the whips of the anxious, desperate shepherds and the fierce barking of the mastiffs.

Countless lambs would die on the way in such nights. Some were frozen even before they fell to the ground. Their bodies would be buried shortly in the snow, which would sink farther into the frozen earth of the marshland in the next summer. After the herdsmen drove the sheep all the way to the pen behind the tents, they counted the sheep and sadly found that nearly ten lambs were lost to the storm. Their helpless sighs were quickly blown away in the whistling wind. The herdsmen patted the mastiffs on the head. The dogs had snow all over their bodies after chasing the sheep in the storm for almost a whole day. The masters took them into the tent and fed them.

This is the memory about the blizzards shared by most of the herdsmen.

In the winter when she was eight, there was another blizzard. A young, tough shepherd counted the lambs after he returned and found over twenty were missing. He could not rest with the loss, so he took two mastiffs the next morning and dashed into the snow with clenched teeth in the search of the lost lambs. He made up his mind to bring their bodies back even if they were all dead.

There were still drifting snowflakes in the day after a whole night's storm. The shepherd walked farther and farther until he reached a slope and found a black spot on the celestial burial platform. On closer look, the spot turned out to be the body of a vulture. On the platform where generations of the tribe held celestial burials, the creature spread its big wings and its black feathers shivered in the biting wind like prayer banners. The shepherd panicked. A legend had been passed in the tribe for generations, that vultures would never leave their bodies on the ground. Ancestors believed that dying vultures would leave their fellows and fly high into the sun until they melted in the sunlight. Nobody had ever seen the body of a vulture. The legend went that the bodies of vultures were devoured by the light of the sun, as human bodies were devoured by the vultures; "this is why our ancestors regarded vultures as incarnations of *bhiksu*. They are living proofs of the six reincarnations," said Grandpa once to Kazan.

Now in that ominous winter, however, a dead vulture lay on the celestial burial platform. Fear-struck, the shepherd hurried back at once and came all the way to find Kazan's grandpa. Hearing his loud, fearful cry from outside the tent, Grandpa pulled the felt flaps open, which were long frozen in the icy weather. Wind and snow poured into the tent instantly, drowning the dim flames on which butter tea was boiled. Kazan did not hear clearly what the young man said, but Grandpa snatched the leather hat hanging beside the felt flaps immediately, put it on, and turned around to take her hand. Kazan, Kazan, come over. Grandpa called her gently.

When Kazan was taken out of the tent by Grandpa, she was so dazzled by the bright snow that she had to shut her eyes in pain and felt dizzy. She could hardly move a step, as she was too short and her knees were buried deep in the snow. Unable to drag her forward, Grandpa carried her on his back and strode ahead. Lying on Grandpa's back, Kazan saw the plain, white land and the snowflakes all around. The snow-clad highland was quiet and solid as the reticent herdsmen and silently sprawled to the boundless horizon. The freezing gale afflicted Kazan's face. She did not cry out in pain, but lowered her head and nestled her face against

Grandpa's back. Grandpa's cassock had a strong smell of cypress and juniper incense.

When Grandpa put her down, she saw a vulture's body crouching frozen on the celestial burial platform. It was as dead as all the bodies of the past generations that were placed on the platform. People surrounded the body horrified and turned the prayer wheels and hummed prayers in the storm. Kazan saw the thick snow piled on their hair and all over their bodies. These people had been kneeling there, trembling with cold and anxiety. They had identified the dead vulture as the head of the celestial flock.

They continued praying until it was dark. The fine snow finally came to a halt after an entire day. The people began to leave, but none of them dared to budge the vulture's body. Kazan thought she could no longer feel her body. Having stood still for so long, she was stuck in the snow, first by the knees and gradually up to the legs. To her surprise, the body of the vulture was not buried in the snow. The snowflakes that fell on the black features were blown off by the wind.

It was not until dark that Grandpa said gently, Kazan, Kazan, let's go back.

When she and Grandpa went back to the black tent, the grassland was enveloped in deep night. The starless firmament was as solid and fathomless as Grandpa's dark red cassock. It was a rare clear night though. The bright moon lit up the expanses of the silvery landscape. Everything was immersed in white stillness, like the memory that always hung on Grandpa's trembling lips but never gave way.

Kazan groped in the black tent to light the oil lamp. She saw Grandpa sitting silently on the bed like a Buddha. An idea came to her suddenly. She got up and led Jinmei, their mastiff, from the sheep pen into the tent. Jinmei entered, bow-wowed in a low voice and lay on its stomach beside Grandpa. Kazan stroked its long hair and patted off the thick snow on it. The animal lay there at rest, its eyes half closed.

When she passed the re-boiled butter tea to Grandpa, she saw muddy tears rolling from Grandpa's eye sockets along his bulging cheekbones. She said nothing, but gently held Grandpa's hand with her hand. Jinmei rubbed its back against Grandpa's legs understandingly. Grandpa's lips trembled again, but again no words escaped him.

She saw the little changes on Grandpa's face and missed her mom and dad.

That night was extremely cold. She fell asleep while huddling with Jinmei's tough, warm body. At a moment, she was woken up by Jinmei's slight stir and mumbling bow-wows. Kazan opened her dreamy eyes and saw Grandpa had made a torch and was about to leave. What are you doing, Granpa . . . ? she asked in a trembling voice.

But Grandpa seemed not to have heard her; he took a large leather bag and filled it with suet, stood up, picked up the torch, and was about to set off.

Kazan shut her mouth. She got up at once and stumbled her way in the snow after Grandpa. She looked back at the tent and found that Jinmei had run out and stood outside the pen, barking indistinctly in the distance. She did not know where Grandpa wanted to go; all she could do was quicken her pace to catch up with him all the way.

The moonlit silvery highland was expansive and dreamy. Everything was utterly still in the sea of darkness. No paths. No ends. The cold air weighed on the wilderness thick and frozen as a gigantic block of ice. Kazan heard clearly the crunch of the snow under her feet and her rapid breath. The coldness of the night numbed her feet, hands, face and nose . . . even her lungs were pricked as if stuffed with big slabs of ice. Voiceless and helpless, she followed the man into the depths of the wasteland in unutterable pain and fear. What she went through that night became a taboo in her life. She bore in mind that blindness was more terrifying than death in a trek through the directionless, snow-clad highland.

Grandpa did not turn to look at her until he reached the celestial burial platform. Kazan thought she was numb all over. A large part of the vulture's body was hidden in the thick snow, which made the rest of it look almost like a fledgling. She saw Grandpa draw the torch close to the bag and melt the frozen suet. He unfastened the bag and poured the suet on the vulture. Then he laid the torch down and drew back.

A flame blazed up and rapidly devoured the vulture's body. The huge, black feathers pricked up in the heat. They caught fire instantly as if absorbed by the tip of the flame and curled up and disappeared. Kazan experienced the power of the fire for herself. It struck her with a sense of life's dignity in the endless cold night. The snow kept melting, exposing a small patch of the earth. She was suddenly grabbed in an unquenchable desire; she wanted very much to soar high like a vulture and look over this tiny spark on the snowy, night-cloaked land.

The flame quickly went down and died out. A large patch of black earth was now left over, like a dubious scar on a smooth back. Grandpa said, only fire can exorcise the inauspiciousness and foul spirit here.

No one visited the celestial burial platform after that. The scorched earth was now ashen and gloomy like a corpse. It was an inexplicable spell that was seared on the herdsmen's home.

Grandpa fell ill in bed that night and looked much older and pallid. His bony hands, now wrapped in the gnarled brownish black skin, were always pointing to an unknown direction. No one would come to him to hold celestial burials after that, as it was believed by all that he was somewhat suspicious in the horrible incident . . . Grandpa's career as the celestial burial master came to an end with the life of the head vulture.

Grandpa emaciated day by day in the black tent. He moved about so slowly that he looked like an oil lamp at the point of extinction. Day in and day out he kept mumbling verses from the scriptures as if rendering an obscure oracle. He sank in bed in that cassock blacked with juniper incense, the wrinkles on his face running interlocked as the mountains on the highland.

Kazan dreamt again and again about her blind trek that night in the depths of the moonlit, snow-white highland.

Grandpa had been a celestial burial master for forty years. He used to be a monk in the temple and was taught how to hold celestial burials by the abbot. He later replaced the abbot and stepped onto the platform in that dark reddish cassock, which turned dark black after forty years' fumigation of juniper incense.

After many years of evolution, the doctrines of the Hindu scripture Diamond-Cutter Sutra gave rise to a popular belief: every man has in his flesh several *lunshi*, or rooms for the transmigration of the soul, which are arrayed in the shape of a lotus along the spine all the way upward from the tailbone to the vertex. Once the "petals" are destroyed or the "root" is rent, the lotus will fall apart and lose its life. In other words, when the flesh falls apart and perishes, it is time for the soul that lives in it to fly away and look for a new home.

"So Kazan, bear it in mind;" Grandpa told her after they came back at dusk, "our flesh is but a lotus and will perish in time, but our souls are immortal. Always guard the beauty and goodness in your soul, Kazan. Only in this way can you receive eternal life with the blessing of the Buddha."

That was Grandpa in Kazan's memory. She always remembered the picture in which Grandpa stood between the azure blue sky and the wide celestial burial platform, the cypress and juniper incense curling upwards and the vultures hovering around. This picture had been stamped on her childhood.

All this time Grandpa was murmuring her name in a low voice: Kazan, Kazan . . . his voice was as feeble as the crackling of the burning cattle dung.

Kazan was making *Tsam-pa* without a word. Jinmei, that mastiff of hers, lay silently by her side. It was tall and covered in long, black hair and as tough as a yak. A glimpse at its paws, which were as big as a tough man's fists, would reveal that the dog was a brave, pure-blooded mastiff. Kazan raised her head and scented the approaching winter through the opening of the curtains.

White snow was spread on the soft, boundless undulations of the earth as a huge *hada*. Inside the dark tent, the oven with the boiling butter tea was the only source of light. It brought along a sense of security in the time of scarcity, and constituted the most primitive sense of survival.

Kazan, Kazan. Grandpa was murmuring by himself.
This old man sat squarely on the carpet like a rusted bronze statue. He sensed the approaching steps of death the way a vulture did, and just in the way a dying vulture would draw itself close to the sun, he strived to get on his feet in the desperate wish to walk

out of the black tent and watch the gorgeous golden flag-shaped clouds on the distant snow-capped peaks. But hardly had he stood up when he fell down. He was not able to reach the bright, solemn white world outside at last. His life ended in a silent and profound reverie, together with the black juniper incense on the celestial burial platform, the broken, withered corpses of lotus, and the hovering vultures.

Panic-stricken, Kazan collapsed on the ground and knocked over the butter barrels and buckets by her side. She was unable to move her body. Not a sound was heard in the stillness, except the rattling wind of the wintry wilderness that flapped on the black, yak-skin tent.

A draught tore the felt flaps open suddenly and thrust in a chink of bright snow. Kazan's eyes were sore with pain. By her side lay Grandpa quietly, like a river that had run thousands of miles and gone dry in the end. Jinmei got up, bow-wowed in a low, restless voice, and roved around him.

2

The sky.

The sky was a sacred existence to Kazan and her ancestors. In a land closest to the sky, these people proudly partook of the red birthmarks born in the eternal sun. The purplish color on their faces was the sun's lip prints. They were blessed with the thinnest, cleanest air, the most rampant sunshine, the bluest sky, and the vastest land. Generations of these primitive, noble-blooded creatures set root and blossomed in this place next to the sun.

Our little girl acquired the name of Kazan before she was born. It was given by Grandpa. It meant: yesterday. She was born in this boundless land. Her horizon was always delineated by continuous peaks, and the highland barley on the slopes would bend down in the strong wind. Large herds of cattle and sheep floated about on the grassland like clouds.

Every one or two years, when autumn came, men would drive horses and cattle across mountains to barter goat skin and yaks for highland barley flour and salt. Late in the autumn when Kazan was six, Dad and Mom drove the horses and departed with several young men in the village. Grandpa and Kazan saw them off. She watched the men and the horses walk away until they disappeared one by one over the mountain ridge.

On and on Dad and Mom and the horses walked, Kazan remembered, as if they walked all the way from the mountain ridge into the sun.

The men and the horses made their way amidst the endless mountains. On the back of the nameless desolate mountains, they trekked along with sporadic pilgrims, who measured the highland with a kowtow at every step. The pilgrims kissed the land all the way. By this ritual they paid homage to the rustic, fragrant land and to their sacred faith.

No one had any idea how long this journey would last. Men spent endless days and nights on horseback. They passed countless sacred boulder piles that remained reticent in the sun. The seven-colored wind-horse banners quivered in the wind, stirring the rampant sun beams into varied shades. The journey became intolerably long with the many hardships and dangers. The footsteps of the wayfarers were like gods' hands that gently stroked the elongated lineament of the mountains.

They passed lama temples on the high mountain. The high white walls with the brightly colored Tibetan window paintings cut clear contours in the azure sky. Inside the temples the smell of butter was dense and incense was burnt. Lamas sang Buddhist prayers in a low, solid voice. It was always dim in the long, narrow passages between the high walls. Only a row of pious, purple-faced worshipers were heard silently turning the golden prayer wheels. Each and every worshiper had a black hump on his forehead, which was the badge of glory of true Tibetans for doing ten thousand Tibetan kowtows. Occasionally a young lama would pass by, his palms put together, his head bent, his forehead shining with a golden luster. The dark red robe gradually faded away at the narrow corner, leaving only the prayer wheels turning as gently and evenly as the cycle of life.

Outside the long, narrow temple gates, the rampant sun beams hoisted the azure firmament. They poured down from the top of the lama temples and dazzled the worshipers into tears.

There existed such a species of creatures. They survived on the nutrition of faith. To them flesh was negligible. It was but a lotus flower, a grail that held up the solid, clean soul.

Autumn came to a close and the weather became colder and colder. When a day passed, distant stars splashed on the night curtain and the Galaxy wound its way through the sky. People rested in the lap of the land as hawks in the lap of the cliff. In freezing nights, horses snorted and exhaled smoky steam. When the mountains were lit by the first ray of the sun, the people and the horses set off again.

This was the eternal lure of the journey. In her long life, Kazan had gradually realized why she always had the passion to say goodbye and set off time and again. It was born in her blood, an irrevocable stamp that Mom and Dad had left on her since childhood. Because it was only on the road that life was worthy of respect.

The people trekked through the upper Qinglunzhuo grassland. Looming ahead was Mount Qinglunzhuo, the highest, most dangerous sacred mountain on the way. They climbed over the sacred mountain, entered the lower Qinglunzhuo grassland, and the Salt Village was not far ahead.

Led by the head horse, the cattle and horses trudged along the old path and arrived at the Salt Village after five days.

The people bought food and salt with the yaks and goat skin, but met with the first snow of the autumn. As winter was coming soon, they headed back after a short day's rest in the fear of being deterred by more snows.

The lower Qinglunzhuo grassland was all white after the first snow in the late autumn. Mountains, rivers, and grasslands were all clad in silver. The mottled surface of the grassland was set off by boundless whiteness, which slightly undulated with the land, like the corpse of the land wrapped with a white *pulu* before the celestial burial. Large patches of whiteness undulated in the rampant sun. Mount Qinglunzhuo towered in the distance. The mountain path was hardly discernible in the snow. Journeying through the snow-capped mountain became very slippery and dangerous. People could no longer locate the path to return; they had to depend on their memory and experience to trek ahead.

Clouds were gathering in the sky. People were disheartened. Without divining with stones and salt, they scented snow in the air.

Dad picked out the toughest and bravest old horses as the head and the secondary to lead the way for the team. They set off again in the dim dawn light.

Unsurprisingly, they came across another blizzard at the foot of the mountain. The snow piled up on the way and the sky was obscured by sweeping gales and clouds. All they could see and feel was the piercing wind that hit them in the face with large snowflakes, which made it difficult to even move a step. But these people had no choice but to forge ahead.

The men and animals made their way on the lee of the mountain. Snowflakes flew into their faces in the gale and piled up on the slope at a rapid speed. After a while the snow was as high as people's legs. Fortunately the head and secondary horses trod a narrow, trench-like path with their hooves; without them the people would have been helplessly stuck in the deep snow.

The head horse was cloaked in thick snow, its mane icy frozen. It bent down its head and forged a trail ahead. The secondary horse, the mate of the head, followed it. It trod down the snow on the path so that the following horses could pass.

The blizzard raged on and on. Both the people and the horses were on the verge of collapse. Mom's and Dad's feet and hands had turned purple in coldness, but they dared not stop. As they knew, any pause on the way would result in death. The snow did not stop either; when they finally reached the top of the mountain it was deep night already. On the peak the steam that the men and animals exhaled was quickly turned into ice. The biting gale whistled through as if about to blow them away.

For an unknown reason, the team gradually slowed down. Mom and Dad hurried up, only to find the head and secondary horses kneeling down, gasping in pain. Their heads and necks were covered in snow; the tears from their eyes were frozen like a deep icy lake that shimmered in the night. The dying horses fixed their eyes on their masters. Dad and Mom knew that the head horse was exhausted.

The people dare not stop; they drove the rest of the horses ahead. They passed by the head and secondary horses and reached the top of the mountain. The head horse lay in the snow and saw the rest of the team off. It rested peacefully, knowing that its mission had been accomplished.

Dad surveyed in deep worry the broad upper Qinglunzhuo grassland and the peaks at the end of the grassland from the mountain top. That was the direction of home. He knew they could not afford to delay. They had to abandon the head and secondary horses for the rest of the animals to get down the mountain as soon as possible.

People stood on the top of the mountain, staring at the two crouching horses in the snow. The two horses were raised by Dad and Mom since they were born. They were the children of the wind god and had aquiline speed and beauty. But now they were old. They wore themselves out to forge a trail for the people. Dad took the reins off them with tears in his eyes.

When the reins were finally taken off, the two horses were rimmed with tears. The long threads of water left icy traces on their faces and dripped into the white snow. The head horse snorted feebly, exerted to move its legs, but failed to stand up. It exhaled deeply and gave up at last.

The head horse bent down its head and looked at their masters in deep sorrow and attachment. Hot tears kept rolling down from its eyes to the ground and melted the snow. The wind brushed its body, blowing the thick snow off its mane. Dad and Mom stroked the necks and foreheads of both horses in tears. They were the heroes of the highland. Carrying the highland barley of the village on their backs, they used to lead the caravan to traverse the highland all the way through the upper and lower Qinglunzhuo grasslands and over the snow-capped sacred mountain. They were the totems of the village that gave people hopes of survival. Like the paths they trod in the snow, they led men in innumerable journeys back to home.

Now they were exhausted for the caravan.

Dad and Mom could no longer hold back their sorrow and returned to the caravan in tears. The people trekked full of hope on their way down the mountain, thinking of the script banners of their home in the distance.

The neighs of the head and secondary horses resounded throughout the quiet snow-capped mountain. They must have been looking over the distant landscape at their last gasps and could not reconcile themselves to not being able to return home and end their lives around the masters. Their neighs were so bleak and forlorn that it seemed as if the fine snow were the tears that the sky shed for them.

Dad could no longer bear it. He headed back to the horses alone. Unable to stop him, Mom returned as well. They left the caravan and went back to the top of the mountain. They saw the two horses, now buried in the snow, huddling together in desolation. Dad and Mom put reins on them again and tried to help them stand up. The two horses were so feeble that they could barely open their eyes, not to mention stand up. Tears of gratitude kept flowing from their eyes when they saw the masters return.

Dad and Mom sat down by their side in sorrow and stroked their cold foreheads with frozen hands. The horses gradually closed their eyes peacefully, their eye sockets frozen with tears and their eyelashes coated in frost.

When the dawn came, the horses had long died quietly. The sky and earth were all enveloped in silver stillness, except for the black hawks that hovered about like vultures at celestial burials. Dad and Mom dug a hole in the snow, buried the horses, and went down the mountain. Their faces and limbs were seriously bitten by the frost. The snow covered the path of the caravan and they could no longer catch up. They walked on without food, water or direction; all they had was the visage of home looming beyond the snowy highland.

Dad and Mom had never returned. They slept under the icy azure sky and on the snow-capped mountains.

Everything was quiet as if in a pantomime. No forlorn neighs of the horses, no crunches on the snow. The gigantic slope of the quiet snow-capped mountain bulged in the view. Below it lay the white land, and above was the azure sky and sober sunshine. The stillness, it turned out, was death.

Kazan, your dad and mom returned to the land of your ancestors. There grasslands were like green seas, flowers bloomed in all seasons, ballads flowed like limpid streams, and the sky was as blue as in legends. There men did not bleed for battles, and women did not suffer in childbirth. There the moonlight was not freezing and the land was no longer ravaged by snowstorms.

Kazan, they slept on the road. Said Grandpa to her in a calm voice.

The long journey of life was now open for Kazan to go through alone. She did not feel sad. She knew the capriciousness of fate. Our flesh was but a lotus flower that lived and died by itself.

The nightmarish tragedy ended on the road. As time passed by, the scar it left was gradually faded away. After the death of Mom and Dad, Kazan became more and more silent. She lived with Grandpa. The old man brought home a little newborn mastiff, so that she would not get too lonely.

The little mastiff had grown soft black hair all over its body. Its dark red pupils shone like gems. It cuddled in Kazan's lap like a most tender and innocent baby, mumbling for food and water. It needed to eat much to grow up quickly, so as to guard the sheep in the austere environment. Grandpa told her its mother was the hero of the ranch and bit two leopards once. Born with the pure, noble blood in its veins, the little mastiff would grow up and become a rare, brave dog. Grandpa gave the mastiff the name of Jinmei, meaning "fearless", as the old man believed that it would become a fearless fighter. Kazan liked this name. She held little Jinmei in her lap. The vigorous, high-spirited whelp began to bite Kazan's fingers instinctively, although it was slightly more than an itch with its budding milk teeth. Kazan's life turned a new page with the appearance of the little mastiff. She fed the little animal patiently and followed its growth closely. Its rapid growth testified Grandpa's judgment. At the age of four months, Jinmei was already far tougher and taller than any of its peers. Its hair was long and purely black, not mingled with any other color. When it ran at the speed of the wind, its hair would flow upward and undulate like waves with a metallic luster. Its eyes shone brightly like two drops of red lava, which reflected cleverness and loyalty.

Women on the grassland did not go out often. It was men's job to farm and ride horses. So Kazan usually left Jinmei in the care of the cattle, and stayed in the black tent awaiting Grandpa's return, making Tsam-pa and blood sausage, burning dairy manure, and boiling butter tea. When there was no celestial burial, Kazan would stay up by the side of Grandpa in nightlong prayers.

The black tent where she lived was sewn with the skin of the yaks on their ranch. In the Tibetan area, black tents were most common abodes for herdsmen. Dad and Mom had lived there when they were young. There was no painted lacquer ware with gold drawings or gilded closets in the poverty-ridden home. All the family's belongings were packed in several big sheepskin sacks and placed in a circle around the tent, which could hold out in the storms and was convenient on the move. There were a couple of old carpets at the center of the tent, their complex, exquisite patterns worn out in the passage of time.

Kazan felt an incomparable sense of security in the black tent. Since her parents' death, she had been more and more reluctant to go out. When she peeped at the bright world through the opening of the curtains, when she glimpsed at the white, thick clouds that fell heavily on the backs of the cattle, the azure sky, and Jinmei's lightning gallop, she felt that life was both beautiful and distant.

Kazan was too young and had too many questions about the world. She chose to stand by instead of setting foot inside it anxiously.

3

Kazan was eight when Grandpa left the world abruptly. Jinmei bow-wowed in a low voice and roved around Grandpa's fallen body restlessly. Kazan was choked in tears. She felt tremendous fear cramming her throat. The unfinished Tsam-pa had dropped from her feeble hands. In the silence of the black tent, she could hear clearly the little crack of the slow fire on which butter tea was boiled. Kazan felt as if she were seeing the expanses of the moonlit, snow-clad highland that night again. A white world. As still as death.

The death of the celestial burial master caught the entire village on the hop. The mourning herdsmen surrounded his tent in silence. They were not men of words. Their faces were always calm to the point of indifference, especially at such a moment as this. Later Rilan, the richest man of the village, walked out of the crowd and sighed to Kazan, let Gibu hold a celestial burial for your Grandpa.

Gibu was Rilan's distant relative. He was a typical reticent Kamba macho from Nangqian grassland. He was tall and strong with a sharply angular contour, small and silent eyes, and a purple face. He was a *regaba* (the corpse carrier, or the celestial burial master). He was also known as a skilled nomadic doctor and later came here alone.

Surrounded by the crowd, Kazan looked at the man timidly and bit her lips.

Gibu left and fetched a brown *pulu* robe from his tent. According to the customs, the deceased should wear nothing but pulu, be tied by ropes in a cuddling posture like an embryo in the mother's womb, and stay in the tent for three days before being carried to the celestial burial platform. Gibu said to Kazan, go away.

Kazan dodged aside timidly, followed by Jinmei. Gibu entered the black tent and pulled the thick felt curtain instantly.

The crowd began to disperse. When Gibu reemerged from the tent, Kazan alone was left standing outside. Gibu faced her awkwardly. He did not know what to say, so he gave her a consoling look and left. He said in passing, I'll be on the guard outside the tent tonight. Don't be scared.

Kazan stood still until she saw Gibu walk away. She lifted up the curtain with shaking hands and saw that Grandpa's corpse had been wrapped in white *pulu* and bundled into a cuddling posture in bed, like a little baby. Kazan put a hand on her mouth and caught her breath. Sitting cross-legged far away from Grandpa, she trembled all over.

She kept sitting there until sunset.

All of a sudden she heard Jinmei gnarring and startled with a jerk. She recollected herself after a while, stood up, and walked outside to see what happened.

It was Gibu standing at a distance from the tent and looking at her in silence. Kazan dragged Jinmei to her and patted its head to calm it down, but Jinmei went on barking in a low voice. Kazan looked at the stranger with alert eyes. She squatted by the side of Jinmei and said nothing.

Gibu did not say anything, either. When Jinmei calmed down, he turned around and sat with crossed legs against the earth wall of the sheep pen.

Kazan watched his back for a while, patted Jinmei, and took it into the tent. The instant when she put down the curtains, she caught a glimpse of the wilderness bathed in desolate moonlight.

Three days and nights. Kazan kept vigil beside Grandpa's corpse alone. No one entered to disturb her. Many years later, she thought of the three nights that she spent by the side of Grandpa's corpse and realized how more dignified death was than life. The thought worked its dim way to her that maybe the other world **was** better, or how could so many family members leave her without any promise to return.

The fourth dawn. Kazan was kneeling on the ground with a hazed mind when she felt a draught behind her. A beam pierced through the darkness in the tent. She turned her head and saw the Kamba man looking at her in silence. She could not see his face clearly for the bright light behind him. All she could see was that his tall body blocked the sunlight outside the tent, the edges and corners in his face as tough as a huge paper puppet.

He told her, Kazan, it's time we saw Grandpa off.

Many herdsmen in the village attended Grandpa's celestial burial that day. Kazan prepared Tsam-pa and butter tea and followed the crowd to the new celestial burial platform. Gibu and several other herdsmen carried Grandpa's corpse and walked in the front. Kazan quickened her pace to catch up with them. They finally got to the platform. She knelt down to kindle the firewood and began to boil a pot of butter tea. The tea was for the celestial burial master. Kazan had learned the rituals by heart.

The familiar juniper incense in her memory rose up again. Gibu stood aside and cast spells. Black spots appeared in the pale sky; they drew closer and closer. The vultures gathered together and waited for the feast. Gibu stopped his spells, unfastened the *pulu* neatly, and began to dismember the corpse with an ax. Kazan bent down her head instantly. When she looked up again, Gibu was throwing chops of flesh with mingled barley to the vultures. After a long while, he went on the dismemberment again and mingled the bones and other remains with barley and fed them to the vultures.

Gibu stood aside and began to pray. The burial went on smoothly. Grandpa's corpse was eaten completely. To the Tibetans, this meant that the deceased was good and honest and would go to heaven. Kazan passed the Tsam-pa to Gibu to clean his hands. Gibu took it and rubbed off the bits of bones and flesh. When Gibu finished, she gave the boiled butter tea to him. Gibu gave her a silent look and drank it.

Gibu turned around, waved his arms to disperse the birds. Vultures and crows flapped their wings and flew away, their rustles sounded sonorously in the depths of the sky. The crowd gradually scattered, and Kazan was left staring at the empty platform helplessly.

She could no longer see the eternal fire in Grandpa's eyes; no more could she see of Grandpa in that dark reddish cassock, standing under the sky to welcome the celestial birds.

All she could see was the snow-white sky. She felt again the gift of silence from the world of white stillness.

4

Gibu told her, Kazan, Rilan is looking for you. Follow me. Kazan pursed up her lips and followed this man. This was another blind journey. She followed Gibu's steps on the way back, the way she quickened her steps to catch up with him to the platform. The man walked fast and turned back to look at her again and again.

Gibu took her to Rilan's big tent. The white sheep-skin tent was spacious and bright. Rilan was sitting on the carpet when she entered and waddled to her, the silver ornaments jingling clearly. Rilan was the most opulent among the herdsmen. He had innumerable sheep and cattle. His yaks were said to be hybrid offspring of wild yaks and were exceptionally tall and tough, almost as tall and tough as hills.

There was little interflow of goods and materials in the village. People were still in the age of barter economy. To have the most and the strongest yaks and the fattest, biggest sheep was a sign of opulence in the villagers' minds.

Kazan's memory of this man Rilan was almost blank; all she remembered was that Rilan was not tall but will a big belly, which set him apart from the masculine, tough men in the village. It was said that Rilan's ancestors were chieftans and there were many treasures at his home.

Now Rilan was standing in front of her. He stooped down and looked her up and down. The child closed her lips, bent down her head, and said nothing.

Your grandpa is dead, Kazan. How are you going to survive alone?

Kazan did not speak.

Rilan paused and said, Kazan, you are my neighbor. Your grandpa was good and honest and had always been our celestial burial master. He passed away, so let me take care of you. From now on you will be my family.

Kazan bit her lips and remained silent.

Rilan was a little impatient. He stood up and said to Gibu, all right, it's settled. Now you go to her tent and help her move her stuff here.

Gibu looked at her silently.

Let's go, Kazan.

She was taken back to the tent by him. Inside the black tent, the man's silent, grim face was lit in the faint gleam of light. Sitting far away from her, Gibu asked, do you have anything to move? Kazan began to feel grieved and helpless with tears rimming from her eyes. She crouched down to cuddle with Jinmei, buried her face in the long hair of its neck, and sobbed at last.

Gibu stopped talking. He watched her patiently.

After a long while, Kazan stood up. She folded Grandpa's cassock, put it in her arms, pulled Jinmei along, and fixed her eyes on Gibu. Gibu frowned a little; he understood that these were the only things that Kazan wanted to take with her. So he searched about, picked up a couple of utensils, took off the sleeves and the front part of his robe to pack the things up with, and wrapped the stuff around his waist.

Kazan, follow me. Your cattle and sheep will be given to Rilan, 'cause you will be part of Rilan's family from now on.

Kazan remained silent. The tears that she wiped with her dirty hands left a black trace on her face.

The man drove the cattle and sheep along while Kazan followed him with Grandpa's cassock in her lap. Jinmei could not tolerate the stranger's control of the master's sheep and howled vigilantly again and again and almost dashed to him. Kazan patted its head, checked it in a low voice, and calmed it down.

Gibu took her to Rilan's home again. When they got to the tent, Gibu told her, wait a minute. Then he walked inside himself. After a while, Gibu stepped out and drove her sheep and cattle into Rilan's pen. He turned back and fixed his eyes on her. The man had not heard a single word from her since the first meeting. He sighed slightly.

Kazan.

He called her name. He seemed about to tell her something, but he paused a long while without saying anything. Hurry up; go inside. Gibu said at last.

This orphan walked into Rilan's white sheep-skin tent timidly. She thought the tent was too bright and spacious for her to feel comfortable. Rilan and his family were sitting on the carpet, gazing at her.

The poor child stood rigidly in the strangers' gaze. She knew that this would be her home from now on and she had to serve these people. She looked up and saw Rilan's wife and two sons sitting there condescendingly and staring at her expressionless. A maid was standing aside.

The maid gave her a butter tea. Kazan took it over and drank it in silence. She heard Rilan saying, go change and clean yourself. From now on, you will be part of our family.

The maid led Kazan to the little stone hut behind the tent. You will stay with us here. Remember to stand aside when the masters have dinner. We cannot take the food here to eat until the masters finish their meal. The maid tenderly stroked Kazan's head with her hand.

The girl's hair was stuck together and very dirty as it had not been cleaned or combed for a long time. The dirt on her face was thick as well. The maid gazed at her for a long time with her soft hand on Kazan's shoulder. All of a sudden Kazan began to miss her mom. The maid hugged her, don't cry, child, she said gently,

Kazan, I'm Renso. Let me be your sister from now on. Don't cry, sweetie. Your sister will take care of you. Renso brushed away the messy bang on her forehead and said, let us go clean yourself. You will be part of the family after the bath and change.

Renso took Kazan for a bath. She pulled a horse along, helped Kazan to mount the horse, threw some clothes on the horse back, and led the horse out of the hut.

Kazan feasted her eyes on the tall horseback. She saw the endless undulating grassland that sprawled to the horizon where it met the azure sky. The lakes scattering on the highland glimmered in the rampant sun, as if they were made of innumerable fallen stars. She rode the horse through the many cattle and sheep of Rilan's, the silver bell on the horseback jingling sonorously on the way. Renso began to sing songs in high spirits, her voice as bright as the clouds that floated in the sky.

Renso took Kazan to Pumu Lake. It was a hot spring lake. Pumu meant "girl". The local girls bathed themselves here, so this was indeed a lake for girls. Hot steam rose from the lake, forming a smoky cloud from a distance like a natural, misty screen. Generations had settled and multiplied here and regarded her as the sacred lake. Men would keep away from it.

Renso took Kazan's hand and jumped from the horseback briskly. Renso said, Kazan, let me help you take off your clothes and you go to the lake yourself. Remember, don't go to the middle of the lake, just hang around the lakeside.

Kazan walked into the hot lake naked. She took a deep breath, immersed herself in water, and rubbed her skin and hair. She could not remember that she was baptized here as a newborn baby. After the many years, all she could remember was the soft, warm water that surrounded her and the waves that tapped on her body when she stirred, like Mom's hands in her dreams.

She lingered in the lake for a long time. The smell of the minerals in the mist grew stronger and stronger. She was dizzy and exhausted. She heard Renso call her name. She tried to get on her feet and return, but found herself too feeble to even stand up. She had a little panic as if she scented the approaching steps of death. She closed her eyes involuntarily and saw the same visage again—the white snow-clad land and the silver moon on the sky. All was still. Your dad and mom slept under the sacred mountain, Kazan. She heard Grandpa's murky voice.

When she opened her eyes again, she saw Renso's face. Renso held her in the lap worriedly. Kazan, you almost fainted and died in the lake. Said Renso stroking her wet hair.

I'm hungry. Kazan said.

This was the first time that she opened her mouth after Grandpa's death. Renso was perhaps the only person she could depend on, so she expressed her need to her. At times of helplessness—during the days and nights when she kept vigil for Grandpa, on the way when she stumbled her way following a stranger, or in the deep, cold nights on the highland, she bit her lips and kept to herself.

Because she believed that our flesh was but a lotus flower that lived and died by itself.

On that day, she was rescued by Renso, put on new clothes, and was taken back home. Renso basked by the oven and combed Kazan's hair. Kazan, do you miss your family? she asked.

Kazan did not answer. She looked like a Tibetan antelope whose parents got killed by poachers. Her black eyes were limpid, innocent, and pitiful.

At Kazan's first meal at Rilan's, she cautiously stood aside with Renso. Zamecho, Rilan's elder son, saw her and said out loud, you, come sit down and eat here! Rilan was a little surprised at first but said at once, um, come sit down and eat with us from now on. Kazan nodded and sat down.

You're not gonna say thanks? Zamecho asked.

Kazan was startled. She looked up into the boy's eyes squarely like a wild fledgling. She fixed her eyes on him and said, thanks, her stare straightforward and unruly. Then she bent down her head and reached for the beef.

The boy said nothing.

Spring tiptoed its way onto the highland as always. But Kazan could remember clearly the moment when migrant birds flew over the sky back to their home, ushering in the first crack of the ice on the snow-capped mountain and the melting of the frozen earth under her feet. The warmth of the sun, though slow in coming, urged the herdsmen to make preparations to move to the summer ranch. After the long, severe winter, the cattle and sheep thinned away out of shape. Kazan was busy working with Renso every day. She collected and dried dairy manure, drove sheep, made Tsam-pa, ground flour, made blood sausage, dried the meat, fed the mastiffs, and boiled butter tea. Jinmei came with Kazan and began to guard Rilan's sheep and cattle. Gibu dropped by occasionally. From time to time, in the midst of all the fire burning, tea boiling, and barley flour grinding, she would find the man upon looking up, who stood outside the door in the distance, gazing in her direction silently.

She would not have expressed her gratitude for this simple, kind man had she had any.

Renso, however, would turn her head in curiosity and steal looks of the man merrily with a red flush on her cheeks. That was the first time when Kazan keenly noted that such a flush would only appear on Renso's face when she saw Gibu. Only in his presence did her face light up as brightly as the summer sky. But Kazan was a smart, sensible child. She shut her mouth whenever necessary.

When spring came, the herdsmen gradually began their migration. They packed up their belongings and drove the bullock carts towards the summer ranch. Which was the same way as the migrant birds.

Rilan and his family always rode on tall horses ahead of others. Kazan and Renso sat on the bullock cart loaded with luggage and followed them. Zamecho, the elder son, galloped about wildly and dashed into the yaks every now and then, creating chaos in the calm, dense herd. This aroused Jinmei, the ward of the cattle; the mastiff dashed in front of Zamecho's horse bawling and jumping up to attack. The boy's horse was taken aback, raised its front hooves, and skewed its body to one side. Zamecho was caught unawares and fell off from the horse. He cried in pain when his feet hit the ground. Many people stopped and shouted, Zamecho fell!

The noise drew Rilan close in this direction.

Zamecho lay on the ground, grimacing and crying in pain. Rilan jumped off the horse. He took up the boy's leg and pressed it by inches to locate the injured part. When he came to the shinbone, Zamecho cried loudly, aw! Rilan said, shut up! The father's warning startled the boy. He bit his lips and made no sound.

Your bone is broken! Said Rilan. Then he turned around and called Gibu up. He told Gibu, Zamecho's foot is broken. Can you handle it?

Gibu knelt down and examined Zamecho's foot skillfully. At the end, he said, nothing serious. I can cure him. But he cannot move today. I'll stay with Zamecho and set his bone. Rilan took an anxious look up at the sky, and said, all right, we'll stop and camp here today.

Inside the temporary tent, Gibu took out herbal medicine, two planks of wood, and straps of cloth and prepared to set Zamecho's broken bone. Kazan and Renso waited by his side. Gibu said, Kazan, Renso, hold him down by the shoulder in case he moves too much and messes up with the bones. The two girls came over and held Zamecho down. Renso lowered her head in a lovely flush.

Gibu looked at the boy and said, son, be brave! At these words he suddenly clamped the boy's foot with his hands.

Zamecho gave a horrible shriek. A crack was heard in his bones when they were jointed together. The boy trembled in great pain. He would have been twisting about in pain had he not been held tightly. Gibu immediately applied a thick coat of herbal medicine on Zamecho's foot, flanked it with the two planks, and fixed them tightly with the straps. Gibu breathed out in relief and said, all right. You'll be ok in three or four months' time if you don't move. Kazan saw the little drops of sweat all over Gibu's bare arms and forehead.

Gibu stood up and walked out of the tent. After a while, Rilan came in. He sat down by Zamecho, patted his head, and asked, did it hurt? The boy bit his lips and shook his head. Rilan said, be brave, son, if it hurts. Be a man.

After these words, Rilan turned to the two girls and said, take care of Zamecho. Call Gibu if there's anything. Gibu is a doctor. He's known for his skills throughout Nangqian grassland. Then he turned around and left too. When he turned around, Rilan said, your mastiff is called Jinmei, right? It's good, but a shepherd dog shall not hurt its master, whatever you call it. You shall give it more discipline from now on.

That night, Kazan and Renso stayed inside the tent. The night grew darker and the wind whistled by. Kazan dozed off in this plain black tent. She saw Grandpa's face, which was interlocked with wrinkles like the highland with the mountains. In her reverie she saw the low fire on which butter tea was boiled and the blurred shadows delineated by the firelight. Inside the black tent, the fire cracked gently and Grandpa was heard mumbling.

Kazan, remember. Every man has in his flesh several *lunshi*, or rooms for the transmigration of the soul, which were arrayed in the shape of a lotus along the spine all the way upward from the tailbone to the vertex. Once the "petals" are destroyed or the "root" is rent, the lotus will fall apart and lose its life. In other words, when the flesh falls apart and perishes, it is time for the soul that lives in it to fly away and look for a new home.

"So Kazan, bear it in mind," Grandpa told her, "our flesh is but a lotus and will perish in time, but our souls are immortal. Always guard the beauty and goodness in your soul, Kazan. Only in this way can you receive eternal life with the blessing of the Buddha."

Grandpa. Kazan murmured. She felt a pair of hands on her face. She felt them after a little hesitation. They were like a warm, wet cloud that skimmed over the dry land, bringing rain and hopes of life.

She opened her dreamy eyes and found it was the boy's hands that were still on her face. She jerked her face aside to dodge them, stood up in alert, and looked at him without a word.

The boy said, why are you dodging me?

Kazan said nothing. She wanted to call Renso, only to find she was not there. She suddenly felt uneasy at heart, so she dashed outside and searched for her everywhere. Not a ghost was seen outside. Nothing but the darkness of the night and waves of piercing coldness brought by the damp mists. Not a sound was heard. So she ran to Gibu's tent. Actually she did not know the meaning of this blind search. She was just shrouded with this inexplicable anxiety, as if she were fleeing for her life.

Outside Gibu's tent, she called in a nervous, terse voice. Gibu. Gibu. She found her voice so negligible, as if she were a mute who exerted to shout out in vain. She could only hear her breaths in her chest, heavier and heavier after the running, and the clear thumping of her heart. She dare not enter the tent. While she hesitated, the curtain of the tent was lifted up by a draught and the dim light leaked through. Someone was talking in the tent in a low voice. She was excited and lifted up the curtain gently.

She caught sight of the intertwined bodies of Gibu and Renso. She heard them murmuring strangely and panting in a low voice.

The firewood by their side had died out with a couple of sparks flickering in the darkness.

She was very ashamed and terrified. She closed the curtain, turned around and ran away.

The highland was shrouded in deep night. Sporadic stars cast down dim light. In the misty, distant moonlight, the remote ponds were still and quiet and scattered on the land like lost memories. Kazan was struck by the vast and boundless land and its stillness. She felt as if her body and soul were about to snap under a stubborn, forceful fate like a long, crisp bone.

For the first time she felt homeless. She did not feel it even at the moment when Grandpa passed away. That night she was keenly hurt by loneliness and desolation. She knew she had nowhere else to go, so she went to the sheep pen and found Jinmei there. She had no choice but to cuddle down with it. Jinmei was as warm as fire.

Hot, shameful tears of loneliness and helplessness were rimming in her eyes. She wiped them off determinately.

Kazan! Why are you sleeping here?

Someone woke her up with a push. She opened her eyes difficultly as they were itchy and dry after the weeping, and saw Renso. I've been looking for you for a long time! Renso said to her. Kazan was silent. Renso pulled her up nervously. Kazan's eyes looked as stubborn as an unyielding cub. I looked for you for a long time last night too. She said to Renso.

Renso was startled. She pulled Kazan to her quickly and said in a low voice, what did you see?

Kazan was silent.

Don't tell anyone, ok? Don't tell anyone! Renso said to her in a half threatening, half begging tone.

Kazan said nothing. The two of them looked into each other's eyes. After a while, she nodded.

As if relieved of a heavy load, Renso straightened up and smiled to her vaguely. Kazan. Some day you're gonna understand it.

In this world, Kazan, said she to her, if a woman can find a man who gives her shelter when she has nowhere to go, if she can stay by his side and partake of his warmth and passion, then she is truly blessed. He should be as solid and broad as a fertile field and she should endure drought and coldness like highland barley. She will be planted into him by fate; through various unpredictable difficulties, she will bud, sprout, grow up, and droop with heavy ears in extreme pain at last.

This is the long journey of waiting destined to us. A sin and blessing that we are willing to carry on our back.

Renso patted her head in a melancholy smile. Behind her, the first sun ray was spurting through the sky.

After two days, Rilan came over and said to them, the herdsmen cannot afford to wait here for Zamecho to recover. They have to move on in time, and he has to go ahead with the others. So he told Gibu to stay behind and take Zamecho along when he gets fine. Rilan told Kazan and Renso to take good care of Zamecho. With these words, he turned and left.

The herdsmen drove their cattle and sheep and departed. The three of them were left to take care of Zamecho.

The grassland was bared suddenly. No cattle or people around. During Zamecho's recovery, Gibu stayed with them and set up his tent next to theirs. Naturally Gibu visited them daily to see to Zamecho's recovery. The atmosphere became ambiguous as soon as he got in. The amorous glances that Renso and Gibu exchanged silently all the time embarrassed Kazan greatly. Zamecho groaned painfully now and then. Whenever he groaned, Gibu would give him a bowl of herbal medicine. The young master would fall asleep in a while. Then Renso would take up Gibu's hand and run outside. Most of the times she would not return until the next morning, leaving Kazan alone in the care of the boy.

The other evening, Renso hung out with Gibu as usual. Kazan looked after Zamecho alone and dozed off. She was woken up by the noise that Renso made when she came back. Happy and exhausted, Renso crouched next to her quietly.

Kazan could not fall asleep again with her back towards Renso. She suddenly asked Renso, why did you fall in love with Gibu?

5

Renso always remembered the day when her mother sent her away.

Her mother took her hand and said, Renso, follow me. She took her to a stranger, who put her onto a cart. Renso cried and struggled; but her mother was only frowning slightly. The tears in her eyes did not even roll down.

She jumped off the cart desperately, but the stranger caught her and dragged her onto the cart again. Her mother saw the scene, but she put her face in her hands and ran away. Renso was so numbed by her mother's escape that she totally forgot she was sitting on a cart farther and farther away from home. The tent and cattle of her home gradually became a black spot at the end of the horizon. The spot finally disappeared, leaving only the endless undulating mountains.

The night before she was born, her mother dreamt of a golden Buddha statue in the oven. But when she reached for the statue, it broke into pieces all of a sudden.

This ominous dream gave an unlucky sign to Renso's birth in her mother's mind. Her mother thought she would be a son, as there had been two daughters in the family already. Seeing the birth of a third daughter, her father became disappointed and impatient.

Renso and her sisters trudged through a long, difficult childhood. They were busy working from early morning when stars still shone till deep night. Then the next day would come and they had to rise and work again. They did not feel bitter as there was no alternative around them. This was the life for all women of the past generations. Except for their drunken father's occasional abuse, they did not find the life hopeless.

At the age of twelve, she was hit by an intense, inexplicable pain in her abdomen one day. The pain eased up after a couple of days and she gave it no thought. But it revisited her again the next month. This time it was so intense that she passed out while working. She had been sick ever since and suffered from more and more frequent fits. Her lips became dark purple and she was too weak to even get out of bed. She felt the lower part of her body was swelling unbearably for no reason as if it were seized by a continuously downward-dragging force.

Her mother began to worry about her. The symptoms seemed to suggest an ominous disease.

One day a well-known roaming doctor came to their grassland at last. He saw the smoke of the damp dairy manure in front of Renso's tent, so he walked in to check up on the patient. Renso's mother was plighted by Renso's weird disease. She saw the doctor as if she clutched the straw and pleaded him for diagnosis.

Renso knew nothing about the doctor's arrival. She was even unconscious during the examination. The doctor made a diagnosis after he heard about descriptions of the girl's illness, examined her purple lips and felt her pulse. He looked a trifle mysterious.

He called the girl's mother aside and told the latter in an elusive tone that this was a "stone girl". The lower part of the girl's body is congested with blood and she is weak with qi and blood disturbance all over and jammed regular channels.

Her mother was numbed by the doctor's diagnosis. This was a terrible sign to them. Only people that committed serious sins in their prior life would suffer from such a disease. Her mother said to the doctor immediately, honored guest, please don't spread this around . . . With these words, she began sobbing quietly in shame.

The roaming doctor said, I might be able to cure her. But I need Notoginseng root. I'll collect some.

When she woke up one night several days later, the roaming doctor put her on a cart and took her into a big tent. That was his only abode when he roamed about. The doctor held her in his arms and stepped into the tent. Her abdomen began to hurt again sharply for the curling position. She thought she was about to die.

In fear and anxiety, she was too feeble to even utter a word. The doctor put her down. A big fire was blazing in the middle of the tent, the firewood crackling loudly. The doctor wore a black mask on his face; the long drape of the mask covered his neck entirely. He took out some herbal medicine from the leopard-skin bag and put it into a blackened tiger's stomach. Then he took a golden vial out of the leopard-skin bag and instilled several drops of black, thick liquid into the stomach. He propped the stomach up by filling it with water from the sacred spring on the snow-capped mountain. He began to decoct medicine with the tiger's stomach the way people boiled water with a bronze bowl. Renso was stunned speechless. She thought the black stomach would burst immediately and the water inside would put the fire out. To her surprise, the man decocted the medicine successfully in the manner unheard of on the highland. The medicine was bubbling in the stomach and gave out a strange sound like an old wizard's spell.

Renso looked at his tall figure in exhaustion. She squeezed a question between her teeth, who are you?

The man did not say a word. When the medicine was ready, he took it to her lips. Drink it. The doctor said stiffly. She held the bowl, but the hot liquid in it kept spilling over as her hands were trembling violently with pain and feebleness. The man saw it and took the bowl back at once. He propped up her back with one hand and held the bowl and fed her with the other. Vague as her mind was, she felt that the man's hands were very firm and strong. The man's vigor made her unable to resist or hesitate. All she could do was submit. The medicine poured into her throat. It tasted very bitter.

Then the roaming doctor laid her down and turned around to decoct another medicine.

Renso lay there and found the pain gradually ebbed away; however, somewhere deep in her body was burning as if in flames. She caught a fever and had sweat all over. Her body was as light as ashes.

At that moment, the man sat by her side and began playing the genka. She seldom listened to music before. Except the profound tunes of suna, jailing and tongqin she heard at temples, she had almost never heard any music. The tunes that the man played with genka were intense and pleasant. They were spirited like the gallops of a steed, which sounded novel and marvelous to her.

While the girl lost herself in music, the man got up and danced to the tune he played around the fire. The black mask on his face began to sway to and fro in his bold movements, revealing part of his mysterious face. Like an esoteric religious ritual, his dance was pregnant with a charming sense of mission. He would even bend down over Renso when he danced around the fire and the tassels would brush over her face swiftly. But he danced away from her immediately, leaving only a strong masculine smell that was mingled with an odor of medicine.

The man began singing aloud. His voice was like the golden sun rays on the top of the snow-capped mountain. Renso saw one after another illusion in the unbearable heat.

She heard that the man was calling her, come dance with me, Renso. Renso.

Caught in the illusion, Renso began to follow the man in dance. Her bright skirt spread around the raging fire. She felt as light as air and as hot as the flames. She longed so much to stretch herself.

The man had been playing tempestuous tunes continuously after he led her into dance. She danced after him excitedly and kept trying to lift up his mask to peep into his mysterious face. She stretched her body to the utmost in exaggerated movements, like a string that vibrated in a powerful sound field.

In her illusion, Renso was sure that she had become a bonfire on the wilderness in the deep night. She was tearing at her life like the faithless in the immense darkness.

She rained with sweat all over. On the verge of collapse, she felt her body erupt with a stream of blood. The blood seemed to be flowing forever like an endless night. She had never thought that so much irresistible energy was hidden inside her.

She felt she was light like a feather.

So she fell down in the grip of the everlasting illusions as conjured by the medicine.

The man had actually long stopped playing music and dancing. Renso was in a state of hallucination during her last dance. He held up the second bowl of medicine and fed it to her.

He saw this pale, pallid girl lying there in exhaustion, like a blooming snow lotus. Under her Tibetan skirt flowed out a thread of black congested blood, forming a strange line that extended slowly on the ground.

He added wood to the fire to keep the tent warm.

Walking out of the tent alone, he sat down with his face towards the east and watched the first pale sun rays on the highland that lit up the sky gradually. The air was as fresh as a ballad.

When Renso woke up, she was terrified to see the black blood beneath her.

At this moment, the man lifted the curtain and walked inside the tent. They looked into each other's eyes.

Why don't you take the mask off, Renso asked. The man said nothing, but carried Renso in his arms, placed her on his carpet, and fed her with another bowl of medicine. While drinking the medicine, she slyly raised her hand and tried to take off the mask. But the man warded it off instantly.

He said, remember, you must not know who cured you. Now it's time you went back.

Thus the roaming doctor helped Renso to the cart and took her home. The man gave a bag of herbal medicine to her mother and then left. Renso gazed at his tall figure and could not but become suspicious of the illusion she saw in the tent the other night. Her mother stared at her perplexingly from the corner.

For a long time afterwards, she kept bleeding every now and then and her face was as pallid as paper. She asked her mother, what's going wrong with me? Her mother never answered.

In the days that followed, Renso had a daily potion of the medicine the doctor left her. The medicine was a mixture of ginseng, Astragalus root, Atractylis ovata, roasted licorice root, huoshen, polygala, Aucklandia root and Notoginseng root, etc. It was a prescription invented in the Song Dynasty by Han people. The doctor added xanthoxylum seeds and crocus powder to it. Having drunk up all the medicine, Renso began to recover and the bleeding gradually stopped. The long-standing heavy load in her body disappeared.

The other night after her recovery, her mother said to her, we're gonna send you away.

She was astonished and asked her mother helplessly, why?

Her mother sighed, Renso, you have to pay the debt that was born with you. This is your fate.

Early in the next morning, before the fog passed off, another stranger came to their tent.

Renso's mother took her hand and dressed her and combed her hair. Her mother said to her, come, Renso, follow me. She loaded the daughter onto the cart. The daughter began crying desperately; she was all desperation and hatred in such abandonment.

She never understood what exactly the so-called sin was that she was born with. Was it the blood of pain that flowed out of her body? If yes, who was it then, that chose her and stuffed the black mystery into her body?

Despite her persistent questions, the mystery remained unresolved for her after all these afflictions and misery that resulted from it.

At the first night of Zamecho's injury, when Kazan and Zamecho were asleep, Gibu said to her suddenly, Renso, come with me.

She was excited at the sudden, ambiguous invitation and followed Gibu into his tent. Inside it she saw that genka fiddle and the blaze in the middle again. The mask-less man had a craggy face.

She murmured haltingly in surprise, you said I mustn't know who it was that cured my disease.

The man frowned a little. He sighed, you don't understand nothing.

6

With her back towards Renso, Kazan asked suddenly, why do you like Gibu?

For a moment, Renso did not know what to say. She said at last, because that day, I saw he was holding a genka . . . I saw that genka before.

Kazan was baffled by the odd answer. Just because of a fiddle? she asked.

Renso was silent. She closed her eyes and said, Kazan, stop asking me, 'cause I don't know what's going on with me either.

Kazan did not ask again, as she believed that she saw tears slipping off from the corners of Renso's eyes.

Zamecho was taken good care of and recovered quickly. He was finally able to get out bed and walk. Kazan looked after him silently as if it were her natural duty. Every now and then he would press his hand on Kazan's face like what he did the other night, and Kazan would always dodge him quickly. The boy kept smiling at her vaguely and asked, why are you dodging me?

Several days later, the four of them decided to set off. They had been held off for a long time. The other villagers should have set up tents at the summer ranch long before. They headed for the distant mountains. Zamecho and the two girls rode the carriage, while Gibu rode ahead of them.

Kazan watched the boundless field. She remembered sentimentally the night after the snow when she trudged blindly after Grandpa. She remembered how difficult it was to make even a step with both feet stuck in the snow. She could even hear the crunches when she set foot in the snow, which was all the more clear in the white stillness.

Now she heard Zamecho singing an ancient ballad aloud by her side, his voice coarse and puerile as a fledgling.

> If the sun never rose in the east,
> Then never would the ice in the west melt,
> Nor would there be Lake Manasarovar,
> The dense sandlewood trees,
> Or the green parrots.
> If no birds sang,
> Then never would there be songs
> On the snow-capped highland . . .

Dark night followed the gorgeous sunset and stars splashed all over the sky. They were on the road day after day. One midnight, Kazan felt again the stroke of a hand over her face in sleep. She woke up suddenly, but kept her eyes shut at a loss. She bit her lips in shame and nervousness. She heard Zamecho ask her, are you asleep? But she remained silent. Zamecho said, Kazan, you're very pretty. I wanna marry you.

Kazan had been sleeping lightly since that night. As she knew barely anything of romance, she constantly watched out for Zamecho in the fear of anything that might happen between them.

They finally got to the ranch after another couple of days' riding. Even the air on the ranch smelt of water and luxuriant grass. Looking from a distance, she saw big and small tents scattering on the grassland and herds of cattle and sheep strolling about grazing at ease, like clouds that floated in the sky. The broad and peaceful land was like an innocent baby that slept in the lap of the azure sky. She realized after many years that the reason for the peace there was that men could not see the passage of time. So everything was at a still.

7

Life on the summer ranch was even busier. Kazan collected dairy manure with a huge basket on her back, which towered over her head. Jinmei kept guard on the sheep every day. All of a sudden Rilan's shepherd dog began howling, so Kazan hurried over to see what happened.

It turned out to be a young couple of tourists who approached the tent. Kazan halted the dog and saw a woman coming up to her and pointed a camera towards her. Kazan looked up at the young tourists, their clothes, hairstyle, traveling bags and the small box in the woman's hands in all curiosity. Suddenly the woman pressed a button on the box which flashed and startled Kazan. After this, the woman said to her in a big smile, sweetie, you are beautiful!

Kazan could not understand a word of hers. But she saw that the woman waved for her to go over. Kazan walked to her timidly; the woman gave her a warm smile and tried to pat Kazan on the head. This was a rude gesture to Tibetans. Zamecho saw what she did and shouted at her from far away, hey, what are you doing! His voice was so fierce that the woman withdrew her hand instantly without even understanding what he said.

Zamecho rode over at a rapid speed and jumped off the horse briskly. He said to Kazan, did they take a photo of you? You fool! You have a photo in the world and your soul will never be able to go up to heaven!

The two tourists did not know what happened at all. They were about to take another photo of the boy when he blocked off the camera. He shouted at the woman, don't shoot! When he finished these words, he grabbed Kazan's hand and took her away. The two travelers were both baffled and amused by the boy's odd behavior. It was the first time Kazan's hand was seized by Zamecho. She made an effort to withdraw her hand but failed. While being dragged along by Zamecho, she looked back from time to time at the woman who had taken a photo of her. The woman was still standing there with a bright smile.

When Kazan walked into the tent at dinner time, she was surprised to find the two travelers sitting on the mat. Rilan was throwing a feast for them as honored guests. Zamecho lowered his head and remained silent. The woman seemed very happy when she saw Kazan coming and greeted her graciously.

Rilan and the two travelers got very excited during the feast. They exchanged words of courtesies in their respective languages and kept toasting when they could not understand a word of each other. The barley wine in the big bowls was pungent and sweet and exhilarating.

Rilan began singing and dancing in high spirits. The woman looked up at him with a bright smile and clapped her hands to the song. She had a natural air of innocence and mirthfulness about her. The young man by her side was looking at her with a slight smile.

All the while Kazan was fixing her eyes at her white complexion, her exquisite features, and her lover's silent face.

Outside the tent darkness was closing in.

Kazan still lived with Renso after they got to the summer ranch. That evening the two travelers decided to stay for the night and set up a tent beside hers.

Kazan saw the blue, water-proof tent of theirs while working. She was attracted by it naturally, so she paused and went over to have a closer look.

Seeing the shadow outside the tent, the woman opened the small window. The two of them caught each other's eyes. The woman asked her in a smile, what do you want, little girl?

Kazan heard a strange language. It was soft, exotic, and feminine. She did not answer but shook her head instead. The woman emerged out of the tent and pulled the curtain open for Kazan to have a look. The red down sleeping bags, gas lamps, big mountaineering bags, water bottles, compact books and notebooks, knives, cellphones, compasses, maps, made-to-order light aluminum sketchpads, as well as big bunches of paints, painting knives, brushes, and paper.

Kazan was amazed by what she saw. But she was so shy that she ran back to her own tent with a blush and would not come out.

Chapter II

When I can no longer comfort you or you no longer care for me, please remember that once upon a time, in our short lives, we saw twelve white egrets flying over the lake of autumn.

Jian Zhen, "Rending Silk in April"

1

Come with me, Jiansheng. Don't leave me. It's beautiful there, more beautiful than you can ever imagine. I'll photograph and you'll draw.

The year when Jiansheng and Xinhe returned from Russia, they were invited by the painters' association on a sketching tour of the Tibetan highland. Jiansheng hesitated, but Xinhe persuaded him to go along with her. She persuaded him by pinching his head to her abdomen, a habit with which both of them had been familiar for years. Her hand stroked his short hair gently. Xinhe said in a low voice, Jiansheng, one Spring Festival when I was small, I visited the Lama Temple with my family. The grownups did many kowtows to worship the Buddha and burned incense in their hands. They said that prayers at Lama Temple were always answered. But I thought doing kowtow was vulgar and stood outside the temple. At that time I said to myself, I missed happiness by inches for so many times. Later I thought that maybe Buddha took what I said as a wish and realized it. To this day I'm still within inches to happiness and yet unable to reach it.

So, Jiansheng, go with me, like what we've been doing for so many years. Jiansheng, you are my happiness. She said earnestly.

Xinhe paused for a long time. She was anxiously waiting for Jiansheng's response. His handsome face was distracted as usual. Sometimes she could not see any hope on it. But his face was also as clean and thin as many years before. At least she was familiar with his face.

And as what he did repeatedly in the past, he conceded to her pleading at last. All right, we'll go together, said Jiansheng.

Then she gave him a sweet, content smile like an innocent little girl. Jiansheng knew it clearly. This woman had a simple, pure, and genuine nature. Whatever meager response Jiansheng gave to her, she gleaned whole-hearted happiness. Because he was the love of her life.

He often felt bitter and exhausted whenever he saw her sweet smile over these trifling matters.

2

One summer evening towards the end of his childhood, Jiansheng went back home after fish-catching in a pond. Yellow Tiger, his dog, bow-wowed from the distance and wagged its tail in welcome. He darted into the door, shouting, Grandma, I'm back! The door creaked open, and the boy immediately saw that by the square table of the living room sat Grandma and a strange woman. He was surprised, but was careful not to blurt a word out. He stood there in silence, waiting for Grandma's introduction.

Grandma stood up and said, sweetheart, come and have a look at your mother . . .

He was stupefied. He asked, Grandma, what did you say?

Tears suddenly came to Grandma's eyes. Sweetie, come have a look at your mother, your real mother . . .

The woman stood up with her hands wringing uneasily on her belly. She gave him an awkward, ambiguous smile with tears in her eyes. My dear boy, Mommy is coming. She walked up to him with open arms, as if she could not wait to stroke his fluffy hair. The boy stood still.

The woman leaned towards him carefully as if he were a festering scar that had not healed for years. Now the boy saw tears trickling from her eyes and felt her hands stroking his head anxiously yet hesitantly. She seemed to have a lot to say, but her words were choked with tears. My boy. She called him.

The woman kept caressing his head for a long time. A relieved smile gradually surfaced on her face. Her hands were soft, affectionate, but strange to him.

The boy asked, you are . . . my mother . . . ? Tell me then, what is my name?

The woman said, you are Jiansheng.

He said, Jiansheng?! . . . No. I'm not Jiansheng. Grandma doesn't call me Jiansheng, nor do teachers at school . . . you are not my mother. You are wrong.

The woman smiled bitterly. Jiansheng, you are my son. I'm not wrong. Jiansheng is the name that your dad gave you.

The boy asked, then where is my dad?

She said, your dad, he is gone . . .

Yellow Tiger's distant bow-wows were heard from outside. The moon was up in the sky. A thick steam gradually enveloped the field in front of the earth-brick house. The living room was permeated with the smell of burning weeds and the fragrance of dried earth after a long day's roasting in the sun. The crude tea on the square table had long cooled off.

After so many years, Jiansheng could still remember that evening.

That was Jiansheng's first meeting with his mother in his memory.

Two days later, he was taken away by his mother. The woman held his hand and walked out of the courtyard. He was taken aback by the abrupt change and had anxious sweat in his hands. He saw Grandma leaning against the door post and watching him in dismay. She raised her lean, coarse hand up. She did not wave, but raised it in the air. The thick morning fog gradually drowned Grandma's face. Yellow Tiger barked loudly and could be heard from far away. Nothing was left on the empty field except the fog and Yellow Tiger's bark. Grandma was farther and farther away.

The boy cried suddenly. He dragged his mother's hand and would not make another step. She had to stop; the boy seized the chance by flouncing out of her grasp and galloping all the way back to the house. Grandma! Grandma! He let out heart-rending screams.

The mother saw the boy run back and stood still in tears.

So the return trip was delayed. The boy was finally persuaded by his grandma and the woman he called mother after two days to set off again. Panic-stricken, Jiansheng pleaded with Grandma to go along with them. The old woman shook her head silently, her muddy eyes rimming with withered tears. She sighed, go away. It's time you both went away . . . Her voice was hoarse and melancholic, which reminded him of the sad call of a lost wild goose in dusk.

Before he departed, the boy put a thick rope around Yellow Tiger's neck and tied it to the door post. The dog barked and jumped forward desperately, the wooden post trembling under its pull. The boy stroked its head and said, Yellow Tiger, heed Grandma's words. If I come back and find you are disobedient and tramp the crops again, I will never give you any upper arm of roe deer! Yellow Tiger, don't forget me . . . Yellow Tiger . . .

The dog's barks gradually turned to plaintive sobs. His round, black eyes were glistening.

The other morning the boy set off with the woman. They spent a whole day in a bus, transferred to a train, and finally arrived at a strange world.

On the train, the boy sat by the window all the time and stared at the fleeting scenery outside in nervousness and curiosity.

The woman looked over the distant north and suddenly realized that nothing had gone away. After being away for so many years, she finally found the courage to return to her old home. The old home was the wet, distant grassland in the north, the lingering fog in the morning, the birds' song in the wilderness, the deep golden forests on the autumnal mountains. Where her youth was buried.

She used to think that the grassland was no longer there. It was lost at a certain tranquil corner of time, together with the pale, blurred shadows of her youth. At one uncertain moment, someone might knock open the thick, rotten lids of the coffins as boldly and curiously as a tomb plunderer, and these withered corpses of youth would reappear in the regretful face of history. Among them lay the corpse of her youth.

3

That maddening, tragic era. The hotbed for stupidity, ideals, enthusiasm, hatred and poets. Tong Suqing, a standard "Lao San Jie", or "Educated Youth", left Beijing at the age of eighteen. Like a dizzy cell stirred in the red, hot artery of history, she was sent to a place in North China far away from cities. The red blood was a metaphor for the most impetuous and innocent sacrifice. It flowed forward vigorously and hurled out several cells on its way. It threw them on the way as farmers sowed seeds to the mercy of the cold land of wilderness.

She was but one of those cells.

That year, she went to work in the country in North China with several youths whom she did not know. They spent two or three days cramming in a train, transferred to a military truck, and arrived at a farm on the Three River Valley when the truck stopped for supply.

The eyes of these urban youths shone when they saw the boundless land: the sky with the white clouds looked like a deep, blue sea with white icebergs floating on it. The cool sunlight glittered on the boundless field and the summer ponds. The wild flowers gave a colored lining around the ponds. The leaves of the grass gave a glazed luster. The ponds were flowing with a wet and fresh green color, as if the waves were dyed by the grass on the bank.

The field was boundless. The green wheat field undulated softly under the repeated strokes of the wind, and the ridges of the cornfields and bean fields lay in an array and stretched to the horizon. Between the long, dark ridges stood robust crops. The land was a huge, finely interwoven web and covered the entire span of the youths' blooming years. The land retained the primitive poise:

though the ridges were combed smooth by the iron rakes of the tractors, the land was still scoffing at human beings' rude, ignorant transformation with its expanses—it had nothing to yield except for the black, fertile earth.

These were the mature fields in the development project of the "Great Northern Wilderness". Many companies of educated youths came to be rooted here. Where she would settle, however, was a more remote place close to the Lesser Khingan Forests.

The youths who arrived earlier cut down trees, erected the wood as poles and beams, and covered them with thick blankets. This would serve as their tent. A hole was left on the top of the tent to funnel smoke in the winter. Several big holes were cut on its four sides as windows. The bed frames in the tent were made of big logs. The beds were soft with hay on them and smelt of the forest. Several weed mats were hung in the middle of the tent to separate the men's "bedrooms" from the women's.

Among the youths there was a young guy called Jian Weidong. To be able to play the cello he would rather lift weight with the shoulder pole than taint his hands with earth or coarsen them with the iron hoe. With a delicate cane case full of books, this young man was packed up and left to the forest farm. His hands were made to play the cello and write poetry. That pair of white, slender hands left Suqing with a deep impression. The "reactionary" attitude of this young man naturally courted many troubles later.

The night when Tong Suqing and the other two girls arrived at the farm, the youths threw a welcome party for them on the yard in front of the tent. It was at that party when she fell in love with Weidong on the first sight. A young man played the guitar; the Soviet ballad flowed across his fingers into the thickets of birch of the frontier and the dark night. Lit by the small, flickering light, all the youths' faces were immerged in a tune more touching and elegant than model operas. Then an older guy got up on a chair and recited poetry of Pushkin and Petofi in a silver voice and with deep feelings. Then Jian Weidong began playing the dark brown cello. His white, slender, hand held the bow and moved rhythmically, which composed an ardent poem that burst into blossom in the dark night and the lamp light.

Suqing admired this young, crane-like, cello-playing poet. She followed his show by playing the nostalgic song of "Hawthorn" with her beloved harmonica.

While she was playing, the poet fixed a destined gaze at her with deep feelings. He saw a dark blue luster around the girl's thick plait in the lamp light, her shining black deer-like eyes, and the shy, sweet contour of her face. The young man did not forget to stop the girl at the door before they parted deep at night.

He was wearing a white shirt that night, which was rare and extraordinary at those times. His pants were in indanthrene dark blue. His sleeves were rolled up, and his neckline was open in an unruly way, exposing the pale neck and collarbones. The veins in his arms stuck out clearly. His slender fingers that held the bow a moment before looked so lonely and melancholic. His pale face had a rigid lineament characteristic of men that lived in freezing places for a long time. His face was distracted, but on it often emerged a mystic, detached smile that was hard to overlook.

He gave her a handmade wooden box and said, these are my poems. Please read them if you like.

She felt embarrassed and ran away with the box. Her blushing, smiling face disappeared in the fragrant birch woods. That night the moon was high. The bright and clear light sprayed over and enveloped the steamy forest.

She returned to the tent and opened the box impatiently by the dim barn lantern. It was a pile of pliable birch skin; on each piece was written a poem in ink.

In the days afterwards they spent many days and nights at the woods. The days were exhausting with the excessive workload, and the nights were sleepless with the excessive yearning for each other. The bright and clear moonlight lit up the secret paths to their dating place. In the off evenings, when they finished supper at the nearby tent, they would often stroll to the valleys hand in hand. They would sit chatting on the cut down logs and hug each other for a long time with trembling arms.

He said to her there, are we going to belong here forever?

She did not know what to say. She could never guess his mind. Blindness was a precondition for love.

The bright moonlight pulled the night curtain aside and flowed from the high boughs. The two of them felt as if they were sitting in the dark bottom of the sea and watching the rays radiating from above. Clouds drifted in the sky and covered the face of the moon every now and then, casting varied shadows on the ground. The chirping of the birds in the forest was a night tune most familiar to them.

Spurred with their ideals and youth, these young people made light of—or rather, bore—the hunger, pains, labor and nostalgia. No one knew how long they would go on living like that. Their young, ordinary lives and wills were too fragile to support the heavy weight of affliction and disappointment. After countless days and nights, in the long years when ideals and youth deserted them, their vigorous faces and warm youth gradually slumped to the ground and quickly withered like the reeds in the frost.

They did not know to what awkward and hopeless place the stupid, audacious conspiracy of history was going to push them and their youth.

Winter came. The youths became busier with lumbering and land clearing. The thick cotton coats and the fox-skin hats made them very clumsy at work, but sheltered them from coldness. The thick snow squeaked under their feet. The snowflakes were dry and soft like French chalk. When they felt thirsty, they would grab a handful of snow and fill it in their mouths. The snow froze their teeth, but it soon melted into sweet water and soothed their throats like mint. The warm steam that they exhaled from behind the masks frosted on their eyelashes and made their eyelids ache.

The men chopped the woods and the women cleared the grounds. The work was exhausting, but they were able to admire the rare, gorgeous scenery during the break.

The hills were covered with dense pine woods. The white snow on the top of the gloomy forests presented a sharp contrast in color. Both banks of the brooks were iced, which formed a crystal silver galaxy winding through the forest. A stream of water gushed from below the ice, giving out a melodious sound like that of the chime bells. A marsh was frozen on the surface like a piece of glass, through which the grass and yellow flowers in the summer below could be seen. The icy marsh with these fresh and bright forms looked like a great piece of delicate, transparent amber.

After the snow, the high birches were dressed in white against the blue sky. Their leaves were all fallen and all that was left was the bare, white trunks with the aromatic sap running within.

A look around brought one the sight of the trunks covered by snow and lovely birds' nests decorating the twigs like black eyes.

The birches stood upright and halved the blue sky behind them like silver swords. The sunlight coated the birches with a golden fringe. What a sight!

Besides the birches, the snow-capped forest was also home to hollies in dark green color. As cool as late summer's sun rays, they were green and lush throughout the seasons, and pleasant to the eyes against the dazzling firn. In late winter and early spring, the azaleas would coat the hills like spilled ink on a piece of paper. They would occupy every twig of the bushes with their shiny pink flowers.

When the birds left, the silent woods received snow by fits and starts. The field was all vast and hazy. The sky would soon show its icy blue after the snow. The faint blue sun rays would also light up the forest from behind the hills. The thick snow extending through the forest was turned into dazzling gold under the sun, like a huge piece of fur, soft and gallant.

But in those endless winter days, the tent was as cold as a huge ice silo. The beds were made of wood. They could not make fire underneath. In the nights as cold as −30 degrees, they had to keep warm with a stove. The youths took turns to stay up and look after the fire. They put a big iron bucket upside down and dug a hole on its bottom. A funnel attached to the hole rose up high through the roof of the tent and made the bucket into a big stove. The one on duty needed to add wood to the stove from time to time to keep the temperature so that the other ones would not feel cold. At about 2 a.m., he or she also needed to go out to the ice-free spring in the valley to fetch some water and put it on the stove so that the others would have warm water to wash their faces in the morning. However, the next day, he or she could take a day off and sleep in the tent during the daytime.

Jian Weidong was on duty that week. He happened to get hold of a ragged hand-written book, *Nine Waves*. He could barely hide his ecstasy and swore to finish the book in two days. In those book "famine" days, nothing could match the excitement of finding such a popular underground literary book and reading it in bed stealthily.

It was late at night. All the other ones had fallen asleep. Weidong was reading by the stove. Feeling the light not bright enough, he lit a hurricane lamp and an oil lamp. He was so into the book that he was not willing or afraid of forgetting to add wood to the fire, so he put a lot of pieces of wood to the stove each time when he remembered to do so. When the fire was mighty and the stove was burning hot, he would return to his book, hoping the fire would hold longer.

Weidong was so entranced by the book that he did not remember to fetch water until three o'clock in the morning. Before he left the tent, he took out the ashes stuffing the stove. He couldn't find the dustpan, so he left the ashes by the stove temporarily so that the heat would not be wasted. He intentionally put a lot of firewood into the stove so that the fire wouldn't go out when he was out for the water. Seeing the fire flaming brightly, he put two wooden buckets on his shoulder pole and went out, yawning all the while.

It was a dry and windy night. It was very difficult to walk in the snow up to his knees. He finally treaded to the spring in the dim moonlight. He slipped and hit his nose and face. However, he still rose from the ground gulping his pain, scooped two buckets of water in the dark and walked back stiffly. The pain in his knees was acute, and he was almost frozen. Worrying about the injuries in his hands, he cursed this bad luck that befallen him while he was on duty. He stopped now and then on his way back. When he finally got to the camp, he was only to be petrified by the sight. The funnel was already flaming red, and the felt roof surrounding the funnel was on fire. A strong gust of burning smell thrilled him. He ran up in haste, but he was hardly up the slope when a flame bounced up at the wind, and the felt roof collapsed with a light sound. The oil in the tent was immediately on fire.

The two buckets were overturned. His legs slacked and he knelt down to the ground. Screams of panic were soon heard from inside the tent. He covered his eyes with his hands and his body shook on the ground in weakness. When he came to himself and ran up to the camp, the fire had already gulped in the whole tent. The burning stove, the burning ashes by the stove, the diesel pot, the oil lamp, the hurricane lamp, and even the hot felt itself had become accomplices to the ghost of fire. The tent was wrapped by the fire in an instant. The burning felt sent off a smoky smell. Tiredness had put the young people in a fast sleep. Even if some jumped out of the tent quick enough, they were already on fire. They dashed into the snowfield meters away like crazy.

There was no water to quench the fire but ice and snow. Cries for help and screams out of pain from the panic-stricken young people could be heard in the depth of the forest. Those unprepared young women held under the bed boards and girders were not able to escape from the fire. What they could do was to hold their hands together under the beds, waiting to be swallowed by the fire.

When they were forced to face the sudden doomsday, their young age and inadequate education were not able to help them escape calmly and cleverly. They left their hollow smiles just like the victims in the Pompeii city left theirs on the fossils. And they all disappeared as time passed.

Luckily, the trees surrounding the tent had all been chopped down for construction. People who escaped from the fire smashed snow on the fire and prevented it from escalating to a forest fire. The dawn broke late in the winter of the Small Xing Anling. The next morning, people not quite recovered from the fright tried to approach the debris from the smoke. And then, they saw four bodies of the women burnt black, and their humble prayer for life. These four were held beneath the girders and the bed bars, their hands tightly jointed, or stretching out to the void, as if held by the King of Terrors. Their bodies had turned into black coke, and oil was dripping through the cerecloth. In front of the sculpture made of the four burnt bodies of the young women, all souls were being questioned and tormented.

These young, vigorous and supple bodies the night before now became withered, blackened corpses covered in shrouds.

These girls used to sing the Internationale together at the party. They came from all corners of China, but now became lost souls of the People's Republic.

That night, after the grievous disaster, Jian Weidong hid himself in the dark forest in deep fear and howled in derangement.

The forest in the freezing winter night was as still as dead. A dense fog penetrated it and gave a halo to the bright moonlight on the snow. The sky and the earth were no longer distinguishable. The high, leafless birches stretched their bare limbs in plain sublimity. The swaying boughs reached the depths of the dark blue sky in a sweet, melancholic posture. The water mist through the forest was as ethereal as sashes of transparent silk. Sporadic stars twinkled in the sky; the birds flew away, and the forest sank deeper into the sea of stillness.

He trembled in fear for his grievous mistake. In the still forests, he wrapped himself in darkness and shame. Tong Suqing woke with a start and escaped, but she did not find Jian Weidong in the depths of the forest until the next evening. He was dirty all over, listless and shaken to the core.

Jian Weidong received serious punishment. Reading corrupt "underground" novels, reactionary behavior, arson, and serious interference of production and revolution . . . not to mention his exclusiveness and pride in the past. The disaster besieged him with hostility everywhere. He was publicly denounced and grounded. Several youth men urged the leader of the production team to hang him on the tree and lash him. They were even shouting to put him into prison for his arson.

After a series of disputes, Jian Weidong could no longer stay there. He was finally reposted to another production team outside the Small Xinganling. It was an outposted team in a large marsh. Tong Suqing could not bear a life without him, so she requested to leave with him.

When they came to the new production team, they were told that there was no spare lodge for them but a shanty deserted by a peasant for its ominous reputation. They built this shanty into a temporary shelter with a fence in the middle. This became their house. She and Jian Weidong decided to go ahead regardless of the small talks of other people. They removed the fence and started to live together in the despicable attitude and gossips of the crowd.

Years passed. Young intellectuals came and went. Some of the peers returned to the cities, which made Jian Weidong very jealous. The ones devoted to Maoism were reposted to factories, the sick were sent back to their origins, and the bold ones rebelled or sneaked away. Jian Weidong did not belong to a good social category. He had a "criminal record". He had an extremely scurvy reputation for living together with Tong Suqing. Both of them were isolated, and on bad terms with the team leader and the political instructor. They had little hope to return to the city.

If he could not return to the city by official dispatch, his family could not get the coupons for rice, oil and cloth in his name. Even if he did get back, his family had to squeeze the resources from everybody's part to feed him, which would make life difficult for everyone.

In those hopeless days, Jian Weidong almost gave up his poems and cello. Art is always a derivative and dependant of life. If living could hardly be insured, what was the point of highbrow art and literature?

The man's chin was now stippled all over with irregular stubble, which made him look gray and hoary for his age. He was growingly tempestuous, arrogant, and incalculable. He no longer went out to work, but idled about with the other youths, drinking and fighting gang fights every day. As he earned no work points, his ration tickets ran out. When he was hungry he would even steal and commit other petty crimes. At that time he lived with Suqing; the young couple fell in and out, thrusting curses to each other.

To make bad worse, Suqing was pregnant. At that time, youths would not be free from gossip even if they fell in love and entered into lawful marriage, not to mention that the two of them did not register at all. They did not dare to tell their families of the news. They could do nothing but grind their days in endless scorn and desolation.

Even in her pregnancy, Suqing had to earn work points. She had to get up early in the morning with a bun in her hand and a basket on her back, and went into the boundless green curtain of tall crops breaking off corn cobs until evening. Dizzy and exhausted, she had to bend her body and dibble in the field in a difficult, awkward posture. Her waist became so painful that she could not stand up. When she returned burning with hunger, she often found the rice jar and big pot empty; sometimes she could not even find a drop of drinkable water. She was immersed in desperation.

That year, Weidong was dissatisfied with her pregnancy and became irritable without any compassion or sense of responsibility, like a scoundrel. She could do nothing but bite all the sufferings by herself. She did not return home even once in the entire year.

The bitterness of those days struck into the narrow of her bones and she was on the verge of collapse. The days were so bitter that she could live through whatever difficulty that she met with in the later years, as long as she compared them with the hardships she endured in youth. This was perhaps also the only spiritual wealth that these wasted days left with most of the "educated youths" in the pursuit of the lofty cause of "transforming the earth".

She fought through the pregnancy and childbirth alone in the countryside and gave birth to a natural son, Jiansheng.

When Jiansheng was six months old, Jian Weidong's father was knocked down with the many changes and frustrations of the difficult time and passed away. Word came that his family pleaded to the Party for Jian Weidong to take care of the funeral affairs, as he was the only child of the family. He knew how precious this opportunity was, and burst into tears and wild joy at the same time when he got hold of his father's obituary. He finally got an excuse to go back and swore that he would never return.

He said to her, follow me; we'll never come back to this place again. You see, new batches of youths have been dispatched here and almost all of our fellows have gone away . . . last time when they enrolled new workers, those sons of bitches turned my application down once again. We will never be able to go back to town if we just stay here and wait . . .

She heard his words calmly, and said ruefully, what are we going to do after we go back? How are we going to do with Jiansheng?

4

Snowstorm at the tail of the year. It was all white under heaven. Dusk rose from nowhere like flood tide and submerged the last daylight. The large frozen lake took on an icy blue under the dim sky. Withered reeds and fleabanes were hidden under the floppy snow drifts by the lake. Snowflakes were transformed into thin soft white wools tossed to and fro by the wind.

They crouched in the shabby earth shelter and gazed at the empty stove. There was no firewood. A pan too huge for their food reserve was on the stove, not a drip of oil in it, as if it would rust in a second. He put on the dark gray cotton coat and lay on the hard bed. Still so cold.

Weidong said to her, follow me. Let's go back to the city.

She knew he planed to run away and would never come back. So she said, let's take Jiansheng with us. He frowned and replied, we cannot take him.

This is our child. We cannot abandon him like this!

What a whimsical idea! We can give him to Grandma Li. Surely she is a childless widow.

What a heartless man! How can you cast away your own son!

The quarrel intensified. She execrated him desperately, and in another minute, beseeched his favor beneath her dignity. In the end, Weidong was silenced with a livid face. Given his consent, she held the child in a shuddering and humble clasp.

On the night before departure, she carried Jiansheng in her arm and lay beside Weidong, shivering with cold. The sight of her baby groaning out of hunger and coldness grieved her so much.

In fact, she herself did not know what a hard and uncertain life was awaiting her even if she succeeded in fleeing to town. And the child—what trouble he would bring up?

The last night seemed longer than ever. At last the day broke up. The roaring gust raged outside against the adobe walls. All of a sudden Weidong opened the door. The boreas surged in together with damp air. The child was provoked into wailing by the cold wind.

On that cold winter morning, amid the mist, they and other several "educated youth", and Grandma Li who came to see them off, went to take a lift in a truck of the forest farm, and were leaving the land soon.

On the way to ride, he said to her: Hand Jiansheng to me. In an ecstasy of delight, she took it for granted that Weidong was determined to take the child with him, so she put the child into his arms joyfully. When they came to the parking place, they found that many youths and farmers had been waiting in the truck carriage, surrounded by people sending off. Weidong helped her up to the truck and then passed the luggage to her, ordering her to put them away in a corner.

He lingered under the truck. Till the very moment when the truck started up, the young father suddenly put the child onto the ground and climbed over the carriage all by himself.

After the truck drove away for quite a distance, Suqing began to notice that Weidong sat among the crowd with a ghastly pale look, clenching his teeth. Jiansheng was not in his arms. She came to herself and asked him: Where is Shengsheng? Where is my Shengsheng? The wretched mother's voice was trembling with panic. She climbed over the crowd of people and luggage, and climbed to the back end of the carriage. But it was too late to see anything. She even did not see how Jiansheng was thrown by on the road like a piece of trash, and then how he was picked up and carried away by the grandma . . .

The truck drove on. In a split second, Suqing shrieked out madly, exerting her utmost strength to jump off. Weidong stuck to her hands like a leech, never to unloosen her regardless of her desperate struggle. The youths and the farmers in the truck fell into confusion. Some were shouting. Some were scolding. Some asked her to get off. Some pulled her back. Hands and figures were in a tangle, hard to tell apart.

Weidong still clasped her hands. She turned back and threw off two slaps in his face, cursing aloud: You son of bitch!

Weidong roared: Listen! Since we even cannot feed ourselves, how can we manage to raise the child! How can we explain it to our family?! I have already made Grandma Li adopt him. She will take care of him well. Don't get yourself into such a fucking bother!

She wawled, shaking her head wildly, losing her mind. She burst into incredible tears . . .

The contours of the village faded away. The forests and the fields made an obscure and vast break against the skyline, leaving a roll of freehand brushwork, sheltered in the depth of the mist. Weidong gazed at all of these calmly, without a single tear in his eyes.

They spent a day and a night in the truck. All the way she was as pale as ashes. She leaned silently against a corner, with scraggly hair and palely chapped lips furling and unfurling. Her look grew old all of a sudden, just like a lunatic and vulgar old woman. He recalled the night when they first met each other. Her pitch-dark plait was glittering, turning lustrously indigotic against the candle-lighting. Her eyes were quick-witted as deer. Her rosy cheeks were blooming as the azaleas in spring hills. She was playing a harmonica. He recognized the song—"Hawthorn Tree". He passionately sent his poem to her, a poem written on a piece of bark.

But all of these passed away. Life and circumstances are able to change all, easily and downright.

His heart ached. Conscience-stricken, he put out a hand to pat Suqing on her head, trying to comb her scraggly plait. She startled and dodged, looking up with eyes full of stabbing hatred; Weidong drew back helplessly, whispered: This is not our fault.

This is not our fault, he said.

Surely, this is not our fault, she replied. But Weidong, she said with subtle bitterness, you are so cruel. Not every man is as cruel as you.

He clenched his teeth and uttered no word.

It takes many years of chaotic and solemn youth to learn an inevasible fact: Fate is beyond control, especially when born in a mistaken age.

At the moment of debarkation, she was heading towards the south, and he was going to the west. She said to him: It's time we part. Dragging his luggage, he turned back and stared at her calmly. Silent countenance returned to his haggard face. He was speechless. Lifting his luggage, he walked ahead without turning his head.

This scene symbolized his divided character: the most melancholy and romantic poetry, and the most selfish and ruthless choice.

That was her last impression of him. The silhouette leaving all alone was just like a hurried and disordered exeunt, announcing the total disappearance of the youth, in this hurried and disordered world, and age.

It is said that a young "educated youth" was seen to go deep into the forests of Xiaoxing'anling, to knock his head before the bleak grave on the hill, and to kneel down for a lengthy while.

He was Jian Weidong. When he was determined to leave this land and come back no longer, he at last had the courage to look upon the grave. Once, he put too much firewood in the chimney. It was broiled so hot as to set the clothing on fire. Finally several people were burnt. Four girls were buried in the conflagration. Their smiles were deserted in the strange land, escaped into a secret corner of the time, and left no trace behind.

It was a dusk before the dark night closed in. Jian Weidong was standing before their grave and gazing at the immerging of their familiar and yet unfamiliar smiles into the ridges of sunset. He knew that these young lives must have retired to a paradise that he could not approach in this world. The broken remnants of tombstone covered with luxuriant grasses appeared as a painstaking and solemn beauty across the silent years.

The smiles slumbered underneath a strange land, not attended to by anybody. In the days to come, they would be keeping asleep as they had always been. The clusters of wormwood and wild flowers scattered nearby wavered gently with the wind, facing the bright and graceful sunset glow spreading over the sky. They too were the judges that had remained silent. He stood alone for a long time, gazing through the cold dark green tombstones at the eyes of these seventeen-year-olds who died at his hand. Like the tide under the moon, time was reduced to pieces of film with full and rich light, rolling before the eyes driven by the screws of time.

At the first gathering for the group of "educated youth", he was the poet with pale and slim fingers, playing a dark brown cello—his fair and slim fingers were holding the bow, the obvious joints on his hand protruding rhythmically like a poem with flying rhymes against the night and candle light. Before he left in a hurry, he handed a box of poems written on birch bark to the beautiful girl, saying: these are the poems I wrote, and you may read them if interested.

What followed was the nightmare of the fire. The black smoke was not yet gone, and the four girls burnt alive curled together hand in hand. Their bodies turned into pitch black charcoal, and thick black grease kept oozing from beneath the shroud.

The lengthy paths leading to the lover on the midsummer's night, those goodbye kisses on the foggy mornings in the birch woods, and those youthful days when the young figures were cloaked by the sea of green fields and eventually vanished, had all gone completely, and not to return.

Jian Weidong stood for a long while before the grave. There were vast and oblivious waters far and away. Fogs and reeds spread all over. The night thickened in the hills. Facing the starlight and the moonlight, he was fully aware that he should have no more regret or greed towards the fate. Compared with these slumbering smiling faces, he still owned life, omnipotent life. Nothing but his years as an "educated youth" could accompany the beings in the grave, whispering to the hills day and night.

He, together with those girls, are the sacrificial lambs dedicated to the ideal of the republic. Ignorant and innocent sacrificial lambs, just like the era itself.

5

After Tong Suqing fled from the village, her parents who had suffered prosecution in every possible way were involved in her desertion case and were humiliated for another time. She was absolutely forbidden from both education and employment.

Without food and cloth coupons allotted to her, she lived a hard life. She was forced into a desperate situation. In this case, she made up her mind to steal into Southeast Asia with some ambitious fellow youths, to start a new undertaking overseas. It took them many years.

She also had a rough time in Southeast Asia, where she soon married a businessman of Chinese origin and learned investment and business under his guidance. They kept their company going by painstaking efforts. When her economic condition began to improve, she was impatient to begin her college education, in order to make up for the youthful days when she was forced to drop out of school. Several years later, the businessman died from an accident. She inherited from him and took over the company. Her business kept enlarging. Finally she secured a foothold throughout all the hardships and struggles. She didn't return to her native land until ten years later.

During a span of over ten years, she acted like a stalwart soldier who washed the wound with the atrocity of war. At every moment of choice, she hesitated at nothing and advanced towards the most risky goal. Her peer educated youths (or "Lao San Jie") all succeeded in their careers. Sometimes she realized that after she left the countryside, no more tribulation could compare to those years of hard and hopeless manual labor and survivorship. And when a person had survived the most awful tribulation and become indifferent to the ways of the world, and when time was so pressed that she could not afford to waste even a minute on matters of no use, what was left before her was nothing but the so-called success. For in her youthful days, the price for it had already been paid in advance. And the enormous injury and regret could not be compensated for only by a heroic and passionate slogan—"no regrets for our youth", even concerning the whole era.

In the lengthy years, it seemed that the aim of life was no more than a justified and impatient revenge. In nature, she was still the very sacrificial lamb, ignorant and innocent. Even the reminiscence of the faraway youth, and the years buried deeply in the farmland and the earth, had become too costly a lamentation. Although in any case, the memory, by right of its irreplaceable magnificence, can always match the present and the future.

After all these years, she came to erase Jian Weidong from her memory, the lover to whom she had paid out all her youth. Afterwards she came to realize that Jian Weidong's choice in casting away his child and parting with her was actually understandable. However, on a night ten years later, she dreamed of Jian Weidong and of those years at which she could not bear to look back. She also dreamed of the harmless baby who was forsaken by his parents and adopted at such an early age. In her dream the pale and slim hands of Jian Weidong were as vivid as those of yesterday, but the owner of the hands was endued with a ferocious face—snatching a baby, the hands closed upon her, silent as a grave. The crying of the baby resounded, extraordinarily sonorous, thin and feeble. She was awaken by the approaching ferocious face, surrounded by a blaze of horror . . .

She woke up in the middle of the nightmare. Sitting up from the bed, she felt so exhausted and tired, relapsing into an endless sentimental mood.

On the next day, in an unspeakable guilty humor, she decided to return to the countryside where she once settled as an "educated youth", and to pick up Jiansheng.

It is a journey overdue for years, heading blankly towards an island standing in the depth of memory. The end of the journey was the vast oblivious water.

It is a journey of reminiscence. Suqing came to the forests.

The horrible shock stirred at the sight of the burnt bodies of the girls always stood in her memory. Following the calling of her heart, she went to visit them.

The afternoon was ending. The daylight had turned so dense. It was another excellent spring day. The fine weather and the brilliant spring scenery were just the same as what they were years ago.

The shabby and deserted grave in which the four girls were lying had been covered by wildly grown grass and trees. Only a corner of the dark green tombstone emerged askew from the depth of the layers of green. Pulling aside the fluffy green foxtail tassel and the leaves of wormwood, one would see the plain and doleful names carved in the stone, already obscured by the thick moss. The expressionless sunlight shed rays of light onto the forgotten tomb. No one knew what solitude and coldness the youthful smile under the tomb had suffered through over ten years until today when an intentional yet casual visit was paid at last.

The mountain wind blew over the land and woods with pungent scent, bringing an ancient and peaceful caress to her face. She was standing still on the quiet mountain with blank memory, accompanied by the silent green foxtail and wormwood. Like a young child eager to have fun, she was greedily enjoying the pleasure beyond time. She seemed to have returned to over ten years before. The hard times seemed to have never existed, and she was still the girl in the oversized cotton coat walking in the depth of the forest, lingering for the birch, holly and azaleas, or later the girl who was wearing a soldier's coat over her big belly and carrying on her shoulders a basket full of corn cobs despite the disturbing heat. Her braids were greasy and messy with crumbs of leaves sticking. She walked through the extension of green fields in a pair of soldier's shoes already worn.

Yet time was so calm and dry. All these had gone and become the past.

The past, lying sideways arrogantly in the middle of lifetime, received the examination of the memory and gave off beautiful light from the brewing of time. It seemed to have become the dream that one had never acquired, and even reason was intoxicated by it. However, it was bitter when the past was still the reality one had to experience.

The setting sun was blown beneath the horizon by the wind like tumbleweed. Looking at the silent smile, she felt calm, almost indifferent. It was time to leave. She touched the cold tombstone, saying her silent goodbye. Perhaps she would never come back to visit again. After all, no visit of mourning could pay back those unknown years of strength and endurance in life, for life itself was but a piece of silent stone on which were carved the words long forgotten by the world.

She departed from the forests and returned to town after several transfers. On getting off the bus, she came across an old-timer sitting idly at a tea-stall. The man was just the political instructor of the former production team. He looked much older than before, and failed to recognize her. She did not intend to chat with him, for it was no longer necessary for her to solicit those people for applying to return to town by obtaining a job vacancy.

Things are still, but people are not. All of a sudden, a familiar poem of her childhood was called to her mind:

I left home young. I return old.
Speaking as then, but with hair grown thin.
And my children, meeting me, do not know me.
They smile and say: "Stranger, where do you come from?"

It is not her home here.
However, isn't it her home here?

Having returned to the site of the subsequent production team, she walked towards the house of Grandma Li. The way had

changed. The people were no longer familiar. On the way she came
upon some aged farmers. They looked familiar, but she failed to
recall their names. At that time both Jian Weidong and she were
unpopular among the people, and had little social intercourse. In
her memory, except for the neighbor widow who had kindly looked
after her, other people were all fatuous, selfish, and unpredictable.
She asked the way several times. The farmers were kind. After she
passed by, they talked for quite a while to guess which "educated
youth" had come back for a revisit.

On the doorstep of Grandma Li, she found that the adobe house
had been repaired a few times and looked different. But the old
wall stood as of old. The hole in it was filled up with bricks, which
appeared so genial. With all kinds of feelings welling up in her
heart, she knocked at the door with trembling hands.

The elder woman looked just as she had more than ten years
before. She led Suqing into the room. The main room was equipped
with electric light now, and also some plastic chairs. Their recall
of the past sounded plain and dull. Her attention was distracted
from the elder woman's nattering. At the thought of the coming
reunion with her son, she could not keep her excitement in check,
feeling a mixture of sorrow and joy.

He came. Feeling that her son was running from afar, she rose
uneasily at once. The old woman looked up at the mother sadly.

It was a small boy, wearing a dirty shirt and having slightly
outgrown his pants. Dots of mud and crumbs of grass leaves were
scattered all over his hair and body, giving off the scent of plants
and soil soaking in sweat. His delicately shaped face shone with
the sunlight, a touch of crimson from basking showing in the fair
skin; his eyes were large and bright. He was very pretty.

The fair-skinned boy, thin and tall, bore clearly the expression
of his father. He was her flesh and blood, the continuation of her
life. Right away she felt gross guilt and remorse.

It was in that summer that she took her son back to the city. They were silent on the train, each immersed in their own thoughts. The huge change took place so suddenly and it took time to sink in.

Right after they returned to the city, she was busy going through the procedures to settle her son's identity, looking for a school for him and shopping for clothes and furniture.

The first night he went back to the city, Jiansheng could not sleep. He felt all too strange; it was like a hasty journey instead of the reality he had to face from then on. The boy rose from the bed at midnight and, turning on the light, looked at the carefully prepared room. It was still unimaginable that a mother who just appeared from nowhere was now sleeping in the next room. He gazed outside the window, the street lamps quietly on and vehicles passing.

He walked out of his room, self-conscious, to knock on his mother's door.

The mother opened the door and asked him curiously, what's wrong?

The boy looked at her and felt like calling Mother, but could not say it. He stood in silence, carefully examining his mother's face.

Finally, he asked, where's my father?

His mother extended her hand and touched his head gently, saying, it's late and you should sleep. You only need to know that you are my Jiansheng. You father ... I will let you know about him when you grow up.

6

That was the summer when Jiansheng's life was utterly changed.

In the city, his mother sent him to the best junior high school where, because of his strong northern country accent and rustic temperament, he became an alien among his classmates. Ridicule and alienation was hard to stand. He was educated in the country primary school and naturally his grades were rather bad. His hatred for the school began to grow stronger and his fear of the classroom and his classmates and teachers was profound. Very often he would sit by the playground for a long while, looking at the playful students kicking balls and attacking each other jokingly, wondering repeatedly why his mother abandoned him for no reason and took him back to the city at an inappropriate time.

He was sure that he was suffering. He talked less and less. And he began to spend long hours sitting under the row of poplars along the secluded playground at the back, thinking of Grandma and the carefree life in the country, until he almost broke into tears. When the thoughts wore him down, he spent the pocket money his mother gave him on picture-story books and read them one after another. He did not know his homework and was unable to finish it. He hated the classroom, the teachers and the classmates. He couldn't understand a word of their dialect, and when he spoke, he only received vicious mockery and guffaws from his classmates.

He didn't attend the classes and his grades were too bad. The teachers would not stand him longer and asked the parent to take him home.

On the night when the teacher told his mother of his truancy, she was busy with work and came back late. Jiansheng was too scared to even turn on the lights. He didn't eat dinner and was very hungry. His mother entered the room with a weary and annoyed face as if covered with frost. She shuffled up some leftover food and put the dishes on the table, making harsh noise. She snapped, go fetch the chopsticks and eat.

Obediently he took the chopsticks and then the bowl quietly and began to swallow the food.

It was all dark outside. The pendant lamp in the dining hall was dim and seemed so exhausted that it would fall asleep instantly. It was the first time his mother talked to him with a long face. In his memory, the chopsticks in his mother's hand froze in the air for a long time with the food on them, and her left hand was holding the bowl edge with such force that the china would break into pieces anytime.

The air was stiff and tense, like that in most of the days to follow.

At last, the mother articulated each word he said. Your father dumped you when we left there, and I know you don't remember. But after all these years I can't forget the pain back then when our car was farther away and you were no longer visible. Life was hard, and I had no choice but to leave you. It was a sin for a mother. Now I brought you home because I want to redeem it. Everything I give you, clothes, shoes, bags, and the schooling, is paid by the money I made in Southeast Asia as a vagrant; I risked my life for the money and suffered disgrace . . .

You are too young to understand my hardship as a woman. We have but each other in this home. If you don't listen to me, neither of us will have an easy life. Our family can't compare with others. Your father failed you, and I replace him to raise you alone as both father and mother. You may not know the difficulty, but you have to understand and can't be unreasonable like other kids. Don't bring me trouble.

Don't play truancy again.

The tone was fierce and the words cold. Gapemouthed, Jiansheng looked at the tears rushing to his mother's thin chin, dripping like the raindrops beneath the eaves of Grandma's old house during a shower. Mother choked with sobs, and he was afraid.

He listened in silence. When his mother finished, he put down the bowl gently, walked in his own small room and plugged the key slowly. He went down, held his knees, leaning against the door, and cried silently, exerting all his strength not to make a sound. He felt very cold.

Not a sound was heard from the dining hall. After a long time, when he was tired from crying, Jiansheng heard a shrill noise. His mother threw a bowl onto the floor. Jiansheng shuddered at the sudden noise, immensely frightened. Before he realized it, the door slammed, and his mother got out of the room.

It was the first time that his mother got angry at him. After that, Jiansheng turned submissive and clever, but more reserved. His mother hired tutors for him to catch up with his class. His handwriting was bad, and his mother sent him to learn calligraphy. For him to have accomplishments like a city boy, he was required to learn to play the piano and English in his spare time ... his mother didn't know how to express in other ways the great expectation she had for him.

She grew up in an era when books and education were not available. The best years of her life were wasted in the countryside, as a result of the desolation of education. She shared the feeling of urgency with other parents of her generation, those who graduated from junior or senior high schools in the special years of 1966, 1967 and 1968. They took pains to invest in the education of their children and offered them the best possible conditions, but in a stubborn and impatient fashion.

It was more the compensation for the unrealized education in one's own youth than the cultivation of the younger generation: as if when one saw their child sitting in the best classroom studying, or playing the piano well, or going to a prestigious university, their own unfulfilled youth was brought back shining again before death and the long-cherished wish came true. Otherwise, they would die with lasting regret.

And the blank period of the first twelve years of Jiansheng's life forced his mother to be more anxious about his education. She offered him all the best conditions, but the slightest hesitation on Jiansheng's side to accept the good will would break his poor mother's heart. Jiansheng tried to express his unwillingness, but gradually learned the futility of rebellion after many times of persuasion by his tearful mother. Finally, he chose passive obedience as the alternative.

He no longer sat by the playground thinking about the hard

questions. However, he would not say a word while sitting in the classroom. When the teachers called his name and required an answer to a question, he stood up and would not utter a thing. The teachers were angry at first, then turned impatient and finally gave up calling his name. When the cocky team leaders in charge of him came to him specially to collect his homework, he gave his blank notebooks and waited for the teachers' scolding. Attacked by the teachers' language, he had no enthusiasm for study and remained low, which naturally resulted in bad grades. He didn't like the piano and never practiced playing after class. On weekends, his mother prescribed practice on the piano and left for work or other social occasions. He stayed home reading picture-story books and played his childish trick by pulling the cloth covering the piano and dropping the scores on it so that when his mother came back it would look like he had played, and then spent his time drawing freely. The piano teacher didn't know how to handle him in piano class. His mother, hearing the teacher's sighs, could not help her anger. And scolding was inevitable after they returned home from piano lessons. While scolding, his mother, in tears, told Jiansheng how she herself had loved music when she was young. She nattered that she never got the access to music because her family couldn't afford it.

One of her neighbors had a handmade dulcimer; envious, she couldn't control the desire to play the instrument. She would sneak into the neighbor's home and play for a while and then leave. A while later, she returned to play it again . . . eventually, her neighbors were so annoyed that they always shut the door. By telling the story, his mother said sternly to Jiansheng, look, Jiansheng, you have such favorable conditions, but you never cherish it, and it casts a chill on me.

Every time when he heard such words, Jiansheng bit his lips without saying anything, tears in eyes. While his mother was forever complaining how Jiansheng failed her, she had no idea that such a life cast a chill on Jiansheng as well. He began to see that his mother seemed trying to make him realize what she failed to do as a young woman—no matter the opportunity of education or of developing talent—and he became the second youth for her mother to make up her own regrets and impose all her unfulfilled wishes on Jiansheng: twelve years after Jiansheng was born.

At the end of his childhood, during the first days back to his mother, he seemed never to have tasted the tenderness and favor he imagined a mother should give the son. He grew to believe that a true mother should not be like his own mother. Although Jiansheng never stated it, what had brought him the greatest pain was why his mother gave birth to him and abandoned him and then took him back for a life of suffering.

He started continuous secret rebellions against his mother's instructions. When his mother demanded a lot from him, he demanded a lot from his mother. But all his demands were for materials, just like all her mother's demands were only for his study and playing the piano. To a certain degree, he did that to desperately express his hatred.

Those were the darkest days during Jiansheng's growing up. The only motive for him to go to school was the two fine art classes each week. He still remembered how, in the first class, the pretty young teacher asked the students to draw whatever they wished on the drawing books and to draw their favorite things. Some students drew their mothers, some chose pastures, and some preferred toys or cakes. Jiansheng drew with crayon his Grandma's old house and Yellow Tiger; he wanted to draw more: the crystal clear pond and the fish, and the ice lake in the winter snow . . . and roe deer, mallards, water birds, durra fields, cornfields, or the wild geese flying to the south . . . he wanted to draw so many things that when the bell rang for the class to end, he was still working on his second drawing and hadn't finished drawing all that he liked. His classmates had left the classroom one after another. The teacher went to him to collect his drawing and asked patiently, do you want to go on drawing? Let's draw together in my office. The teacher talked in a northern dialect, familiar to his ears.

He didn't speak but nodded obediently. He collected his things and followed the teacher to the office.

The class was over for the school students. The setting sun moved over the wall covered with ivy; the yellow light in the office was cut clearly, shed on the floor. Jiansheng bent over on the table and worked. He forgot that the teacher was beside him; she didn't talk either, but patiently waited for him to finish.

He finished four drawings at last, satisfied and happy, tiny drops of sweat on his forehead. His arms had left sweaty and warm marks on the table. He gave the drawings to the teacher. He would not forget the joyous surprise on the teacher's face and all the praises. The teacher's pretty young face left a deep impression on him. Immersed in the peaceful rays of the sunlight, it made the only happy memory since he left the old country home. Finally the teacher said, work hard on drawing, and you are surely to become a painter!

When he came back home that day, Jiansheng said to his mother, I want to learn drawing. His mother asked, why? He said, because the teacher praised me today, saying if I work hard on drawing, I will surely become a painter!

The mother, weary and fretted after a day's hard work, only replied expressionlessly, oh, really.

After a long pause, his mother said, what about the piano?

Jiansheng said, I don't like the piano. I don't want to learn to play the piano.

The mother said, I spent a lot of money to buy you the piano and now it's garbage. Do you think I make money that easily?

Jiansheng bit his lips and stopped talking. After a long time, he said in a low voice, you didn't ask me what I wanted to learn.

His mother replied indignantly, why do you always talk so coldly? You . . .

The words were on the tip of her tongue, but she stopped, looking ready for whining again.

Jiansheng was so tired of such scenes between his mother and him. It went beyond his endurance. He said, I will not say I don't like it lightly if I can learn drawing.

The look on his mother face was surly. She gnashed her teeth and said, what if in a month you say again you don't want it?

In a low tone Jiansheng said, I won't.

He remembered his words and started to learn drawing as if fighting against his mother. Nothing much changed, but the air seemed now icy at home, because of Jiansheng's intentional avoidance of his mother.

Jiansheng had a born talent and a hearty passion for painting. He took classes in Chinese painting at the Children's Palace at first, but he soon grew tired of the crowd and noises there. He found a private teacher from the Academy of Fine Arts and began to learn sketch drawing, the fundamental skill of western painting. Unlike other children who were whipped by their parents to idle through painting lessons every week, Jiansheng displayed great talent for painting. Always the first to come and the last to leave, the boy was often absorbed in silent observation of the solid, plaster geometric shapes.

Jiansheng would live the entire week in the expectation of the drawing lessons at weekend. He never got up late on those days. He would take up the oversized, olive-drab drawing board on his back in the early morning, buy breakfast downstairs, and eat it on the bus. He always picked the front seat in the drawing room in order to watch her drawing closely. He returned home very late every Sunday.

The rest of his spare time was spent on the roof garden. He would always go up to the garden and take care of the plants the first thing after school. When his mother occasionally went up there to hang clothes, she would see him crouching on the ground with flax gloves on and a shovel in his hand, talking to the plants and insects, or sitting on a stool sketching a gardenia with the drawing board in arms.

He asked for plenty of pocket money from his mother to buy books. Every now and then, he would stay a while in the bookshop after school and walk home leisurely with a bag of books. He did not like pop songs or watching TV, but he loved tending the flowers in the roof garden, buying a lot of books to read, crossing the city in the curtain of night with books or the drawing board, and watching the stream of people and cars. The bustling world would gradually quiet down and dissolve into extreme stillness. This would make him happy.

This was no false sentimentality. He was just a solitary boy and could not get adapted to the people and things around him.

7

He painted his childhood away slowly; actually he grew up so slowly that his mother seemed to lose her patience. She soon entered the menopausal period, and he soon approached adolescence. The two of them formed an upsetting juxtaposition. In the following days, Jiansheng became habitually silent, while his mother grew more and more fretful. Jiansheng often quietly watched his mother busying over the chores restlessly with her teeth clenched. The less she said, the more turmoil Jiansheng would feel inside her, as if it might explode at any time. Mother's temper became unpredictable. In the end, Jiansheng would sometimes intentionally provoke her and gain vengeful pleasure over her tearful yammer. He felt a cutting pain inside, too. The relationship was totally pathetic.

From then on, Jiansheng would hear his mother curse somebody in a low voice when she was working alone. She was cursing constantly. The words were harsh and the hatred was impossible to conceal, which made her teeth-grinding sound rather terrifying.

At other times, when she was cooking in the kitchen or taking a bath, she would make exaggerated, protracted sighs. Her voice was fretful and full of boredom and disappointment. Her sighs made him feel cold to the bones. At such times, Jiansheng would withdraw into his own room in disgust and sit alone with his legs bent for a while to get rid of his fear. Then he would indulge in random, endless guesses at who she was cursing and why she sighed so sadly.

Jiansheng spent his adolescent years in guesses and fear.

His mother had always been hateful. She had never been blessed with contentment in her life. At that time, Jiansheng was not sympathetic with her endless complaint at all.

She never explained to him the cause of her hatred, nor could he ask her. Such things became unspeakable taboos of the family.

Young Jiansheng began his habitual confrontation with his mother. Even when their relationship was broken beyond repair, he was cold at heart and would only feel occasional disappointment.

He did try to rescue the relationship, though, before it wrecked.

That was not long after they came back to the city when he was thirteen years old.

Jiansheng got to know his mother's birthday from her ID card. He bought a gift—a scarf—for her and had it carefully wrapped, planning to present it in the morning of her birthday.

It was a Sunday morning. He could remember it clearly. He was supposed to take a painting lesson that day, so he woke up very early. After getting up, instead of washing his face or brushing his teeth, Jiansheng took out the gift and ran to his mum's room. When he opened the half-closed door, before he could say anything, he caught sight of two naked bodies lying together. The muscles on the man's back moved in excitement, a movement that was incomprehensible to Jiansheng. The two of them were so preoccupied that they did not notice Jiansheng at first. Jiansheng held his breath and closed the door softly.

At that time he did not know the truth about lust, nor did he understand what Mother and the man were doing. He even heard Mother's vague laughter. But he was struck with an enormous fear and shame. Jiansheng quietly returned to his room, bent his legs and crouched on the ground to calm down. A few minutes later, Mother came to his room abruptly. She embraced Jiansheng tightly with rattled tears—the hug was so tight and unexpected that he could not even breathe—and between Mother's arms, he saw that the man hurriedly put on his shirt and fled.

Mother held Jiansheng up and put him on the bed. She asked him anxiously, what did you see . . . you . . .

Jiansheng thought for a while. Then he told a lie for the first time in his life: I saw nothing.

Mother seemed not to hear this obvious lie; or rather, she did not care about it. She began her long, broken monologue about her agony, the same as all the women in love, only more desolate and tragic. Mother grumbled to her son, who had been with her for no more a year, you are too young to understand . . . this is nothing serious . . . mum loves dad . . . surely he loves me too . . . it's just been too long since he left . . .

As his mother went on talking, tears came out of her eyes again.

And that was when young Jiansheng became bored of his mother's tears.

These choked, unclear words were the only mention of her emotional life that he ever heard. Since then, the only thing he could remember was his mother's hatred of various people, including his father.

Once in a while, she would talk about Father in a calm tone. When Father was young, so she said, he would wear a white shirt with half folded sleeves and indanthrene blue trousers. He was a striking young man with pale skin and poetic beauty. But he was also selfish and schizophrenic. In the age when poets abounded, Father and Mother in their late teens were driven by fate to the northern countryside as educated youths. Mother fell in love with Father for his rather naïve yet extravagant talent—he was a young poet then. In those bleak years they had a romance that was equally bleak. Soon after Jiansheng was born, his father abandoned him with his own hands.

Those years were buried in the northern countryside. The continuous forest of the Lesser Khingan and the icy lake covered with snow were silenced in the sad and remote nightfall. The blue sky and the clear moon in the northern country were too far-off to be true. The land and the youth and passion on it were now scoffed off by the present social values. That piece of memory was worthy of nothing but destruction.

Mother would often use Father as an example in her ambiguous complaints about men's hearts of stone. She said, don't trust men. They are capricious and selfish. They are so cold-hearted that they can even abandon their own children.

Young Jiansheng was fed up with such complaints. He was only an innocent child then. Mother's pessimistic way of life profoundly shaped his understanding of the world. In a time before he set foot into the world and felt its heat and cold and after his carefree childhood in the countryside, Mother broke in abruptly and constantly poured into him her hatred of the world, telling him the world was more indifferent and ruthless than he could ever imagine . . .

Mother was bitter. She could find no one except Jiansheng at whom she could pour out her pain. It was not her fault, either.

But after all, he was only a child. Such bitterness was incomprehensible to him, and he was not ready for it.

He was a son, and was destined to grow up into a man in the

future. With Mother's endless complaints about men and the world, he lost himself. In this unfortunate world, he was deprived of a father in the first place. A son without a father as a male role model, and living with a mother whose personality was totally twisted in frustrations, would become baffled about the role he should play.

On that Sunday morning, he had all the good intentions to celebrate Mother's birthday, only to find Mother in such an embarrassment. He was put on the bed by Mother. He had to listen to her long-winded monologue about her affairs with those men.

Jiansheng did not hear a word. The only thing he felt was shame. It was like being on pins and needles. For a boy in his age and knowledge, the joy of the bed was an unendurable shame in itself, not to mention the fact that the man was not his father.

For the first time, Jiansheng roughly interrupted Mother, who was still immersed in her sorrowful monolog. He said, don't talk to me about this. I need to take the painting lesson. I'm going.

So he went, with incomparable disappointment to each other, and from each other. He was disappointed. So was Mother. As for the scarf, it was never presented.

Later, he ran into Mother in the company of a strange man several times again. He was not as scared as the first time though. He still felt hurt, but he would walk away in silence. Then he closed the door of his room, quietly did his homework or read books, or made paintings for the most of the time. He was so tired that he had to lean on the desk with his heart thrilling in sadness. There was nothing he could do.

For the long time afterwards, there was no conversation between them, except for "Come and have dinner" and "How is school?"

Mother still had the traditional responsibility of a parent. She asked about his lessons and grades whenever possible. Unfortunately, it was also what he was weary of. He had bad grades. With exam papers home, he was sure to be scolded.

He was scolded so often that he became numbed about it. He no longer felt sad for being scolded. Even if he was slapped in the face, he just went to his own room gloomily. Then he slammed the door shut and refused to come out.

Because they were each other's closest family, many things were taboos between them. Communication was shame. Intimacy was shame. The only proper way to express each other's love was to over-critically hurt each other. What a tragic fact.

Through the years, Jiansheng did not know the truth behind Mother's affairs with other men. The only thing Jiansheng knew for sure was that he no longer had hope for this family, nor did he have hope for Mother, even if he saw her aging with saddening speed.

Someone has said that if a child is disappointed about his own family, he is sure to be disappointed about the world.

8

When the seventh grade was finished, Jiansheng learned that their young and beautiful drawing teacher was going to quit the job and take advanced lessons at the Academy of Fine Arts, and teach in its training courses at the same time. He was flurried. He did not want to part with her, so he decided to attend her painting class.

That was how this life began.

Crossing the umbrose streets in the beginning summer of his juvenile period, he went for her for the first time. Jiansheng anxiously found her home in the Academy of Fine Arts, and gently knocked on the door. He waited for a while before Huai, in a casual dark nightgown, with a charcoal pencil in her mouth and a pile of paperboard in her one hand, used her other hand to open the door. Her hair was done up in a bun, leaving her long neck uncovered. Her collarbone was as prominent as that of slim teenagers. Her face had a clear and tight outline. For unknown reasons, she was much thinner than before. She had pure white skin, just like the blossoming magnolia downstairs.

Jiansheng was stunned by her beauty. He was too anxious to say a word. Huai questioningly looked at this double-minded boy.

Standing at her doorstep, he asked anxiously, may I attend your painting class?

Huai was thrown by him for a while, and then she smiled, of course you may.

Getting her permission made the young boy so excited that he lost his words. Thank you, thank you, he said it again and again. On his laddish face was a sincere smile, faint and soft, young and shy, yet too impressive to be forgotten.

On his way home, he walked blithely as a happy young boy for the first time in his life. The air in the southern summer was hot and humid. The shady trees stood along the streets. He happily jumped, picked a piece of green leaf and rubbed it with his fingers as if it had been the fine skin in his imagination. The city was immerged in the afterlight of the setting sun. The dusk crawled over the ivy walls, the light sad and mellow. He tended the flowers on the roof garden, humming. The jasmine and gardenia he had planted with his own hands were blossoming with pleasant aroma. Sweats dropped from his forehead. He swiftly wiped them with his sleeves. His mind was full of sweet imaginations about Huai. He had never been happier before.

For the days following, he was addicted to painting. On many evenings when he was supposed to be doing his homework, he could not resist the temptation to begin drawing on the draft paper or sketch book. Most of his drawings were casual portraits of Huai.

He wrote a diary on the sketch paper. When he was hidden in his room practicing the gouache painting, he dared not go out to change the brush washing water, so he just did abstract painting with dry brushes.

At times when Mother suddenly assaulted his room, she would fly into anger and scold him endlessly for wasting his time when she saw the paintings. Sometimes she even grabbed the sketch book and pointed at the female portraits, angrily cursing and tearing them into pieces. Then she would thrust the assignments into his face, ordering him to finish it before 12 p.m.

Often, after Mother went out, Jiansheng felt so depressed that he could no longer control himself. He would even climb up the window sill and be caught in a desire to jump down. But he did not have the courage. So he often sat on the sill until late in the night.

At such times, he despised his own life deeply.

Jiansheng went to Huai's classroom at the Academy of Fine Arts to draw still life sketches every weekend. Huai had a special classroom for weekend lessons. The classroom was full of standing easels and wasted paint. The ground was covered with a thick layer of pencil ash and irremovable paint left by former students. The walls were spotted with colorful stains, too. If someone leaned on the wall, he was sure to be tainted. However, the room had a special beauty with all this.

Jiansheng walked through the shady flagstone street of the Academy of Fine Arts to the red brick three-storey building covered with dark green vines nearly every day. The plants had a bright and saturated hue. Their leaves swayed in the muggy midsummer breeze, glowing like green daggers. The ceiling fan ran with a loud noise, which was mixed with the drone of cicadas and thus made a perfect summer atmosphere. The classroom had large glass windows, with hefty and dusty curtains. The lighting was very good. Outside the windows were high deciduous trees that remained green for the whole year in the warm south. The cicadas buzzed more and more loudly. The shadows of the trees were sparsely spread in the empty classroom. The shadows seemed to contain some spice rustling down. He was focused on drawing those dull plaster models. If they were too tired or could not find their way, Huai just let the students have a break. Huai chatted with them about the Eagles band that she was addicted to as a student of the Academy of Fine Arts and the dormitory 517 that was said to be haunted. Jiansheng listened and hung around in the classroom, feeling matchlessly joyful.

Sometimes Huai talked to Jiansheng about her boyfriend at college. Jiansheng did not feel any jealousy at all. He was even happy to listen to Huai talking about how they had been in love at college and how they parted after graduation. Jiansheng asked her, surely he loved you very much?

Huai looked back at him and said,

Never presume that others are faithful to you.

This sentence left a deep impression in Jiansheng's mind. It was a long time later when he realized that it was true indeed, though hopeless.

Since that time, Jiansheng fell in love with, or rather, became attached to this young woman who used to be his teacher. Huai had a pair of mild, peaceful eyes; she was patient, nice, and very pretty. She was his painting teacher. Jiansheng felt immensely happy around her. He thoroughly enjoyed every moment by her side and did her many little favors to please her in a cunning yet childish way, such as delivering paintings, pouring water, washing brushes, passing paints, and even getting meals and answering calls. He would often stay in the atelier until dark to walk with her alone for a while after the painting lesson.

The boy's passion for the teacher was always straightforward yet humble. His earnestness and clumsiness often filled Huai with blank dismay and tender affection.

Thirteen-year-old Jiansheng spent the entire summer at the atelier in this way. Huai liked this special boy and insisted to charge him no fee. So Jiansheng visited the atelier regularly even in weekdays after school was open. He would fly to the atelier after school and attend Huai's lesson to the big boys. He waited behind the high easel until dark, only to walk Huai to her dormitory after the lesson or chat with her over supper at the gate.

This young, sensitive boy had a short haircut that made him look like a Japanese. The long fringe on his forehead covered his eyes. He was spare, pale like his father and had an introverted disposition that kept him apart from his peers. He grew up alone with the big, sweet secret fermenting in his heart.

Nothing in school could arouse his interest. He would sit through the lessons quietly, sometimes painting, sometimes getting lost in reverie. He carried the sketch book in his bag, on which he drew many sketches and poured out the secret sentiments. He was such a silent, low-profile boy.

Only in Huai's presence would he light up and become talkative. After all the years, even he himself was not clear what role Huai played to him, be it the fair, patient teacher, the affectionate, beautiful mother, the understanding friend, the intimate sister, or the faithful lover. To him Huai set up a paragon for each role that he could imagine. In his long adolescence, he kept the firm belief that life would not be worth living without Huai.

His only wish was to live in a world with Huai. His heart was filled with immense happiness when she was around.

Meanwhile, his mother was still busy flying around cautiously with men and money. During the first night when his mother stayed out without notice, Jiansheng stayed up alone at home and waited for her. He finished his homework, drew several sketches, and had a shower to wash off the fatigue. His mother was not back.

The boy became uneasy, anxious, and troubled, with a nibbling feeling of shame. He waited on the sofa in the same dismay as the first time he saw his mother in bed with a strange man. His heart began thumping fast and his throat was choked. He could not help missing Huai.

So he left home and walked towards Huai's dormitory. The street in the deep night was damp and still. He came to the building alone. It was a cool summer night. Under the blooming magnolia, amidst the transparent moth wings in the gauze of lamp light, the boy prowled to and fro. Whenever he looked up, he could see Huai's window. The moon was as bright and clear as what he saw in his childhood in the countryside in North China. The sporadic stars above his head splattered in the night curtain. He closed his eyes and missed the summer nights at his hometown and Huai's gentle smile. He felt peace at heart.

He stood through the entire night and walked slowly home with stiff legs.

Mother was not back yet. He felt hollow at heart. He would rather be greeted by her scolding than find the house chillingly empty. The boy withdrew to his room quietly, turned the lamp on, opened his sketch book and began painting a blossoming magnolia tree in the night. He wrote on the back of the sketch, Mother did not come home tonight.

He was sleepy that morning. He did not go to school, but slept until noon. When Mother came back, she did not know he skipped the lesson. Jiansheng asked her quietly, where were you last night?

Mother answered in a playing tone, I was busy writing a proposal at the company. Then she turned around and went to her bedroom to change. The boy remained still until she closed the door on his face. He returned to his room without a word.

He was fifteen at that time.

In the sleepless nights that followed, he would often linger around Huai's dormitory building. He indulged himself in this clumsy yet earnest game. Sometimes a storm would pour down in those sweltering nights. The cool rain would flow into streams, bringing a damp smell of plants and earth and washing away intoxicated flowers. When the petals were washed over his insteps, some of them would be hooked by his sandals and leave a slight itch on his skin. At those times, he would bend down and pick them up. He would feel the delicate flowers as if they were that pair of smooth, white hands in his memory. He would put the petals in his pockets and fold them in the sketch books when he returned in early morning. The sketch books became thicker and thicker as more and more flowers were folded in them.

The lonely lad danced on the chords.

He had never told her about his waiting. When he was alone with Huai in the drawing room, he tried hard to hold back his sentiments. Such a brooding, melancholic lad. At moments when he was lost in thought, he would recall every detail of his meeting with Huai. A happy smile would crawl onto his face unwittingly. A most innocent smile.

Sometimes Mother came back at midnight and could not find him anywhere. She would scold him and ask his whereabouts anxiously when he returned. He told lies calmly at first. After several times, however, Mother began to be suspicious.

He went out one night. Mother followed him to Huai's building and suddenly appeared before him when he strolled to and fro idly.

He was stupefied for a moment. Before he realized what happened, he received a hard slap on the face.

His mind went blank. His eyes were dizzy, and his eardrums vibrated with various noises as if rubbed by sharp metals. His face was set on fire; it was not the first time that Mother had hit him like that, but the pain and shame that he felt was more than ever. He stood there pondering difficultly whether he should strike back.

Mother questioned him in a stern voice, what are you doing here, are you looking for that woman?!

Jiansheng felt his heart was about to be torn apart by the blood that gushed out. He was filled with anger and shame and began to walk back silently with clenched fists. Mother did not stop, but trailed him and besieged him with questions and bitter curses.

Fuming with anger, Jiansheng turned back and blurted out, did I ever ask you where you had been when you hanged out with men?!

Mother was petrified. She stared at him unbelievably and was about to slap him again. Jiansheng seized her hand. The boy's hand clamped her wrist forcefully like steel pliers. The mother and son glared at each other in cold hatred.

She could not bring herself to the fact that her relation with the boy would escalate beyond repair. Helpless tears gushed out of her eyes.

Jiansheng felt sour at heart in the face of his mother. He could not find anything else to say. With his face still burning, he swung Mother's wrist aside and walked ahead alone. He looked so much like his father, who turned and left with the luggage.

This little boy used to catch fish in meadows with his face in suntan and muddy spots and crumbs of leaves scattering all over his hair. Now he had grown rapidly into the same stature and face as his father, only with a more indifferent, melancholic, and distracted disposition.

For the first time, she was struck with the idea whether it was a mistake to take him back.

In the dream that night, he saw clearly his father, that man who gave him life but never appeared in his life. In the chaos of the dreams, the boy pleaded with his father to take him back to the watery haven in the North in his childhood. The summer there was full of endless sunshine, noisy cicadas, and lush tree shades. He would swim in the river, catch red dragonflies in the sunset glow, enjoy the cool in the garden in bright summer nights, and read the twinkling stars in the galaxy.

In such dreams, he was the silent boy who never knew how to forget the pains in the past or shoulder the pains in the future. He inched ahead in the violent sun in the strange city with his shadow as his only companion. He would not even look ahead. In the nights when Mother did not return, he would draw tirelessly in his dark little room. When he stopped painting, he would often find that, outside, the dim dawn light had gradually drowned the thick, stuffy night. The notes he jotted down on the thick sketch books accompanied him through one rainy summer after another.

9

He graduated from junior high school when he was about to be sixteen. When summer came, Huai took several kids of the painting class for a sketching tour.

They visited remote scenic areas far away from the city. The boys and girls were plainly dressed with canvas bags and sports shoes and carried painting boards, little buckets, watercolor paper, sketch books, and many paints and brushes. The young painters took a long ride on bus and reached the picturesque country.

All the students loved Huai. Everyone wanted to sit by her side on the bus. But Jiansheng would never jostle for a seat by her like the other noisy boys; he would sit behind her and watch her from behind silently on the way. The road wound its way through the nameless mountains with the streams in the valleys flapping heavily against the shore. Huai and the students got off the buss on the way and climbed the mountains with bags and painting stuff in the search of sketching spots.

Jiansheng fell behind the other students. He picked up a wooden stick on the way and slowly made his way up the mountain.

It was a sunny day in July, but it was not hot in the mountains. It had just rained, so the air was damp and the forest was lush green. The purple flowers broke into blossom along the road. Noisy cicadas repeated their songs in the tranquility. The students trudged along the winding mountain path for nearly two hours. The sunlight was rampant and the children became thirsty. Some of them began complaining and grumbling uneasily. Huai had to coax the kids and had sweat all over. Jiansheng walked behind everyone and remained silent on the way. He felt thirsty and hot as well, but he found it worthwhile when he saw Huai's figure from behind.

They finally reached the top of the mountain. The mountain peak presented a most invigorating view to them. The light blue contour of the peaks gradually melted into the sky. The breezes were very refreshing.

Huai asked the children to rest under the tree. They rushed to the cool shade and put down their bags, gulping water and gasping exaggeratedly.

Jiansheng walked to Huai alone. He gave her a cool towel wet with spring water. He told her sincerely, Miss Huai, you can wipe the sweat with this.

Huai looked up into the boy's suntanned face. The hair on his forehead had sweat all over and was slightly rumpled, exposing the bright and clean forehead. His white shirt was wet through as well. The vague, sincere smile on his face had a unique boyish charm that was hard to forget. Huai said, thanks.

Jiansheng left with a smile. He settled in the shade by himself and had some drinks.

The children recovered a little after eating the food they brought for lunch. Huai asked them to pick an angle for sketching. The children immediately bustled around, filling buckets with water, washing brushes, setting up painting boards, spreading the paints, and what not. Most of the children had rarely been to scenic areas in the past and they were full of curiosity and excitement at the first sketching tour in their life. To a certain extent, this was not like a sketching tour but an adventure. Jiansheng took out his sketch book, sharpened the charcoal stick with his knife, formed a frame with his fingers and looked carefully for an angle. When the other children were busy preparing the tools, he had already turned a new page and begun painting.

Huai sat in the distance and watched this special boy. He was such a gratifying child, she thought. She walked over behind him and watched him painting for a long while. Jiansheng noticed her and began to feel nervous. He became hesitant and even trembled with the brush in his hand. Huai was completely amused by the cute boy.

Jiansheng turned around and looked up into her eyes. He immediately turned back and buried himself in painting without saying a word. In curiosity, Huai knelt down and took up his sketch book. The boy made an attempt to hold it back, and was caught in a complete daze. Huai got hold of it at last. She saw her own portrait on every page she turned.

She was taken aback, put the book back in silence, stood up and left.

Jiansheng glimpsed at her figure from behind, as if his unspeakable secret were disclosed in the public. His heart was filled with shame.

They passed the night at Lingxi County at the foot of the mountain. The ancient county was settled in the embrace of the mountains and faced a green lake in the front. A brook ran through it with limpid water jingling on its way, and hence the name "Lingxi", meaning literally "a jingling brook". Huai and the children sat around the table and had supper in the folk house. The children were all exhausted after walking a whole day. It was dark after the supper, and the children lined up impatiently to have a shower one by one at the plain bathroom behind the hotel.

But Jiansheng walked out of the courtyard alone and strolled on the path.

It was a cool night with a full moon in the sky. The trees cast down swaying shadows in the bright moonlight. The lonely wild goose sang sad songs in a low voice like a vague, ancient lullaby that lulled the village to sleep. Smoke curled upward from kitchen chimneys in the depths of the dusk and licked the stooping sky in melancholy. A wooden boat that anchored by the reedy lakeside gently swayed to and fro like a humble leaf falling prey to the wind of fate. The air was moist and cool. Broken stars quickly emerged in the dark blue sky. The mountain breeze kissed the waves, swam through the weather-beaten fences of the courtyards by the lakeside, and carried the distant dogs' barks and the roosters' crows far away.

Jiansheng closed his eyes. He felt as if he returned to the countryside in his childhood. Once again the expanses of dark green lakes and the world of wilderness appeared before his eyes.

Huai found Jiansheng missing when she counted the students. She went out of the yard anxiously and, after walking for a while, saw the lad standing by the pond, alone, resembling a tall and slender young crane. She went up to call him gently, Jiansheng, Jiansheng.

The boy turned back and saw Huai coming to him. He could not see her face clearly but felt the all too familiar yearning pressing like a sweet dream within his reach. His heart was tranquil and well at the moment.

She said, why aren't you back?

The boy smiled a little smile, saying, it's so pretty here. I forgot the time.

Huai looked around and saw the moon was bright and light and felt the cool breeze. A kingfisher plunged into the water to catch fish, stirring a ringing noise to break the silence. She couldn't help saying, it'd be nice to walk.

The two went for a walk leisurely around the mountain village. Moonlight overhead, they were at peace and contented. They didn't talk. After a long walk, they returned to the inn and found the waiter was ready to shut the door and turn off the lights. Frost-like moonlight was on the dark wood porch. The boy bid her good-night. She stood there, looking at his thin back in the white shirt disappearing under the moonlight into the narrow corner.

When the boy turned to leave, happy tears filled his eyes for the walk on such a perfect and unforgettable night with the beloved one.

10

They were drawing sketches in the mountain village. Everyday they brought solid food with them and sat drawing all day long. Huai patiently modified the children's drawings; every kid was eager to have her modify their work. Jiansheng was always sitting beside in silence, looking indifferently at the others around Huai like passionate and blind bees. He only remembered the cool moonlit night when he walked with her in silence. The very thought of the night would fill him with profound sweetness and while drawing he always wore a subtle smile.

She came to modify his drawing. It was not the first time she discovered the lad's talent. Many girls could draw elaborate and fine pictures but most were mediocre; many boys drew clumsily rather ugly pictures. But as for the truly talented boy, his first strokes would reveal his gift, and one look at his work could recognize his unique character, the nimbus in every stroke, the unforgettable touch. The curious local passersby came to see the children's work and talk to them. Only Jiansheng didn't talk much and focused on drawing.

In several days the children had drawn all the old houses, fields, lakes and streams near the village. Huai planned to climb to the southern mountain to the village to see if there were suitable places to bring the children up for sketching. The other children were sleeping late; when Huai had set off, however, Jiansheng couldn't help following her. He quickened his steps to catch up with her and said, teacher, I want to go with you. Huai looked at the uneasy boy and smiled, all right, you come with me.

So they went up the mountain together. They stepped into the deep forest and walked along the Ling river. The streams were clear and bright like a lover's tears. When they stopped to rest, they could see the mountains and peaks looming behind the old trees. The howls of tigers and screams of monkeys were mingled with bird chirping. The early morning fog in the mountain wrapped the skin like silk. He followed Huai closely, imaging how he would rush to her rescue if she should fall ... the sweet imagination unfinished, Jiansheng himself fell to the ground inadvertently and in a fluster. Huai turned around. He got to his feet quickly despite the pain and looked at her with a red face. Huai said, come, Jiansheng, come over.

Huai supported him and examined his scrape carefully. He felt that he had lost face and tried to endure the pain for fear that Huai would laugh at him. Huai asked worriedly, let's go down the hill to apply some liquid medicine? Hearing the words, Jiansheng said quickly, feeling anxious, no, no, I can move on.

After a brief rest, they resumed the journey. Along the way, Huai tried to support him with her hands. When she got close to Jiansheng, the boy smelt the floral scent, free from the odor of perfume. When she stretched out her feminine and lovely fair hands to hold his arms, the coy boy was flushed. For the first time he tasted such strong and complicated feelings and so unforgettable.

They kept walking and spoke little. As if they had forgotten the original intention of the climb; instead, it had become an adventurous excursion whose goal was ignored. Huai was not weak as many city girls; she walked nimbly and showed good stamina. Finally they reached the mountain top.

Standing on the top of the unknown mountain, they saw deep green around them and extending far away, like ocean waves. Occasionally the green was disturbed by a row of egrets flying across like kites, which brought liveliness to the color as if one could touch it. He felt that everything was better than dreams—walking through picturesque mountains with the one you loved right next to you.

That day he stood with Huai on the mountain top overlooking the endless mountains; the cool breeze refreshed the heart. Several times he almost told Huai about his love. However, the two of them, standing on the mountain top, did not say anything, and went down in silence.

Huai didn't let the children to go up the mountain and her reason was that the roads were too slippery and risky. Jiansheng, for obscure reasons, felt secretly glad about the decision. The beautiful mountain and forest, quiet like a virgin, was a memory that belonged to Huai and him. He didn't want anyone to tread rashly.

The next day, carrying a whole pile of drawings, Huai and the children set off on the way home.

On the bus back, Jiansheng was again sitting alone in a seat for two. Seeing him, Huai went to sit with him out of compassion and care. The instant when he saw Huai sitting down by him, his heart was trembling like the wings of a flying butterfly and the feelings were full of colors.

The bus circled the mountain body along the highway and through the forest road. The green vines shook by the bus window, dripping sweet dews. Even the sunlight took on the color green and the light shed into the bus in the shape of a column. The breeze cool as green jade brought Huai's hair slightly by her ears. Sitting next to her, he was drowsy and shut his eyes. In the dreams, he seemed to be saying to Huai, Huai, how I've missed you.

The journey back ended in the city. It was ten at night when they arrived at the station. The parents had been waiting for a while at the station gate, but no one came to meet Jiansheng. Carrying his bag on his back, he took a taxi and went home by himself.

Jiansheng took out the key to open the door and found that again his mother was not home. Disappointed and tired, he dropped the bag and drawing kit in the bedroom and went straight to take a shower. He stood for a long time under the shower and allowed the water to fall vehemently on his body and washed it. The wounded knee was wetted and hurt much. He covered his face with his hands, standing in the water, thinking of Huai in the keen pain.

His mother still wasn't home after he took the shower. He thought that again mother would not come back tonight, so the boy put on clothes, drank a glass of water and walked out. When he was not far from home, he saw a car pulling in. A man got out and went affably to the other side to open another door, and his mother came out.

The boy saw his mother and that man hugging and kissing. He saw his mother's soft hair falling onto her shoulders and couldn't help wondering what happened between his mother and the man a while before. Every time faced with such a scene, he could not control himself but begin to wonder about the shameful things, even though it was proved later that things were not always as what he imagined.

He didn't know who the man was and didn't want to know. He had wanted to call his mother but suddenly found it unnecessary, and walked round the car lights and left quietly.

That night, he went to Huai's building again. It was most familiar to him. He looked up and saw the light on in Huai's room. The magnolia blossom was still clean and white. He lingered by the building for a while, the indecent imagination about his mother and those strange men troubling him like nightmare and making him feel extremely vexed and ashamed. The impulse arose in

Jiansheng to go up to see Huai. Without thinking, he climbed up the building quickly.

The knock on the door sounded. Huai's voice was heard, surprised and careful. She asked, who is it?

The unnamed dryness stuck in the boy's throat. He answered, it's me, Jiansheng.

The door opened. Huai still looked surprised. She was wearing the same dark sleeping gown of materials tending to fall that she wore the first time when Jiansheng came to see her. She looked like she had just stepped out of the shower and was extraordinarily beautiful, her face soft and moist and her wet hair gracefully bound. The fair neck and the thin girl-like collarbone were bare. The lad smelt the cool fragrance on her body and felt sharply the uncontrollable sorrow in his heart.

He remained silent, gazing at her in the dark. It was the face that had repeatedly appeared in his dreams, his home and his love. Tears dropped on the boy's face, and he held her without a word. Huai was held close to him and tightly. In amazement and uneasiness, she felt the boy's burning body. His tears dropped unto her shoulder. Huai hesitantly flicked the boy's head. She asked, what's the matter?

The boy didn't answer. He clung to her stubbornly like a baby. Finally Huai pushed him away forcibly and held his shoulders, shaking him, and asked, what's the matter?

Jiansheng was pushed away; a fit of pang seized the sensitive boy. He couldn't help but feel hurt. He looked at Huai, poked her hands aside, turned around and scurried down the stairs.

Huai stood by the door amazed. She didn't follow him down the stairs.

11

After the incident, Jiansheng didn't have the guts to attend Huai's drawing class any more. Time was flowing without changes in the lonely and hot city. During the days when he didn't draw with Huai, life was as empty as if he were in prison. He missed Huai and everything about her. When he became restless, he would go to bookstores to spend the time and came back slowly with the albums and books he liked when the street lamps were on. Sometimes he turned on the tap to water the plants on the top of the building and fixed with a spade the drain stuck with fallen leaves. Or he would spend long hours with the silent plants. He picked a large bunch of gardenia buds and kept them by clear water in the vase and together they spent the last of summer before the season to blossom.

When September came, he started the senior high school.

Instantly he grew up. Wearing a white shirt and trousers and sneakers, carrying a schoolbag, he looked tall and straight. On his forehead there were still fringes shading his eyes. The face had some childlike air left but the lines were becoming solid daily. Just like his father, he bore certain absent-mind expression, looking handsome in a style of someone down and out. And his faint but sincere smile was unforgettable.

Sitting in the new classroom, holding new textbooks, surrounded by new classmates, he had bid goodbye to the gray days of junior high school. On the new starting point, no one knew about his past. Wearing the decent clothes his mother bought him, he didn't look any different with the city boys. However, he was still the quiet lad who was easily neglected by people.

He had nothing much to say with his mother at home. Because of their disappointment for each other and family life, the gap grew deeper and the two of them felt more like strangers. When they ate together at home, only the sound of the tableware was heard; not a word was said. The mother and the son lived separate lives; she was busy with business and the people related to business and often left early and came home late. From time to time the mother would leave plenty of cash in his room for him to arrange his life. Jiansheng only spent the money on books, a lot of books, in order to spend time. His heart was immerged with the longing for Huai, but he lacked the courage to see her.

Since he entered the senior high school, he had formed the habit of finishing his homework in the classroom before going home, because he would have only faced an empty home if he had gone home too early. Although they would still behave like two strange tenants when his mother came back home, at least he was not home alone. He stayed in the classroom alone and worked on his homework until it was late. Only when all the lights were turned off in the building and it was dark would he clear up his bag and leave. The empty hallway, reflecting some dim yellow light from nowhere, was like an endless path leading to uncertain youth. Humming a tune, he left the classroom, kicking an empty bottle with his canvas shoes. The echo of the bottle lingered in the hallway.

One day he finished his homework and was ready to leave as usual. He carried his bag on his shoulder, walked through the narrow space between the messy tables and chairs to the door and turned around to lock it. He couldn't help but stop midway at the hallway; he crouched down against the wall, looking at his own long and dark shadow so alone in the hallway. The empty bottle he kicked away was rolling away, bumping.

He lowered his head and closed his eyes. He missed Huai so much.

He saw Huai's face. Dazedly he felt her hands stretching out to hold his arms. The cool fragrance when they hugged. His aching brought tears to his eyes and before they dropped, he stood up suddenly, flung the bag over his shoulder again and ran down the stairs fast.

The lad rode his bike blindly through the turbid city. On an overpass, he leant against his bike and gazed for a long time at the constant flow of crowds and vehicles. The evening was getting darker and the city was weary. Fewer and fewer people were in the street. The boy left the overpass with his bike and went home slowly.

The city was falling asleep, but Jiansheng was hanging around in the cooled city. When he passed a phone booth, he thought for a long while and decided to call Huai. He was apprehensive. When he heard Huai's voice, he was unable to speak. Huai asked repeatedly on the other side of the line: hello? Hello?

Jiansheng said two words despite the lump in his throat, it's me.

Huai, however, sounded like she had just received a call from an old friend and blamed him laughing why he hadn't come to draw for so long. The boy on this side of the line listened quietly, red-faced. The chat was a little now and a little then; Jiansheng spoke little. Huai was speaking all the time, lightly.

They talked for quite a while and it began to rain. The drizzle was flying on the early autumn night. It was all dark except for the dim street lamp light. Jiansheng immediately felt cold. He said to her, I am cold.

Huai said, where are you? Go home quick. Jiansheng said stubbornly that he didn't want to go home. Huai had no choice but sigh on the phone. Finally she said, wait, I'll bring you clothes.

It was just like that. At one in the morning, Huai arrived in front of Jiansheng in a taxi.

They had been apart only since the end of the summer, but it felt like a long time since he last saw Huai. Jiansheng saw her approaching from across the street, within his reach. She walked through the ray of rain dyed yellow in the dim street lamp light carrying a coat. She appeared a vague figure in the dim background against the sharp difference of colors, but was like a promise exposed in desperation, striking on the peace of the rainy night in early autumn, leaving a clear mark in time.

Huai walked close and put the coat on him and pulled the collar. Then she touched his head gently. The moment she came close, Jiansheng felt distinctly the warmth from another body and the sympathetic response of kindness rich in redemption. The body didn't play a game with him but only hoped to warm him and told him that it was the way between people. He looked up but could not see clearly Huai's face in the darkness against the light.

Many years later, that scene still had its long reflection in their memories, making them a bit low. The warmth was so dense that Jiansheng believed his latter life would be devoted solely to the repetition of that scene and the negation of it by real life.

Indeed, as it is said, for most short and banal destinies, human beings are just a bunch of blind and useless enthusiasm. The everlasting beauty and excitement of love is just based on the tragedy that the estrangement between human beings is eternal.

Jiansheng raised his head and looked behind Huai. Under the street lamp resembling a spotlight, the night wind made the drizzles sway like a school of silver fish gently tossed about by an ocean flow. And he imagined Huai had a moonlight-like gaze as that of Lingxi, merging with the thickest autumn night.

That night, Huai and Jiansheng sat on the steps of the front porch of a shopping mall, chatting while waiting for dawn. The young boy tried carefully for the first time to express his affection, but every time he came to it, he diverted his topic. He talked, brief and jumbled, about his countryside childhood without his parents' presence, and his disappointing life with his mother when he came back to the city. In the intervals of the chat, this sensitive boy dropped his head, not knowing how to continue. And Huai would stretch her hand and gently stroke Jiansheng on his head, like a senior person.

The boy nerved himself and said, shaking, Huai, I love you so much.

Huai did not respond. She turned around and gazed at him gently. Jiansheng looked back, into her eyes. She was so beautiful.

A fit of planned hugging and kissing. He was fierce, but Huai dodged without hesitation. She pushed him away and said, low but firm, Jiansheng, don't do that.

A long stalemate, and silence.

In a while, Huai started brokenly, tears in her eyes, Jiansheng, you have to know that you are still a kid. I did this only because I don't want you to be hurt, and I want to tide you through this period. It is just like that. And now I don't really know how I should get along with you. I'm afraid my care for you would trap you in the mesh. But if I intentionally stay away from you, I could hurt and disappoint you.

Jiansheng, I don't know what to do.

Jiansheng felt terrible. For a sensitive lonely young man, he could feel real pain in her words. Disappointed, he turned to look at her silhouette. The memory of his first drawing in her office a few years ago flooded back. That was not long after Jiansheng returned to the city. It was a shiny but peaceful afternoon. Huai asked the kids in her art class to draw their heart's desire. Huai gave him such a beautiful impression. In these years, the yearning for her had accumulated to the fortitude of a first love and had deeply rooted in Jiansheng's life.

The young man said to her, I won't leave you, Huai. Stay with me, please.

He hugged her in his arms. The light shaking of his thin and weak body aroused her pity for him.

12

That autumn, Jiansheng's mother got a returned check she sent to Grandma Li in the countryside. The post-office remarked that the recipient did not exist. She made a phone call to the county, only to learn that Grandma Li had passed away. When mother told Jiansheng this news, she said, I'll go to the countryside to see her when I have time. Hearing this, Jiansheng agitated, When you have time? Grandma Li brought me up for ten years and you have to wait until you have time to pay respect to her? She was all alone. Who's going to arrange her funeral?

Mother was silenced, Jiansheng, I'm your mother. Don't talk to me like that.

Jiansheng said, ok, mom. I won't ask you to go with me. I can go alone.

Mother showed a bitter smile, all right. You can go. I don't want to go there any more.

Jiansheng asked Huai to go with him. Huai hesitated, but agreed finally.

They took the train northward, accompanied by the regular clanking between the wheels and the rails. In the midnight dark, Jiansheng could not fall asleep. He sat by her sleeper, gazed at Huai fast asleep, and tugged the quilt for her.

Another chance to stay with Huai exclusively brought Jiansheng utmost pleasure.

They got off the train and onto the bus and finally arrived at the county. Jiansheng saw scenes he had been familiar with many years ago. The late autumn in North China was rough and stern. The first snow lay on the deserted county. Amid the leaden low buildings were age-old lanes. The windows flocky with frost in the early morning, the plastic cloth hung on the doorway of the small shop rustling in the wind, the dirty snow on the streets, the tractors stopped on the roadside, and the red paper-cut patterns of the yesteryear, all were conveying this roughness and sternness.

They took another shuttle bus from the county to the countryside, to the lake of indigo. The reeds had been dyed scorch by the frost and brought down by the wind in melancholy. The wild geese carried the leaden clouds heading South. Their flying silhouettes were all over the sky. They took a slow sail across the big lake, leaving some silent diffusing ripples on the virgin water. Jiansheng pointed at the other side and told Huai, look! That was my home.

Grandma's house was empty as expected. The neighbors were not the old ones. The two asked about the whereabouts of Grandma's grave, but were told how the village committee managed her funeral and buried her on the hill in back of the village. People said hers was such an evil fate, that her adopted son raised into his teens was taken back to the city . . .

Jiansheng heard this and felt a sting at his heart.

The two searched the hill in back of the village, one grave after another, and finally found a new one, with a tombstone made hastily, crude and lonesome, as if a parody of the lonely old woman. He did not know what he should present to her, a bouquet or a large plate of fruits with incenses; it seemed as if anything he did would be ridiculous and absonant. Jiansheng knelt down in front of the grave. He bowed his head in such sorrow that he could not utter a word.

Black birds were swirling in the sky, melancholy and ominous. Dusk rose from everywhere and it became bitter cold. Huai watched him silently, aside.

At the end, Jiansheng rose and said, let's leave here tomorrow. This place makes me so sad.

They spent that cold night at a peasant's, and he dreamt of his childhood.

Midsummer's moonlight shed its light on the dreamy lakes. Their mirror-like surfaces glittered in soft luster. Only when water spiders dipped their long thin legs into the water, there would be circles spreading and tossed back by the reeds in the lakes. Then the ripples would spread mussily further into the night.

The reeds in the dark were coated by the luminous moon in a fluffy purple halo and swayed to the melodic night wind that was like Grandma's lullaby. An occasional splash of a fish jumping into the water would startle the harmonious bugs' song to an excited disorder, and the hunting roes and bitterns, and the dreams of those wild ducks, which would respond with uneasy quacking. But soon, all these would lapse into boundless night again. Only the frosted reeds were left, regularly swaying like a pendulum.

This was the most peaceful summer night of his childhood in his deep memory. Having spent the daytime in the marsh, fishing and swimming, he would surely be very tired and lying on the reed mat on the floor of the sitting room, and fall into sleep at the squeaks of Grandma's fan. The moonlight flooded over the doorsill and chopped a silver block off the floor. It was so glaring that he had to turn his back on the door. In the second half of the night, the reed mat on the floor would become bitingly cool. The burnt wormwoods were hung highly on the eaves of the old house to keep mosquitoes away. Inhaling their strong smell was just like gulping the spring in a well. In summer, the day would break right after 3 a.m. The barks and crows could be heard from afar, and he was still in sweet dreams. He would not get up until the cool morning sun shed its light into the sitting room and Huanghu, the yellow dog, licked him with its warm tongue.

In winter, large pieces of water were all frozen. They were metallic blue under the moonlight. The wind would bring clear, cold air directly into your lungs and thrill you. The snow on the reeds turned them into veils, leaving only a few white fluffy spikes swaying in the wind, as if they were bidding farewell to those sad days. Occasionally an inexperienced yellow goat slipped on the ice and failed in its rattled struggle to stand up. It took people little effort to turn it into a rare delicacy in the winter. The pure white snow would not melt until the sprouts of spring made their presence. In the enduring harsh winter, children would fish on the icy lakes with steel drills. As long as you poked right on spot, a hole would attract fish jumping out in a string for fresh air.

And there was life in the mild springs and sober autumns.

He woke up from this midnight dream and felt nostalgic. He shivered off the bed and sneaked under Huai's quilt like a helpless child. He said, Huai, I dreamt of the lakes.

Huai cuddled this young boy into her arms and stroked his head gently. He fell into sleep again in her warm bosom.

Maternal love like this had left deep impressions on Jiansheng's life. Reminded by the warm sense of touch, he felt reminiscent from time to time. The mellow memories always made him quiet.

13

The day he returned home, he had supper with his mother in the kitchen. Mother asked, with whom did you go there?

He answered calmly, with Huai. Mother responded, how could you be with a woman much older than you? What would people say about you?

Jiansheng didn't raise his head: I don't worry about what they would say. It is my own business.

Mother became angry: You can ignore them, but how could I? Those indecent gossips! You cannot be like this! Foolish! If you muddle on like this, you are doomed!

Jiansheng talked back agitated: Am I foolish? Do I muddle? Even if I'm a muddling fool, why you come to my rescue so late?! Are you entitled to do so? You care about how people talk about me, but why don't you care about how they talk about you first?

Mother was shaking with anger, you shameless . . . I'm your mother anyway. What's good about that woman that amazes you so? It was so blind of me to spend money and send you to her painting class!

Jiansheng turned hot-blooded at these words. He burst into cries: I don't deserve to be your son! Does this satisfy you? You are not in a position to interfere Huai and me. It is not like what you think!

The young man's face was distorted by anger and impulsion. His mother slapped him twice more. He tumbled back, buzzing in the ears and smart on the face.

He knew it was the old trick again!

Mother dashed into his room and nattered: You think I'm an idiot? You think I didn't know what you were doing while pretending to do your homework? She was shaking with anger. She pulled open his drawer, grabbed his sketch book, tore open his palette, routed up his drawings and tossed them onto the kitchen floor. Pointing at those paintings, she started again, my hard-earned money! You were not studying and not doing your homework. You wasted the paper and pens on drawing her! You are shameless and hopeless!

Her rage was so fierce that her words were taken to the extreme. She picked up the paintings and tore them into pieces. The young boy could not stand this humiliation anymore. He dashed over and rescued some of his paintings from his mother. He said bitterly, give them to me. If you tear one more, I won't let you get away with this!

The harsh response was clearly out of her expectation. She put up her hand again but it was held by him. She couldn't release her anger, so she turned around, got an iron clothes rack and thrashed on his arm.

It was so painful that Jiansheng had to hedge all the time. His mother wouldn't stop. She was outrageous. Jiansheng couldn't stand it any more: Enough, Mom, enough! He hid aside and crouched in a corner, his bruised arms protecting his shoulders, his feet stroking the floor. He was still trying to hide, like an injured cub.

He felt the acute pain in his heart and could not stop crying. He cried so hard as if to throw up all his internal organs. Countless fragments of memory flooded back: a childhood without parents, the isolation and grievances at school when he returned to the city, the insatiable mother, the frequent scolding and lashing, the witnessing of his mother making love with a stranger, the heartbreaking family relationship, the passing away of Grandma Li, and his hard love for Huai. All these splashed on his heart like waves on rocks. He was not a muddle-headed roguish boy who could turn a blind eye to everything or forget about the pain when his trousers were pulled up after a lash.

In his character there was some inborn sensitivity and fragility suited to his talents. For a boy, this was just the original sin. He felt he could no longer bear all these.

She heard his cries, not loud but heart-rending. He never cried in front of his mother. Seeing his terror, she stopped and stood there silently with a livid look.

She calmed down, with remorse and anger deriving from her high expectation. She stepped over and stretched out her arms, wanting to pull him up. But her son tossed off her hands like an extremely frightened bird. He pled hoarsely, don't touch me.

He crouched in the corner like a scolded child, head buried, sobbing weakly. His mother was standing right in front of him. After a while, he stood up slowly in her gaze.

I should not live in this world, he said, mom, everything would be fine if you and dad had not brought me to this world . . . I am an immoral debt in essence . . . Forgive me, mom, I know I should have loved you rather than Huai.

His words were sincere, but his mother was hurt by them. She could not accept his not loving her, and his love for that woman. She could not refrain from hitting his head with the rack.

Shut up, you freak! You know nothing! If you stick with her all day long like this and ignore your study . . . I don't believe I cannot kill her hope if I cannot kill yours. I'll sue her for sure!

The boy was put to despair by her words. He took up a knife from the kitchen table. His mother was terrified. But hardly had she asked him to put it down that he stabbed himself right in the chest, right in front of her.

She screamed.

The lad closed his eyes at a fit of the pang, and coiled down to the floor, hand on hilt. Warm blood sprung out like tears. He felt his body was again in the wrap of the sweet amniotic fluid, as if he were home again.

14

Mother was shaken to the core when she saw his blood.

In the emergency treatment room, his broken body was repaired bit by bit under the surgical instruments. For a moment he thought his heart would stop beating—or how could he not feel any pain and see Grandma by the dark green lake, waving a palm-leaf fan and humming an ancient nursery rhyme. He felt as if he were as light as a soul.

He began to regret deeply at that moment. Huai was still in this world with which he was so impatient to part. He was afraid that he might never be able to be with her. No longer could he sit in the spacious drawing room painting still lifes all day and watching the sun rays outside the window stroking the small exposed part of her white, smooth neck. No longer could he chat with her over the phone until morning and when he felt chilly, watch Huai hurry over and hand him a warm coat. No longer could he hang out on impulse with Huai in the suburbs in a certain afternoon during the May holiday; on and on they would walk, the breeze bringing the scent of the dry earth of the countryside and sometimes of the animals. There was but little wind; the boughs of the high trees swayed gently and the leaves sang songs. Dogs and boys ran wildly about, stirring up the dust behind them. The sun's tears splashed all over their shoulders and faces. On and on they walked; they saw many deserted warehouses and factories on the outskirts of the city. He shambled behind Huai on the way as if he were a small leg-dragging child. When the sun stooped low, he would stand by the riverbank in high spirits with an exhausted smile.

Would Huai, whom he never had a chance to bid farewell, remember that sketching tour in the summer after he graduated from junior high school? Would she remember that picturesque town, where limpid brooks trickled like lovers' tears? The two of them climbed to the top of the mountain, feasted their eyes on the innumerable peaks and enjoyed the orchestra of tigers' roars, monkeys' cries, and birds' songs. The morning fog wound around them like silk, and the lush green landscape extended into the distance. He could almost touch the green waves of grass, which livened up with a line of kite-like egrets. Would Huai know that while the two of them stood on the mountain top and were pierced by the wind, he was constantly caught in the desire to confess his love for her.

How could he ever forget this wordless obituary that he had been writing for so many years since that summer at the end of his childhood. Huai probably would not understand even a ten thousandth of the meaning of this metaphor.

He thought that at such an age when memory of life was but meager, he would have nothing to care about in the world. But now that he looked back on the short years he lived in the face of the phantom of death, his heart was filled with gratitude and regret. In his long adolescence, he always had the company of painting and Huai. If everything had not begun in such an abrupt way, he would have presented her with a blooming bouquet of camellias. In his short memory Huai had always been beautiful and cared for him in a plain way. On her blouse nestled the fragrance of Jiansheng's entire childhood.

At the age of seventeen, Jiansheng had the inconceivable courage to stab a knife into his own chest. Not everyone in this world has the courage to assassinate himself, unless he is fed up with the world, or too immature to live on, or both.

The wound was a half centimeter away from his heart and was very dangerous. Because of hemorrhage in his chest cavity, the surgery took a good fourteen hours, in the course of which Jiansheng had a lasting dying experience in paralysis. He felt himself lightened up as if his soul had broken free from his young, broken body. He kept a sober watch over his fragile body lying on the bright operation table, which was repaired and mended by the cold, dazzling surgical instruments. Is that me? he asked himself.

He believed that once he opened his eyes, he would find Huai sitting by the bed and waiting for him patiently.

Life was resilient. Maybe fate decided that it was not the time for the boy to leave and deterred him.

Jiansheng's mother called Huai to the hospital. She could find no one else to help after her son's grievous accident. Huai told her while waiting out of the surgery room, let Jiansheng live with me when he gets out of the hospital. He'll need me to take care of him.

Mother was completely deranged. She said in a trembling voice, how dare you say such things to me at this time? Now I only wish my boy could survive. Had there been any conscience left with you,

you should have known that it's you who killed him! Her words were drowned in sobs.

Huai did not argue with her. She understood that reasoning was no use at such a time. She comforted the poor mother and said, Jiansheng will be all right. Everything will be all right.

Jiansheng sank into a long coma. When he woke up, his face was as pale as paper as a result of blood loss. He opened his eyes and found Huai sitting by him. He wanted to say something, but failed to mumble a word at last. The moment when he tried to speak he was seized with a sharp pain with the small twitch of the muscles. Huai read only one word from the shape of his mouth, "painful".

She gazed at this poor child and could not hold her tears.

Throughout four months in the hospital, Huai visited him daily. She would bring him meals, chat with him, read for him, and help him walk around. The boy's deep trauma gradually healed.

She always told him, sleep a while. You've been awake for a long time. The boy would close his eyes obediently, but he would not fall asleep until he grasped Huai's hand on the edge of the bed. He was such a frightened child.

It was not time for him to leave, so he had to carry on.

The pang in his chest accompanied his long life. Mother was shattered. For a long time afterwards, she was haunted by a nightmare, in which her son stabbed at his chest in her face.

Mother was at her wits' end. When Jiansheng recovered and left hospital, she could not bring herself to face him any longer. Their relationship had been too heavy and entangled; the affinity in blood made it even harder for them to face each other and plod on together.

She turned the thought over in her mind; she found Huai at last and committed Jiansheng to her.

She said, I know you are not kin to my boy and don't have to take care of him. As his mother I should have been taken up the responsibility. But I've been thinking it over after that incident; I know I was not a good mother. I wanted to make amends to him, but things went contrary to my wishes. I can see he staked a great deal on his feelings for you. It's no puppy love; it's deep.

I wished him good, if this was good for him at all.
I'll pay for his living expenses. Don't worry about those things. I would take care of them. I beg you to take good care of him for me. Please.

15

He lived in peace at Huai's home. She took care of his life, cooked his meals, washed his clothes, and took him for walks. Like a real family, she gave him a normal life as a boy.
She would often bring him small surprises when she came home, which made him infinitely happy. Living with Huai made Jiansheng feel as if he had sunk into the dark bottom of the sea and his body had been surrounded by the sea water everywhere, warm, irresistible, to the point of suffocation. He would have loved to stay like that and never wake up.

Jiansheng filled Huai's balcony and windowsills with plants and watered them patiently like waiting for a promise to come true. When the flowers blossomed, he picked them off and placed them in a vase on the dining table. The fragrance of the flowers saturated the entire room. He would get up early every morning, nip off the dewy jasmine buds, arrange them on a white ceramic plate, and place the plate by Huai's side. When she woke up in the sweet, refreshing fragrance and saw his vague, handsome smile: Good morning, he said.

He stayed in the room painting. He painted the plants in the vase on paper every day. He painted the still life at Huai's home, the small plaster statue on the bookshelf, the cups on the tea table, and the foreign wine bottles. On fine mornings, when he drew the curtains aside, the oil painting that he finished the night before would harbor in refreshing aroma and bright light. When dusk settled in, he would play Debussy's "Nocturnes", the piano solo shimmering in the night like waves on a lake. He and Huai would dine in the small living room, chatting and laughing over the light, simple dishes. After the meal, Jiansheng would wash the bowls, while Huai would go to the living room and make a pot of Russian-style honey and lemon tea. The tea shimmered with a mellow, charming luster in the simple, dark-striped glasses. On pleasant weekend mornings, when he got up and saw Huai's sleeping face, he would take out his sketch book, draw her with a pencil, and leave the date or a short note at the bottom of the page.

He carefully examined Huai's paintings that she had kept for years. Huai took up advertisement designing and teaching after she finished her studies at the Fine Arts Academy. After Jiansheng recovered, he would often audit Huai's lessons at the drawing room. He would sit at the back of the classroom and watch Huai over the many high easels. When Huai was out, he would take her place in teaching. He had surpassed most of his peers by far in talent and techniques.

The beauty and peace of these days made him lust for life; once, on a sleepless night, Jiansheng told Huai about his days in the countryside in North China and the vague omens of fate that he met with in his childhood. He said, in all these years, I've always wanted to have a look at my father. For me a look would suffice.

But I could only see different men who came and slept with my mother and disappeared immediately. Why didn't Father show up after so much time? At these words his throat was choked; he felt blood gushing silently and fiercely out of his chest. It ran with such a huge momentum that he felt as if he were stabbed by a knife again. His eyes were burning and tears ran down from his cheek. He shaded his face with his hands.

Huai gazed at this sensitive, sad boy and gave out a low sigh. After a long while, she reached her arms to embrace him, but the boy struggled in resistance. Huai said, don't be like that. Come over, Jiansheng.

She said these words in a determined yet gentle voice. Huai held Jiansheng's head and combed his disordered hair with her fingers in silence.

He felt exhausted and fell asleep gripping Huai's hand in his, like a sweet, contented kid after being given a piece of cake.

That night Jiansheng dreamt of Huai. He dreamt that he and Huai were taking an old bus to a damp forest. They could see fragrant plants fleeting outside and the air was wet as if it were rimming with tears.

He was sitting next to Huai on the long bus trip. He could not see Huai's face. It seemed that Huai's face never appeared in his dream, but he knew it was Huai all the same, his beloved one who kept him company through the entire journey of growth.

He told her, Huai, I missed you so much.
Huai gently stroked his head again and said, don't you know I missed you too after so many years?
Don't you know I missed you too?

Jiansheng woke up for these words. There was a dull pain in his chest. Beside him was Huai's sleeping face in the dark. In this capricious world, he was so fortunate to spend so many sweet, peaceful days and nights with his love.

She did not play games with him; rather, she told him simply that people should treat each other like what she did to him.

So Jiansheng sat up. He did not turn the light on, but took out his sketch book in the moonlight. He turned it open, and wrote a line beside Huai's portrait. He wrote, I want to trust someone. Very much.

He wrote the date below it. Then he folded the book and put it back.

He called her name in a low voice, Huai.

What, Jiansheng? she asked gently. Huai was a light sleeper; she would wake up from time to time at nights. She opened her eyes and saw the boy's shadow sitting on the edge of the bed in darkness.

Huai, I never thought if I loved you. After all a man cannot choose his fate, and you've been my fate. Living with you these days makes me wonder what better things life has in store for me. What can happen besides this?

She kissed the boy's forehead: Goodnight, Jiansheng.

Memory and time came to gel in the moonlight.

He did not know what better things life had in store for him. What could happen besides this?

16

He had not contacted his mother until he got her call on his eighteenth birthday. Mother told him over the phone, Jiansheng, come back home. Today is your birthday. I cooked dinner for you.

Jiansheng frowned and remained silent.

Mother's voice over the phone became plaintive, Jiansheng, we are mother and son after all ... today is your birthday. Please come back.

Jiansheng agreed after some hesitation.

He walked out of Huai's home. He had not stepped out of the campus where Huai lived for a long time. The city was still busy and bustling. He walked a long way alone and returned home.

The table was full of fresh dishes. The TV set in the living room flashed variedly in the dark room. One after another advertisement. Mother was coming down from the roof when he arrived. She saw him and said to him smiling, I watered the flowers just now. The jasmines and gardenias you planted are all blooming.

For some reason, Mother's smile was tired and agonizing. She said to Jiansheng in a low voice, come, baby, sit down and eat.

She took out a pretty round paper box from the kitchen. It turned out to be a birthday cake. She cut the red ribbons and took off the lid. The cake immediately gave out a sweet scent of cream. It was made in bright colors, on which it was written in cherry sauce, Happy Birthday to Jiansheng. The cake cost a fortune, Mother twittered, I ordered it in advance and brought it home this afternoon.

Jiansheng looked at Mother's face. The fine wrinkles kissed her forehead like the rough coated tongue of time that licked off the bitterness of fate. Her weary cheerfulness looked more heart-rending than ever with a lifetime of suffering.

Everything would pass away. No need for harsh judgment and hurt. Those days of venting on each other their anger and regret at fate would be forgiven at last. At that moment Jiansheng found he could not but feel sad when faced with warm affection. He had never celebrated his birthday in his growth; before twelve he did not even know which day his birthday was.

Jiansheng passed a slice of cake to Mother and cut himself a slice and ate it quietly.

The mother and son did not exchange any word. The blind eating numbed his senses and he gradually felt less sad.

Having had the dinner and the cake, Jiansheng helped Mother wash the bowls and sweep the floor. He then climbed to the roof to watch the winter night view. To his surprise, he found the roof garden was not deserted. He did not know how much time Mother spent taking care of it when he was gone. As in the past, Jiansheng took up a shovel to dredge the draining hole and trimmed the plants. He stood beside the railings and looked over the city where streetlamps had just been lit, then went downstairs to his study and read several essays. It was eleven when he emerged out of his room after putting his painting tools in order, throwing away several tubes of dry paints and this and that.

He went to the door of Mother's bedroom. The door was closed. He stood there uncertain if Mother had slept already. He was hesitant whether he should knock at the door and say goodnight to her. They had become strangers after the long separation.

He did not knock at last, but withdrew to his room after some hesitation. The bedding at his room was clean with regular creases and a scent of detergent. Mother must have put herself out of the way in every preparation for his return. This shot a strange pang through his heart.

He turned off the lamp and went to bed. But he heard a tap on the door not long after he lay down. Mother said behind the door searchingly, Jiansheng, are you asleep?

Jiansheng said, come in, the door is not locked. Then he sat up. Mother came into his room and sat on the edge of his bed.

Jiansheng, how have you been at your teacher's home these days?

Fine. Peaceful.

Jiansheng, have you thought about going back to school?
. . . I will go back to school, but I want to apply for the Fine Arts Academy. I would not be admitted to common colleges anyway. Miss Huai is confident in me. As long as I keep painting like this, there'll be no problem for me to get enrolled into a top academy on fine arts.
That'll be great. You have a goal to work for. Ask your teacher for help if you need.
She has been helping me all the time.

Jiansheng. Mother's voice was suddenly choked. You are eighteen years old now. I think now it's time for me to give you a share of my money.

Jiansheng startled. Why? I don't need any money. He said.
Jiansheng, listen to me—Mother stroked his head gently. Jiansheng looked at his mother baffled. It was the second time that his mother stroked him, the first being at his first meeting

with Mother in the countryside in the summer evening when he was twelve. Here is a key. Take good care of it. It's to a safe in the Citibank in Singapore. The property is at your disposal.

The boy was shocked. He asked, why do you give me this? Did anything happen?

Mother smiled bitterly. She said, no, nothing happened. It's just your birthday gift. You've grown up, and these are the properties that I prepared for you. I just wanted to give it to you on your birthday, Jiansheng. Remember to cherish your life. No matter what happens, remember not to make light of it.

She said, remember not to make light of your life. These words hit a soft spot in the boy's heart.

Jiansheng answered, I'm living happily with Huai. I cherish my life very much. Don't worry about me.

That's good. Mother said.

Good night, Jiansheng. Mother stood up and left the room.

She suddenly turned around at the door and gazed into his eyes, Jiansheng, can you forgive me and your father?

He heard her words and his chest twisted with a sharp pang. He looked up, stared in a hollow direction and answered in a low voice, we are a family. We have nothing to owe each other or to forgive each other. I am your son. I just wish everyone happy. If you talk about forgiveness, I also wish that you would forgive me. I said once that you are my mother and I should have loved you.

Mother did not say anything; she turned away.

Everything retreated to silence again. He heaved a deep breath in darkness. He knew everything had passed away. They finally came to reconciliation just now.

The night of his eighteenth birthday, Jiansheng dreamt of his childhood again.

The mid-summer moonlight illuminated one dreamy lake after another. The mirror-like surface of the lakes glimmered with a soft, smooth sheen. With the palm-leaf fan in hand, Grandma would wave him to sleep.

In winter, the large lakes were frozen and unfolded a metallic dark blue color in the moonlight. The reed swayed to the wind as if bidding farewell to the melancholy days . . .

The night was too short for him to review every beautiful moment of the past years. Day broke again. Jiansheng woke up and looked up at the white ceiling and the embedded beech patterns in relief. Huai was not around. He was disheartened. Without him the fragrant flowers would not be nipped off and placed on the white plate and Huai would not wake up in the sweet perfume. The boy wanted to go back. He missed her.

Mother prepared breakfast on the dining table. She was serving milk from the kitchen when she saw Jiansheng get up. She said, Jiansheng, are you gonna eat breakfast?

Jiansheng had just washed his face and was about to leave. But he knew his mother seldom prepared breakfast like that. So he said, all right.

He drank milk and peeled off the eggs. Sitting in front of him, Mother saw the clear, stern contour of his face. He was as handsome as his father years ago. This boy was bone of her bone and flesh of her flesh, but was deserted on the way by the young, cruel father and picked up by strangers. After so many years, as the bygones went away, so did the child's attachment to her.

After the breakfast, the boy put down the bowl and chopsticks and said, Mom, I'm going back.

Mother smiled bitterly. This child told his mother, at his home, that he would go back. He did not recognize that this was the place where he should have been back.

She was not in a position to complain, so she said quietly, all right. Go back and learn painting from your teacher. Her twitter amounted to nothing but a humble consolation to herself.

The boy stood up and walked towards the door. Mother hurried over, leaned towards him, and fussed with the collar of his coat. She jingled on, Shengsheng, be obedient. Take good care of yourself when you live with your teacher, all right? Her voice was muffled and trembling with these words.

The boy could not bear such a scene of farewell. He nodded his head and turned away.

17

Soon Jiansheng went back to school. The school had become a strange place to him. The desks, chairs and textbooks seemed to have been hurled from his world long before. Scores no longer counted as he was applying to the Fine Arts Academy. Huai found a senior professor from the Academy in charge of the entrance examinations to provide him with individual tutorship.

One day, the professor assigned Jiansheng to paint a group of still objects as usual. Jiansheng's work was well proportioned and accurate in the colors of the other objects, but something always went wrong with the glass on the top of the triangle setup. He modified again and again but could not fix it. As titanium dioxide was less effective in highlighted areas, the painting grew grayer and grayer. His chest twisted with a sudden pang like an ominous sign. The pain distracted his attention; the glass went out of shape and the color turned grayer and grayer beyond repair.

The professor repeated, no it's not right. Redo it. No, redo it. Later he threw him a pile of paper and asked him to paint on it until he learned how to render the glass from that angle correctly.

The other students had finished their assignments and left, while Jiansheng was still sitting there working. His painting was worse and worse and the professor became more and more particular . . . he had drawn many glasses on the paper, but the professor rejected each of them. Jiansheng hated the excises-stuffed method; he thought it an insult to painting. He trusted only his eyes and brushes. He was driven crazy at the end but the long-faced professor asked him to continue painting.

He said to the professor with his hand on his chest, I'm not feeling well. The senior professor said, have a ten-minute break and come back.

When Jiansheng had learned painting from Huai before, Huai would let him rest and have his attention diverted whenever he could not find his touch. He would always feel better the next day. However, the intensive drills for the entrance examinations were not as easy. They were no different from the drills on mathematics or physics. He had to follow the rules and theories in accordance with the professors' aesthetic views.

The professor's voice tinkled upon his ear not without a sense of pride: every year a couple of students shed tears here in their preparations for the entrance examinations, but they beam with smiles without exception when they get enrolled in the Academy. I was strict with you for your own sake.

Jiansheng gave in at last. He followed the professor's advice and passed the examination by highlighting the glass. He got back very late and kept thinking about the dozen sketches and one mass tone drawing assignment to be finished on his way home. He was tired and sleepy with a growing pang in his chest. He felt down in the dumps.

He hailed a cab and returned to Huai's home. His chest was choked in pain. He dashed upstairs after he got out of the cab and knocked at her door nervously.

Huai opened the door. Rather alarmingly, she stroked his shoulders and froze the words on her lips.

Baffled, he looked over her shoulder and glimpsed his uncle from Singapore sitting on the sofa solemnly.

Jiansheng's heart ramped wildly. Nervous and awkward, he felt his throat choked bitterly. He saw his uncle pass a big envelope to his hand. Uncle said, Jiansheng, your mother asked me to give this to you. Please open it yourself.

Jiansheng was puzzled and opened the envelope tremblingly. He found a will, two deposit books in his uncle's name, a thick letter, and a small key, which was the same as the one his mother gave to him on his birthday.

He was dizzy with a sharp pang in his chest. He never expected that his eighteenth birthday would be the last time he ever saw his mother.

In the major-case investigation on smuggling and corruption, Mother and many entrepreneurs, military officers, political officials, and custom officers were indicted for smuggling, bribery and corruption. Almost all her public and private properties were confiscated or auctioned. When the bells went off, almost everyone involved in the case was busy covering the crimes up or preparing for escape, but Mother did not disclose anything to Jiansheng beforehand to protect him from provocation. Their attempts turned out to be futile. She had to accept her fate.

Drowned in a sea of pains, Jiansheng read his mother's dying words in the long letter.

Jiansheng,

I thought things would quiet down in the end and we would get through all the difficulties. Also I didn't want you to be disturbed by any of those things. So I always held them from you. But things went contrary to my wishes. There is always something inevitable. Mum is indeed not brave enough to take the prison as home for the rest of my life. My only hope is that you can live a good life yourself.

Jiansheng, I never considered myself a good mother, having abandoned you after you were born and not taking proper care of you after I found you again. After all, mum is not a quiet person in character. In the ups and downs of the past decades, I never lived in peace and content. My dissatisfaction with and grudge against fate even affected your growth. After I brought you back, I had the stubborn and foolish belief that with my financial capability, I could provide you with proper care and compensate for what had been missing in your earlier years. So from the start, I was more than eager to mould your growth according to my wishes. When I look back, I find I was imposing on you my own goals that I'd never been able to achieve ... Most parents from my generation fell into similar traps. However, this is the greatest sorrow for me as a woman and mother.

During the time we spent together after I had brought you back to the city, although I was often upset with you as an elder, Shengsheng, you let me experience the joy and pride of a mother. When I recall all these at the dead end, your being with me during those years is the last and only thing I'm happy about and also proud of.

I didn't realize it until now that the only happiness for a parent who struggles in this world is having a child who continues his or her life. It is a true miracle. Perhaps you won't understand this feeling or meaning until you become a father yourself. When you do become a father, never be as hard as nails the way your father was. But now, I hope that you would forgive your father. An unforgiving heart will never be able to find peace in the cruel and unjust world. This is mum's last admonition.

Some twenty years ago, when I first met your father, he presented me with a box of poems written on birch bark pieces. In one of the poems he wrote, I promise you a future of sea breezes and floods and ebbs.

I was once deeply touched by it. I fell in love with the fantasy I created out of it and hence with your father. Our hearts were both filled with yearnings for a peaceful and happy life. But poetry is not life. Afterwards we spent our hard and wretched life in utter despair and curses. It's also from that time on that I almost always lived with a vengeful heart. I tried every means to make a living. I wanted to become independent and tough enough to scoff at my regrettable youth.

In a certain sense, the fate in store for me sets me free. My disappointment with the world started from the time when your father abandoned you and left. Also, you also used to make me feel overloaded with the sense of guilt and responsibility. I always hoped to compensate you for what had been lost in your growth, but I never found a proper way. Although the gap between us inflicted sorrow on me, I suspect it had an even stronger effect on you, because you were a vulnerable child after all. Mum knows that you didn't enjoy a happy childhood. This is still my biggest concern at the end of my life. Honestly.

Shengsheng, fortunately I have prepared some money for you, which I've left in a safe at Citibank. The amount is not large, as most of my property has been confiscated. What remains there is the legacy I legally inherited from my previous husband. Mum used to be able to provide you with whatever amount of money you needed. Although this obviously is not the best compensation for you, I could find no better way to satisfy you practically. As to the money that is left, I made great efforts to keep it in your uncle's name. It'll cover your tuition fee and living expenses. Sorry, Shengsheng. You have to be frugal and independent from now on. Mum is really sorry. Shengsheng. Mum only hopes that you would be strong. Whatever difficulty there is, there will always be hope as long as you survive. This is also the reason your father and I named you Jiansheng, although we didn't expect the name to come true today.

There is still a long way for you to go in your life. Mum is going to give up as there is no hope left. Mum can't imagine how my imprisonment, rather than death, will affect you. I wish that you live with Huai. She is a really good and true-hearted woman. She is a real treasure for you. Her concern and care for you, whatever her motivation is, will give me reason to rest without regret. As the saying goes, the greatest pain for a child is that he wants to take care of his parents but they are no longer there. If Huai were not around, how could I have the heart to leave you alone? I will definitely die with an everlasting regret. Jiansheng, treat her as your family. Always keep her kindness in your mind.

In fact, as I grew older, I became more and more aware of the cheapness of money. By saying this I'm not absolving myself from guilt; I intended to earn more money and leave it to you for a comfortable life. After all, it's so difficult for an abandoned mother and son to survive without money in the cruel world. Perhaps God foresaw that it would do harm to you and forced mum to stop. But how are you going to live without money? Shengsheng, you should understand how difficult the money was obtained. You should make plans for it, because you have to depend on yourself for the rest of your life.

Shengsheng, I'm not sure if you still resent mum or if there is still a great barrier between us. Whatever it is, you must know that mum loves you. Mum really hopes that you would enjoy a beautiful world of sea breezes and floods and ebbs.

Always love you. Bless you.

Mother

Jiansheng held the thin sheet of letter in his hands. Tears fell off his face.

Long after his mother had passed away, his uncle began to tell him, Jiansheng, do you still remember the man named He? You should remember his relationship with your mother. But Jiansheng, don't misunderstand her. You know, your mother found it inappropriate to explain everything to you.

She didn't want you to bend down with any burden, so she never told you this before—after she had brought you back, she was eager to compensate you and give you a comfortable life, so she submitted to He's humiliation. He had been engaged in smuggling long before he met your mother. He took advantage of your mother's weakness; he intentionally created difficulty for your mother's trade ships at the customs and forced her to use them to smuggle goods into the mainland. Your mother had no alternative. Even though she was given seventy percent of the gains, the trade leads nowhere but to a dead end.

Jiansheng, your mother had suffered from his humiliation for a long time. Do you remember those times when your mother lay ill in bed suddenly? It's because she had several abortions. She even had to hide it from you and pretended to be all right so that you thought she merely caught cold.

Your mother's money . . . She hoped to provide financial support for your studies on painting abroad . . . Did you ever know her wishes? Jiansheng, you must remember it. This is the tragedy for little people like us. We are always powerless.

Jiansheng, disasters we can't abide to see do not slow their steps because of us. We need to forget them and move on. I know it's difficult for you. Your mother's death may mean another tomb to the world but for you it means the burial of an entire world.

Jiansheng, forgive your mother. When she was alive, she called us behind your back several times and wept out to us the isolation between you two. She was often sobbing uncontrollably when she suddenly remembered it was time you went back home, and she would hurry back to cook meals for you. She waited and waited and all the while you were staying with Huai. How could she stop her heart from breaking?

Your mother was not agreeable; she was sturdy, bitter, harsh and impatient. Her character determined her fate. Being a woman like that, she knew that her character would not bring her any luck or shortcut to success.

No one loved her, not even you in the past, am I right? She didn't hear even a whisper of concern. As a woman she struggled alone in the business world and endured countless hardships.

She did not want to influence you in character. She knew whom you loved; she knew Huai was gentle and nice. She even hoped that from your relationship with her you could receive the attention and love that you lacked in your childhood. But you have to grow up like a man. You must remember that there are certain responsibilities you have to shoulder yourself.

After so many frustrations, your mother's dying will was nothing but that you face everything in tolerance. After all, cruelty and injustice are so common in this world and you will meet with more of them in the future. But as long as you remain calm and contented, no hardship can beat you.

Shengsheng, I know the cruelest thing in the world is that the son wants to take care of his mother but she is no longer alive. But now you have another choice rather than death, that is to live on bravely—as bravely as your mother did—even in her will, she did not reveal to you the shame inflicted on her as a woman.

After all, she lived a bitter life, but she loved you so much.

18

At the age of eighteen, Jiansheng lost his mother before she was sent to prison. He held her will in his hand with a pang in the chest, as if he were pierced again by a sharp knife.

No one showed up at Mother's funeral except Uncle and Huai. Mother used to have a large circle of acquaintances because of her job. But all the blandishments, intrigues and false displays of affection were as transient and ephemeral as a fleeting cloud. Life was like the sails on the ocean that come from different places but set out for the same destination.

At the end of the road, they threw a handful of pale ash to the wind. How much filial love could make up for the gap of love when the dead was alive? How can the living strike the ending note of the elegy and console the lonely souls under the silent gravestones?

In the short cycle of life, how many bitter souls sank into eternal oblivion before their corpses turned cold?

The boy suddenly felt as if he were immersed in a world of stillness, as if in a boundless snowy land, where black clouds floated on the sky like humble souls that met and parted, foreboding the eternal redemption of death.

He forgave Mother. But as his forgiveness came too late, he could never forgive himself.

Jiansheng knelt before Mother's tomb. His adolescent years came to an end in pangs in his chest and threads of tears.

Uncle helped Jiansheng apply for a special leave at school and took him to Singapore. From the safe at the bank, he got his mother's 500,000 RMB and two estates. Uncle told him, your mother left with you some other savings in China in my name. They are all in the deposit books that I gave to you. Don't use the money here, but save it for the future. I'm only following your mother's will by showing what she left for you. Jiansheng, now everything is at your own disposal. Behave yourself for your mother's sake.

Jiansheng, it's time you grew up.

Uncle stayed in Singapore, while Jiansheng returned to China and lived with Huai.

For a long time after Mother's death, Jiansheng kept vomiting for no reason. He could not eat anything and lost ten kilograms in a week. He collapsed in a state of serious prostration while painting. Nervousness inflicted a spasm on the main artery in his head, which resulted in lack of oxygen in the brain. He was more sleepy than ever and yet lost sleep every night. He suffered from a splitting headache and was beset with nightmares when he did fall asleep.

The professional examinations were approaching. Huai knew that Jiansheng was in no shape to pass them, so she suspended his intensive painting drills with the professor and let him stay home. She sent him to a clinic, but did not follow the doctor's advice to put him in hospital. She knew clearly it was not a disease that could be cured with medicine only. She followed the doctor's prescription, fed him with light potions, and spent much time in Jiansheng's company.

Huai was no kin to the boy, but she willingly accompanied him through his ups and downs. Tired as she was, she always attended to him physically and mentally. Sometimes she was more than a mother to him. Jiansheng knew how precious this was to him and acted in concert with her. He finally recovered after several months. He began to sleep well, then dined well, and finally his depression was alleviated.

19

When spring was approaching, Jiansheng asked Huai, can you go with me to the countryside in the North?

She did not know if he was fit for the trip, so she consulted the doctor. The doctor told her as long as he avoided deep conversations on sensitive matters or contact with sad memories, a trip would do him good.

So she was disarmed and set off with Jiansheng again.

With the rattling rails under their pillows, the two of them made their way to North China. Huai asked him nothing on the train but: are you hungry? Wanna eat?

He would say, as you wish. Then he would stare at the fleeting scenery outside in silence. He was calm at that time. The greatest love needed no words and the greatest speech lay in silence. No matter what pains he had to endure in this harsh world, he felt utterly contented as long as his beloved stayed with him all the time and lavished him with love and care.

Whenever the train stopped on the way, Huai would get off and buy some warm food for him. But Jiansheng was used to light meals in his convalescence and had a running stomach after eating the chicken leg that Huai bought from a stand. Huai was sorry for him and sighed in worry, but Jiansheng joked it off and took some medicine.

In his subconsciousness, he knew that he was an orphan now in this world and had to take care of himself.

After the long trip on the road, the two of them arrived at the village where Jiansheng had lived with Grandma Li. In a week's time, Jiansheng revisited the lakes and meadows to which he used to have a sentimental attachment in childhood. Most of them were frozen and the landscape was only gray and white.

Winter was passing, but spring was slow in coming. The pale end-of-winter landscape looked exceptionally desolate. The lakes were still frozen, through which children poked holes with ice rods and fished. Jiansheng gazed at the innocent children and saw for a moment the clear track of the time. The humble hovel in the midst of snow and weed was the one where he and Grandma Li lived for ten years. The hovel not far from it was Dad and Mom's home.

Jiansheng and Huai entered into that hovel cautiously. The roof had collapsed; pale beams of sunlight leaked from the holes and cast luminous spots on the floor. The deep black clay-plastered walls were beds to mosses and the corners were infested with weeds. The hearth was empty except for a beetle that crawled slowly across it. Not even a bed frame or an iron pan was left. Maybe someone removed everything. Jiansheng fixed his eyes on what he saw in the house. He could not imagine that, years ago, this used to be his mother and father's home. His own life was conceived from a short eruption at this dilapidated place. He was depressed at the sight of this house, but he forced himself to face it.

After all, one can only leave the shadows behind by turning his face to the sun, thought Jiansheng to himself. He felt he was mustering his courage and growing up again, or in other words, he was aging.

He took out a scarf from his bosom.

It was the birthday gift that he had wanted to present to Mother when he was thirteen. He did not know at that time that he would never be able to give it to her until her death. He gently placed the scarf on the smeared oven and stepped out of the hovel in silence.

Pushing open the old squeaking wooden door, he looked over at the vast ice lake and heaved a deep breath of the freezing air. His mind went blank; he just felt himself lightened up in peace and emptiness. He held Huai's hand and said, Huai, look, this is my home.

Jiansheng stood still; between the frozen wilderness and the sky, he missed his mother sincerely and her obscure course of life as a humble, tragic figure in a wrong time.

They stayed there to draw from nature. He painted on the canvas the dark green lake in the distant haze, which was as impenetrable as dusty memory. He had not touched his brushes for a long time; he even felt strange when holding them again, but he liked this piece of work very much.

The night he revisited the old places in North China, they stayed at a local folk house. The night was chilly and the two of them had to cuddle with each other. He buried his head by Huai's neck and smelt her familiar scent of plants from a comfortable angle. The scent of home in his fantasies. He kissed the smooth, moonlight-like skin on Huai's neck for a long time with his eyes shut. He did not fall asleep.

In darkness and silence, he told Huai in a low voice with his eyes closed, Huai, how lucky am I! If the past is the price for such an evening, I'll pay for it with all my heart.

Huai.

Chapter III

The longer I know you, the more I feel that you are a limpid, delightful creek on my way.

I tried to forget you, but I met with you again when I thought everything was over. Perhaps this is because I could never tear myself away.

I know I can't be your companion on the journey of life. For what we can hear and see in this world, God will not place my hand in yours. I've recognized them all.

For all these years, I have been lucky to be your biggest sharer. Every time we met, you never withheld from pouring the rimming vigor of your heart into my chalice.

By being obstinate I am not censuring you for any of your practical decisions; it is the faith I commit to myself. You are so beautiful. You are always more beautiful than me.

Jian Zhen, "Rending Silk in April"

1

What is your name? Xinhe asked Kazan.

Kazan did not understand a word. She raised her head and looked at the woman. Jiansheng came to help by taking out a manual. Not without difficulty, he pronounced the question with the pinyin annotations: What is your name?

Kazan. She answered softly.

Xinhe. She gestured in front of her chest and smiled at the girl.

Come, Kazan. Xinhe called her name and tried to invite the girl to her tent. Kazan ducked. She ran back to Rilan's tent. There were tons of chores for her to do.

Renso asked her in curiosity, who are these two people?
I don't know. They may be here for fun.
Why would anybody come here for fun? What's fun about here?
I don't know.

That night Gibu was waiting outside in the dark again. Renso worked with a wandering mind, which Kazan picked up. Kazan asked, why don't you marry him? Renso flushed crimson with embarrassment and said half annoyed, who said I was gonna marry him! Kazan said understandingly, go outside. I'll finish the rest myself. Renso couldn't thank her enough and flew out immediately.

Kazan finished the rest of the zanbas, refilled the bronze basin with a bowl of sheep milk, and cut half of a sheep leg and threw it to Jinmei. Jinmei jumped in the air and held the leg in his mouth. He cut it in halves easily and shredded and swallowed it all in a minute.

Night enveloped the boundless landscape and remote stars were twinkling in the sky. Kazan closed her eyes and sank into a dream again. She always saw boundless snow in her dreams.

The dark snow-capped highland was dead quiet and endless. She stumbled her way after someone and kept sticking in the deep snow at every step. Every step was difficult.

The snow on the sunlit sacred mountain. Mom and Dad were left on that majestic mountain and never came back. Grandpa told her, your Mom and Dad are sleeping on the snow-capped mountains. They will return to the land of their ancestors.

Grandpa's voice sounded like a delusion. She never thought how long this dream would take.

The next morning, Jiansheng and his companion packed up to leave. The upper and lower parts of Qinglunzhuo Grassland were the most beautiful mistress of every photographer. Those were the places they headed for.

Before they left, Rilan's wife served fresh blood sausage. Blood was taken out of newly slaughtered sheep before it congealed, mixed and stirred with chopped viscera and meat, and stuffed into clean gut. The sausage was then put into water in the pot and was ready when the water boiled. As the air pressure was low here, the boiled sausage was still smelly and mixed with threads of red blood when sliced apart. Jiansheng and Xinhe were not used to the food, but they ate up two slices all the same.

They bid farewell to the Rilans. They took the two rented horses, put the backpacks separately in the two bags on both sides of the horses, and took the reins and set off.

Kazan followed them out and clung her eyes on Xinhe. Jinmei ran after her, his eyes shining. Xinhe made two steps, and Kazan did the same. She was obstinate and silent like a wild cub. Xinhe could feel that this child wanted to go with her. She turned back and looked at Kazan and Rilan in turn and was embarrassed. They all remained silent for a while.

At last, Rilan waved his hand and said to Kazan, go with her. Maybe you could lead the way. Take your Jinmei too, so that he can protect you on the way. With these words he and the rest of the family went back to the tent. Rilan turned back again and leaned his face, if you wanna come back, you are still welcome to this tent.

Renso could not bear to see Kazan leave. Zamecho bit his lip and waved the whip. He stared at Kazan, his eyes still like those of a foal eagle. All of a sudden he mounted the horse, cracked his whip and went away.

Kazan gazed at them from the back until all of them went back to the tent. She walked towards Xinhe and Jiansheng hesitatingly. Jinmei followed with steady steps. It was loyal, meek, strong, and as tough as a yak. Its long hair danced in the wind.

Jiansheng did not say a word. He looked at this skinny child. Her eyes were sharp, resilient, and cleansed by the highland wind. Kazan would make a silent, trustworthy guide. Although he did not know why she was so ready to part and hit on the road at such a young age, he invited her with admiring eyes as if she were a living wonder before his eyes.

The three humans, two horses and the dog jogged along steadily. The firmament took on a light blue after being blown by the wind. Walking on the land closest to the sky and inhaling deep the icy, clean air, one felt as if it were not the thin air in his lungs, but a sky-blue dream. Fatigued as they were for lack of oxygen, Jiansheng and Xinhe held the reins tightly and jogged ahead in even steps.

They planned to go out of this farm and then hike northward along the route the locals used when they bartered for corn and salt. That was her third camping site for shooting. She would stop by the legendary upper Qinglunzhuo grassland, pitch camp at the best angle for photography, and wait for the perfect combination of light and color. No one knew what would come out of such waiting. Maybe the only result after a good week's waiting was just another snowstorm when they ran out of their supply.

2

Xinhe carried on her back a black pack of tools for professional photographers. It contained a complete kit: a external carbon fiber tripod, a lens hood, backup battery, UV filter, regular detergent, oil-free lens cleanser, a whole bag of resin cotton, lens tissue, a dust bump, brushes, photoflash, extension wire, cable release, dust- and rain-proof plastic bags, a dark bag, film, a regular rangefinder camera, a single lens reflex camera, and $^{24}/_{1.4}$, $^{85}/_{\frac{1}{2}}$, $^{300}/_{4}$, etc. She used the fixed focus to get better photos even though she knew it would add extra weight on herself. The wide angle end of the fixed focus was less affected by distortion and glare. As dust was heavy in some parts of the highland and the temple was full of dust and smoke, the fibers and dust were easy to get into the less wind-tight fixed focus lens due to the wind box effect. The lens was difficult to clean even with the single lens filter dust bump, and sometimes even the film got scratched. Besides, wide-aperture lenses were also necessary for the fixed focus.

While they had made as many preparations as possible, they met with unexpected troubles on the way.

They started from Chengdu and trekked into the highland along the Sichuan-Tibet railway. Their first camping site was Laigu Village on Ranwu Lake and its upper reaches. The name of the village came from Laigu Glacier. Almost no hikers along the Sichuan-Tibet railway stopped here. In this wonderful small village a lake could be seen that was divided in halves by a terminal moraine in the Laigu Glacier. The landscape on the two sides of the lake differed greatly and set up a gorgeous contrast. When they arrived, they were greeted with pink and yellow wildflowers on the open ground of the village. In front of them lay the twin glacier lakes in dark blue, and farther ahead was the splendid Laigu Glacier bathed in the summer sun. The black moraines ran in parallel amidst the white snow. The scenery reminded one of the Scandinavian landscape in North Europe.

From Laigu Village they walked onward through Linzhi, Gongbujiangda, Mozhugongka, and arrived at Lhasa. They had a short stay in Lhasa, and headed northward for Namucuo. When they made their way over the 5000-meter high Nagenla Mountains, Jiansheng was tortured by altitude stress and felt pain in his chest. At last they reached Zhaxi Peninsula of Namucuo. The two of them feasted their eyes on the gorgeous view of the Nyenchen Tanglha Mountains. Jiansheng sketched for several days there, but his work came to a halt as the paints were frozen every now and then.

While shooting at Namucuo, Xinhe found on the film traces of static electricity due to the dry weather. They left Namucuo in regret and headed southward. They trekked along the China–Nepal Highway through Rikaze and Dingri, and entered the natural reserve of Mount Jolma Lungma. The lubricating oil between the apertures of Xinhe's single lens reflex camera could not stand low temperature, so Xinhe left the camera outside when she waited at the Everest Base Camp to shoot the sunrise, as the difference in temperature was not good for the camera. But the apertures did not contract regularly in the full-aperture metering, as the machine was exposed in coldness for a long time and the lubricating oil congealed. The overexposure made her shooting efforts futile. She wanted to redo the pictures, but the battery quickly ran out in the low temperature and died completely before long. It was a shame.

Jiansheng could not sit and paint slowly as usual, as it was freezing. The paints were all stiffened. He had to do sketches and wait to resume the work when he got back.

She was not detained by any of these difficulties. Out of the natural reserve, they returned to the interior of the North Tibetan Highland. They met with a pilgrim on their way. The old man had a big, dark purple bump on his forehead, a stamp left from the prostrations he did in pilgrimage. He stopped on the roadside, stood by a Holy Mani Stack. He took out of his bag some tsha-tsha, or Tibetan Buddhist sculptures, and placed them on the stones of the Stack reverently while repeating his prayers all along. Jiansheng approached in curiosity and found the tsha-tsha rugged, irregular in form but not without simple, classic beauty. He thought of taking them, but the Tibetan folks warned him not to do it, as the tsha-tsha had the pilgrims' prayers on them and might bring bad luck for the family. So he had to give up the idea.

3

They trekked northward after a brief stay at a simple hotel on the roadside. They rented horses and headed for the Qinglunzhuo Grassland. It was there that Jiansheng entered Kazan's home.

Now when they started off again, they had the company of Kazan. The pass towards Qinglunzhuo Grassland was an ancient one which villagers followed to barter for corn. The road was convoluted, so Kazan became their guide. On the expanses of the North Tibetan Highland, the land surface was as deserted as that of the moon. White clouds drifted freely in the sky overhead. The land was bare except for two light furrows in white, which floated into the distance like a white mourning dress at a funeral. They walked a long time without finding the so-called highway, so they followed the furrows instead. Jiansheng took out the compass for direction from time to time, and to grab a rest to alleviate the thirst brought by heavy breaths. At other times Xinhe often took out her shooting kit, placed them at the right angle, and photographed. The landscape in her camera was bare with nothing but the vast, boundless earth in the pepper-salt color of a weasel-hair brush, and a sky that was even more vast and boundless. Only the blurred contour of the black mountains in the distance broke the bare vision.

Walking in silence replaced everything else in the trek. Jinmei led them all along in steady footsteps. The gales blew through its black fluffy hair, which made it flutter like the rippling wheat in the open field.

Towards the evening of the first day of their hike, the setting sun on the highland greeted the stooping night with its unchanging grandeur. The winds on the sky threw themselves into different colors, and the last sun rays pierced through the thick purple-blue clouds and cast down golden beams. The nameless streams wound their way through the land and shone like gorgeous silk in the sunset. Jiansheng was always struck speechless at such sights. He took the rangefinder camera for snapshots. The instant he saw the landscape outside the lens through the narrow view-finder, he was soaked in frustration. The sky and the earth were too vast to be contained by a camera. The thought hit him strongly that they had better remember the landscape by heart than by photos.

Xinhe took out the carbon fiber tripod. As the wind was fierce, she hung the camera kit on it for stabilization. But the fleeting scenery had faded away before she got everything ready, and the bleak, cold night presided instead. She sighed softly. The landscape was like a proud lady blessed with perfect beauty who scoffed at the exhausted suitors prostrating at her foot. Xinhe felt herself petty and low when faced with the expanses of the highland.

4

They stayed on the boundless highland farm at night. The dark night settled unnoticed. A silvery crescent rose up on the dark night sky. In the distance the snow of Geladandong could be seen close to the starlight, like the lines in Gitangali they read in childhood, stars were born at the end of the journey.

Jiansheng put up the tent. He made a fire on the open ground in front of the tent and took out the beef cans and bread from the backpacks. In the depths of the wilderness, they cuddled together in the comfort brought by food and fire and faced the doubts and uncertainties of life in the most primitive way. Nothing was on the land except the darkness. The remote stars were still twinkling in the sky. Jiansheng and Kazan were not on familiar terms. The language deadlock made them rather look like strangers that met with each other on the road, took care of themselves, and treated each other kindly in silence.

Jiansheng divided the food and passed to Kazan her share. He saw the bony kid burying her nose in the food like a hungry newborn cub. He felt for her from his heart and stroked Kazan's head softly. The sensitive girl stopped eating at once and stared at him with her limpid eyes. She did not say a word, but her pupils were shining in the firelight. To a certain degree she was like Jinmei, or any other soul on the highland, or a nameless highland lake. She was silent and introspective with natural born courage.

He thought of Huai when he stroked Kazan's head. It dawned on him now what deep compassion the kind girl must have felt when she stayed by his side during his growth.

Jinmei was standing vigilantly, his eyes surveying the roundabout. His body was drowned in the darkness; the only thing that could be seen was his red pupils shining like a mysterious fire.

The cow droppings that they collected were not enough and the fire went out after heating the cold cans. They ate the food in silence, and Kazan fed a good half of her food to Jinmei. Jiansheng was abashed to realize that he had forgotten to feed Jinmei at all. Xinhe immediately put two sausages by Jinmei's mouth, but Jinmei did not take a bite and ate only the beef that Kazan gave to him. Jiansheng did not understand it. It was not until Kazan fed him the sausages with a smile that he opened his mouth and ate them. He was a loyal and smart creature. Such a stark difference from the pet dogs in the cities that begged for food with a swagging tail or squirmed to please their masters.

It was dead quiet except for the howling wind that pierced the land. There was no sign of life, as if they were on a human-less planet after the end of the world. Jiansheng was excited about this experience. The bustling urban life two months ago now appeared to him like nightmares in sci-fi films. He entered the tent and began to write in his journal.

For a moment, he thought of the urban life. The towering man-made jungles, the noisy flow of traffic and humans, and the lurking danger everywhere. The law of the jungle was a lot darker and meaner there than in the animal world. The ticking of time was always ringing in the ear around the clock to remind you of the deflation of youth. It was so messy and tiring.

His contact with Kazan this day revived many reflections and memories in Jiansheng. He was infinitely contented with the experience. This was more meaningful than the trip itself and all the painting and photo-shooting.

They were tired out after the day's hiking, and they still did not know what would happen tomorrow. Outside the tent Kazan sat on the ground and looked over the boundless dark land in solemnity. It was like the end of the world. She began missing vaguely the deep interlocked furrows on Grandpa's face.

Jinmei crawled by her feet silently. Its long black hair fluttered in the wind like the sutra streamers. Kazan sat for a while in silence, then stood up to check the reins of the horses, and patted Jinmei's head. As usual, it stayed out of the tent to keep the night watch.

They slept early that long night. No sound was heard on the highland except the bellowing gale. Jiansheng turned his head and found Kazan wrapped in a black sheepskin jacket and sunk in sleep between him and Xinhe. She had a sweet, innocent sleeping form. The girl looked lonely in sleep. Her inborn nature lent steadiness and composure to her.

Because for them life was a lotus flower that bloomed and withered by itself.

Jiansheng tried to breathe deeply to fill his lungs that always felt hollow. He tried to lull himself to sleep. Anyway he had to make the best of tonight's rest, as there was a long hike tomorrow.

5

At midnight Jinmei suddenly became restless. Muffled low bawls came from deep in its throat, and its pupils were hot and alert like mysterious flames in the darkness. The horses outside the tent began snorting and spinning in agitation. Their hooves clanked on the ground.

Jinmei crawled calmly and hunted for the smell of wildlife in the air. The animal was approaching and the smell became stronger and stronger. The masters were still asleep, but it knew that the wild animal with which it was all too familiar was impending. Its inborn sense of mission gave rise to its desire to protect. From its stern performance of duty as a shepherd dog it knew clearly that the protection of its masters and their tents and cattle was more important than its life. It would lay down its life to fight against the malicious wolves and leopards that risked sneaking up on the cattle in cold winter.

Since the ancient times, Tibetan mastiffs had been fighting fearlessly against whatever beasts of prey. With the rich fighting experience and the strong desire to accomplish the mission, they often exhibited astonishing strength and courage and fought to the end for their dignity as loyal and powerful kings of shepherd dogs. Jinmei gained absolute confidence in its courage and skills from the first time when it bit a hungry wolf to death in a close battle one night. From then on, every wild animal it fought with ended up bitten in the neck until dim, thick blood gurgled out of the throat and the body slumped lifeless.

It was its duty. It was not a killer, but it had to slaughter at times of duty. So did it this time.

It stood up quietly, the body tensed up, the hair erect, and the four paws stuck deep into the ground. It stared in the direction where the smell came, its throat giving low, powerful bawls in warning. The night was dark. The restlessness of the horses did not affect its composure at all.

At last a silver shadow appeared. It was a leopard, a silver Himalayan snow leopard. Jinmei could even feel from the smell that the leopard grinned and bared its crimson tongue. It was gigantic in size but walked as lithely as a cat.

Jinmei gave out a more menacing bawl from the depths of its throat.

The leopard ignored it and drew close. Obviously she was hungry. There were fewer and fewer preys on the grassland. The yaks and the blue sheep on the rocks disappeared, and the Tibetan antelopes were killed off by poachers. She was feverish with want and there were starving cubs in the nest. She smelt humans and animals and took the risk to attack. The vague smell of humans and beef in the tent almost drove her mad. She had a sturdy build; her sharp ears were tilted forward alertly, her front paws crouching low to the ground, and her supple body was already bent and tensed up like a slingshot. Her stomach contracted and the muscles in her legs protruded under her skin. The perfect prelude to a lethal attack.

Jinmei was fearless. Its hind legs stamped the ground firmly. It growled in a low but powerful voice, and its hairs were all erect. The fight could break out at any moment.

Both sides cast covetous eyes on each other. Evenly matched, they took enough caution in this head-on struggle.

Snow leopards certainly knew the capabilities of mastiffs.

As was recorded in "Er Ya", "dogs that are four chi long are called Ao, or mastiffs. . . . The meaning of 'Ao' is pride." In the forty-sixth chapter of his famous travelogue, Marco Polo also described the mastiffs as "shaped like Tibetan mules with a bark like lions. They were good at hunting for buffaloes and could fight with leopards."

Indeed, when Genghis Khan's troops swept Europe in 1240, he had a legion of 30,000 mastiffs. These pure mastiffs brought royal and courageous blood to European dogs. They were so exceptionally tall and tough that even the grandsons of their grandsons became world-famous excellent large breeds in today's world, such as the Great Dane in Germany, the Caucasian in Russia, the St. Bernard in France, the Newfoundland in Canada, and the English mastiff.

Although the leopards could neither read about the ancient literature nor hear of the Mongolian mastiff legion, they knew that the big black shepherd dogs were the kings of the pastures. It was said that in the mating seasons, female dogs in heat that were not mastiffs would keep away from the male mastiffs, as they could not bear the crushing weight that the sturdy male mastiffs imposed on them. This was obviously a joke, but it reflected the dominance of the mastiffs. Even when they faced the wolves alone, they would fight till death and inflict heavy casualties on the enemies.

Jinmei was not without experience in fighting against leopards.

These handsome beasts lived around the snow line and were covered with a gorgeous coat of fine silky hair. They were as ferocious as wolves on the highland. With lightning speed and the suppleness of slingshots, they were not daunted even in the face of tall wild yaks. They often made sneak attacks on lost calves. When they ran short of food, they would even risk preying on cattle. They did not attack in groups like wolves, but usually hunted alone or in mated pairs.

The situation was grim. Jinmei's only concern was its little master in the tent. It could not imagine how terrible it would be if the leopard attacked her. It had to make a last desperate attempt. It would give anything to keep its master from being hurt.

At the moment when the tension between both animals reached its height, the leopard sprang forward, its white stomach shooting a silver blade across the night. Jinmei gave out a thundering roar and threw himself forward like a black lightning bolt. The two beasts gripped and bit each other, their black and white shadows wrestling in the dark and the barks and bawls muffled in their throats. They fought in a heap and rolled a long distance without being able to bite the vitals of their foes. They separated instantly and confronted each other again. The left shoulder of the leopard was torn and blood was visible flowing out of the silver skin.

They gasped heavily, their stomachs swelling and contracting in heavy breaths.

The snow leopard knew it was no use continuing the fight, so she turned around slyly. She was lured by the smell of horses and food to launch another attack on the tent. Jinmei discovered her plan instantly and stood in her way while bawling warnings. Thwarted from implementing her fast-raid plan, the leopard became furious at the mastiff. She faced the dog again gasping and preparing for the next attack.

All of a sudden, Jinmei leaped forward to bite the leopard on the hind leg. The leopard soon recovered from the shock of the sudden attack and dodged the dog's teeth swiftly, its gigantic body as agile as a pussycat that jumped over a wall. The movement prevented Jinmei from snapping her leg off, but the leopard's about-turn exposed her neck completely to Jinmei. Like lightning, the dog jumped at her and bit her in the neck. It drove its sharp canine teeth into the tough muscles with all its strength. The startled leopard struggled and a flap of skin with flesh and blood was torn off her neck.

Well-trained shepherd dogs on the pastures were very cautious when they bit enemies. As their masters often needed to sell the skin of the beasts and torn-up animal skin was worthless, they would often snap the beasts' necks as soon as possible without damaging the skin. Jinmei felt sorry and hesitant for a moment when it saw the leopard's skin was torn.

The leopard was fuming with pain and shame. She rolled to the ground and got rid of Jinmei's bite. She snatched at the lower jaw of Jinmei with her forepaws and tore it apart, while her hindpaws cut into Jinmei's stomach. Jinmei gasped and jumped aside. The blood oozed from its skin and stained the thick hair red. Jinmei felt a sharp pain.

The horses fastened aside neighed in panic and stamped the ground with their hooves. The horses' stamping, Jinmei's bawling and the beast's gasping sounded like a drum-roll on an ancient battlefield.

Kazan was woken up by the sudden barks and neighing. Jiansheng and Xinhe were petrified. Obviously a bloody battle was going on outside the tent. They could not believe that such a scene from comic books and magazines was really taking place right before their tent. Xinhe felt cold in her hands and feet and was at the point of fainting. She leaned herself in Jiansheng's arms and asked in a trembling voice, are we gonna die?

Jiansheng struggled to remain calm and grasped the Tibetan dagger beside him. His hand broke out in a cold sweat. The dog's bawling, the horses' neighing, the beast's gasping and the noise of clashing teeth became louder and louder. Jiansheng suddenly thought he should do something, so he took up the dagger and tried to stand up. Kazan dragged him back and shook her head at him. They remained silent in the darkness. The stupendous tension and horror grabbed them speechless. Kazan shook her head and said, you'll be no help in the fight. Don't make trouble. Jiansheng could not understand a word, and stood there in a cold sweat. He did not know if he should thrust out his head to see what happened. He would rather put on a last desperate fight than be shredded by the wild beast in the wilderness. He used to sneer at life, but it was not until this dramatic trial of fate that he found in himself the instinctive lust for it.

As he was turning these thoughts in his head nervously, Kazan crawled over and found the solar-powered flashlight and the gas lamp. Kazan turned the flashlight on in the tent abruptly and the light dazzled everyone in the tent. The leopard outside was also startled by the bright light and drew backwards, which gave Jinmei a precious break.

Jiansheng calmed down. Light and fire. These are the only weapons they could take up to ward off the beast, besides Jinmei. He took out the cameras and gas lamps immediately and collected some combustible stuff, such as his notebooks and clothes. If necessary, he could even burn his sleeping bag. He took out alcohol from the medical kit, sprayed it on the paper and clothes and kindled them. He thought of the flash lamp, so he grabbed the rangefinder and the external flash lamp and dashed out of the tent.

The instant he pulled aside the tent, he saw Jinmei struggling with a leopard right under his nose. The leopard was battered and bloody on the neck, and Jinmei was bathed in blood too. The crimson blood spilled on the ground. It was his first time to confront such a dangerous animal. His heart was thumping wildly and his legs sank under him out of control.

Jiansheng threw the burning stuff to the open ground where the animals fought. The fire balls that descended from nowhere threw the leopard into panic. Jiansheng pressed the shutter immediately at the leopard's eyes. The flash lamp shot one after another sharp white lights in the dark and startled the leopard. Jinmei grabbed the opportunity when the flash lamp was running and the leopard flinched back. It took a deep breath, bumped against the leopard's body with all its might and turned her over. Its paws punched her stomach and its sharp teeth closed on her throat.

The snow leopard put up a deathbed struggle. Lying on her back under Jinmei, she drove her paws into its stomach and inflicted a slash across it. Jinmei's blood poured out and stained the leopard's white skin in crimson red.

Jinmei felt torn apart by the intense pain; it did not let loose its teeth, but took a firmer grip on the leopard's throat because of the pain. It tasted the warm, smelly blood that gurgled and bubbled out of her neck. The leopard was still struggling, but she became weaker and weaker and her paws finally slackened off.

She died.

Everything was quiet as if in a pantomime. Nothing was heard except Jinmei's pressing, hollow gasps. It collapsed on the leopard's body like a sandbag that was poked through and slackened off. The two animals stuck to each other in flesh and pulp.

Jinmei's eyes were slightly closed. It seemed about to doze off as if nothing had happened.

Jiansheng and Kazan carefully approached Jinmei with pounding hearts. The desultory stains of blood spread on the dark ground like blooming snow lilies. Kazan knelt down by Jinmei and stroked its thick hair in sobs. When they gently separated it from the body of the leopard, they caught a glimpse of the long, ghastly wounds on its lower jaw and stomach underneath the stained hair. Its black intestines were spilled out of its stomach, and its flank was badly bruised.

Jinmei only lifted its eyelids in response to Kazan's stroke. It then closed its eyes again as if about to fall asleep. It breathed heavily and wearily like a kid who tired himself out by playing all day long in the depths of the grassland.

Jiansheng dashed into the tent and bound Jinmei up with all the first-aid medicine they had. The thick blood immediately soaked the gauze. Jinmei was as tender and meek as a kitten and only trembled in pain with its eyes shut when Jiansheng's hand touched its wound. Kazan could not bear it any more. Her big tear drops rained on Jinmei's body like blooming lotuses.

Jiansheng wanted to carry Jinmei into the tent, but it was too heavy and the moving would inflict new pains. The man had to give up the idea. He stayed beside Jinmei and watched its long hair fluttering in the wind, as if the hair were melted in the night. Not yet recovered from the fright, Xinhe emerged out of the tent in panic; she immediately buried her face in her hands at the ghastly sight of Jinmei.

The wind was still bellowing on the highland. The blood-thick night gradually paled away; dawn was approaching. After they did not know how long, Jinmei finally opened its eyes. Like a comatose vegetable who slept for years, it stirred its lips and budged its paws. Jiansheng noticed its small movements and was overwhelmed with joy, Jinmei, Jinmei is awake!

In all the excitement, he woke Kazan up with a push. Kazan looked up at Jinmei; she remained calm and silent, but her face was in deep anxiety. She reached out her hand and touched the tip of Jinmei's nose. Breaths were ebbing away at the dry spot. She felt the thick hair under its neck. Jinmei fixed its limpid, peaceful eyes on her in the darkness, like a family member unable to tear himself away. All of a sudden it tried to get to its feet. Its body was so heavy that the ground was shaken when it did make it. Dust rustled from its body and soon scattered in the wind. It stood up with difficulty.

Jiansheng was filled with unspeakable joy. He admired the sturdy vigor of the creature when he saw it stand up. But that happened within a blink of an eye. Jinmei turned around and looked at Kazan. It looked grave and solemn, like a soldier who swallowed the words on his lips when it saw the waving father on the platform. The moment was so touching.

Kazan and Jinmei gazed at each other. She could not help remembering the late autumn when Dad and Mom went away. It was sunny that other morning. She was roasting the juniper incense when Grandpa came in with a new-born mastiff in his arms. She held the mastiff up carefully like a city-born kid who received a beautiful doll for her birthday. Small Jinmei had a pair of bright, ruby-like eyes and black smooth hair. When it grew up, it always guarded the master's tent and cattle with a desultory yet vigilant air. Jinmei's eyes were profound and piercing. At times when she stood right before it, she felt as if its eyes penetrated her, the tent, and the cattle and reached into the depths of the distant snow-capped mountains. It was almost as if Jinmei were confiding in silence with some unknown yonder friend. The grass grew and withered on the pasture, and the cattle returned every day in the pale sunset. Day in and day out she saw the increasingly strong figure of Jinmei galloping all the way from the skyline like a hawk that soared from the top of the mountain.

During the many cold, desolate nights after Grandpa left, Jinmei was her only loyal and trustworthy companion. She could go to sleep quickly only when she held Jinmei's warm, solid body.

Kazan sank into a deep reverie. At this time Jinmei had turned its head and gazed at the distant wilderness. The dark gray horizon was as unfathomable as the border of the world. As if called on by nature, Jinmei dragged itself ahead in heavy steps. The two horses snorted loudly and stamped their front hooves. They fixed their sorrowful eyes on Jinmei as if bidding farewell to the friend.

Jiansheng and Xinhe were astonished. They instinctively wanted to hold Jinmei back, but Kazan murmured to them in the strange language, Grandpa told me that dying sacred mastiffs would leave the pasture and the master's tent for which they dedicated their entire life and walk alone into the distance. In their lifetime they devoted themselves to the masters and cattle, and after they were dead they devoted their souls to the sacred mountains. The holy, mysterious yonder land was their only home. They would return to the gods and the golden flag clouds on the Everest and look over the pastures that were once their home. They were all offspring of gods. Like the vultures, they would melt their bodies in the rays of the sun.

Jinmei's black figure gradually disappeared in the depths of the dark night. It followed its ancestors' footsteps and embarked on the last return journey. The vision of the snow-capped peaks at the horizon was calling on its inmost soul.

The dawn broke gorgeously that day. The purple sun blazed up over the horizon, the clouds in the sky dyed in deep crimson as if they were shreds of silk soaked in yesternight's blood. The colored clouds varied in radiance in the pale sky, the golden beams leaking through and setting fire to the dark wilderness. The gilded tides of crimson clouds poured their way through the interlocked furrows in the land.

Jiansheng and Xinhe were so awe-stricken with the sunrise that their chests almost burst in pain. Xinhe wanted to take the scenery down, but she suddenly felt disappointed when she stared from the camera at the landscape in the size of a fingernail. It dawned on her that this land was not to be contained in even the widest angle. Even if it were taken down in photographs, who would ever know that this landscape copied with the man-made optical apparatus was the last home to a Tibetan mastiff?

She gave up the idea to record the monumental moment. It was enough to leave the moment in her memory. Memory retained the best image.

So she walked up and held Kazan in her arms. This child lost another family. She did not cry; her slender shoulders did not even tremble. She was as resilient and silent as the highland barley under the deep snow. Or the land itself.

6

This world abounded in sorrows fueled by imagination and cowardice. Some would cry to heaven and knock their heads on earth to gain others' sympathy or excuse their own weakness. Those bent down in profound sorrow, however, more often than not remained silent.

Jinmei departed. It was loyal, heroic and honored its blood. Kazan knew this was perhaps the best ending point of its life. Jiansheng and Xinhe decided to return and send Kazan back to the grassland. With the death of Jinmei, it would be heartless to invite her farther on their trip, now that she was alone.

In the early morning, the three of them started off quietly. They followed the same path and climbed over the peak that gave them nightmares the other night. It was already dusk when they cast the mountain behind. At last a gray gravel path lay before their eyes not far away in the cornfield. Jiansheng and Xinhe were not over the shock yet and felt exhausted. They gasped, but still found themselves out of breath as if they were muffled by plastic cloth. They were so troubled with the breath problem that at times they wanted to post their hollow lungs back to the inland and have them refilled with oxygen before reinstalling them in their chests.

The two of them waited on the roadside to hitchhike. They had weak legs when they stood by the road, but they dared not sit down. The doctor warned them not to sit down and rise up rapidly, as their hearts would not stand the sudden change.

At last an engine was heard bellowing from far away. The presence of these iron machines that humans created to make up for their physical fragility was as awkward on the highland as that of dinosaurs in New York. Jiansheng walked to the middle of the road to stop it. Drivers on the highland were usually willing to give a lift to strangers. Men on a lonely trip were more sympathetic, as they realized that they would need the same help some time in the future. Such a good deed might prevent them from karma when they asked for help from others. It was out of such concerns that since the ancient times, the Buddha and gods had been promoting the idea of accumulating virtue like today's insurance salesmen.

The big truck stopped. The driver was a young Tibetan guy. His small, narrow eyes were like a pair of scabbards. He looked shy at the beginning, but was very patient. He talked with Jiansheng in awkward Chinese and made sure that their destination was on his way. Jiansheng took the reins and saddles off the horses, and the guy helped Xinhe load the backpacks and equipment on the truck. Jiansheng patted the horses on the neck and said, horse, go over to Jinmei. You must be missing your home too.

At these words he was plunged into sorrow. The three of them jumped in the raised seats and shut the door. The two horses lingered around the truck and stamped their hooves in anxiety. They had been rented from a shepherd in Gaize with a high deposit and accompanied them through most of their journey. They were so tame that Jiansheng doubted if they could survive without being fed by humans. But they could neither go back on foot nor take the horses in the truck. Seeing the tarrying horses, Jiansheng was worried that they might get too close and be run over by the truck.

The truck roared its way along the road. The two horses began neighing and galloping parallel to it. Their manes and tails were blown into straight lines in the wind, and their slender legs galloped regularly like fluttering wings. They ran neck and neck with the truck for a while, but the truck gathered speed and the horses gradually lagged behind. They were farther and farther behind. When Jiansheng turned around again, he saw the lonely figures of the two horses left on the narrow road in the distance, their heads still turned towards the direction of the truck. The sight of them standing against the blue sky made him feel guilty as if he abandoned two babies to the mercy of nature.

The dust was settling down and the sky turned dark blue. The clouds presented the same gorgeous colors as in sunrise. The sky with the setting sun was like the seabed with clusters of colorful corals.

Jiansheng was seated beside the driver and Xinhe and Kazan sat on the back seat. Xinhe did not feel well and crouched in the seat silently. Glad to have company on the long, boring journey, the young driver chatted with Jiansheng in high spirits. He asked, why did you guys come all the way here? Man, we don't have nothing here, not even air. Not like your town, right? Jiansheng laughed without answering him.

He was tormented by the altitude stress. The drumming in his ears became more aggravated; he could not hear a thing except the roaring engine. He felt queasy as if he were hit by a carsickness. But he knew he had to keep his head up.

He leaned on the seat and closed his eyes in exhaustion. The journey continued. He groped through his memory slowly.

7

When he turned eighteen, Mother passed away and he was ill for a long time. When he recovered and returned from the countryside in North China with Huai, the professional entrance exams were six months away. They found the senior professor again and began preparations again for the application to the Fine Arts Academy. He lagged too far behind his peers at school and had to work hard to catch up with them. So he attended the lessons at school in the day and took the painting training with other students at night. After he returned from the extra lessons at school on the weekend, he had to hurry over to the professor's studio. The lessons at school were increasingly difficult. He had wasted too much time in the past and felt helpless at them.

While he was at school, he had to bury his nose in exercises during the break and at noon as he could not stay for night study. He would snatch a quick meal at the small restaurant at the school gate and return to the empty classroom to study alone. From the gloomy winter of his mother's death to the next summer his life had been busy and regular.

He could always remember how patiently and quietly Huai accompanied him that year. She mothered him in every respect. His lesson at the professor's studio ended at eleven, and Huai always waited for him whenever she was free. They would walk from the east gate to the west gate of the academy deep in the night. The green, lustrous plants bathed in sun and rain during the day now swayed in the dim lamp light, like the forgotten shadows of the past.

The young man followed Huai with dragging steps. It was the most beautiful moment in his day.

He heard Huai ask him, are you tired? Sleep early when we get back. I heated a glass of milk in the kitchen. Go back and drink it.

He suddenly became agitated. He felt himself immersed in her endless grace and the happiness almost suffocated him. He stepped forward and embraced her from the back. Both of them were nervous but strived to remain composed. Huai heard the boy's choking voice. He called her, Huai. But he did not utter another word. The southern magnolia trees were blooming again and the boughs were studded with big, white flowers.

He kept dreaming about Huai and Mother at night.

In his dreams, he took an old, empty bus with Huai and went deep into a damp, luxuriant forest. Green vines dangled outside the window dripping with sweet dew, and green sun beams penetrated the dim space in the bus. The sapphire-cool breezes lifted the hair by Huai's ear.

He smiled contentedly and sentimentally by Huai's side. But she disappeared when he turned around again. As if trapped in a conspiracy, he sat alone in the dim bus panic-stricken.

Not long after, the bus stopped. The door opened and a voice was heard from the luxuriantly green woods, Jiansheng, come. Follow me, Jiansheng.

He rose up unconsciously, got off the bus, and followed the vague voice into the endless green world. Gradually he saw his mother waving at him at the end of the road, as if she were greeting him on the platform in the moonlight. He placed his hand on Mother's palm, and she took him to the depths of the forest.

Do you know where you are heading for, Jiansheng?

I don't know, he answered.

Jiansheng, I can't go on now. You go ahead by yourself.

Mother let go of his hand. As if dragged by an enormous power, Jiansheng went on and on. He turned back from time to time, only to find his mother fading away in the distance. The bus was gone, so was Huai. The forest seemed to open its arms and cover everything up behind him, as if it wanted him to forget the past.

The forest became denser as if he were in a rain forest. It was as solemn as a grave. Jiansheng walked ahead over the lush green leaves. Two exceptionally big trees appeared before him, between which stood a rusted iron door. He pushed open the door, which startled the gigantic green-winged birds that perched on it and set them crying plaintively.

A big white grave was half-hidden in the woods. Moss crawled along the white gravestone. He walked up and flicked away the leaves and wild fruit on the stone. It was inscribed with Mother's name.

Jiansheng woke up in sweat. He opened his eyes, only to see the ceiling with the dancing shadows of the trees outside. He tried to recollect the dream he just had, but it became blurred immediately and escaped his memory. The boy, however, was clear about the metaphoric implications of this dream. It was a microcosm of his growth.

He felt thirsty and unable to breathe, as if under a heavy weight on the chest. He tried to call Huai gently in the darkness, but his throat was too dry to give out a voice.

He knew he could not get any sleep again, so he rose up from the bed and drank some water. He walked to the door of Huai's room and pushed it open. He stood at her door silently and watched her in sound sleep till dawn lighted up the room.

Jiansheng knew that he had tarried in this dream for long, but sooner or later he had to part with it. It made him even more nostalgic. To a certain extent, he was even blinded by this dream and refused to grow up.

When the Spring Festival was approaching, the exams were impending too. The sessions at the professor's ended, so Huai tutored him in painting when he got back from school. She trained him on such exercises as quick sketch, sketch, colors, and composition. She smiled in relief like a mother when she held Jiansheng's painting in her hands. She was always encouraging him, you are the best.

From February till April, Jiansheng traveled to two or three cities and entered for the exams at the fine art academies there. Huai had to ask for leave to accompany him to the exams. She stayed at hotels, prepared charcoal sticks, pencils, brushes and paints for him and gave him helpful tips.

While Jiansheng took the exams, she waited for him in the freezing wind of early spring.

Their efforts were rewarded. Jiansheng did extremely well in the exams. He was not a student of the affiliated high schools, nor was he a student of the famous professors of the academies, but he was ranked top ten in all of the professional proficiency exams. This was a miracle.

After he came back from the exams, he began preparing for the National Entrance Exams. The preparations kept him busy until July. He persisted, for he knew it was only in this way that he could repay his debt to Huai.

During the three days of the National Entrance Exams, Huai waited for him in the scorching sun. He repeated, don't come by. It's not necessary. But Huai came all the same. When he got out of the classroom alone after the last exam, the sun was setting and he discerned Huai's figure in the crowd from far away.

That was his story when he was nineteen. From twelve to nineteen, that was how he spent the seven long years.

8

It was graduation season again, a season to bid farewells. Jiansheng got the letter of admission from the top fine arts academy of the country. Huai was greatly relieved. Jiansheng told her, Huai, the letter is but a piece of paper to me. I'll give up anything if you want me to stay.

Huai said, Jiansheng, you've got to understand that this is exactly what I've been worried about. I stayed with you only because I wanted you to grow up. I'll never retain you here. You cannot rely on me like this forever and refuse to grow up. You have to return to the world of your peers and to a simple, independent life like everyone else. You have to love and marry a girl of your age and live a normal life. So you must leave.

But I only want to be with you. Forever. He said childishly.

Jiansheng—she stroked his head in deep sympathy—don't let me down, Jiansheng. If I ever expected anything of you, I wanted you to grow up like a real man. A flawless man who is tough, kind, independent, and forgetful.

They strolled together one cool night that summer. They passed the dense, tranquil garden and came to the three-storey red brick building. Huai took him to her studio.

At the age of thirteen he came here to learn painting from Huai. Seven good years had passed, and the studio was still full of high easels and cast away paints. The ground was covered with a thicker coat of lead dust and indelible paints, and the walls were full of stains in all colors. On the huge full-height windows hung old curtains and the faded flannel was thick and dusty.

He would always remember this place. The tall deciduous trees outside remained green in all seasons in the warm south, and cicadas' songs surged non-stop in midsummer. The trees cast well-spaced shadows in the spacious studio. He could almost smell the acrid scent that rustled off the shadows. In those summers he would tread the flagstone walks of the academy that led all the way to the three-storey red brick building covered with crawling vines. The plants on his way thrust their bright green color into his eyes like blades, and their leaves swayed to and fro in the damp breeze in midsummer. The electric fan in the studio clanked and swiveled, which, together with the cicadas' songs, were suffused with an air of summer.

When the students were tired or lost the hunch, Huai would let them rest a while. Huai chatted with them about the Eagles with which she was infatuated as a student at the academy, the haunted Room 517, and her boyfriend. Jiansheng had asked her, he must be madly in love with you, right?

Huai had turned around, looked at him, and said,

Never presume that others are faithful to you.

Jiansheng was thirteen then. Now the lonely kid who used to linger in the studio painting plaster statues was about to turn twenty.

In the dark, spacious studio, Jiansheng sat on the tall stool before the easel. Huai could not see his face. She only heard the boy say, Huai, I don't know how I could repay the debt I owed you. One cannot choose his fate, so I could not help but meet you. No words can describe how happy I've been these years. Huai, I know I will have a difficult time getting used to being alone again after I leave.

You may not know that in my infatuation with you, I used to roam in front of your apartment for a whole night when Mother did not come back. At that time, I thought how lucky the man would be if he could live with you every day. I did not know that my fate and your kindness turned me into that lucky man. I'm really content with the short time in which we have lived together.

We used to be infinitely close to each other, but like blood relatives, everything but hugging was prohibited between us. I know you are unwilling, so I did not even try. We are not kin, but we spent so many years together intimately without becoming lovers. Am I right?

Huai, tell me you don't love me. At these words the lad looked at her through the tears.

Thanks to Huai's company, he had not cried since Mother's death. But now he was weighed down by the beautiful memory. He could no longer stand it.

In this dark room, he talked on and on like a blind man who calmly told lies about light to another blind man.

Huai remained silent all the time.

That night the young man could not get any sleep. At midnight he rose from bed, walked out of his room, and came to Huai's door. He found a ray of lamp light through the door. So he pushed the door open and found Huai sitting in bed reading. As he had been doing in the early days, he got under Huai's quilt. He embraced her, felt her face, and kissed her with trembling lips.

That was his first kiss in all these years. He turned the lamp off and the room sank into darkness. He was almost stifled by his own nervousness; his heart was thumping as if it were about to burst into pieces, and the wound in his chest was painful.

He did not say a word, but took Huai's pajamas off. His hot, trembling hands stayed on her slim, cold shoulders. He kissed her neck deeply and smelt the familiar scent of plants.

Huai burst into tears. She closed her eyes and pushed him away again all at once.

Jiansheng, if you think you still owe me, don't do that again. We are not lovers and never will be. My affection for you is not that simple. I need you to respect it too.

At these words, they were frozen in silence in the darkness. His hand became still. After a long while, Jiansheng sadly withdrew and leaned to the other side.

Huai, I'm sorry. He apologized.

Huai, we human beings have no shortage of happiness in life—why would we always keep the painful memories only and neglect the tiny but real happiness? My mom was like that.

Huai, I did not understand how blessed I was until I came to live with you. I've been thanking God ever since. No matter what pains I went through or what bad fortune I will face in the future, I will gladly savor them all if these are the costs I have to pay for the happiness of living with you. Huai, you are right. How greedy I would be if I dare ask to prolong it.

9

He regained his composure and spent the last days with her in deep respect. He painted portraits for her in sunny mornings and gave a dignified coloring to all the oil paintings. While he was painting she would sit there quietly and stare in a hollow direction. Sometimes they climbed mountains together. They followed the winding path through the green forest and listened to the songs of the wind at the peaks. When they got home, he would help Huai tutor the kids in their painting lessons, modify their sketches, clean the rooms and cook delicious meals. They even bought fresh grapes and brewed red wine in glass jars at home. At dinner, they would pour two glasses of homemade wine at the table. When they strolled past a cafeteria, he would go over and play a piano piece for her. He was out of practice and made a lot of mistakes. She laughed. In the rainy days, they would visit his mother's grave with large bouquets of white violets in their hands. They grew plants together and picked the gardenia flowers off. They plucked the flowers, put them in a vase and added an aspirin to the water. The scent of flowers accompanied them through their last summer.

The wild geese flew southward and cast down their last shadows from the sky. When autumn came, he got on a northward train and began writing letters for her.

Huai,

How are you doing?

Yesterday when you sent me off, we didn't say much. As they say, great lovers do not speak and great music has the faintest notes. I guess they are right. I've been sobbing for a long while, but when I took up the pen, I did not know where to start. I could not but feel the power of time. But my heart is rimming with all the thoughts of you and I have to write them down.

A couple of years ago today, we were on a sketching tour in the Lingxi hills. I heard that there was construction underway and vehicles were not allowed to pass. Do you still remember the limpid brooks and the lush forest there? I wanted to revisit the place, but I was afraid I would only stir up trouble when I did. Maybe we don't need to go back. Maybe you are right.

I was so impetuous and restless when I was small; I was filled with shame whenever I reflected over the past. Now I've come to understand that for such a long time, what tremendous a blessing and forgiveness that life, or rather, fate, has endowed me with, despite my scoffing. I was upset when I expressed my gratitude. You know how pathetic I was when I and Mother treated each other badly out of our hatred and harsh demand for life.

In the future I will be faced with a serious problem, that is, how to arrange my life strictly and put my heart into doing the right things. Uncertain as life is, I can still find tremendous meaning from it if I finish every job with perseverance and rigor. I need to discipline myself, but I know it is going to be hard. It may take a long time.

I miss you so much. I appreciate all the time and energy you spent with me. Some say that true gratitude is beyond any words. I will never forget what you did for me.

When I reflect over my growth, I find those incidents I used to take as heavy blows were but commonplaces. I felt sad indeed when I saw myself helpless in the marsh of time. Recently I often thought about my childhood deep at night. I was living at my own house then and was but a common kid who wanted to do well at school. I got used to sitting in the study and reading every night, but I could not help painting. Later fate stepped in and I attempted suicide out of ignorance, only to hear about my mother's death soon afterwards. Then I lived with you and was saved by your goodness. It is such a pity that all those good old days were over. I cannot help missing the care and concern I received on my way.

I regret the trespasses I did to you in the past out of my impetuosity and ignorance. I am truly sorry for it.

I love you. I don't care about expressing—neither do I want to talk about—what this love means to me.

Seven years elapsed without our notice. As I knew I had to grow up and be independent, I remained calm all the time. Your existence for me is the echo of the night wind. It ripples to and fro and ends up in eternal silence.

Maybe it is because you kept aloof from me that I could continue my dreams of growth. If I could hold your hand in mine and listen to the songs of the wind one day, maybe I would remain indefinite about my happiness. After all my frivolity and fragility in the past, I now warn myself to remain tolerant and calm. To be smart and to be as good as possible, to not contradict each other.

I'm just wondering when and where I can meet you again and present you a bouquet of camellias. In my memory you were as beautiful and full of hope as the camellia. I could smell the scent of my youth from the edge of your blouse.

I had a peaceful mood when I visited my mother's tomb in North China. The world is worth being forgiven for the many regrets in it. Now I can even re-read Mother's will in peace. I feel deeply about her instructions. Is that a sign of aging, to appreciate the great pains my mother took? We were so pathetic those days when we hated each other and hid from each other. I regret what I did to her. It is such a pity that all the understanding and reconciliation take time. I was always late for them.

How can I ever forget that wordless condolence letter that I have been writing since I was twelve! You probably would never understand even one ten thousandth of this metaphor.

I am going this summer. You can take up this opportunity to testify your view that my feelings for you were out of ignorance, as if one fell in love with a brook before he saw the ocean. It does not really matter what the conclusion is. As long as your doubt exists, it does not matter if the conclusion is recognized. It is true that I will go through many new things on my way, but they can never replace what I've been through. Neither can they prove that I will forget the past at all. I am sure that man should not base his expectations of the future on scoffing at his past and the indifference at his present.

A boy bids farewell to the ignorant, wanton years of shallow sorrows and begins to live honestly with a peaceful and resilient mind. Such a change certainly involves pains in life. I also believe that the change is a good thing. I changed after I lived with you. Growth is the badge with which you honored me. Small and petty creatures as men are, they will get stuck in more uncertainties than what really exist if they are not patient. I used to be greedy and unsatisfied. I never had a chance to express my gratitude for all the tolerance and care you lavished on me. Maybe you would think such an expression is unnecessary.

I saw a movie years ago with the name, "There Used to Be a Fool". I still remember one exchange from it.

Mom, is the cross the symbol of love?

Yes, my child. And love often means the cross too.

I was touched by the lines. If everything leads to perdition, is it necessary to go through it at all? If one knows he will die, is it necessary for him to go on living? We are always too weak to face such questions of life. Ignorance is bliss.

I am ignorant and a coward. Because it is you I love.

It has been raining all the way. The clanking of the railway set my mind at rest. At dusk the streets were soaked in the rain and slackened off. The dim yellow sky looked like the tea stain in a porcelain cup. This is the hometown in my memory, the place where I grew up. It is ambiguous and commonplace. It strives to be good but cannot escape from ugliness at times. I am grown up in this beautiful world of regrets.

My feelings for you have been too long and too stable for you to believe them. This also coincides with your prediction that all will perish.

You know that is not what I wanted.

But, isn't that what I wanted?

All the best,

Yours,

Jiansheng

Not long after he went to college he received Huai's reply. There were only a few words in the letter.

Jiansheng,

I've got your letter.

Actually I regard all the things that I take up willingly as but pleasure and self-redemption. I did not feel any sense of

burden or toil in doing them. After all, I was only responding
to your feelings, and that was not wrong.

Jiansheng, I am married.

I've been doing great. Don't miss me.

Yours,

Huai

He thought he was mature enough to remain calm at any time,
but he could not help feeling painful in the chest when he read
the letter. Holding the letter in hand, he bent down his head. She
was married. She was gone forever. There was still a long way
ahead for him.

But he knew that this was perhaps the best ending of their
story.

Chapter IV

Perhaps aging played tricks on me. I began to realize in this world of toil how hard it is to live as beautifully as the ideals. What I could see is but incomplete fragments. I would be waging a futile battle against myself by bewailing the imperfections of the world. So I turn out more easygoing when I cheer up. I will take whatever comes to me wherever I go. I never question about where everything is from, nor ask for more, nor if our first meeting will be our last one.

Jian Zhen, "The Fallen Sunflower"

1

Xinhe. Sometimes I thought about what feelings Huai had for me, and why she made up her mind to live with me. She did not just put me up for a day or two; she lavished her affection on me for years. But somehow she would not confide her feelings to me or hear me talk about them. We became a family who, weighed down by the tie between us, hid ourselves from each other, skimping on the love for each other, and even hurt each other.

Xinhe. When I met you for the first time, I thought I saw her in you. You are both very beautiful women. I could spot the purity and goodness in you at the first sight. I said to myself if I really wanted to be with you, I had to let you know about my past. So I told you all about her. I hope you won't feel that I am another boring man that shows off his exploits. You know I am not like that.

My mother and I, out of the fear of the bluntness and cruelty of language, refused to talk and constantly hurt each other. I don't want to have such regrets again, so I decided to tell you everything.

Jiansheng was in college when he said the above words. At that time he had grown into a handsome young man with fine features and a tall, trim figure. Smiles often dawned on his distant, aloof face, which made him look handsomer. He was a magnet to girls.

He was not tempted by these young women, but he did not know how to refuse them either. So he was always surrounded by them. He met and parted with them and the relationship never went further, at least on his side. The girls were always brokenhearted when they broke up, but they moved on soon and found new boyfriends. Breakups always ended up like that when one was young. Many of his ex-girlfriends still missed him and cared about him many years after their breakups. Jiansheng would receive their letters occasionally, in which they claimed their attachment to him and inquired about his life in ambiguous words. Most of the letters were signed with pet names, and he could not even figure out to whom these names referred.

The relationships were as flimsy to him as that.

These girls who fell in love with him and vanished from his life flashed bright smiles on his heart as fresh, dewy flowers spread on his path. He knew he did not stop for them. The reason why he forced himself to stay with them was that he panicked in emotional disability after he left Huai. He could not bring himself to love anyone else.

For all his aloofness from school life and infatuation with Huai, he was never blessed with simple love affairs and amusement with his peers throughout his adolescence. It was no surprise that he found college life boring. He had no other entertainment than dating.

He remained unperturbed at heart due to his perseverance. Painting was still his priority, into which he poured all his passion. He was one of the few students who spent their spare time at the studio painting in the ghastly light of the fluorescent lamps.

At times he would browse the sketches he did as a boy. The childish strokes of the portraits, the broken, obscure lines, and the remote dates would suddenly plunge him in deep memory.

But bygones were bygones.

His heart was shattered when he knew about Huai's marriage. After all, among many other things, Huai was his lover in his mind.

He was not grown up after all. He could not dismiss the loss of Huai with merry meet, merry part. He could not make light of the past. So he was scared of his emotional disability and forced himself to move on.

At the age of twenty, he made love with a girl for the first time. She was perhaps the only girl whose face he could remember clearly. He knew nothing about her except that she was madly in love with him. He never refused any of her dates. The girl loved him so much that she wanted to hold him with her body and promises in the first couple of dates.

The girl was pushy at their first time. It was her first time too, but she was so anxious to offer him all she had as if in a desperate effort to prolong their relationship.

The girl removed Jiansheng's shirt and discovered the ghastly scar on his chest. Her sympathy was sincere, but not without curiosity. She touched it gently and asked him, what happened?

People always took pride in partaking of the important secrets of their lovers and regarded the confession as testimony of their possession.

The girl asked him twice, but he only shook his head and remained silent. He did not want to commit himself to them, so he remained silent all the time.

Jiansheng bent down and kissed the girl's face. He habitually buried his head between the girl's neck and shoulder, but could no longer smell the familiar scent. He felt hopeless and sentimental at heart, so he closed his eyes and indulged himself in lust. His mind gradually went blank; he did not think of anything, not even the strange face and body under him.

After the first time, they had a second and a third. For a while after their first night, he made love with her again and again. The girl complied with his desire every time. He knew how cruel and unjust he was, but he could neither control himself nor find another outlet.

He began to call her for perfunctory dates, and rushed for third base shortly afterwards. Many young men who were not yet tired of lust had the same demand. Jiansheng was not exactly indulged in it; he was just lost after the loss of Huai and eagerly sought refuge elsewhere. This girl madly in love with him happened to be the first straw he grabbed at that time.

That day the two of them strolled to Taoran Pavilion. The park was bleak and deserted in the cold winter of Beijing. The lonely pavilion stood on the bare ground like an outcast of time. They strolled slowly in the park and stopped at the famous tombs of Shi Pingmei and Gao Junyu. Half hidden in the rough, sere grass, the gravestone stood in silence as witness of the love in the revolutionary age. The story buried in the tomb went around from mouth to mouth and was enveloped in a shroud of mystery and immortality. At that age love was at the mercy of politics. There was indeed no difference between the regret and sorrow of the red lovers that lay here in silence and those of all the other lovers of all times.
The girl stood still and asked him sentimentally, Jiansheng, do you think we will be always like this?
Jiansheng did not say a word.

He did not love the girl, and felt only sorrow and even sarcasm at the girl's wishful ideas. As the cruel saying went, when the scales of love are uneven, contempt and distain are added in.

That night they stayed at a hotel and made love in the strange, narrow bed. For he did not know how many times, he repeated the same drill, bumping and sweating with a blank mind. The girl under him burst into tears, but she did not say a word.

He happened to feel the tears on her face. Why are you crying? he asked. He was suddenly frustrated and upset. He stopped moving and turned over. Exhaustion and desolation drowned him.

Tell me why you are crying.

The girl was silent. She turned her back on him.

Jiansheng sighed deeply. He felt more hollow after the sex than before. His head was gradually filled with chaotic thoughts. For a moment he felt he was about to be drowned by them.

In his boyhood he used to catch his mother in bed with someone. At that time in all his self-righteousness he distained her and thought sex vile and dirty. He was dejected to find that he himself turned out to be as dirty and vile as a dog in heat.

Besides, he thought he could not bring himself to face Huai any more. Even the thought of her humbled him to the dust.

Jiansheng could no longer stand this thought and turned his back on the girl as well. The two of them lay there in silence. He fell asleep soon, but she did not.

After he did not know how long, he felt tears in his face. The girl pressed her lips on his forehead. He woke up suddenly, but lay there stiffly without opening his eyes.

In the darkness and silence, the girl's tears rained on Jiansheng's face. She kissed his forehead gently and murmured to him in heartbreaking sobs.

I know you don't love me, Jiansheng. But I'm still happy that I could be so close to you.

I'm pregnant. Sorry, I've got to leave you.

It's all because I'm too much in love with you, Jiansheng. Please always bear in mind we are each other's first ones.

The girl was in tears when she said these words. Jiansheng's face was sopping wet. He listened to her with his eyes shut and was deeply moved by her confession. But he still lay there silent, stiff, and unable to open his eyes. He did not know how to face the girl's tears and pains. He was more ashamed and scared than her. He could not move a limb at the heavy blow.

The girl was all dressed up. She left a last kiss on Jiansheng's face and left without a sound. Everything was still. When he tried to open his eyes a trifle, he found the bed was empty and the room was enveloped in darkness.

In the acute pain, Jiansheng turned over, grabbed the quilt, and wrapped himself completely. He forced himself to bite his fist so as not to give out a cry. He curled up with the pang in his chest. Tears were rimming in his eyes, but he bit his fist without making a sound.

To his surprise, the girl went away for good. She never returned to the academy. At that time, rumors and prejudices could destroy a young unmarried mother, not to mention that she was raised up in a traditional family. He could not imagine what she went through afterwards.

Jiansheng lost track of her. He was upset all day in anxiety, regret and fear. He trembled to think what the poor girl might go through, if she sued him, if her parents came after him, if the school would punish him, if she would give birth to the baby, if she would never come back, and if she did come back . . . He was so much panic-stricken that he dare not even inquire of her whereabouts.

He spent a long time in anxiety. Nothing that he feared took place. For the several decades afterwards, he was in the dark about what happened to the girl. His memory was gnawed by infinite regret.

The girl madly in love with him thus disappeared abruptly. Of course it was only abrupt for him. In fact after she knew her pregnancy the girl calmly made every preparation before she left without telling him a word. By leaving secretly she completed her love for him. In this way the man she loved could continue his life as if nothing had happened.

After many years, Jiansheng could still remember the girl's face. Her selfless love added to her beauty and youth in his memory. Every time when he mentioned the Taoran Pavilion and the famous tombstone, he would think of his cruelty in shame and the lovely girl who loved him so madly.

For nearly two years afterwards, Jiansheng did not have any girlfriend. He imposed on himself a self-restraint and resistance to sex for the rest of his life to repent his sins and cleanse his soul. He was essentially a clean man.

After the affair he lived an austere life in every way. He focused on painting more than anything else and did not go back home during the four years in college. In a way he dare not go back and face Huai's marriage and family. He had not even contacted her ever since. He did part-time jobs in the cities in North China by painting for advertisement companies and teaching painting lessons. He was still diligent and busy and got straight A's in the courses. He was the professors' favorite student.

In his junior year, he met with Xinhe when he selected the works for the students' exhibition.

He was amazed at first sight with the likeness of Huai in Xinhe's face. The girl was so beautiful and resembled Huai so much. This irresistible face instantly determined the trajectory of his love.

At that time the two of them contacted each other frequently for the exhibition. Xinhe soon began to chase after him. He accepted her after some hesitance, as he found himself attracted to her as well and could not resist her face.

They made a perfect couple on the campus. She was from a scholarly family and her parents were graduates from the same academy. Her father was a well-known painter who used to study in Russia. In the Cultural Revolution the man was battered and humiliated and was sent to the farm to undergo reform through labor. He caught a disease there and passed away. Her mother recovered her post at the academy after the Revolution and re-married an art collector. Her family had been happy and peaceful. Her step-father was an elegant, poised man and cared for Xinhe deeply. Brought up in this artistic family, Xinhe showed her talent in painting in childhood.

2

He was a man with whom women easily fell in love, and she was a woman whom he thought he could love. They hit upon each other as a matter of course. To this day he still could not say he loved her as much as Huai—in fact he had not loved anyone ever since—but he had a liking for her all the same. Jiansheng did not like a complicated life. By settling down with Xinhe he warded off other girls, which he considered good. Thus the two of them began their relationship as if predestined by fate. His amicable experience with her proved his deliberation right.

He did not rent a flat on holidays, but lived with her at her request in a vacant apartment that belonged to her parents. They paid a visit to Xinhe's parents that Spring Festival.

He was formally introduced to Xinhe's parents as her fiancé. Thanks to her step-father, Xinhe's family was well-off. Having lived with his mother since his boyhood, Jiansheng was not unsophisticated either. With his handsome features and stable manners, he was loved by the elders.

Xinhe's mother was a quiet, dignified woman. She told him in private, I give my blessing to you. Please treat each other well in the long journey of your life.

He nodded his head understandingly. Thank you very much for your trust. He said.

Turning around, he could not help but be baffled. Was he thus settled for good? Lost in thought, he fixed his eyes on Xinhe, who was sitting in a distance chattering away with her family. A splendid smile lighted up her innocent face, a smile he thought Huai would have had when she was a girl.

That night they lay flat together like two children. She said, Jiansheng, will you marry me? He answered, yes.

She said, I don't know why, dear, whenever I saw you, I felt as if you were distant from me, as if we were a whole world apart from each other, and I were only standing at the threshold to your world. I knew I was never gonna enter it. But I hope to lead you out of the pains of the past into the simpler and happier world. I want to live the rest of my life with you. You know my love for you, don't you? I don't know how long it'll take, so all I wanted to know is, Jiansheng, are you really ready to be with me at all?

He listened to her quietly and was deeply touched. Innocent and outgoing as she was, she was also a kind, sensitive girl. He had been awed by the goodness of the female sex. He knew he had been warmly protected all along by their bounty and affection. Deeply moved, he held her hand and said, Xinhe, I'm ready to be with you.

At these words a faint smile emerged on Xinhe's face. She said, Such a fool I am, to ask you for a promise. Jiansheng, no matter what happens, at least you made a promise to me. I understand how hard it is for you. I'm contented really.

He was deeply ashamed by her words. Maybe she had long been clear that this relationship was but unidirectional. To a certain extent she was still another Huai to him.

At this thought he felt sorry for her. He embraced her and kissed her gently on the forehead. The girl fell asleep in his arms.

Outside the window the first snow of the new year was falling. It was snowing all night long. He could not help thinking about Huai from the depths of his heart and the icy, dark blue lake in the frozen landscape in his childhood.

From time to time, the farewell song of his youth resounded in his ears. He was like a hastening wayfarer who was lulled astray by the blooming camellias through the trim fence of time.

When he looked back, the figure that he thought would leave an indelible stamp on his memory had long faded away. The lonely swan had sunk into the heavy twilight and left only a sad song behind.

3

In their senior year, Xinhe began making preparations for her master studies in Russia. She learned a bit of Russian from her father, who used to study there. Jiansheng did not intend to follow her to Russia, but he was brought to the decision under Xinhe's pleading and her mother's encouragement. He began cramming Russian and was utterly exhausted from overwork.

Huai wrote a letter to him and asked about his plans after graduation. He replied that he would further his studies in Russia and had been busy making preparations.

He had not got any letter from Huai ever since.

At that time he was extremely busy with the graduation project, the memorial exhibition of the anniversary of the academy, Russian lessons, and applications for graduate schools. He and Xinhe led a busy life struggling for a common goal. Their projects were excellent and their applications were admitted. The result was thrilling: Rapin Academy of Fine Arts in St. Petersburg, like the National Academy of Fine Arts in Paris, was one of the top academies in the world. He could not believe his eyes when he got the letter of admission. He got his visa after waiting for a long time, and booked the tickets immediately.

Everything went on smoothly. He wanted to tell Huai the good news, only to realize that they had not called each other since she got married and moved.

He had to write a letter. He and Xinhe had flown to Russia before he got any reply.

They flew to Moscow first and then transferred to St. Petersburg. Xinhe was affected by the tremendous momentum of the plane before it took off and said to him, I remember the words of a German photographer that I liked very much. She said, the plane has to fight against tremendous resistance before it takes off, but once in the air it can fly freely, as the resistance there is but negligible compared with that on the ground. It's just like life.

Jiansheng, look, we are in the air now. She said with a sweet smile.

He smiled faintly, but could not help worrying at heart. His Russian was still terrible. Problems were heaping before him: the language barrier, the living expenses, the social upheavals and racial prejudice in Russia, and the pressure of the studies. He was really unsure about his future in this foreign land. It took so much faith to forge ahead.

While they went through the customs formalities at the Moscow Airport, a blonde, blue-eyed Russian policewoman looked up and down at Jiansheng with his Chinese passport in her hand. For no reason, he was held up from the queue. He intended to speak Russian, but before he could even utter a sound, she yelled at him, no English!

The policewoman indicated for him to stand aside. His passport was suspended for no reason, and another policeman led him to an office. Hardly had Jiansheng opened his mouth for inquiry when the policeman locked the door with a bang. After half an hour, two policemen came in and babbled something to him in a heavy Scandinavian accent. They spoke so fast that he did not understand a word; maybe they did it intentionally. Then one of the policemen took down Jiansheng's passport number and called the other side for confirmation.

Jiansheng heard from the boarding announcement of the plane to St. Petersburg. The policeman put down the phone and heard the broadcast too. He finally asked, are you taking this plane? Jiansheng said, yes. The policeman turned his face aside impatiently. After a while, he tossed the passport back at Jiansheng and nodded him out. No apology was offered.

He was handled roughly, all because he was holding a Chinese passport, and he met with a policewoman in her middle age crisis. Xinhe did not know what happened and was waiting for him anxiously at the gate. Without any time for explanation, he dashed to the counter to sign the boarding card and to the departure gate.

His face remained purple when he finally got on the plane. Xinhe tried to comfort him. Are you okay? she asked.

He shook his head without saying anything.

Perhaps it was because his preparations went too smoothly. He met with such an ominous episode the moment he set his foot on the foreign land. What happened later proved that his road was bumpier than he imagined.

It often snowed heavily in the freezing winter of St. Petersburg. Food became very expensive and heating cost a lot too. The nights were endlessly prolonged. They had to pinch every penny. On religious festivals all the stores on the street were closed. They had to snatch a bag of potatoes or baguettes before the supermarket was closed too. One day when Jiansheng was hurrying back with a bag of potatoes, a gang of bald youngsters popped up from behind him and beat him up in a quiet block. He threw the potatoes at them and tried to run away, but he was kicked in the stomach and squatted down in pain. He picked up a brick by his feet and lashed out in all directions without even opening his eyes. All of a sudden a scream was heard. He must have hit someone and blood spilled all about. The youngsters were panicked and tried to raise the injured man up. He had just time to run away and screamed for help. The red blood on his hand trickled along his way; he did not even know whose blood it was, his or the injured gangster's.

He returned to the apartment badly shaken. Xinhe was shocked too. The two of them spent the next week trembling in fear.

Their life in Russia was as rough as that.

Asian faces were conspicuous at the Rapin Academy. Jiansheng and Xinhe attended the junior courses first. They could not proceed with the master studies unless they got the professors' permission after they finished the junior courses. Jiansheng was eager to excel; in his supervisor's studio there were over thirty talented youths from all over the world. They took lessons together and studied sketching and composition. During the holidays they would go to draw from nature and study the masterpieces at the museums. Jiansheng was as talented as anyone and was very diligent. However, the European standard was different from what he accepted in China. He felt lost at the beginning and had difficulties communicating with the professors. But for Xinhe's help, he would have had a much tougher time. They supported each other through the years of hardship.

During the three years when they stayed there, the government was tightened up and old St. Petersburg was in bad shape. An atmosphere of desolation permeated the city. It was built in 1703 by Peter the Great as a waterway fortress. It was later expanded into a city and derived its name from him from then on. In 1712, the Russian Empire moved its capital from Moscow to St. Petersburg and it remained the capital of the country for twenty years. Most of the architecture in the downtown areas was dated two or three hundred years ago. While the architectural styles of Baroque and Rococo should have been extremely extravagant and elegant, most of the buildings were worn down by the years without repair. Their walls were smeared, the power supply was unstable, and the huge chandeliers were gloomy. The entire city was a scene of desolation.

The era of the Russian Empire left its trace everywhere in the city: the palaces, squares, and the tall statues of Peter the Great. The warships on the Neva had been bathed in flames of war and seemed to repeat histories of war and peace in a choking voice under the lead sky. Places of historical interest scattered the city as well: the small black river here where Pushkin dueled and the old apartment there where Tchaikovsky lived. The ancient Orthodox Church towered under the sky, its grayish contour half hidden in the fog. The doves that flew around the spire gave the sight an ominous, melancholy touch. Bitterness and abjection filled the students' hearts.

There were good days too. In midsummer, they would stroll on the bank of the Neva like every other couple in St. Petersburg and watch the white night in the setting sun. At midnight, the sun that was just stooping low would rise up again on the other side of the horizon exactly as described by Dostoyevsky. The sky was in a white glow; they could almost see the sails on the distant Baltic

Sea. Occasionally a white-skinned woman walked past them in a fashionable dress and a frozen, dignified face.

This used to be Leningrad. The cannons that bombed the Winter Palace in the October Revolution were still standing quietly, while the red era of heroism and ideals was long past. The young Russian ladies were no longer tragic Anna Karenina who struggled between love and fate or Katyusha who stood on the cliff and missed her lover. Heroes had left, but the bloody dawns were still quiet under the hawthorn trees in the country, in the suburbs of Moscow, in the dense birch woods, and on the Don River.

> Man's dearest possession is life, and it is given to him to live but once. He must live so as to feel no torturing regrets for years without purpose, never know the burning shame of a mean and petty past; so live that, dying, he can say: all my life, all my strength were given to the finest cause in the world—the fight for the liberation of mankind.*

These were the stamps of the past heroes and ideals. But could these glorious oaths that inspired a generation of people retain their purity when they emerged out of the mist of history? Look at the elegant girls on the bank of the Neva who fixed their blue eyes on the fashionable dresses in the luxuriant European and American stores on both sides of the Neva street. They consumed their ideals there. Their parents who spent a lifetime fighting for the Stalinist ideals, meanwhile, were perhaps counting a meager pension and worrying about the heating expenses in the coming winter. Such a tragedy of the society could only be redeemed by individualist struggle. That was why the slim, pretty Russian girls left their homeland in the pursuit of ideals. They drifted into the fashion industry in West Europe and to the bustling commercial

---

*   From *How the Steel Was Tempered,* by Nikolai Ostrovsky.

streets in North America. How many bitter tears would they shed on the way when they left such a beautiful country!

The girls were just like them—Jiansheng and Xinhe. Their parents' generation ended up in the mistake of the times, which dragged a long shadow on them as well.

4

Jiansheng worked very hard at painting. At the college, he spent most of his time at his supervisor's studio. During holidays, he followed his supervisor's suggestion to intern at museums and studied the masterpieces there. The Winter Palace Museum, or the famous Hermitage Museum, was one of the four top museums of the world on a par with the Louvre in Paris, the British Museum in London, and the Metropolitan Museum of Art in New York. It boasted a collection of 2.7 million artistic works from all corners of the world and at all times. If one lingered for one minute in front of every work of art and spent 8 hours a day in the museum, it would take him 15 years to finish browsing all the exhibits. Familiar Chinese exhibits at the Winter Palace included relics from Dunhuang and Qi Baishi's paintings. While he appreciated the masterpieces, it struck Jiansheng that European and American museums seemed to take shameless pride in showing off the exploits of their invasion and plunder. He sighed deeply for his motherland when he looked at the exhibits there.

The Winter Palace was astoundingly magnificent. From that time on, Jiansheng found he always felt panic and dizzy in spacious rooms with columns and porches. He got worse when the space was also gloomy. The hollowness of the Winter Palace was made up by the extravagant decorations, but he was still upset with the feeling as if he were inside a magnificent grave. The uneasiness, on the other hand, made him more susceptible to the masterpieces in front of his eyes. He would spend five or six weeks on end copying the works there in deep intoxication.

While learning painting at the Academy, Xinhe also studied photography by herself. During the holidays, she took advanced photography lessons in Moscow, while Jiansheng went to Pushkin Hill and the Black Sea for a sketch tour with the younger students. Standing by the Black Sea, he watched the waves in Pushkin's poetry. The sea and sky were of one hue in the gorgeous sunset, and the seagulls flitted on the surface and let out startling cries. He spent all his holidays in the sketching base of the Academy. Sitting all day on the freezing seaside, he felt his heart was opened up.

He and Xinhe supported each other and kept an intimate relationship. Three years elapsed without their notice. They persisted to the end and graduated with top grades. Xinhe also won an international youth photography award in Moscow. When they returned from Russia, Jiansheng took up a teaching post at his alma mater and Xinhe began taking up photography by working at a studio while furthering her studies. With their studying experience at Lapin Academy and Xinhe's mother's support, the couple soon became the rising stars of the circle. Invitations showered on them to art and photographic exhibitions, arbitration of competitions, China–foreign artistic exchanges, and so on.

The busy life numbed his senses. He was often worn out when he flew between different cities and spent nights at hotels. He said to Xinhe, maybe we should have a rest.

Xinhe answered, let's get married and go for a honeymoon trip.

He smiled gently and kissed her face, but his mind suddenly went blank. It had been over a dozen years since he had been taken to the city by his mother. Now he was at the threshold of marriage. He did not know how Huai lived in the distant South. Sometimes he could not but feel his cruelty. Since he met Xinhe, he almost severed himself from Huai.

She used to be the only care of his life. She was his only love.

But he would still accept his fate in all sincerity. Xinhe was a real treasure in his life. He liked her and cherished her. He was going to marry her.

She said, Jiansheng, if you are tired, let's go for a trip for our honeymoon. I received an invitation from a publishing house to photograph for a large album. The theme was Tibet. Jiansheng, let's go together. You can sketch there. The place is more beautiful than you'll ever imagine.

Jiansheng frowned. He was not ready for it and felt hesitant. But he complied with Xinhe's pleading.

He never refused her, neither did he know how to.

5

On the land that was more beautiful than they ever imagined, the loyal, courageous Jinmei left them in a most dignified way. Now that Kazan was all alone, Jiansheng had no heart to hold Kazan up further in their trip, so he and Xinhe decided to send her back home. After the loss of Jinmei, the little girl was extremely lonely.

They hitched a ride with a nice, young Tibetan. On the long, monotonous journey back, Jiansheng saw the expansive horizon undulating outside the window. Kazan was carsick and looked uncomfortable. Xinhe found her some medicine from the backpack and fed her. She held the little girl in her arms; the Tibetan child remained remarkably silent.

At times Jiansheng fell asleep. When he woke up from time to time, he found that Kazan closed her eyes and endured the discomfort. He felt this scene was somehow familiar, as if he were seeing his own silent, painful adolescence right before his eyes. The difference was that Kazan was a truly strong-minded kid. She was a tough creature of the highland.

They hiked a long way after they got off the truck and went back to Kazan's pasture at last.

No one bid her welcome except Renso. She was picking cow droppings with a basket on her back in the distance. She straightened her back at the sight of Kazan and called her name, Kazan, Kazan.

That night Jiansheng and Xinhe put up a tent by that of the Rilans. They were worn out by the hike in the last couple of days and went to bed early. But they were not able to get any sleep as their heads ached and their chests felt tight with altitude stress. They felt too miserable to utter a word. With their discomfit, the couple sank into silence in the darkness.

Without Jinmei, Kazan felt strongly that she did not belong there. That night, she wandered in the wilderness by the tent in deep thoughts. As poor a kid as she was, she was too small to feel any pity for herself. She was just missing her dad and mom, her grandpa, and Jinmei in silence.

She used to have the loyal, silent company of Jinmei on such nights in the past. When she tired herself out in nostalgia, she would crouch by Jinmei and fall asleep in the vast landscape. Jinmei's warm, tough body used to be a home to her. Now that Jinmei was gone, she was left alone in this expansive highland under the expansive sky.

Is the other world so beautiful, that so many family members left her for good?

Zamecho went to Renso's tent, but did not find Kazan there. He knew she was wandering alone in the wilderness again. He used to see Kazan sleeping in the wilderness with Jinmei many times. He wanted very much to go over and sleep with her, but either Jinmei's presence or his lack of courage deterred him from approaching her in such an intimate way. The defiant boy had been missing her badly in the days when she was away. He liked her in his blind way.

He mounted a horse and searched for her in anxiety, his heart thumping wildly in his chest. Kazan was startled by the rustling sound behind her; she turned around and found Zamecho on horseback within a few steps. For a moment she thought of the amorous way he stroked her face and his vague, arousing words during his rehabilitation. Kazan had always held a vague resentment towards him. Now that Jinmei was gone and he showed up in such an abrupt way, she was caught in panic as if some bad omen were approaching. Without a word she drew back and began to run towards the depths of the wilderness like a helpless Tibetan antelope.

In his frustration Zamecho galloped the horse after her. He jumped from horseback when he was close and like a beast on its prey, he threw himself on her recklessly. Both of them rolled to the ground. He never thought of holding Kazan in his arms in this way. Out of impulse, he gazed at the girl and said, Kazan, I missed you very much when you were away. You are so pretty, I wanna marry you.

Kazan looked at him with fearful eyes. She shook her head desperately and wanted to shout, turn me loose, let me go! But for no reason her throat was choked and she lost her voice in the tremendous horror. She burst into tears, she felt helpless and panicked, but all she could do was struggle desperately in vain.

The more she struggled, the angrier he got. The two of them were almost engaged in wrestling. He never expected such defiance from anyone, not to mention from his dreamed girl. He could not stand a refusal like that.

Carried away in such selfish conceit, he robbed her of her poor dignity while defending his own.

This was part of her memory when she was ten years old—when she was pinched on the meadow by Zamecho, the blades of grass cut into her exposed body like knives. Amidst the splitting pain, she was frightened to the marrow, her tears streaming down onto the ground. She was unable to utter any sound, as if she were taken by the throat by utter aphasia for a brief time.

In tears, she looked at the faint galaxy and the broken stars in the dark blue sky. They were so familiar and silent like the land beneath her.

The next morning Renso woke Xinhe and Jiansheng up and asked if they had seen Kazan. Jiansheng did not understand her question, so he mumbled a vague reply and walked out of the tent with dreamy eyes. He came right in sight of Zamecho, who led the horse and came over from the distance. Kazan was sitting on the horse's back as if in a dream, her hair disheveled and her face ghastly pale. She had lost focus in her eyes and stared in a hollow direction. The sorrow and fear about her made her look almost like an old woman.

Not knowing what happened, he and Xinhe looked at each other in consternation. They watched Zamecho getting her off the horse's back and walking inside the tent. Renso followed them in a complete daze.

Zamecho's parents were having their morning tea. Gibu came by to say hello and happened to be there as well.

The boy caught his parents unprepared. He said, I wanna marry her!

It happened so quickly that Rilan answered in perplexity, what are you talking about?

The boy would not let the subject get away, so he blurted out, Kazan became my bride last night!

Everyone froze for a moment. Baffled, Rilan asked again, what did you say?

The boy raised his voice and said, last night Kazan became my bride!

Rilan was shocked. He fixed his eyes on Kazan's pallid, despondent face. He gradually became black in the face, picked up a whip and lashed out at his son. The boy bit his lips defiantly and stared back at him without saying another word.

Rilan was fuming with anger and began whipping Zamecho again.

The tent was in a big row. Zamecho's mother came up and stood between Rilan's whip and her son. Renso was shocked speechless and held Kazan in her arms. Jiansheng and Xinhe watched them from outside the tent and guessed what had happened the night before.

Held back by Zamecho's mother, Rilan rattled away with a torrent of abuse in anger. How dare you talk about it as shamelessly as that! You bastard! How dare you do such a thing! Didn't we arrange a bride for you? Kazan is our maid! How can you . . .
At these words Rilan stopped. But he was heard all too clearly by everyone. Renso looked down at Kazan in her arms and shook her head in deep pity.
I don't care! Zamecho stood up stubbornly and turned away.

Gibu went out of the Rilans' in silence, but his face was still blank. Renso took Kazan back into their little tent. Gibu watched them from behind and sank in deep thought. He stopped and followed them over.

Renso asked Kazan in the tent, tell me, what happened last night?
Kazan remained silent for a long time. She squeezed between her teeth at last, he wanted me to sleep with him . . . he was strong . . . I could not help . . .
Renso held the child in arms silently and stopped her. She looked up to find Gibu lifted the curtain and walked in.

Gibu sat down grimly. He asked Renso, if the Rilans cannot allow Zamecho to marry Kazan, how can we deal with the poor girl? Renso looked at him and shook her head in silence. She did not know what to do. Nobody knew. Gibu did not say another word. He sat for a while in silence and went out.

That day Gibu found Jiansheng and Xinhe. The tough man went down on his knees before them. Jiansheng was surprised. They did not know what the man was up to.

Gibu said to them in raw Chinese, please, if you like Kazan and feel for her, take her away. Take her away from here.

They were astonished at the man's request. They helped him up and asked, what happened exactly?

Gibu said, it was I who brought Kazan over to the Rilans when her grandpa died. They raised her and she worked for them. But something happened yesterday. Zamecho ... violated her. He has a bride, and Rilan doesn't want him to marry such a lowly maid as Kazan. I thought I could see her get married and live a happy life, but now that she was violated, there is no hope for her here ... I beseech you, sir, if you have a heart of mercy, take her to the outside world, treat her kindly and bring her up ... this poor kid just lost her Jinmei ... please do her the favor for the sake of Jinmei, who died for you!

The kind-hearted man was begging them for Kazan.

Xinhe was deeply touched. She said at once, okay we'll take her with us. We'll raise her up in good care.

Jiansheng turned around and looked at Xinhe with an ambiguous expression. He was deeply moved too, but it was no small matter to shoulder another life all of a sudden. The commitment was not a matter of days, but might affect Kazan's entire life. He said to Gibu in sincerity, thank you, Gibu, I thank you for Kazan. You are a good man indeed. We'll think about it and talk with Rilan later. Put your mind at ease, Gibu.

Gibu nodded and went out in silence.

Xinhe cuddled Jiansheng and said, let's adopt her, darling. Can you bear to leave her alone in this place? She is deprived of all her family, even of Jinmei, and she was raped ... Jiansheng ...

Jiansheng answered, you misunderstood me, Xinhe. I'm not without sympathy or fondness for her. But this decision is a major one. We have to be a hundred percent sure about it. Once we are committed to her, it'll be a matter of a lifetime. We'll be responsible for her and make sure she lives a good life. We have to work hard together. It's like giving birth to a baby.

I was once adopted by a stranger and lived like an orphan for some dozen years in North China. I understand what great fear and shock a child has to face when he is taken to a bustling city after living in the country for many years. The change is very painful and not easy to swallow at all. Kazan will face the same adjustment period if we take her to the city, no matter how much we care about her. Besides, she is a real orphan, a pure-blood Tibetan child, a victim of rape at such an early age, and she doesn't even know Chinese. We need to take good care of her. Are you sure, Xinhe, you want to adopt her?

Xinhe nodded. Yes I'm sure, Jiansheng. I'm gonna adopt her. She will only be in more pain if she stays here.

Jiansheng looked at her and thought about Huai suddenly. He thought about the debt he owed to Huai. After his mother's death, it was Huai who kept him company, mothered him in life and study, and helped him get enrolled in the academy. He was once again struck in awe by the kind nature and maternity of women. He nodded and said, okay. Don't forget that we made this decision together.

That night Jiansheng and Xinhe called Gibu over and found Rilan. Jiansheng said to Rilan, it's your bounty to have adopted Kazan. Now that you are in difficulty, please give her to us. We want to adopt her.

Gibu translated Jiansheng's words to Rilan. Rilan and his wife looked at each other in consternation. He remained silent for a long while, and then turned his head and said, if you want to adopt her, take her away. My son Zamecho was a bastard. He committed a terrible sin to Kazan. Please forgive him.

Gibu translated Rilan's words to Jiansheng. Jiansheng nodded and said, we have to ask Kazan if she is willing to go with us. We cannot just decide her life by ourselves. Kazan has the last word.

The three of them went to Kazan. Renso was busy working, and the poor girl was still demented in the nightmare.

Gibu went over and said gently, Kazan, are you better now?

Kazan, do you want to leave here? These two travelers, they want to be your mom and dad. They want to take you with them and take care of you. Do you want to go and live with them? Kazan?

The girl raised her head and looked into Xinhe's eyes in a heart-rending way. Gibu watched her and suddenly remembered the scene he saw two years ago when Kazan's grandpa had passed away.

That winter the land had been covered in silver snow. Kazan stayed in the black tent alone and kept vigil beside her grandpa's shrouded corpse for three days and nights. Jinmei was with her. On the fourth morning he appeared in front of Kazan's tent and said, Kazan, let's go. It's time for us to send Grandpa away.

At the celestial burial the girl had lowered her head and held the butter tea up to him with trembling hands. It was snowing heavily. He took her to the Rilans' after the burial. The poor kid stumbled her way after him. She was so fragile and yet so strong-minded.

Now that the poor girl was in such a wretched situation, Gibu felt truly sorry for her. He hoped that she could go with the kind couple. The grassland was too expansive and too desolate. How lonely she would feel if she stayed here.

Kazan did not speak. Gibu squatted patiently beside her and asked her in a gentle voice, do you want to go? Kazan, answer me.

Xinhe watched the silent girl and began to worry about her. She went down next to her and stroked her head gently like a nice, patient mother. She pressed her lips on Kazan's face and said to her, Kazan, we both love you. Come with us. Our home will be yours and I'll be your mother. I'll take care of you. Kazan, come with us please.

The child did not understand a word, but she was touched by the woman's warm affection. She gazed at Xinhe in helpless tears like what a hurt child would do to her mother and mumbled gently, he wanted to sleep with me . . . he is strong . . . I couldn't help . . .

With these words, Kazan locked her arms around Xinhe's neck. The wretched child kept calling in a low voice, Ma . . . Ma . . .

Tough as he was, Gibu was brought to tears by her words.

Xinhe held Kazan tightly and looked at Gibu in anxiety, what did she say?

He said, the girl called you Mom. Kazan called you Mom . . .

6

A couple of days later, one foggy morning, they set off with Kazan on Gibu's bullock cart in the curling juniper incense. Renso was the only one who came to see them off.

Nobody saw Zamecho in the distance, who watched them on horseback over the small, undulating hills. Under the blue sky, a floating cloud glanced off the boy's head.

Xinhe stayed close to Kazan in the fear of arousing her anxiety. The child was silent and obedient on the way. She did not even look back at her homeland often. In her blood resided a thirst for new starts, as if she were the reincarnation of a steed's soul.

She left this expansive land that had brought her life and pleasure as well as death and desolation. If it was her fate to depart, it was useless casting lingering eyes at the past. Her homeland had been inscribed in her memory long before. She knew she would never forget it.

That was enough.

Gibu's bullock cart sent them to a faraway town. Jiansheng and Xinhe found the local police station and had Kazan's domicile changed. There were a lot of other complicated adoption procedures for them to undergo when they got back to the city.

Gibu went back after dropping them there. He wanted to tell them something before he left, but he was reassured at the sight of the young, kind couple and simply bid farewell to them.

They took Kazan to Lhasa after a long ride and flew back to Beijing.

On the plane, the three of them sat together like every other family. Xinhe sat close to Kazan to take care of her. She kept asking her what she needed in a low voice and trying to teach her Chinese. Overcome with emotion, Jiansheng sat by and watched them in silence.

Is this the so-called samsara of life?

This was exactly what had happened to him when, out of the blue, he had been taken to the city some ten years ago. Sitting on a train, he had stared at the window in curiosity and felt everything strange. He could well remember how he panicked and fretted in the next few years. Amidst the frictions and fights with his mother in the later years, both of them could not help wondering if it had been right for him to go to the city at all. For years they had been isolated from each other by so much misunderstanding and hatred that their final reconciliation came too late.

He hoped that in this samsara, he would not have the same irretrievable regret. He owed too much to this world. Maybe it was a way of paying back. He was sure he was ready to do it.

He felt happy for the goodness in himself.

Off the plane, Kazan was amazed by the enormous Beijing Airport. She had never seen a city before. She felt both excited and insecure when the depths of the Tibetan Highland shifted to a dense forest of concrete walls and steel rods. She grasped Xinhe with her hand in sweat. Xinhe understood the child's fear and never left her company for an instant.

Jiansheng drove across the city and took the family home.

Kazan looked back time and again from the back seat. But she could see nothing clearly except the bright car lights on her face. Night settled in Beijing. The heat of the summer had not consumed itself yet, and the city rippled with a mellow luster of red wine in the splendor of the lights. Amidst the streams of cars and men, buildings ablaze with lights were scattered here and there, which gave the city its unique grandeur. The modernity of the city stood in sharp contrast to and yet complemented its history as the ancient capital, which used to be full of richly ornamented columns and beams, exquisite jewels, and phoenix-patterned robes. The classic image of the city was a sinking gigantic dragon boat with gorgeous corridors and balconies and magnificent singing and dancing scenes. It sank further and further into the dark night and never came up again.

She felt from her heart the giganticness and loneliness of the city. All of a sudden she had to face a brand new world alone. Fear suddenly preyed on her mind.

After they were back, Xinhe helped Kazan to wash and put on new pajamas. She was very gentle and careful when she touched the child. She combed Kazan's hair in the bedroom and saw the child's simple, pretty face in the glass. She had purple skin, a lean face, bright eyes, and slender arms and legs.

She embraced Kazan gently and kissed her on the cheek. Kazan, from now on you are gonna live with me. The girl smiled shyly and quietly.

That night Kazan slept with Xinhe. At midnight, she had a light fever and a headache. Xinhe was worried and did not know what to do. Jiansheng frowned and said, let's take her to hospital tomorrow morning.

The doctor's diagnosis was "deadaptation to high altitude".

The doctor told them that there was some truth in the long-standing superstition that highland women residents would catch diseases when they came to the central plain. As they have been accustomed to the thin air on the highland, they will feel uncomfortable with the low altitude and feel dizzy, weak, and a tight chest, etc. This is exactly the same with the inlanders who have altitude stress when they go to the highland. Besides, the child has low resistance to bacteria and viruses as she grew up on the clean highland, while the air in Beijing is polluted and contains many microbes. The child will need a long time to adapt herself to the new environment. You need to take good care of her.

For a time after she came to Beijing, she was not in good shape and suffered from the deadaptation. Jiansheng and Xinhe looked after her carefully and hired a nurse to take care of the housework and the meals. They also hired a private tutor to teach Kazan Chinese. The girl was very sensible and tough. She never moaned when she did not feel well but endured the discomfit silently. She also worked hard at Chinese.

Jiansheng and Xinhe were afraid that Xinhe's mother would not agree with their adoption, so they went through the procedures without informing her, and took Kazan to her later.

Xinhe was anxious when she told her mother how the child came to their family. The old lady was also shocked and moved by

Kazan's experience and her sensibility and toughness. She finally understood them and accepted the adoption. She ended up with the same words as Jiansheng, this is no small matter. I hope you have considered it well before deciding.

The old lady stroked Kazan's shy face gently. Her reddish face beamed like sunshine and her slender figure was sinewy and healthy. She had a pair of bright eyes and long, dark, and fluffy hair that stooped in two big plaits. Dressed in the fancy garment that Xinhe had bought her, she was an exceptionally pretty and exotic little girl.

Everything went on smoothly. They were all kind-hearted people in this cold world. Kazan was very lucky to meet with them.

Xinhe's photographic works got collected in the large album of the publishing house and made a hit at the joint photography exhibition. At the exhibition, the dozens of works that she carefully selected were all exhibited. The photos presented the visitors with the most primitive and touching landscape and life.

> On the golden land, the grazing cattle lowered their heads
>   and shouldered the tranquil dusk
> A golden flag cloud on the dark purple peak where the sun
>   and the moon shine together
> The short whip was raised and the melancholy setting sun
>   hid its face between the peaks
> When the wind passes, the highland barley undulates under
>   the knees of the reaper
> In the shepherds' village, the juniper incense curls up in the
>   dawn light and licks the stooping sky
> The black hawk hovers past the fluttering wind-horse ban-
>   ners. Its wide wings flit over the nameless graves to the
>   end of the sky
> The jolly wild flowers kindle the cowboy's songs on the end-
>   less wilderness as if they were telling a tear-less legend

The high, milk-white walls and the gilded skylight of the
lama temple cut a clear contour in the azure sky
Outside, the horse stands at the end of the long, narrow path
and looks in the direction of the truck
The path behind us flows to the distance like a Khatag in
the wind, a heart-rending scene under the blue sky
Dusk settles in the Lower Qinglunzhuo Grassland. The sky
with the clouds looks like the deep blue sea bottom with
the exuberance of colorful corals
The limpid, nameless lake murmurs a legend of the shadowy
past, which is swiftly pecked away by the singing bird
The lonely pilgrim leaves a trail in the starlight like the
Buddha's hand that strokes through the undulating spines
of the mountains

. . .

In the prologue to the exhibition, Xinhe placed a couple of
special works.

The upside-down image was obviously captured in a flurry.
Amidst the blurred, staggered light and shadow, a badly injured
Tibetan mastiff was fighting fiercely with a snow leopard.

They introduced the photos in full length in the prologue.

I took the photo accidentally when I tried to scare the leopard
away with the flash lamp. The courageous mastiff was the only
family of a Tibetan orphan. That night the mastiff fought the
leopard to the last. Blood gushed out of the mastiff's wounds and
spilled all over the ground. The next morning, it sensed impending death and left us alone for the distant snow-capped mountain,
the home of its soul.

It was the guardian god of the grassland. In loyalty and valiance,
it bled the last drop of its blood for its small master and her lambs
and black tent.

This photo is dedicated to our everlasting friend Jinmei.

Jiansheng took Kazan to Xinhe's exhibition. He held her hand firmly in his palm and stopped over every work. Kazan stood for a long while before Jinmei's photo without a word. She knew Jinmei was waiting for her in the distance and they would rejoin each other some day.

7

Jiansheng and Xinhe were very busy. They were both young artists. Jiansheng taught at the Academy, and Xinhe designed and produced photographic works at the studio. Xinhe often came back very late at night.

Jiansheng worried about Kazan. He was worried that she would feel lonely and deserted, as he felt when he was small. He tried to play a good father. He tried to be close to her at home, ask her about school every night, and talk with her. He and Xinhe took her out for excursions on weekends. In the fear that Kazan might meet with difficulties in study, they arranged private tutor lessons every night to help Kazan with her Chinese and schoolwork.

After all, she was out of school for years. It was not likely for her to be outstanding at school and they had nothing more to desire except that she might lead a happy life with her peers.

To their consolation, they got along well with each other. The family relationship was blessed with a harmonious beginning. Jiansheng had always feared that he would repeat the mistakes of the past, but he was greatly relieved with the result. The child was very sensible and studied hard. She took good care of herself and never bothered the nurse.

Her life was smooth at the ethnic primary school. In the graduation exams she got 70 or above in every subject. This was a feat for a child who used to be illiterate and had not been able to speak Chinese at all. Xinhe and Jiansheng were immensely gratified.

That summer after her graduation, Jiansheng and Xinhe were

kept very busy working at the studio and atelier. Kazan was very sensible and took their meals to them at work with the nurse every noon. Xinhe was touched greatly when she saw the child came in the hot weather and told her, don't bring meals for me any more, sweetie. The studio offers working lunch, and I can order meals from the restaurant if I need. All you need to do is take good care of yourself. Sorry for being busy. It's your graduation summer, but Mom and Dad have no time to stay with you.

That night Jiansheng and Xinhe returned home earlier and the whole family had dinner together. The jasmine flowers on the balcony were blooming, so Kazan nipped the flowers off and placed them on a white ceramic plate on the dinner table. The sweet scent of the flowers immediately permeated the entire room.

Jiansheng was astonished. His memory flashed back to his boyhood. Many years ago he used to have the same habit by nipping the fragrant flowers, placing them beside Huai's pillow and waking her up in the sweet perfume. Now he was a man in his thirties and everything had changed. How time flew!

He reached out his hand and stroked Kazan's head affectionately.

Xinhe lay awake that night. She kissed Jiansheng and woke him up. She crouched beside him and stroked his handsome face in the dark. Jiansheng, Jiansheng. She called to him gently.

What? he answered.

Are we gonna be like this forever?

What do you mean?

I am saying, don't we want our own baby?

He was silent. At last, he said, is there anything wrong with the life we have?

Xinhe said, no, it's just that . . . maybe we should have our own baby.

Jiansheng answered, Xinhe, we are both in our thirties now. We would wear ourselves out with Kazan and another baby. How are we gonna take care of the baby if both of us are so busy? Kazan is a sensible child and gets along really well with us. Don't you think we are just perfect together? Why bother to add anything else?

Xinhe was silent. After a long while, she asked him plaintively, Jiansheng, we've been together for seven, eight years. I once said that when I looked at you, I often had the feeling that you were far away from me. I know it's your past that separates us and I can never be part of it. But I've always wanted to lead you out to a happier life.

Tell me, did my wish come true? Do you feel truly happy with me, like you did when you were with Huai?

He felt a pang in his heart when he heard Huai's name from Xinhe. They were both kind and beautiful women and he did enjoy infinite love and happiness from both of them. But somehow he knew they were different.

He did not know how to tell her about the difference, so he held Xinhe in his arms in the darkness and kissed her forehead. He said gently, don't worry about it. We're always gonna be like this. I'm very happy and I love you too.

He felt for her. Her love for him was an enormous blessing. They supported each other through the long years of hardship. In those days when they were young, they spent their college life together, graduated together, studied in St. Petersburg and returned to China together. They got married, went to Tibet, brought Kazan back, and decided to raise her together. The relationship was lasting and treasurable.

Time flew. He felt as if he were a boy who played on the way back and got lost while admiring the beautiful view. He could never retrieve what he passed in his youth. He might have forgotten it, or might not. Many years later he would plunge into memory when he saw the fragrant flowers on the white ceramic plate, feel a vague pang when he heard the name of his beloved from another person deep at night, and thought about her when he stroked the peeling oil paintings. Only then did he know that the first bright rainbow had been inscribed on the horizon of his life and he was never going to forget it. After all, that was the dawn of his life.

He closed his eyes. He saw Huai's fresh, beautiful face again, in that dream that he'd had repeatedly in his childhood.

In the dream he and Huai got on an old, empty bus that drove slowly into a dense, moist forest. The green vines dangled outside the window and dripped with sweet dews. The green sun beams shone down into the dim bus and the cool breeze lifted the hair by Huai's ears.

He sat beside Huai and said to her in the green world, Huai, I missed you so much.

Huai reached out her hand, stroked his head, and combed his disheveled hair on his forehead with her hand as before. Huai told him, don't you know I've been missing you too, for all these years?

He smiled contentedly and sentimentally. But when he turned to her again, Huai disappeared. As if trapped in a preconceived parting, he was left alone, frightened in the dim bus.

The forest became denser and he felt as if he were in a rain forest. The solemnity in the air made him think of a grave. He stepped over the lush green boughs and went on and on. Right before his eyes appeared two big trees, with a rusted iron gate standing in between them. He pushed open the gate, which startled a huge green-winged bird. The bird flew to the sky and cast down a sad cry.

He found a big, white grave half hidden in the shrubs. Moss sprawled along the white gravestone. He wiped the leaves and wild fruit off the stone. It was inscribed with his mother's name.

Jiansheng woke up with a start. The dream had been visiting him for years and he could never forget every detail of it. He opened his eyes and found Xinhe sleeping in his arms peacefully. Her sleeping face brought to his mind the nights he had many years ago, when he lay by Huai's side, kissed her neck and smelt her fragrance, and sank in sleep in her arms. He felt a vague pang in his chest again. So he called her name in a low voice in the dark.

Huai.

They did not have a baby at last. Jiansheng remained restrained, even frigid to sex. This was not normal compared with most other men. Xinhe gradually sank in despair; she knew she was unable to drag him out of his past at last. With all her love for him she had no choice but to pour all her hope on Kazan and she cared for her like a child of their own.

8

Kazan became a high school student. The teacher arranged seats for the students and she sat next to a very pretty girl.

It was still scorching towards the end of September. The girls wore white shirts and blue skirts and sweat was dripping from their temples. The neighbor said to her, hello, my name is Ye Lan.

Kazan turned around and saw a smile beamed on the girl's face.

She answered, hi, I'm Kazan.

Kazan, that's a special name. Where are you from?

Kazan did not know how to answer the question. She finally turned around without a word.

Kazan made few friends at school, and Jiansheng and Xinhe were aware of it. This was not because she was unkind or not easy-going, but because most of her schoolmates were Han children and they seldom came up to talk with her.

Ye Lan, however, was different. Kazan talked about the girl when Jiansheng asked if she met any new friend at school.

Ye Lan was the prettiest and richest girl at school. She was from a single-parent family. Since she attended junior high school, her former classmates had been, out of envy, spreading malignant, dirty rumors about her among the bitter-tongued girls. Her audacity, puerility and uncompromising attitude added fuel to the flame, and she had been isolated from the class since primary school. The rumors made her both lonely and widely known on campus. Wherever the pretty, solitary girl went, she attracted eyes in envy or distain.

It turned out that her isolation even worsened in junior high school. Quite a few boys took a fancy to her, and she was indulgent in character and did not mind the company of different boys. Her unrestrained behavior aroused even more resentment among the girls who thought she robbed them of the boys of their dreams.

This was perhaps a common phenomenon among many kids. Almost in every class and grade there were one or two such girls who were isolated for whatever bizarre reasons. Sometimes it was because they were too pretty and unruly, and sometimes it was because they were the opposite.

Cruel slanders and rumors were always directed at them. The rumors were mostly not true. Even if they were, they were results of misunderstanding. Envy and cruelty set their roots early among the innocent kids. It has always been the case. But the kids committed the mistakes unwittingly, so one cannot blame anyone for their wrongdoing.

Most of the wretched, isolated kids, were innocent. Their adolescent years were more or less shadowed and cruelly distorted by the unfair isolation. Friction with peers was a commonplace to them, and the quarrels led to nothing but the pleasure in fighting and their teachers' hollow instructions. After all, who would remember those elegies for youth, even if the sorrow that the songs unfolded haunted the victims' entire lives?

Ye Lan used to tell her, Kazan, believe it or not, they thought I had many good-looking boyfriends, but I've been alone all the time. No girls wanted to be near me, so the boys came. There are only two kinds of people around me, lovers and enemies.

Maybe I have to count you out, Kazan, 'cause you're my only friend.

Kazan told her mom and dad about Ye Lan. She said, Ye Lan treats me as her good friend at school. Jiansheng smiled and said, Kazan, are you happy to have a friend? She answered, yes. He stroked her head and said, great, then don't mind what others think about her. Do whatever you think is right, Kazan.

On and on the veins of time ran towards the unknown gateways of life. The boys and girls in white shirts were standing on the cool, mossed stone staircase, and gazed into the garden called youth in front of them with exploring eyes. With throbbing hearts like the fluttering, colored wings of butterflies, they pushed open the gate of time timidly and looked at the lush, magnificent, and yet desperate illusions in curiosity.

Friendship at a young age was always sincere, touching, and yet hollow. Ye Lan was a child in the spotlight, while Kazan was in every way the opposite. The two girls were drastically different and yet they were the same in a certain sense.

It was always easy for children to get along well with each other. They exchanged gifts and calls; sometimes they would turn a cold shoulder to each other for the loss of a gift, and come together again a few days later with a note of apology.

It was the trick of the innocent, lonely teenagers. They exchanged a lot of greeting cards on the New Year's Day and each other's birthday and wrote letters to each other. The letters were full of innocent sentiments but aroused their sympathetic responses. They treasured each of these letters.

Kazan's adoptive father and mother were both vigorous artists and her life was very comfortable. However, she was amazed by the affluence of Ye Lan's family when the latter took her home.

It was a large suburban mansion in the European style, surrounded by precious, towering trees that were transplanted and grown with delicate care. The trees separated the mansion completely from the crowded area of the upstarts' villas. There were as many as seven cars in the garage at Ye Lan's disposal, and the mansion was only one of the many estates that Ye Lan's family owned. It was really amazing.

For no reason, Kazan had only a vague idea of Ye Lan's house despite the many visits. Like every other magnificent place, the house had an air of melancholy despite the wearily extravagant decoration. Ye Lan had a nurse and a driver and there were many bodyguards around the mansion. They were there to protect the cars and antiques, she said, not her.

Ye Lan's mother came back occasionally, but Kazan never met her.

She would go to Ye Lan's on weekends. Since the mansion was far away, Jiansheng and Xinhe would always spare some time to drive her there and never pressed her time-wise. The first time when Jiansheng and Xinhe sent Kazan there, they met Ye Lan. The pretty little girl wore a polite, graceful smile and told Jiansheng like a grownup, don't worry, sir, I'll have the chauffer drive Kazan home.

The two children frolicked in the garden. They helped two handsome, precious sled dogs to wash, and ran and played with them. When they wore themselves out, they entered the house and lay on the wooden floor, telling each other jokes, playing computer games, dozing in piles of dolls, or browsing the brand new comic books in the bookshelves. They had a lot of fun together.

In their first summer holiday at junior high school, the handsomest boy at the school began dating Ye Lan. The boy's name was Kang Yijun; he was a great magnet among girls. Most of the small girls at their age were susceptible to vanity. To them, dating handsome boys was a feat to be proud of and a testimony to their charms. The idea was funny, but it was also simple and romantic.

She remembered that it was scorching that day. The flames of the sun were like a pot of melted metal liquid that sprayed all around. The air she breathed in was a carpet made of camel hair that wrapped the heat up tightly. The leaves of the plane trees on both sides of the streets were curled up in the heat like tinfoil paper. Everything was stooping in the sun except the dark green creeper on the trellises on the corridor downstairs, which still beamed with a bright luster and cast down patches of shade.

She had been staying home all day doing assignments for the holiday. In the afternoon, Ye Lan called and said, let's go swimming. She said, all right. At your home?

Ye Lan said, no, Yijun doesn't like coming to my home. Let's go to the indoor swimming pool.

Wait, did you say Kang Yijun? Are you two dating?

Ye Lan's excited voice was heard over the phone, yes we are. We'll talk about it later. Meet you downstairs in a minute.

Kazan put down the phone and went on with her exercises quietly. Minutes later Ye Lan's voice was heard downstairs. She put down her pen, told Mom and Dad she was going out, and dashed downstairs.

She came into sight of Kang Yijun, who rode a bike with Ye Lan on the backseat and emerged from beneath the green shade of dense creepers. He parked the bike at a quiet corner with winding vines. Kazan's eyes were instantly attracted to this handsome boy. He had a brownish face with clear features, and his pupils were bright and watery like a tropical river hidden in the lush rain forest. He was tall, straight in figure, and his shirt was very clean. Leaning against the backseat of the bike with his arms crossed on his chest, he turned his head slightly and watched the two girls, framing a perfect profile to her.

Ye Lan was always with these good-looking boys.

The three of them went swimming. Yijun pushed the bike on the way, while Ye Lan and Kazan talked and laughed hand in hand. The three children disappeared in the waves of sunlight.

They often went swimming that summer. Kazan often sank into the cool blue water of the swimming pool and held her breath for a long time. She could always see the vision on the verge of suffocation, as if she were covered by big snowflakes in silence. The waves surrounded her like her mother's hand and reminded her of her bath experience in the sacred lake with Renso. On and on she sank in a desperate effort to hold the faces in her illusion.

Summer passed by quietly. When the new semester came, the news of Ye Lan and Yijun was spread all over the school. As they were in different classes, Yijun would wait for Ye Lan at the door of her classroom after school. He was disappointed to find that Ye Lan's driver had also been waiting at the gate. He was frustrated that he never got an opportunity to walk her home.

Ye Lan said, sorry, Yijun, but my home is too far away and you can't possibly bike me there. But Kazan's home is close, so why don't you take her home?

Yijun was silent. He looked at her despondently and turned away without a word.

During the first days of the semester, when Kazan walked home alone after school, sharp-tongued girls would stop her and scold her, why are you meddling with that bitch? Stay away, or we'll never talk to you again. Don't you know her nickname was "pickup", 'cause anyone can pick her up?

Come on, do you want her or us? The girls looked at Kazan out of the corners of their eyes.

Kazan looked at them innocently and said, you never talked to me before I met Ye Lan.

The girls stammered with rage. They were on the point of saying something when they saw Yijun standing behind Kazan and staring at them coldly.

They refused to retreat, but shouted behind Yijun, and you, you're shameless! Didn't you speak ill of her before? Don't think we don't know it! How come you follow that bitch around like a fly?

Yijun dashed forward with daggers in his eyes. He stood next to Kazan and said to the girls, go away! His fists were clenched.

The girls fled. Yijun stood still for a long time quiet and melancholy. Kazan knew that he was surrounded by girls. His former girlfriend was very popular among girls. At that time Ye Lan was still juggling love games with boys. But later it got around that Yijun had liked Ye Lan instead of that girl, so the girl broke up with him quickly. Yijun began to date Ye Lan that very summer.

Kazan stood by Yijun and said, don't mind what they said. Ye Lan is a good . . .

He cut her short and said, let's go. I'll see you home from now on.

The days at the beginning of youth were bright and fresh like tender sprouts in early spring. Everything seemed elusive and unreal to them as they were barely teenagers. The fantastic, sweet games they played were sure to be quickly forgotten and would only be remembered jokingly as the follies of youth many years later.

Starting from then, Kazan went home with the boy every day after school. She kept a pace from him, so that she could always look up into the boy's lean figure, so lean that he looked as if about to be melted in the sunshine before autumn came. They did not have much to say at the beginning. It took them a long time to feel natural and comfortable talking with each other. After chatting their way to Kazan's apartment, they would say goodbye to each other, and Kazan would go upstairs while the boy turned away.

Kazan never thought of letting out her sentiments. They were like the precious pine cones in her secret garden that she preserved with care. She treasured them and gained pleasure from them.

Xinhe used to talk with Jiansheng about the boy who saw Kazan home every day. She was kind of worried if the boy was patient enough to carry through, if Kazan would feel hurt when he no long did it, and if the simple friendship between the three kids became complicated. Jiansheng smiled and said, no. Don't you know Kazan? She enjoyed the sweet secret. We have to let her handle it. It's her world now.

I'm happy as long as she remains close to us, and there is smile on her face when she opens the door.

She was indeed very happy. From primary school on, whenever her mom and dad had time on weekends, they would take her out shopping. When the chrysanthemums bloomed at Beihai Park, they would stroll around the lake for exercise and have dinner at the century-old restaurants. During the winter vacations, they would spend the Spring Festivals at Grandma's and visit the Lama Temple to pray for the New Year. In summer vacations, the three of them would go to the seaside, swimming, jogging on the beach, making sand sculptures, and enjoying seafood at the night market. Jiansheng and Xinhe even took her along when they attended an international exchange activity in Russia. As soon as the program was over, they got on the train that traversed Siberia and headed for Lake Baikal. During their stay at the picturesque lakeside, they would stand on the balcony and watch over the lush woods and the vast lake in the distance. Bathed in the breezes, Jiansheng and Xinhe felt peace at heart. Their little daughter was growing fast beside them. To their immense relief, she overcame her twist of fate and adapted herself to a normal child's life.

9

School days were always about waiting. Children waited for the end of school and for the ripe age. The days of innocence slipped by without their notice, and the three kids gradually grew up with the uneventful flow of time.

Ye Lan was strong-willed and independent. She never put on a long face in front of anyone, as if she thought nothing of the rumors and rejection. She always beamed with happiness, or at least, apparently so. She was not the kind of girl who defended herself with smooth pretensions. Actually she was only courageous when faced with slanders. Despite the isolation she beamed with happiness and remained forgiving all along.

Yijun loved her. He loved her so sincerely that everyone could see the futility of envious slanders. For over two years he had been dating Ye Lan, but Lan always said to Kazan, Yijun is too weak, too sensitive. I don't know if I truly love him.

She said, I like you only, Kazan. You are my best friend.

The two girls lay side by side on the wide floor at Ye Lan's house. Their long hair was spread all over the ground and got entangled like two vines of different colors, Ye Lan's yellowish while Kazan's pitch dark. They put their hands together. When Kazan was about to fall asleep, she felt Ye Lan kiss her face and embrace her.

Ye Lan's dreamlike voice went, Kazan, are we gonna be like this forever? Are you gonna leave me like everybody else?

She heard her voice but did not answer.

She liked Ye Lan and Yijun both. Her liking was based on simple, harmonious, sibling-like companionship. Beside the easy, pleasant friendship, she kept the rest of her world to herself.

She worked hard at school and got straight A's. Her head teacher used to advise her sincerely, don't follow Ye Lan's example. You don't follow the same path.

She answered quietly, yes I know, Miss. We don't do bad things at all. And Ye Lan needs me.

One rainy evening towards the end of eighth grade, Kazan was bending over her desk doing exercises. Thunder and lightning were raging outside in the pitch-dark night.

The phone rang. It was Yijun's voice.

Kazan, tell me, does she really like me? Yijun's crushed voice was heard over the phone.

She was surprised and did not know how to answer.

She broke up with me. Kazan, I'm crushed. I don't know what is happening. Tell me, did she never like me before?

Yijun, Ye Lan liked you.

Really? But why is she breaking up with me?

She must have a reason. Didn't you ask her?

I asked. She just told me I was not her type. I asked her, who is your type then? She said it was you. She said it's always you she liked. Is that true, Kazan?

No, Yijun, I like Ye Lan too, but that's different. You're wrong. Ye Lan is just too lonely. What she wants is just simple love, and maybe you made it too complicated. She doesn't want to be stifled, that's all.

Really? Yijun asked.

Yes. Come, don't get jittery.

There was a long pause on the other side of the phone. Then Yijun hung up. She could only hear the busy buzz in the tumult of the night.

Shortly after that the extra lessons for the ninth grade began and they returned to school. Within a week, Ye Lan's textbooks and materials were all stolen. They were found in garbage cans and bathrooms later, all of them torn apart and written with dirty words.

Ye Lan was undisturbed by the nuisance and did not even tell Kazan. As they were deskmates, she either borrowed or shared Kazan's materials. When Kazan asked her, she said in a nonchalant tone, I lost them.

The new young teacher did not know what happened to her and scolded her sternly, how can you come to classes without the books? It's the ninth grade and all you know is muddling, muddling and muddling. You're really beyond help, girl. Go stand in the corridor. Without the books you won't understand the lessons anyway.

She did not say a word, but bit her lips and went out immediately. There was a loud snicker in the classroom.

Seeing Ye Lan standing on the corridor, the president immediately took her to his office and entertained her obsequiously. He found the teacher afterwards and gave him a scolding: Don't you know how much Ye Lan's mother donated to our school? You get all your salary and stipend thanks to her! Thank God the girl never told her mother about all the tricks and bad treatment at school! Her books were thrown away by other kids, didn't you know? Even I know the tricks the other kids play on her! How did you become a teacher? What do you know about your students? Did the donator give you the salary to abuse her daughter? Go back and apologize to her tomorrow in class!

The next day with all his pretensions of justice the teacher bawled at the class, that's too much, all of you! How dare you bully your classmate like that! Don't you belong to the same family? What wrong did Ye Lan do to deserve that? Ye Lan, I offer my sincere apology to you. I apologize to you on behalf of the entire class.

What are you doing? Seeing that the class was silent, he said immediately, come on, every one of you, everyone except Ye Lan, stand up and say sorry to her! Whoever does not stand up and apologize today is going to be punished!

His stupidity escalated into a disastrous episode that afternoon.

Before the night study, all the students in the ninth grade had dinner at the grocery or the restaurant by the school gate, and Ye Lan and Kazan were no exception. Goaded by his girlfriend, a bad boy dashed into the restaurant, dragged Ye Lan up from her seat and tossed her to the floor. He used to chase after Ye Lan but was harshly rejected and had resented her ever since. Before Ye Lan could react, he bent down, tore at her hair, and slapped her in the face. He yelled, you bitch, I'm being polite to you not to tear your clothes off here! Fuck! So you have money, so what!

The restaurant was in dead silence. The students looked at each other in astonishment. Everyone shoved off and looked on in cold indifference, but Kazan dashed out and covered Ye Lan. She bit her lips and stared at him silently.

The boy pointed at her insultingly, this is none of your business, I tell you. Damn, shove off, all right . . . Hardly had he finished the words that Kazan punched him heavily in the nose. Blood streamed out immediately and he grinned and howled in pain. He covered his nose with his hand and found himself bleeding. Fuck! He cursed, and turned around in fuming anger to look for something to fight back with. He picked up two chairs in his hands and was about to hit the two girls with them. Kazan stood in between him and Ye Lan; she did not even duck when the boy came at her and closed her eyes in fear. At this moment a couple of campus securities dashed over and dragged him aside.

When she opened her eyes again, the restaurant was swarming with whispers. The students rapidly dispersed after watching the scene, leaving Ye Lan sitting on the floor miserably. The two girls were completely cast out. Kazan hastened to help Ye Lan to stand up. The wretched girl's white cotton skirt was smeared, her hair was disheveled, and the slap had left clear marks on her face. She caught sight of Yijun when she stood up.

She was in a mess, but she stared at him all the same. Her stern look drew tears from Yijun's eyes. She brushed against him without a word, and Kazan walked with her all along. When Kazan turned back after walking a long distance, she found the boy was still frozen there.

They did not make the night study. Ye Lan was surprisingly calm. She called the driver over and was about to go home.

She said to Kazan, Kazan, go back to the classroom. I'm going home.

Kazan said worriedly, cry out if you feel bad, Ye Lan. Don't wear yourself out.

Ye Lan smiled. She said, what do you take me for? Is this worth my tears? I could've beaten them to hell if I had wanted to.

Kazan, I'm going home.

Ye Lan came over and hugged her. You fought for me today and protected me . . .

She swallowed the rest of the words, turned around, and got in the car.

Kazan watched her car drive away in the evening, when streetlamps had just been lit.

Ye Lan went back home and bumped into her mother. She asked her casually, I heard you were beaten up by a student?

Mm. Ye Lan answered in a low voice and walked into the bathroom to wash her face.

Do you need the bodyguards to straighten things out for you? Her mother's voice was heard from the sitting room.

Don't bother. She answered coldly.

Let's go to the U.K. Don't stay here any more.

At these words Ye Lan straightened up and looked at herself in the glass. She did not say a word.

10

That night when Kazan went back home, she went on with her homework calmly. At bedtime, she went to Jiansheng and Xinhe's room and said, Dad, Mom, I beat up a student at school today.

Jiansheng frowned. He asked, what happened, dear?

She told him everything, and Jiansheng became silent. Xinhe embraced her and stroked her head. You didn't do anything wrong, sweetheart. But you need to take good care of yourself from now on. Look, Dad and Mom would have been worried to death if you had gotten hurt by the chairs.

Kazan nodded and walked out quietly with a good night.

The troublemaker soon quit school. Ye Lan had not shown up ever since. Her little foes were greatly relieved by her absence. It seemed that nothing changed at school without her. The teachers held a meeting to stress discipline to the students, and the episode quickly passed away.

Yijun was still wandering at the door of their classroom. Kazan knew that he was there to see if Ye Lan came to school, as she no longer answered his calls. From time to time he would come to Kazan and hesitatingly inquired about Ye Lan's whereabouts. He asked, is she never gonna come again? Can I call her?

The boy used to be open and clear, but since he met Ye Lan, he was utterly changed and became sensitive and fragile, as he cared too much for the girl. Because of his relationship with Ye Lan, many of his good friends left him. He seemed ashamed to meet with them too and ignored them when they came across each other. He kept to himself at school in silent sorrow and did not care about classes. As his scores plummeted, he became the bad example of those who "ruined themselves in puppy love" in the teachers' mouths when they scolded other students. Many students sneered at him behind his back and said he made a fool of himself by falling in love with Ye Lan.

No one knew that the reason for his change was that he loved her indeed. He was not like any other boy who chased after her out of vanity as if to show off an expensive jacket.

The boy was too sensitive and hurt himself deeply for his kind nature.

The next weekend, Kazan visited Ye Lan's home. The instant she saw her friend, she gave her a big hug. Are you all right? Kazan asked.

Ye Lan was still relaxed. She said, I'm good. I'm finally rid of the assignments, now that I'm at home. Kazan asked Ye Lan, aren't you gonna come back to school?

Ye Lan looked at her and said, my mom arranged for me to study in a high school in the U.K. I'm going, Kazan.

Kazan found the news hard to swallow. When are you going? she asked.

I don't know.

The girls sank into silence. They lay on the floor and watched the exquisite decorations on the ceiling. The long silence made the room more desolate than ever.

Their long hair still got entangled like two vines in different colors. But they were separate.

Kazan asked her, Ye Lan, can you really ignore what happened to you in the past three years?

As if hit on a soft spot, Ye Lan became silent. She said at last, you're wrong. You should've changed "three" to "nine".

She was such a lonely and innocent child.

Kazan understood that to Ye Lan some wounds were like arrowheads that could never be drawn out from the sores. She could try to forgive and forget, but she was damaged all the same. Even if she made light of them with all her might.

Ye Lan left a broken yet indelible stamp on Kazan's adolescent memory. Only Kazan knew Ye Lan's pains. The two friends hugged each other as if nothing had happened. They cuddled together and fell asleep in the grids of sunlight that shone through the white lattices. Before the farewell songs were heard, and after the early days became memory.

Ye Lan, will you remember me?

I said you are my only friend. How can I forget you? she answered.

Kazan told Kang Yijun the news that Ye Lan was about to go abroad. The boy was so sunken and disappointed that he did not say a word.

He skipped the last two classes and traversed the city to look for her in the heat of September. His shirt was drenched in sweat. The sun was sinking and its crimson rays were cut to pieces by the skyscrapers and stitched to the sky in a montage. The boy rode three good hours through the stream of traffic before he arrived at Ye Lan's door. He shouted in a loud voice from behind the iron fence, Ye Lan, Ye Lan.

Ye Lan came downstairs. The boy said but one sentence, don't leave me alone, okay? He pleaded to her with big drops of sweat rolling down his handsome face as if he were crying. Ye Lan looked at him in surprise and did not say a word for the moment.

Ye Lan, don't leave me alone. He hugged her and pleaded.

What happened to you?

Don't go to the U.K. Stay in Beijing, okay?

It's not up to me.

Ye Lan, didn't you ever like me?

Kang Yijun, don't do this again, okay? You are always like this. You're wearing yourself and others out.

The boy suddenly knelt down. Ye Lan, I beg you, don't go away. I like you so much. I can't live without you!

For a moment, she was deeply touched. She could always remember that night, beside the ivy of the garden, when a boy put down his dignity and begged her to stay, on his knees.

This was the first man who knelt before her in her life. At such a dangerously young age, he plunged himself in the torrents of love and hurt himself badly. He was too brave to be strong.

Kang Yijun, I can't stay, she said, but if you still want to live, promise me never kneel before any girl again. Remember you are a man. Don't waste your dignity in pleading. You'll be despised. If you are not able to hold your girl back, you've got to learn to forget her. Pleading is no use. Sorry, I think I don't like you enough.

He was silent. He stood up for a long while and looked into Ye Lan's calm face. The boy said in the darkness, maybe you're right, Ye Lan. But you'll change your idea when you really love someone in the future.

Ye Lan, I'm off. Goodbye. He turned away in sorrow.

The boy rode on his bike and his white shirt gradually faded away in the dim light of the street lamps. His shadow was like a choking memory that was finally forgotten in the depths of time.

11

The autumn was sober when Ye Lan was leaving. Kazan told her parents, Dad, Mom, Ye Lan is leaving, but I still can't decide if I want to see her off.

Xinhe looked at her. She could not understand why this sensible child was hesitant over such a trifling thing. She said, she's your best friend. Of course you should see her off.

Jiansheng pinched Xinhe's hand immediately and indicated for her to stop. He said, Kazan, tell me the date whenever you make up your mind and I'll drive you to the airport. But it's all right if you don't see her off. It's all up to you.

Kazan did not see Ye Lan off at last. She did not even know when Ye Lan left.

During that time, she was still working hard in the classroom on her exercises, lessons, and endless exams. Whenever a plane roared through the blue autumn sky, however, she would look up from the desk and watch in the direction.

Is Ye Lan up there looking through the window at the city below the thick clouds? Maybe she is not. After all, she has no beautiful memory down here.

But, does she not?

One night at 1 a.m. shortly after Ye Lan's departure, the phone started ringing. Jiansheng picked it up. It was Ye Lan. Jiansheng was woken up, but he was still patient. He put down the phone, knocked at Kazan's door, and said, Kazan, it's for you. Ye Lan is calling.

Kazan was overwhelmed with joy. Picking up the phone, she immediately heard Ye Lan's relaxed, joking voice, hello, is that Kazan? I'm in London now. I've been studying English at the language school. I'm sick of it so I called to speak some Chinese with you. How are you doing?

She listened to Ye Lan's voice from the receiver and felt at that moment as if she were back at their first meeting.

. . . Hello, I'm Ye Lan. The girl said to her. Kazan turned around and saw the smile that beamed on her face.

The hair that spread on the floor and got entangled like vines. The letters they wrote to each other in the innocent years. She stood in front of her when she was bullied . . .

Looking back, everything was so beautiful. Although the bygones were bygones.

She still kept the silent world to herself. With the impending major exams, the students were divided into two camps, those who worked hard and those who played harder. Kazan had rarely spoken in the past and was close to no one else except Ye Lan. Now that her best friend had left, she turned back to her old track again and never mingled with the other girls. Her only focus was schoolwork. She was like a lotus flower that bloomed alone and kept aloof from the tides of the world.

In the quietness of home and school, she concentrated on her study and made great progress in the ninth grade. She was such a bright child that Jiansheng and Xinhe did not worry about her at all despite the impending exams. She even had the spare time to visit her mom and dad's exhibitions. She liked Jiansheng's oil paintings and was keen at art, too. She used to say to Jiansheng, Dad, you seem to repeat something when you painted all the different objects. Do you miss that thing?

Jiansheng smiled slightly. He was amazed by the child's keen artistic sense. People always said his paintings were special, but no one else was able to point out in what way they were special. No one knew that it all sprang from his memory.

Kang Yijun ceased seeing Kazan home. He was not interested

in anything. In the summer of her ninth grade, Kazan passed the exam and was admitted to a key senior high school. Yijun lagged way behind. His parents spent a fortune to get him into a common high school. They kept in touch and remained good friends. But they avoided talking about Ye Lan whenever they met each other. It was like an unwritten rule between them. Kazan believed that he had not moved on yet.

After Ye Lan left, Kang Yijun became more despondent than ever. Because of his good looks, he was again surrounded by girls from in and outside his school. Kazan heard that he made some new friends at high school. He meddled along with the other kids so as not to get too bored of life. He changed dates frequently and never turned any of his girlfriends down. Sometimes he even called Kazan to hang out with him. He always rimmed with tears when he got drunk. At times when he could no long control himself, he would lean on Kazan's shoulder and blurt out in drunkenness, will you remember me when I die? He would put on a hollow, lonely smile or begin sobbing beyond control while covering his face with his hands.

He missed Ye Lan terribly.

Kazan never met another friend like Ye Lan after the tenth grade. She was comfortable with the distance she kept from her fellow students.

Like every other girl at the age of sixteen or seventeen, she shuttled between school and home solitarily with a bag on her back in the sunshine of youth. She spent her uneventful days in the well-lit classrooms, went back home in the setting sun, and worked on her exercises under the small lamp in her room. She jotted down formulas all over the scratch paper. Different from most of the girls who found mathematics, physics and chemistry a headache, she did very well in them and made greater and greater progress as time went on, just like some boys. The teachers said jokingly that if she entered for the Entrance Exams as an ethnic

minority student and her scores above the lowered entrance mark
could be spared to others, the average marks of the entire school
could be raised a lot.

Occasionally she would receive letters and packages from Ye Lan.
The letters were often simple greetings written in English and
Chinese on a thick, smooth piece of paper in the classic style. More
often than not she would receive packages of all kinds of strange
gifts. She once received a big bundle of dry lavender. The purple
buds retained their fresh luster and the special perfume smelled
like the splendid sunshine in a flower field by the Mediterranean.
Kazan carefully put them in a glass vase and enjoyed the view
of them. While she studied in the U.K., Ye Lan was constantly
transferring from school to school and often toured around other
countries. For some reason, Kazan's replies could never reach her,
so Kazan decided to write no more. As long as they missed each
other, it did not really matter in what form they communicated.

Ye Lan returned once during Kazan's eleventh grade year. It
was her Christmas holiday. The school was not off yet, so Kazan
skipped classes to meet her at the airport.

At the busy exit for arriving international flights, she saw Ye
Lan walking out alone with a small bag in her hand. She smiled
so casually and happily, as if she had been simply out for shopping. This was hardly a surprise. She had been flying all over the
world since childhood and overseas trips were commonplaces for
her. At the sight of Kazan, Ye Lan immediately put down her bag
and dashed towards her excitedly. She gave her a big hug and said,
Kazan, God knows I missed you so much!

That night at Ye Lan's home, the two of them frolicked in the
room like before. When they wore themselves out, they lay on the
floor side by side. Ye Lan chattered about her life abroad, the places

she'd visited and the people she'd met. Then they started talking about the past again and chuckled at the interesting stories they shared. They took out the sentimental letters of confessions that they kept and laughed while reading them. They held their sides with laughter when they talked about how they were discovered playing gobang games during history class.

They both had a spark in the throat and sounded hoarse after chatting for a long time, and lay down finally. Kazan had been busy with schoolwork lately and suffered from lack of sleep, so she dozed off when she quieted down. Seeing that Kazan was asleep, Ye Lan lay by her side quietly and stroked her hair.

In her sleep, Kazan could feel that she was held from behind by Ye Lan. Ye Lan said, Kazan, we're always gonna be like this.

The next day Kazan went back to school and did not see Ye Lan again. She only stayed in Beijing for three days, then she went to Hong Kong to see her mother, and then went back to the U.K.

Kazan was all alone again and went on with her high school life. The birches on the campus turned yellow in the autumn and turned green again in the spring. The wind rustled past the bright windows, the dance of the sunlight on the small, lustrous leaves outside like the brisk whistle tune of "the young lad". The golden beams of the sun were cut regularly by the lattices of the classroom and sprayed evenly on the white wall full of standard keys and information for the Entrance Exams. Amidst the tireless songs of cicadas, the white shirts, test sheets, and book pages fluttered restlessly in the swiveling blades of the electric fan, like the constant turning of the tides in the youth's heart. The seats of the bikes that parked in front of the classroom building were scorched. Occasionally a blue-winged dragonfly would perch at the windowsill, and quickly got bored and flew away.

That summer Kazan finished the eleventh grade. During the vacation, she and her classmates had to sit through extra lessons for the twelfth grade despite the glare of August. Their toughest year had begun. Sweat dripped from their faces like threads of tears and wet the test sheets when they buried their noses in exercises. Their elbows were stuck to the desk in sweat and ached acutely when moved.

In those long days of rigorous training, they were buried in endless tests. The students spent their days attending classes in the stuffy classroom and reviewing again and again the out-dated textbooks. The sunlight was hot and hard, and looked blind and weary like the students. For their night studies, they had tests in the pale light of the classroom. Night settled in the city and the students' minds gradually felt numb. At times Kazan felt exhausted and looked up to regain her breath, only to find in the classroom a dense black mass of heads bending over the desks. The students' hands and heads moved so uniformly that she was shocked with the horrifying picture.

At that time, she felt as if she were walking on a dead end road and no outlet was within sight.

Eight years ago she was but an innocent girl in the rampant sunshine of the highland. She waited for Jinmei to return in the dusk, and prayed with Grandpa in the black tent through the starlit nights. The butter tea boiled quietly on the low flames and the juniper incense curled up from the land. The moon was limpid in snowy nights on the highland.

Now she was working her head off in the classroom for the twelfth grade of a key high school of Beijing. This was inconceivable to the highlanders.

She had been accustomed to hearing the last bell clanging at the end of the night study and walking out of the classroom amidst the noisy crowd. The lights of the classroom buildings were turned off one by one in the darkness. The students' voices streamed together and flew through the quiet campus, the luxuriant trees by the streets, the brightly lit city with all the bustling cars and people, and the blind fatigue and the humble hopes of tomorrow. One after another, the students went back home.

With the thick reviewing outlines and test sheets in her bag, she got on the last bus and sat in the back row. The orange street lamps sprayed into the bus and cast down varied shadows.

She would meet with two kids at the back row on the bus. They were a young couple in school uniforms with bags on their backs. They always huddled together without saying a word. The girl with long, black hair buried her head in the boy's arms. The two kids turned their faces in the same direction and watched the fleeting scenery outside in melancholic eyes. They were lost in the sorrows of youth.

She went back home, turned on the small lamp in her room, and went on with her exercises after drinking a cup of water. At times she grew tired of the endless, boring drills. When she felt upset, she would copy Buddhist Scriptures in Tibetan.

No one knew that she never forgot her mother tongue after she left the highland. She could not only speak Tibetan but also taught herself writing in the language. The picturesque Tibetan Buddhist Scriptures filled the gap in her heart. When she finished a paragraph, she would read the characters in silence and feel warm and comfortable as if she were back at home. The Scriptures renewed her courage to walk on in the strange world far away from home.

If late at night Xinhe found beams of lamp light through Kazan's door, she would push the door open gently and give the child a glass of milk. Xinhe was always afraid the little girl would wear herself down and urged her to go to sleep. Kazan always answered the mother's earnest, affectionate urges with warmth and patience. All right Mom. You go to bed early, too.

She always stuck to her words and went to sleep at once.

That year she was eighteen.

Kazan, our flesh is but a lotus flower that lives and dies by itself. It perishes. But our souls are eternal. Kazan, always keep your soul clean and virtuous. Only by this will you be blessed with an eternal life.

She heard Grandpa's distant voice. Throughout the many years in which she came to live in this strange world far away from her homeland, Grandpa's admonition was her only luggage. She knew that in the depths of her soul there was such a garden, where grassland undulated like green seas, flowers bloomed in all seasons, ballads flew like limpid brooks and the sky was as blue as in legends. Where men never bled for wars and women never ached in childbirth. Where the moonlight was no longer cold and the storms no longer wreaked havoc on the land.

That was that land of her ancestors. Dad, Mom, Grandpa, Jinmei, they were happily reunited there forever. They were patiently waiting for her. Before joining them, she had a long way to go alone. She was fearless and ready for the future.

During the last days of twelfth grade, she was extremely calm. She had no idea about the Entrance Exams really; to her they were but another exam. She took the exams in a relaxed mood and her scores were ranked in the top four in the grade. She was happy with the result. When they filled out the application forms, everyone thought she could pick up the hottest major at a top university, but she surprised them all by selecting archaeology as her major.

Kazan calmly presented the application forms to her parents. Seeing her choice, Jiansheng asked her, Kazan, are you sure you've thought over your choice?

She nodded confirmation.

So Jiansheng said, all right, go ahead for it. This is your decision.

12

Jiansheng, are you relieved? Xinhe asked him before they went to bed that night.

What do you mean?

I know that you've been worried from the start if we'll make the same mistakes with Kazan as your mother made with you. I know you tried your best. For so many years we've stayed close to each other without any fights or quarrels. You've always attended to Kazan's needs and given her the right to decide for herself. You stayed with her, followed her growth, communicated with her, and let her feel loved. And I did the same too.

Jiansheng opened his eyes and said, yes, I know you understand.

Xinhe said, Jiansheng, the more you cared about Kazan, the more grieved I felt. We don't know what will happen to her. She was brought up in our love. I'm afraid with all her purity, simplicity, and independence, she'll get hurt in the future. I can also see that by raising Kazan you are correcting the mistakes and making up for what you missed in your childhood. Jiansheng, the more you care about our daughter, the more I feel for the breach in your heart. I'm worrying about you.

He sank into silence. After a long while, he said, don't wear yourself out, Xinhe. I'm truly happy that you understand me so much, but don't worry about me. Xinhe, we'll always stay like this. Don't you think everything is perfect?

Chapter V

In the woods leaves are heard rustling under the gentle touch of the autumn's finger. The sun paints warmth all over the wall, while the night blows it cool again.

Autumn rustles the old leaves off. Do you want to hear a new tale? The quiet river opens its eyes wide and says with a smile, there are always as many homecoming pilgrims as leaving sails.

Jian Zhen, "Floating Boat"

1

Kazan remembered very well an age-old bronze bowl that she had used back at home on the highland. Its surface was etched with many scars of time, which gave it a pristine, ancient look. The lack of craftsmanship was evidenced by the bold, abstract, unpolished patterns about its rim. After many years of use, the indented space amidst the patterns was blackened, while the lines in relief became smooth and burnished with perennial rubbing. The bowl was so old that no one could tell exactly when it had been brought home, or by whom. The reason why Kazan had a deep impression of it was that it was always used to contain her favorite yogurt. The sweet and sour drink was so sensuously smooth and tasty that it formed the plainest and strongest allurement in her childhood memories.

She remembered clearly how, on the Shoton (yogurt-eating) Festival, the white curds in the bowls would vibrate enticingly with the jiggle of the hands, giving out a sweet, mellow scent that to her almost equaled the taste of happiness.

She had never had yogurt again after she left home. For a long time the milk in the city repelled her. Only once did she spot a bowl of yogurt at a bakery. The liquid in the white ceramic bowl reminded her of the favorite drink in her childhood memory, but somehow it looked different. She peered at it for a long time.

The memory of the vision was the first to wake up, followed by that of the smell and the taste, until she was embraced again by the long-lost subtle taste of happiness. But the illusion quickly passed away. She knew she could no longer go back.

By that time she had already entered college and grown into a tall young lady with beautifully suntanned skin and a trim, svelte figure. She had a perfect curve in the neck and arms, slender legs, well-defined features and bright, dark-black pupils that resembled those of an antelope. Her rich, pitch-black hair was braided in long plaits that reminded one of the luxuriant autumnal forests.

Kazan was very beautiful. Her unique beauty set her apart from any common urban girl that one easily met with in a crowd. Her internal beauty was so radiant that she would draw many eyes on the street even though she was dressed in a plain student uniform.

She went to a university in Beijing, so she lived on campus on weekdays and visited her parents and grandmother on weekends. She was always a sweet, obedient child. She worked very hard at the university, indulging herself in systematic historical studies and going for field study tours to Shaanxi, Henan and Gansu organized by the departments of history and archaeology. All the while she kept the habit of daily sutra-copying that she formed in the twelfth grade. She spent her college years as uneventfully as any other college student.

From that time she fell in love with relic studies. She found immense fun in learning the skills of cultural relic identification, in which she probed the true face of history by examining a delicate ancient vessel. She would loiter about the antique market by herself and relish the joy of identifying and appreciating an authentic antique out of the bevy of rough shams. More often she would hunt for related literature in the library. Her favorite activity was to collect the auction notices in the newspapers and attend the antique expositions prior to the auctions.

It was at a large expo of Tibetan Buddhist antiques that she met with Jianan.

She loitered about the exhibition hall and examined carefully the splendid Buddha statues, the Tangka (scrolls of Tibetan traditional painting), and the sacred vessels. She was turning around inadvertently when she found a tall, erect man beside her. The man had regular features, thick, curly hair, and bronze skin. Viewed from the side, his profile was as clear as if it had been chiseled by the most skilled craftsman.

Kazan was struck by the first glimpse of him, as if an undefined vision that she had long cherished materialized for the first time.

She decided to give it a try and said to him in Tibetan, hello?

The man turned around in surprise and answered in Tibetan, hello, with a smile beaming on his face. The full look of his face instantly reminded Kazan of her homeland and brought her face to face with an almost irretrievable memory of the past. Such a face must have been blessed with noble blood and ample exposure to sunshine. He was so handsome that she was unable to turn her eyes away from him.

Kazan asked him, are you from Tibet?

The man smiled and said, maybe.

Kazan did not inquire further, neither did the man explain. His smile left a deep impression on her; she almost smelled the mellow memories of the past.

He was not a man of words. After the greeting he remained pleasantly quiet. A ghost of uneasiness, however, gradually rose in her heart with his silence.

For a while the stranger was absorbed in examining the exhibits; then he turned around and said to Kazan politely, excuse me, I'm going over there. It's nice to meet you. Bye.

He did not leave her a card. He bid her goodbye in a reserved, distanced manner and disappeared quickly.

She did not know Jianan's name or his whereabouts when she met him. Later she confided to Ye Lan in a flirtatious and self-mocking tone: he is such a handsome guy that any woman would want to bear his children upon the first sight of him. He was an antiques dealer.

Kazan attended this auction unhesitatingly. She paid a fair amount of bid bond in anxiety and, with a bidding number in her hand, pricked up her ears for his voice amidst one after another auctioneers' calls in the venue.

She did not discover him until he successfully purchased a gilded bronze Buddha statue by offering an astoundingly high bid.

During the break, she caught him smoking a cigar at the exit.

The man was surprised at the sight of Kazan and asked her with a smile, so you're an auctioneer, too?

Kazan did not know how to explain. She said, no, sir, I'm just coming for a look-see.

As he was smoking, he made a gesture with the cigar in his hand and asked her in a westernized manner, sorry, do you mind?

Kazan shook her head.

The man asked her in return, are you from Tibet?

Yes, Tibet is my home town, but I go to school here.

The man did not ask her which university she was from, but said in curiosity, do students attend auctions too?

Kazan said, I'm an archaeology student, so I often come to antiques auctions.

He smiled and said, I see. You like studying antiques?

Kazan answered, yes, it's fun.

The man smiled again. He raised his head and puffed at the cigar.

It's about time we went back. Let's go. He said.

2

The two of them sat down side by side. The man seemed uninterested in the rest of the antiques, so he turned around to chat with her in a low voice. He confined the topics to the auctioned antiques, which saved the conversation from being uncomfortably intimate. He whispered by her ears, look at this Tangka. The pure-gold bris-thang is over 100 years old, but it's actually a replica of replicas. Its original is a gos-thang piece that is said to date from the beginning of the twelfth century. At that time Tibet was beset with the 400-year-long tangled warfare among warlords. Having lost his family in the war, a nobleman named Wangzangmuqin took the monastic vow and had a Tangka made as a tribute to the temple to commemorate his conversion to Buddhism. Legend has it that the nobleman had quality silk as the base, his own blood as the red dye for the thread, and gems from Xinjiang and pearls from the East Sea as the inlays on the brocade. It's said that the completed work was such a splendid masterpiece that it became the crown of the treasures of the temple. Regrettably, it was stolen overnight during the British invasion and its whereabouts had remained a mystery ever since. So an old painter at the temple made a pure-gold bris-thang replica according to his memory of the original. The new work bore remarkable resemblance to the original, but the craftsmanship was entirely different. The original was a tapestry work, while the replica was a painting on common cotton fabric without the silk base, the dye of blood, or the inlays of gems and pearls. Thanks to the painter's superb skill, it looked exactly the same as the original when viewed from a distance. The replica was then taken as the model for quite a few dpar-thang copies, one of which was collected by a painter in Lhasa. The painter died heirless and his collections were appropriated by various people. This Tangka piece is one of the dpar-thang copies. What an irony it is to watch these business sharks eagerly salivating over a replica!

He said, I bid for that statue at my client's request. Gilded bronze Buddha statues have not been popular since the Qing Dynasty. Personally I find nothing special about the statue except for its authenticity, but my client would not listen to me. He wants an authentic Buddhist statue urgently and I don't have one on hand, so I bought it.

Kazan listened to him with a racing heart. She took such a fancy to the stranger that like a drunkard, she would not realize the pains of love until she woke up with a hangover. Groundless and feeble as her infatuation was, she plunged into it all the same. He was such a mysterious man who appealed to her infinitely with his introverted poise, calmness, and easy charm. His adeptness made it natural for anyone to be attracted to him inadvertently.

She was not aware of the danger she was in and threw herself into the spark of love like an innocent moth.

After the auction that day, the man invited her to dinner.

Kazan was not without hesitations. She was afraid to be taken as a light woman who would dine with a stranger upon the first meeting, but she liked him so much that she yielded to the temptation at last.

This complete stranger drove her to a seafood restaurant. Now that she reflected in the afterthought, what a precarious situation she had put herself into! She remained credulous and innocent despite the traumatic experience in her childhood.

She was invited to order, but found herself at a loss when faced with the riddling names of the dishes and the colorful, elegant illustrations. She said at last, I'm overwhelmed. Could you order for me? The man smiled gently over the table and ordered tuna, oyster, sea urchin, shrimps, crabs, and more. The dishes were spread all over the table.

He said to her candidly, sea urchin is my favorite food. When I was in Las Vegas I would linger in the hotel all day eating the sea urchin when the other guests lingered in the casino. Sometimes I would even return to the restaurant shortly after lunch and order another serving of sea urchin. The hotel in Vegas serves the best sea urchin I've ever had in my life. I've never had such delicious sea urchin again.

He was as innocent as a boy when he talked about his appetite.

Kazan picked up a piece and tasted it. She was not used to the flavor and grinned.

The man fixed his eyes on her and said with a smile, you don't like it? You prefer butter tea?

Kazan asked in reply, don't you like butter tea?

He answered frankly, no I don't. My mom used to boil tea for me, and I could hardly swallow it. He smiled.

The two of them chatted about this and that over dinner and became more and more relaxed. Kazan even picked up a shrimp with her hands and peeled off its skin without the least restraint. The table quickly became a mess. The man did not drink alcohol in her face and was neat and refined in his manners. They ate so much that they thought they would burst.

The man asked her smilingly, this is the best dinner I've had for a long time. And you?

Kazan laughed and answered, me, too. I'm full.

He paid the bill with his credit card and walked with her out of the restaurant. At the exit the man said, let me send you back. She silently consented and followed him into the car. She was not suspicious at all, but immersed in blind, childish joy. He decided that the girl was still too innocent to be a desirable companion for him. They exchanged surprisingly scarce words on their way back; all of a sudden the cordiality between them cooled down to indifference and detachment again.

Kazan got out of the car at the gate of the university. It was still early.

He said, I'll go to the auction house to pay for the statue tomorrow and leave for Italy to deliver it. This is my card. You may email me.

He gave his card to her and bid her goodbye in the car. He stopped again after driving ten or twenty meters and leaned forward from the car crying, by the way, how do you address yourself in your mail? He inquired about her name in perfect courtesy, but the belatedness of the question drew a faint smile on his face.

Kazan. She answered.

Is this your name? Yesterday?

She nodded not without uneasiness, and drew herself away without saying goodbye or thanks. Her thin, slender shadow gradually disappeared in the darkness.

3

That was her first meeting with Jianan. That night she turned over the man's face in her mind and found herself inexplicably yet helplessly drowning in happiness. She thought she "might be able" to love him. With the self-suggestion she seemed ready to fill a gap in her heart and forfeit herself in his hands. Such a readiness for self-forfeit was anticipated years before. After the loss of her last family, she used to stumble behind a stranger into the unknown depths of darkness. The blindness of her pursuit now seemed like an ominous prophecy, which lurked throughout the years awaiting its realization.

Beijing was dry, sunny, and restless towards the end of June. Outside the windows, the sun set the ground on fire, and the highway gave out a crunching noise as if about to melt whenever a car passed. The weather was so scorching that Kazan felt as if she were trekking through the Sahara under a heavy raschel blanket.

The semester drew to an end again. She became busy with her final exams and term papers. Quite a few classmates were too busy with paper writing to even snap up a shower in the deadline week. Like many others, Kazan would get up at 7 a.m. to get a seat in the library and sat on the bench through the day until 10 p.m. The continuous intensive reading sometimes gave her dizzy eyes and a splitting headache and she began to see the characters in the books collapsing down into separate strokes that flew about on their own. Never had she seen so many students huddling together in the same places: the reading rooms, the self study rooms, the corridors, and even the benches. Everywhere was swarmed with students. Everyone was reading avidly as if about to gulp the books in one swallow. In front of the water fountains students waited in a winding, endless queue like refugees lining up for relief supplies.

They stayed up for the entire night before the exam and had sweat all over in the narrow, stuffy dorm. It seemed as if they had hardly begun reading before it dawned. When it was time to enter for the exam, the students washed their faces with cold water, drank a cup of espresso and drifted into the exam room like zombies. They were not able to drift back to catch a nap until the end of the first exam.

The last days of the term vanished in such a chaotic scramble.

As soon as they finished the last exams the students left the campus for their homes. Kazan went back for vacation, only to find the house very quiet. Jiansheng was busy preparing for his exhibition tour and rarely showed up. Xinhe went to work at the studio every day and the dinner hour was the only time the mother and daughter could spend together.

During the dinner Mother filled her bowl with food and inquired about her school in a brief, courteous way. This was a habit that she had formed through the years. Her inquiry was more in the nature of exchange than inquisitiveness. She kept her promise by treating Kazan like her own daughter and attending to her needs carefully and patiently. She had been a gentle, dutiful mother since Kazan was ten. Her goodness brightened Kazan's world up and brought happiness to the family.

One night when both of them sat at the dinner table, Kazan asked all of a sudden, Mom, why didn't you have a child with Dad?

Xinhe put down her chopsticks as if controlling her feelings. She looked up with a reluctant smile and said to Kazan, aren't we just perfect, the three of us together?

Kazan knew clearly that it was not because of her that Mom did not have another child throughout the years. Perhaps the reason would always remain a secret between her parents. She did not probe further, neither did her mother go on with her explanation. But the girl was inexplicably sorry and grateful when she witnessed the aging of her mother.

4

Xinhe, are you asleep? Jiansheng asked her at the bedside.
No. What?

Jiansheng reached out and held her in his arms. Xinhe, I've been preparing for this exhibition for a long time. I'm very lucky to have found generous sponsors and it'll be a precious opportunity. But I'll have to leave for a long time after the opening of the exhibition.

Xinhe did not say anything. She gazed at Jiansheng's face, which was half lit in the moonlight and half sunk in the unfathomable darkness. His arms were around her just like any other night throughout the years. She had been familiar with the face and the arms since she was twenty.

She answered, I know. The opportunity is too precious to give up.

But I'll have to leave for a long time. You'll have to stay at home alone if Kazan goes back to school. I'm worried about you.

It's no big deal. I can live and work by myself.

No more was said between them. She had been familiar with the touch and smell of Jiansheng's hands. His gentle, neat manners almost bordered on distanced politeness. But she had been used to everything, including his embrace and the tone of his voice. They had been each other's life companion since the end of their adolescent years. The time they shared together was not too long, but neither was it too short. Jiansheng's gentle, neat manners made her feel safe. She knew she had been used to him and they would always remain like that.

She whispered to him, I love you, Jiansheng.

He kissed her on the forehead in the darkness and buried her head in his arms. I know, Xinhe. He said.

Jiansheng and another tourist painter from the Russian program held a joint exhibition that toured from Beijing to Shanghai, Chengdu and Guangzhou. It was a feat indeed for a painter to open an individual exhibition on such a scale. The organization of the exhibition tour not only exacted a high demand on the painters' creativity but also posed many practical difficulties ranging from funding, to venue arrangement, transportation, participation, promotion, etc. Jiansheng's collaborator used to study in Moscow. They clicked immediately at the first meeting and became very good friends. Jiansheng's partner had a large circle of friends and won the support and sponsorship of a large company. He then invited Jiansheng to hold the exhibition together with him. They had prepared for the exhibition for over three years and now their efforts finally bore fruit.

5

The first stop was Beijing. The exhibition was a complete success from the opening to the end. The sponsors commercialized the exhibition by hosting a grand party at the luxuriant exhibition hall, which ensured the influence of the exhibition from the start. Many of their works were favorably reviewed or ordered.

The exhibition gathered momentum in its tour to South China. Grand advertisement boards were seen on the streets of the cities where the exhibition was to be held. Huge light boxes of their modernist works were made, where the two painters' names occupied a prominent position. The light boxes caught the eye easily among the numerous billboards featuring beautiful models. At the last night of the exhibition in Chengdu, Jiansheng took part in a banquet and returned to the hotel exhausted. He made a call to Xinhe and found himself so fatigued that he started to fall asleep instantly.

When he had a shower and was about to go to bed, a staff person knocked at his door and said to him, someone in the lobby wants to see you. She has visited your exhibition in the past couple of days.

For no apparent reason he immediately guessed it was Huai. He wanted to confirm it with the staff person, but gave the idea up with a bit of hesitation and said, okay, I see. Thanks. I'll go downstairs this minute.

He wondered why Huai was in Chengdu, but did not have time to think it over. His heart began racing and swelling in such excitement that he thought his chest would burst. All of a sudden his fatigue was gone. He put clothes on quickly and dashed to the elevator alone.

He entered the spacious, luxuriant hotel lobby and looked about, but he did not find Huai. His heart sank into anxiety and emptiness.

No one came. He went back to his room.

Huai, was that you?

6

The last stop of the exhibition tour was Guangzhou. It was close to the city where he grew up as a child. The hot, damp air was familiar to him. The young, robust city looked almost transparent under the bright sunshine, like a city of glass that rose from the desert.

He decided to look for Huai.

It was as if he had made up his mind long before. He wanted to see her. Since he heard of her marriage they had been out of touch. He even did not know if Huai was still in this city, but he wanted to visit her all the same.

He only had the address on the envelope of Huai's reply many years before. He knew she moved away at that time, but he decided to visit the academy where Huai lived and worked.

He found the courage to walk back into his memory at last.

He found the academy a sight of sumptuous greenery. After so many years, the urban landscape outside the campus had changed beyond recognition, but the school was like a haven that survived the scribbling hands of time. The only change on the campus was that it became more beautiful. The trees were more luxuriantly green than before like the charming brows of a classic beauty. He was surprised to even find the three-storey building still standing there, the building where he spent his entire adolescence painting. The red brick walls were entirely covered by lush creeper and looked like a sweet, fluffy, green cake. His memory flashed back to the remote years. He felt as if he were still the lad in the white shirt, who, bathed in his first love, painted his longings on the sketch book and lingered all night long under the blooming magnolia tree.

Now everything had changed. Nearly two decades had passed when he looked up at the building again. Is Huai still there? Is there anyone else who would place a plate of fragrant jasmine flowers by her pillow every morning and wake her up with the sweet perfume? Will she remember him, when they have been separated by so many days and nights?

Jiansheng visited the professor who used to teach him and inquired if Huai still worked at the academy. The professor told him that she quit her job after her marriage, but she returned after a year and had been working at the affiliated high school ever since. The professor paused and said, but I heard she had been sick for a long time.

Jiansheng was immersed in mingled feelings of joy and sorrow. He asked the professor anxiously, what's the matter with her?

The professor said, sorry, I don't know.

Where is she living now?

The professors answered, she is still living in that old building. She moved back later.

7

Ye Lan, I still know nothing about him, but I can't help being curious. On first sight I knew by instinct that he was the man who would leave a stamp on my life. Kazan told her best friend over the phone.

That summer vacation Ye Lan did not come back, so they chatted over the phone. Kazan told her friend about her date with Jianan. Having heard of the adventure, Ye Lan said to her in dismay, you are still a child, Kazan. You know you know nothing about the guy and you fell in love with him? Are you in contact with him? He took you to dinner on the first date; did it ever occur to you that he might be a cheater?

No, Ye Lan. I think I'm different from you. You've been surrounded by boys all the time, but I know you've never really loved anyone.

Ye Lan said, Kazan, if this is what you think of me, I'm in no position to say anything further. But you have to promise me to protect yourself. You are not like me. I can face whatever isolation squarely and recover from whatever wound. Promise me that from now on you'll protect yourself bravely the way you used to protect me. Always remember that you can fall on no one except yourself, especially when you are in love. You have to know that not everyone is as kind as your adopted parents.

And, Kazan, I don't know why, but I feel that I can no longer keep you to myself. Will you remember me?

Kazan said, Ye Lan, if fate is full of traps then it's no use trying to dodge them. Entrapment is part of fate. Since we have to face fate, there are certain choices we have to make with all our hearts, be they wise or blind. Besides, it may not turn out as bad as you imagine.

That summer Kazan idled away her vacation at home. Jiansheng was not at home and Xinhe was busy with her work. She missed Jianan, so she wrote him a couple of messages at the address on his card. She asked in the message, where are you? When are you coming back? Her inquiry betrayed an anxiety as if he were a close relative of hers.

The vacation elapsed without his reply.

She was not disappointed and went on with her waiting.

It was not long after the opening of the new term that Jianan came to her school for her. He waited in front of her dorm building. When the janitor told her someone was waiting for her downstairs, she asked the lady who it was out of curiosity. The middle-aged woman said impatiently, a man.

Kazan went downstairs and saw Jianan leaning against his Porsche. He smiled when he watched her coming over.

She blurted out in surprise, why are you here?

Jianan said, one of my buyers invited an expert to identify a cultural relic for him, and the expert happened to be a senior professor of your school. We finished today and I drove him back from lunch, so I came by to see you on my way.

You are thinner, Kazan. He said to the girl and put his hands on her shoulders, as if they had been familiar for a long time.

Kazan was silent. Her face was vague in the dim lamp light.

I'm holding an auction expo tomorrow. I'll pick you up. When will you have time?

He did not bother to ask her if she wanted to go and simply said, I'll pick you up, as if the invitation were not to be turned down.

The next day he picked her up. When Kazan got into the car, she found the man dressed in a Nepalese-style cotton-flax shirt with dark-striped totem-like patterns, exposing the healthy skin about the neckline. The fabric of his shirt had a nice drape, which set off his perfect figure.

He smoked on the way and chatted with her over this and that. He said, I had many of the auctioned articles brought from Tibet. I thought you might be interested in them. Are you still an antiques fan, Kazan?

For a moment she was absent-minded like a child. Her eyes wandered about the windows and she did not hear his question at all.

Slightly surprised at her silence, the man looked up and found from the overhead rear view mirror the girl was absorbed in the scenery outside like an innocent kid. An amused smile emerged on his face.

He showed her around the expo.

Kazan, look at these time-worn objects. We traded them at a high price out of naked, simple purposes. If antiquity means nobility, then there are always cheaters who take any risk to fake the quality of time and history. I have seen innumerable fakes. To replicate the grayish color of the ancient jades as the result of many years of erosion, the cheaters would throw new jades in fire. To feign the shades on the ancient jades as the result of absorption of soil rust, they would make new jades in the ancient form, sew them in sheep legs and take them out a couple of years later to derive the dark red stripes. To fake the black spots in the middle of the jades after thousands of years of erosion of the miasma in the tombs, they would bury the inferior jades with gold- and silverware in the soil. Dark blemishes would appear in the jades under the chemical reaction with the gold ... These are just some of the clumsiest means, which are easy to detect. Some fakes are so cleverly made that they often pass for authentic. Since the ancient times, the cheaters and the relic identifiers have been entangled in this endless war against each other. If time can be fake, what cannot in this world?

Jianan said these words at the expo when he was standing next to her.

She could not but wonder if this man in front of her was real. He fixed his eyes on the precious jade ware with a faint smile. His face looked lively and elusive. He knew the young girl was different from any other woman he had ever met, so he had enough patience and interest to capture her, as if this game of love would make his life less boring.

At that time, Kazan did not know that he was such a bored man who needed new excitement to fill his life.

He grew up in a religious country and came from a big family. Before the abolishment of the hierarchy, his father was the master of a Vaisya family in Nepal and married five wives in succession. One of the wives was a Tibetan and Jianan was the hybrid son.

He told her about his mother. She was very pretty and had always been his father's beloved treasure. After she married far away into the foreign country by herself she cushioned all her complaints and sweated for the big family throughout the years.

Jianan's mother was very pretty, so he derived his good looks from her. He was also very smart, so his father loved him and his mother best in the big family. The Vaisyas were traditionally traders and Jianan's family was no exception. The family had been engaged in trade for generations and gradually accumulated wealth and bought fields. While they still belonged to a less noble class than the Brahman, they were a well-heeled family. Since the abolishment of the caste system in Nepal in the 1990s, they had been freed from many restraints and became more and more prosperous. They acquired large patches of land, the women of the family and the hired staff opened up many restaurants, and the grown-up sons turned into successful traders or politicians. Jianan's father had been engaged in black market antique trading from his early years and had been well known as a major supplier of antiques throughout South Asia.

Jianan said to her, my father loves me very much and paid for my high school and college education in Singapore. He wanted me to be a politician, so I complied with his wish and studied law in the university. But I have to admit that I'm neither interested nor talented in legal studies.

The only reward of his college life was that he picked up English, Chinese and Italian. With Nepalese and Tibetan, which he had known before, he could boast a multilingual genius. After graduation Jianan followed his father into the underground antique dealing trade. For a long time there had been little control over the theft and transaction of cultural antiques and his father made a lot of money by selling many relics from Angkor of Cambodia to Europe. Later Nepal and other countries began to forbid the export of important cultural relics and antique smuggling became more and more dangerous as the antique dealers' networking through bribery sometimes broke down unexpectedly. The dealers had to be more and more cautious and their profits dwindled. With the aging of Jianan's father, the son took his father's place and opened up Tibetan antique stores all over the world and attracted a lot of attention. They sold to curious foreigners legally exported cultural relics and simulated antiques for decoration; meanwhile they accepted secret orders and acquired antiques for their clients either from tomb plunderers at the markets all over the world or in international switch-trades. He had stores in Beijing, Hong Kong, Malaysia, Japan, Israel, Turkey, Italy and Saudi Arabia.

His business was booming in Saudi Arabia and South Italy, which were where oil tycoons and the Mafia gathered. The anonymous clients there were often surprisingly generous and determined in their offers.

In high spirits, Jianan told her about his first antique deal in Italy a couple of years before.

He had a common stone stool with dragon and phoenix patterns that dated from the late Qing Dynasty transported from Beijing. The transportation fee included, it cost him only 8,000 RMB. At that time Italy was not rich compared with other European countries, but the southern part of the country gathered many Mafia members. It was sunny that day, he remembered. A car stopped in front of his store and a stout man in a light suit stepped in and looked around at the antiques with childish curiosity. He walked out quickly without a word.

After a couple of days, a stern attendant in a black robe walked in. Out of ignorance or great wealth, he pointed at the stone stool and accepted whatever price Jianan quoted. They finally completed the deal at 20,000 USD. The attendant flung down the cash and drove away with the stone stool.

The two of them were dining at the restaurant when he shared the story with her.

Jianan was humorous and witty and his legendary experience fascinated Kazan. His eyes sparkled with a boyish, foxy light.

The congeniality at the dinner cooled off again into silence on their way back that night. It was already dark and nothing could be seen except the lamp lights that danced elusively outside the window. Kazan felt sleepy in Jianan's car and watched outside with weary eyes. Car lamps cast bright beams on her face in passing. Here stood the capital before the night curtain. Kazan felt as if she returned to the night when she was brought to Beijing by her adopted parents. It was her first time to see a real city and she was awe-stricken for her own smallness in the face of the brightly lit luxuriance and desolation.

She was further and further away from the land in her memory. Only the large expanses of snow-covered land in the cold moonlight lingered in her memory and cast down a blurred shape in her dimmest dreams.

Jianan's voice sounded in the darkness. Kazan, is it too late for you to go back to school? The man asked her probingly.

The intention of his invitation was obvious. Kazan said, no. I have to be back at night.

The man said no more. A vague smile appeared on his face. When did he become so gentle and patient with a woman?

When she got out of the car at the school gate, the man got out and stopped Kazan.

Without much hesitation, he embraced and kissed her. Kazan found herself unable to break free from his arms. She was still frightened with the smell and touch of any man who approached her suddenly. When Jianan finally let her loose, he found her crying like a startled bird.

He did not ask what happened to her; neither did he bother to find out if she was deeply stirred or frightened. He said to her, I'm gonna be out of town for a couple of days. Contact me if you miss me.

Jianan turned away. He got into his car and disappeared in the darkness.

8

Jiansheng did not go back to his exhibition in Guangzhou. He went back to look for Huai.

He waited several days in front of the door of Huai's old apartment without seeing her. His partner called him and urged him to go back, saying that the organization of the exhibition was complicated and his help and participation were indispensable. Jiansheng kept apologizing over the phone and tucked a note beneath Huai's door. It read,

Huai,

I'm holding an exhibition in Guangzhou. I came by to see you on my way, only to find out that you are sick. I waited several days in front of your apartment but you were not back. I'm worried about you.

If you happen to see this note, please do not leave. I'll come back soon.

My number is on the back.

Yours,

Jiansheng

He returned to Guangzhou. The exhibition was well underway and, as he and his partner insisted that they exchange with the fellow artists in the coastal area, they had been extremely busy with various parties and promotion activities.

Jiansheng grew more and more dissatisfied with the commercialization of the exhibition. He hated attending the occasions, which were nothing but flattering and empty clichés, but he had to undergo all of them for fear of hurting his partner's feelings. He was absent-minded all the time and wished the exhibition to be over as soon as possible so that he could go back to visit Huai.

Xinhe made several calls to him. Over the phone she asked him mildly, is everything going on well with the exhibition?

Jiansheng answered, it's okay except for the commercialized part. Sometimes networking is all it is about.

She said, this is unavoidable. When will you be back?

Jiansheng hesitated. He replied calmly, they want the exhibition to remain in Guangzhou, and we are to give a series of master classes. It is a good opportunity. I have decided to come back later.

Xinhe was surprised and said, okay. Don't worry, Kazan and I are fine.

Okay. I'll come back as soon as possible. Bye.

Jiansheng was sorry when he hung up the phone. He knew he was lying to her.

The exhibition came to a close after half a month and Jiansheng hastened back to Huai's apartment.

He knocked at the door, but he was so nervous that his knock almost escaped his own ears. He went on knocking with his eyes shut. His memory flashed back to many years before.

Many years before, during that night when the white magnolia had been blooming, he'd caught his mother hugging and kissing a strange man at the door and had left home angrily. He'd lingered before Huai's apartment and seen Huai's window still lighted. Deeply upset and ashamed with the embarrassing memory, he had dashed upstairs in an impulse to visit Huai.

The knocks on the door had been followed by a cautious voice from within, who is it?

The boy had felt an inexplicable dryness in his throat. He'd answered, it's me, Jiansheng.

Jiansheng felt an inexplicable dryness in his throat. He answered, it's me, Jiansheng.

The door opened with an old lady behind it. For a moment he was overwhelmed by disappointment. He said, sorry, I'm mistaken.

Hardly had he turned away and taken a few steps before he saw Huai at the door. Both of them were speechless the instant their eyes met. At last she murmured as if to herself, you're back, Jiansheng.

There stood Huai before his eyes, with her calm, melancholic voice. She paused and said, Jiansheng, this is my mother.

Jiansheng nodded and said hello to her politely.

Mom, this is Jiansheng . . . a former student of mine.

He walked into the apartment to find little change in the house after all the years. Amidst the same old furniture a corner of that white, narrow single bed was seen from the sitting room just as before.

Huai was wearing a white cotton chemise and sandals with her hair tied up as high as before, baring part of her slender neck. She looked pale and gloomy as if she had not been exposed to sunshine for years. The wrinkles on her temples and around the corners of her eyes shot pangs through Jiansheng's heart, but Huai wore them easily as if they were emblems of her reconciliation with time. She was leaner than before and her face was sunken.

Huai poured him a cup of tea and served him fruit. He looked about the room while sitting on the same old narrow sofa in the sitting room. Huai's voice was as gentle as before. She said with a smile, this room is as old and shabby as before, isn't it? Jiansheng shook his head quietly.

He smelt her sweet scent again, and the sunshine that was left on his white shirt when he was a boy. Huai's mother seemed very polite to withdraw from their meeting. She said with a basket around her arm: I'm going to the market to buy some vegetables. Make yourself at home.

How long are you going to stay here, Jiansheng?

I'm not sure yet.

I heard of your exhibition, but I didn't have the opportunity to go there.

Huai, I heard you were sick.

Yes.

What is it? Is it serious?

Huai was silent. She watched him from the opposite sofa with the same gentle, polite smile on her face.

You've not changed much, boy. How time flies . . .

Jiansheng interrupted her, tell me, Huai, what's wrong with you?

After a pause, Huai answered brokenly, my mother came specially to look after me, but I really don't think it necessary. A couple of years ago my legs started aching as if they were tied up tightly by something. I felt numb and languid, but I thought it was because of fatigue and did not go to the hospital. Last year my eyesight fell sharply and I occasionally suffered from diplopia. I went to the hospital to have my eyes examined, but the doctor could not diagnose. A doctor asked me about the other symptoms, and I mentioned the leg-ache and languor. He suggested me to have a close examination at the neurology department and I was diagnosed as having multiple sclerosis.

I never heard of this disease before. The doctor told me it is a breakdown of the central nervous system. It is normally chronic or spasmodic and its symptoms are like those of muscle strain. I took it to be muscle strain and did not pay attention to it. But the sclerosis can cause major functional failing and can be multiple with increasingly complicated symptoms. The doctors explained that the root cause lies in the biological electric charge, but I couldn't understand what that meant.

What a joke my fate played with me . . . you know my favorite cellist Jacqueline du Pré. I remember playing her concerto for you here in the past. I used to bewail her early decease and sighed for the cruel fate that made this young, talented cellist suffer and die from a strange disease. It was only later when I read about her that I realized I suffered from the same disease.

I began to suffer from multiple sclerosis shortly after my marriage and it's been on and off for years. I can still work now, so at least I did not burden my parents financially. But I feel very sorry for my mother indeed, as she is old now and I cannot fulfill my filial duties to the end of her life.

Jiansheng heard all this without a word.

At last he said, Huai, you are too tragic. I don't want to see you like this. Please let me accompany you to the end of your life, Huai.

She raised her head slightly startled. The stern contour that Jiansheng acquired as a boy was right before her blurred eyes. She said, I don't need you to do this, Jiansheng. You have your own family and you have to be responsible for them. Don't be a child.

Jiansheng did not listen to her. He asked, is your mother here to take care of you?

Yes.

You shouldn't let such an old lady do the job. Let me look after you. Huai, I've never forgotten how kindly and patiently you accompanied me before and after my mother passed away. I only regret that I was unable to love again after leaving you. I tried my whole life to deny this fact but I failed. Now I only want to come back to you.

Huai, you know my feelings for you and you need me. Am I right?

9

Deep at night she was hit by the acute pain in her head and legs again and could not go to sleep. She bit her lips to fight against the spasm and lay on bed as quietly as she could. Huai's mother was a light sleeper and woke up after hearing her slight moaning and tossing. The old lady got up and worriedly massaged Huai's legs with hot packs.

Her mother murmured in fatigue while wringing water from the towel, so that student is the Jiansheng you told me about. Looks like a trustworthy man to me. You'll be lucky if he really meant to help. After all, I am old and may not always be able to take care of you when you're sick. I can see how he feels for you. I used to warn you not to get too close to him, but now that he came back after so many years, he seems a man of passion and honor. Don't be cold to him if he wants to help. I'll be much relieved if you accept his favor. For better or for worse, baby, let him help us for as long as he can, okay? It's our fate . . .

The further her mother was into her late years, the more she was inclined to being pessimistic when talking about anything.

Huai blurted out sadly, Mom, let's not talk about it any more. I'm so sorry. She turned her face towards the wall with tears rolling down her cheeks.

Jiansheng was sleeping on the couch and woke up at the rustling in the bedroom. He walked up and saw the stooping shadow of Huai's mother through the half-closed door. Huai betrayed a vague moan now and then.

Jiansheng knocked at the door gently and stepped inside. He squatted down and said to the old lady, Mother, please take a rest and let me take care of her instead.

The lady glanced at him, stood up quietly and sat on the other side of the bed.

The bell struck the hour and the sound resonated in the quiet, dim room. It was two o'clock in the morning.

Huai took down Baclofen and Dantrolene pills and said, it's nothing serious. I'll be all right in a minute. Now go to bed, both of you.

Jiansheng would not go away, but waited on her at the bedside. They remained silent under the dim lamp light. After a long while, Huai said to him haltingly, Jiansheng, I remember a writer whom I like very much used to write: What can one ask more from life than passing through some beautiful scenery, writing a heart-rending article, and missing a beloved person?

Huai's voice became softer. Jiansheng knew she was suffering from acute pains. He sat down by her bed, held her feet up, and gently massaged them with hot packs. Women's feet were always the sexiest parts of their bodies. Huai's feet were as slender as the root of lotus and as smooth as jade. But Jiansheng found himself confused and awe-stricken when he touched the woman for whom he had been longing all his life.

Don't go on reading, Huai; your eyesight is falling and this'll destroy your health, he said.

Only those who feared not on the blade of life could retain

such calmness and peace. She was like a bull that bore the fardels without any complaint and sweated under the cross of goodness. She swallowed quietly the many sad and happy bygones and savored the various aspects of life without grunting. She never frowned at any difficulty or gloried in any success. Words seemed superfluous to her. She was only stirred occasionally with the memory of certain people and things and recollected the past alone when belated tears came to her eyes.

After a while, Huai's mother asked Jiansheng out and closed the door to the bedroom.

Standing outside the room, she said to Jiansheng, I've heard a lot about you from Huai and now we finally get to see each other. She needs help now. I beg you, young man, to help her.

Jiansheng answered, I surely will. I owe a lot to her. I'll never cast her aside. Please rest assured.

The old lady said, Jiansheng, I'm putting her in your hands. Time spares no one. Her father passed away a couple of years ago and I'm old. We brought Huai up and we knew how she was hurt for her goodness. Her marriage was unhappy. She got married after you went to college, but she fell sick within two years. Her husband thought of her as a burden and divorced her. She had been living alone ever since. She never told us, but we know her regrets. She has been missing you all these years. I know how cruel the world is, but I never expected to see her end up like this with all her kindness. I appreciate your kind help very much.

The old lady returned to the bedroom. Jiansheng remained at the door and felt relieved. For a moment he felt as if he were looking over the quiet flow of the time. He knew he had finally won the opportunity to reexamine the attachment between himself and Huai. His longings were finally answered after all these years.

It was a month later when Xinhe called Jiansheng again. She said over the phone, how are you doing, Jiansheng?

I'm okay.

Xinhe said, I never thought they would want the exhibition in

Guangzhou for so long. What a pleasant surprise! Where are you living? How are the master classes?

Jiansheng answered, they're all right ...

At his curt reply Xinhe said understandingly, I know you don't like the commercialism. Don't be too sad. Surely there are one or two worthy students in your master class? I miss you so much, sweetheart. When will you come back?

Her words hit a sour pang through Jiansheng's heart. For a moment he did not know what to answer.

Xinhe resumed, Jiansheng, can you come back and see us once? It's been nearly six months since the opening of the exhibition. I miss you terribly and Kazan wishes you home.

Jiansheng was perturbed. He glanced at Huai, turned around and said quietly, okay, I'll come back at once.

Huai looked at him from the back. She knew what was troubling him. Jiansheng, go ahead, I'm all right. My mother is here, and I can still work.

He fixed his eyes on her, his heart gnawing with pains and anxiety. He said, Huai, I have always wished that you all will forgive me.

10

On his flight to Beijing Jiansheng watched over the white sea of clouds on the stratosphere. The clouds looked like the boundless snow-covered land that stood still under the smooth icy-blue dome. The sun sprayed rampant streaks right before his eyes.

He considered whether he should ask for a divorce immediately if Xinhe could not accept his plan. He knew that whatever his decision was he would hurt someone, be it Huai or Xinhe, and he himself would suffer from the gnawing pains of conscience for a long time. Sometimes he even hated himself for owing so much to others that he could hardly repay any one of his debters.

He was especially sorry for Xinhe, who was drawn into the mess involuntarily.

But he knew he had to face the pains and responsibilities squarely if he chose to be a good and grateful man.

The night when Jiansheng returned home, his wife and daughter prepared a big dinner for him. At the sight of him, Xinhe jumped up and kissed him with her arms around his neck. How I missed you, honey!

He was gloomy and dispirited when he saw the innocent joy of his wife at his return. His heart wrung with pain when he thought of her innocence. This pretty, kind woman had been his wife since he was in his twenties. Her hairstyle was tied up high, exposing part of her white neck, which bore a certain resemblance to Huai but struck him as more innocent and tender.

Kazan cried excitedly at the sight of him, Daddy!

The daughter's cry woke him up and he was dragged inside the house.

Xinhe served him his favorite dishes: steamed bass, dried shreds of bean curd with parsley, and salted shrimps . . .

She knew Jiansheng liked salty food. At times he would complain that dishes were tasteless even if she put a lot of salt in them. Xinhe did not like salty food herself, but she compromised to make him happy. Throughout the years she had become used to salty food. Perhaps every woman would be as supple or tolerant as Xinhe when she really loved someone.

Jiansheng felt inextricably stressed after the past six months of living in hotel rooms, dining at restaurants, and socializing with people, etc., and especially after the turmoil with Huai. Now back at home, he found everything cozy and familiar: the overhead lamp of the dining room cast down soft light, the dishes on the table gave out enticing steam, and the food tasted perfect in the mouth. Everything was in peace and harmony and made one feel infinitely relieved. It had been long since the three of them sat down and enjoyed a dinner together. The smiles on the faces of Xinhe and Kazan looked so pleasant and touching to him.

Xinhe kept inquiring about his master classes over the dinner table. This double-checking did not spring from disbelief; on the contrary, Xinhe trusted him so much that she took the lie for truth and was genuinely concerned about his work in Guangzhou. Jiansheng hesitated and blundered; how could he tell Xinhe that there were no master classes, that he had been staying with Huai and had to be called back, and that he was planning all the way to abandon his wife?

Such lies were always painful yet unavoidable.

The thick curtain was drawn at night. The enclosed space of the bedroom gave one a sense of security. He felt relaxed when he sank into the comfortable bed. It had been a long time since he slept with Xinhe and her body suddenly struck him as strange. She crawled over and hugged him, touched the scar on his chest, and kissed the spot as if relieving him of the imagined pain. She stroked Jiansheng's face by inches, her bright pupils sparkling in the darkness. He knew she was looking up at him. The darkness in the room was like the thick patches of paints on the canvas that covered up all lies and truth.

She said, Jiansheng, do you remember our first night?

His breath became heavier. Yes I do.

Women who are vaguely suspicious often demand the proof of love in such a humble way and Xinhe was no exception. He had been accustomed to such hints and reviews and had gradually turned such affectionate questions and answers into part of his life. He had no other choice.

Jiansheng . . .

Xinhe . . .

They paused for a while and spoke at the same time. The atmosphere became slightly awkward when their voices coincided.

What did you want to say, Jiansheng?

He looked at her bright eyes in the darkness and swallowed the words at his lips. He asked back, what did you say?

Do you love me? she asked.

Yes I do.

As if reassured with a definite proof, she was relieved like a little girl and bent over to kiss him. Have a rest, dear. I know you're tired, she said.

Jiansheng closed his eyes again. He knew but too clearly that he and his wife slept in the same bed but dreamt different dreams. She was so naturally simple and sincere that she bought whatever well-meant lies from him. This innocence undoubtedly added to his guilty feelings towards her. He could clearly envision the impending tempest of the family.

What made him feel worse was that he would think of Huai as soon as he closed his eyes, even by Xinhe's side.

He had no choice.

During those days Jiansheng was helpless and anxious. He took up the clumsiest solution by going aberrant and waiting for Xinhe to disclose the cause of everything. This was cruel, but it was decent and indirect. He thought it better than blurting out everything.

A week later he quit his job at the central academy without telling his wife. Soon Xinhe's mother asked her, why did Jiansheng quit?

She was surprised at the news and said in disbelief, that's impossible! I don't know a thing about it!

That was on a weekend. She cooked dinner and waited for Jiansheng to return calmly. She concealed her emotions so well that Kazan did not even notice her change when helping her in the kitchen. Xinhe still trusted her husband so much that she would willfully turn a blind eye to truth even if it was at her door.

The three of them had the dinner in high spirits. Xinhe asked him casually, Mom told me you quit your job?

Yes.

Why?

He paused in silence. Jiansheng was not a man of resolution and decisiveness. Susceptibility and kind-heartedness were the two traces that were deeply planted in his nature, so to a certain extent his original sin had the deceiving look of beauty and goodness. He was doomed in this way. He was doomed to fall prey to the Oedipus Complex.

He did not know how to answer Xinhe's question. Kazan was at the table too. How could he open his mouth and confess everything then and there?

So he struggled to maintain his composure and said, yes, I was about to talk about it with you. Let's at least finish our dinner.

The excessive politeness between the parents startled Kazan. The daughter's limpid, sensitive eyes wandered probingly to and fro between them. She knew that perhaps Jiansheng was avoiding her, so she murmured understandingly, Dad, is it inconvenient for you to talk with Mom in my face? I can go back to school . . .

Jiansheng was intensely grieved again at these words. He immediately put on a gentle smile to Kazan and said, no, it's not like that. It's not you at all. You only come back once a week and we've been missing you terribly. Don't leave us. Have your dinner. Dad and Mom will talk about it later.

No more words were exchanged over the table. Nothing was heard except the rattling of the bowls and the food chewing. The silence reminded Jiansheng of those quiet dinners he and his mother had when they lived together before the many painful conflicts fell out.

11

Jiansheng, maybe it's time for you to tell me everything. She said, looking into his eyes.

That night Xinhe entered the bedroom early. She waited for a long time before Jiansheng entered. She wanted him to confess.

She said, perhaps you thought I was just an innocent, boring woman after all these years. But sometimes even the toughest nut must crack. I know I've been protecting my relationship with you with all the sacrifice and affection to the point of ignoring the disproportion between the give and take between us. To my relief you seem to have been accustomed to our relationship after my repeated cues and reviews, which is why we came this far. It is out of habit that we've been living together. We even built up a comfortable castle to support the habit and disguised it as the illusion of love.

Xinhe, don't you believe that I love you? I . . .

Do you love me? How far do you think my innocence would go? When you muddled with me, do you think I can't see it? Do you think after all the courtesy, we are paying due respects to each other like the ancients did? This is ridiculous, Jiansheng. It seems women are more sensitive than you would imagine. More often than not they put innocence on to deceive themselves or cover up their disappointment. I want to be with you forever, 'cause I love you . . .

Xinhe. Please stop—he was besieged in misery and sorrow and covered his face with both hands—I said my love's different. But Xinhe, you're right. I can't hold this back any more. I need your support for one thing.

There was only one master class in Guangzhou. I have to admit to you that I visited Huai. I meant to visit her only, but I got to know that she had been divorced and fallen badly ill long before. She has been living alone all this time. I want to go over and look after her to repay her kind help in the past. She is sick with a chronic disease. It's complicated and lasts a long time. I was thinking . . .

Jiansheng—she did not want to hear any more of this, so she interrupted him—is this the reason why you quit your job?

Yes.

The exhibition closed in Guangzhou?

Yes.

You've been living with Huai for the past month?

Yes.

So you've been cheating on me?

... Yes.

And now you come to me saying, "to repay her kind help", as if you had to do it against your will? Jiansheng, I'm so disappointed with you. You are a weak liar.

Xinhe raised her voice. This was the first time that he heard her talking to him like that.

Xinhe ... please let me finish, he said. Yes, I could have confessed to you relentlessly that I'm still in love with her after all these years and I have to take care of her. With such a confession I could have appeared like a martyr. But how would you have taken it? Xinhe, I lied because I didn't want to inflict any pain on you. This is all my love is about. I can't inflict any pain on either of you, so I don't know what to do! My only hope is that by providence you would allow me to go and accompany her for the rest of her life. I would ... I would do anything to express my appreciation for her ...

The words drew tears to Xinhe's eyes suddenly.

Look at this man I've been in love with for so many years. Look at his handsome face and his stern contour that I stroked hundreds of times ... She said faintly, Jiansheng, after all these years, isn't my love worthy of your appreciation too?

Her voice attenuated while choking with sobs. It pierced his heart.

Xinhe, you don't need to cry. I'm not leaving you. I'll come back and be with you forever. I just wanted to accompany Huai to the end of her life. She is sick and by herself and needs to be looked after ...

You are too naïve, Jiansheng. Forgive me if I'm sarcastic: what if she gets better and better and pulls through the illness at last with your care? Should I wait for you forever? Even if she dies, will you really have the heart to come back to me? All these possibilities are not my point though. The point is, Jiansheng, I was not your first love. What made things worse for me is that you took your first love to be the one love for your whole life. You've never spared me any love or longing in any form. And now you think I can continue to play the perfect wife and yield to your wish again?

Jiansheng, I yielded to you in the past because you were beside me, and I could still go on with the hope of being with you forever. But you are leaving me now. How can I be as tolerant as accepting your sheer disloyalty?

I am your wife, and you ask me to tolerate your lies and lack of affection, and let you take care of your beloved for an indefinite amount of time until she dies. I'm sorry. I would never dream of accepting such ridiculous terms unless I were one of your mistresses and lived with you for your money.

Even if I agreed, what about our daughter Kazan? What are we going to do with her? You kept asking me if I had thought carefully before the adoption. How are you going to reply if I ask you the same question?

She raised her voice in deep rage when she said these words. Any genuine woman would have been carried away with anger like her.

Jiansheng sat behind her as Xinhe's every word struck home to his heart.

The two of them remained silent while Xinhe turned her back to Jiansheng.

For young feverish lovers silence and darkness were the hotbed for sweet and sour exchanges; for those who treaded a long way to the cliff of love, they were but the autumnal frost that turned affection and tolerance into coldness.

Jiansheng gazed at Xinhe from the back. She was still as slender as a young girl and her back was straightened up like a beautiful marble statue. But her beauty was desolate under the weight of blunt disappointment. She was like a plaintive wife who, deserted by youth, was not without humbleness even when fuming with anger. She gave him youth, love, and practical benefits—education, career, and marriage—she surrounded him with every sign of solid happiness like the mother's womb that cushioned the many sharp, cold edges of fate and promised sweet eternity for him.

He had been accustomed to her deep affection and turned a blind eye to it. From the start, their relationship was doomed for the unbalanced give and take. He was in no spirit to find out what was really going on between them. More often than not one had to follow the tide of fate instead of struggling for control.

Jiansheng, her voice was as dim as the lamp light. Now that I reflect over myself, the only mistake I made is that I shouldn't have deceived myself. Dignity has no place at all when it comes to self-deception. It must have been the same case with you when you chased after Huai. Ironically we share the same affliction, only that we differed in the direction of our love. It's sad to find out at last that we are really not meant to be together. You are a kind and affectionate man; you kept thinking about her all these years and tried to repay her goodness whenever possible. But you are also cruel and weak, because you lingered on the past illusions blindly to the point of absurdity and turned others into innocent victims.

It's a pity that I never had the luck to be your first and everlasting love.

Now that we have come to the dead end, I'm afraid there's not much for me to do. I know well that the last thing I can do for you is to comply with your wish. Any effort of pleading or struggling to rescue our marriage is futile and will only inflict more pains on your side. After all, I love you, Jiansheng, and I will spare you and myself the torment of a broken relationship.

Their conversation sank into a long pause. In the silence Kazan pushed the door of the bedroom open. The doorframe cut her shadow into two halves, one lit by the lamp and the other hidden behind the door. Xinhe walked over and said, Kazan, why are you here?

Kazan did not reply, but embraced her mother in her arms. The girl was already taller than her mother by a head. She held her mother tightly and felt her shaking slightly. Her warm, blood-like tears gradually dampened Kazan's neckline. Kazan held her mother and stared at Jiansheng on the bedside. The two of them looked into each other's eyes.

12

In October the city turned into a mirror that reflected the autumnal scenery. Hardly had the golden leaves fallen from the boughs before they were carried away in the wind. They danced low along the dry road like dust. When the wind stopped, they fell to the ground in despair as they were no longer able to catch up with the flying smoke and dust on the road. When the street was still, one could even hear the echo of the flying leaves.

The echo was light, melancholic. It was as curt and beautiful as the sound of splitting silk and as heart-rending as the sighs of the legendary tear-drinking butterflies that parted with each other in despair. The falling moment of the leaves formed a desolate and hopeless sight like a hollow hand that reached out for something, only to catch the wind that forgot to run away.

Autumn should have been like this in his imagination. In South China trees were green all year long. Greenery was everywhere in any season. He could only detect the alternation of seasons and the passing of time through the temperature. The sky was always damp with rain and looked like a face that seemed about to shed tears at all times. The face of the season was dim and ambiguous.

He and his mother had been living in a city close to the sea. When a typhoon passed by, he would stand on the roof and feel the large patches of dark cloud brushing by his shoulders. The ravenous wind made him falter to and fro, but he derived intense pleasure from the detection of his own smallness and powerlessness. The crown of the tall trees lowered and bounced back repeatedly under the havoc of the tempest. Torrential rain swept the city in minutes and big raindrops swarmed down like misfortunes and fell to the ground with misty splashes. Lightning split the gray-ish, tempestuous sky like the cracks in a broken vase, followed by deafening thunder. The typhoon was so terrible that it seemed as if the gods were venting their anger at their creations after they fought their heads off for the latter's welfare and found out that sin and imperfection were all that the latter brought to the world.

He remembered that, once, before the tempest came, there was a big dust storm. Mother was not back yet and her thick carpet was still hanging on an aluminum pole on the steel bracket in the walls of the balcony. The carpet rocked to and fro in the wind and seemed about to fall down.

Jiansheng closed the door and windows at once and rushed to the balcony to retrieve the carpet. The fence on the balcony was so high that he could only reach the edge of the carpet by leaning out of the window. As it was cloudy in the afternoon, the thick carpet was not dried off and was heavy with water. Jiansheng got hold of a corner of the carpet and tried to drag it back, but he was not strong enough and the carpet fell down from the sixth floor. It was blown by the wind like a feather, became dripping wet in the rain, and was covered in dirt as it fell on the flowerbed downstairs.

He knew he had gotten into trouble; unfortunately his mother had come back and caught him reaching for the carpet but dropping it by accident. He was panic-stricken when he saw Mother dashing in the rain awkwardly, picking up the heavy, damp carpet, and coming upstairs with furious curses. Amidst the noisy wind and rain he could hear clearly the curses his mother exploded out in rage. She cursed her way up from downstairs and her voice was heard to accompany her hasty footsteps from the courtyard all the way to the door.

His mother was a common woman who became bitter and hateful as the result of the many setbacks in her life. At that time Jiansheng did not know that she suffered from menopause hyperthyroidism. Due to the hormonal change she became exceptionally tempestu-ous and could not control her anger.

Jiansheng was shaking with fear before his mother came upstairs. He opened the door timidly and waited for her.

His mother was dripping wet. She strode inside gaspingly and hurled the wet, dirty carpet to the floor. Then she stared at her son silently in deep depression and anger.

The boy's head lowered and his shoulders sagged. He feared her so much, as if she were a stranger to him. The mother was furious and slapped him, clenching her teeth. Jiansheng was hit on the face and drew several steps backward. He blacked out for a moment and turned around to his mother sobbing in grievance and despair.

Can you do a damn good thing for me? Can you do me the favor not to get into trouble for once?

Mother forced these words through clenched teeth. Torrential depression surged within her and she pushed Jiansheng aside forcefully. Jiansheng stumbled to the ground and his nose hit the edge of the cabinet loudly. Blood ran out of his nose at once.

Mother's heart wrung with regret when she saw him bleeding, but she was embarrassed after the intense anger and did not help him wrap up the wound. The child crawled into the corner covering his face with both hands. Tears and blood mingled together and formed a ghastly sight.

He was in too much pain to withhold his tears. He mumbled in a small voice that almost escaped himself. Mom, I just wanted to help . . . If I hadn't meant well . . . I would have been safe . . .

Warm, thick blood. It was the thing that he feared in his childhood. The thing that he remembered most clearly of that memory was not the beating or the bleeding, but the lesson he drew from it: Not every act of kindness would be rewarded. A well-meant action could be wrong. This was the most unfair and yet practical logic of the world—mind your own business, regardless of the appropriateness and urgency of your help.

That had been his motto until Huai changed him with her kindness.

Would it be the same situation as before, only far more complicated than reclaiming a carpet? Had he only wanted to repay, he could have given Huai some money to treat her disease instead of going back to live with her. But he chose the latter all the same, despite the fact that Huai had held aloof from him from the start.

Most stern women were equipped with such shields. They always retained their calmness, even indifference, in love affairs. He could see clearly his dispensability to Huai. She treated him nicely when he came and walked away calmly when he left. Such aloofness and indifference made him wonder what affection she held towards him, be it love, debt, or both. The only result of his observation was that Huai was different from Xinhe. The latter's wish was never complicated. She simply wanted the two of them to go through the journey of life together hand in hand. But he failed her.

This was unfair to Xinhe.

If damage was to be done, then it had better be done quickly. He had to grope his way blindfolded and go straight back to Huai at whatever expense. His determination was solid to the point of bigotry.

But before they could put on a case for divorce, Kazan demanded to end her adoptive relationship with them.

Jiansheng asked her, what are you doing, Kazan? What your mother and I have been doing has nothing to do with you. Don't be childish.

She answered, Dad, I was not kin to you, but you took care of me for so many years and gave me love and a happy life. Words cannot express my appreciation for you. I know you are getting divorced from mother, and I'll pose as a difficult problem between you and Mom. You are going to take care of someone else and cannot take me along for sure, but can Mom support a daughter all by herself, a daughter who is not even in her own blood?

It will be unfair for her to shoulder the heavy burden alone. I've been an independent girl since my childhood and now I'm grown up. So I think I can live by myself and pose no embarrassment or burden on you. I'll leave first, so that you'll go ahead with the divorce without caring about me.

Dad, I've been thinking it over. Don't give it a second thought. Just take this to be an expression of my appreciation for your goodness. It's also the most appropriate choice.

13

It was early in the winter. The sky was gloomy and bleak and wind raged all day. The dry, cold air was very refreshing when it assailed the nostrils and pierced the lungs. Through the windowpanes, wind whistled by, rattling the windows with a ghastly sound all day long. The streets formed a bleak sight as the trees were deprived of their attires of leaves.

That day Kazan and her parents returned from the civil administration department after they had the adoption terminated. This was the last opportunity for the family to be together. The three of them remained silent in the car, their eyes wandering in different directions and their minds immersed in deep thoughts. Kazan got off at the gate of the school and bade farewell to her parents, as she did regularly in the past. But she knew she could no longer go back home after that day. She was back in the world all by herself again. She chose this as a token of her gratitude for them. It was also because of this that she felt calm and peaceful at heart, as if everything had been settled perfectly and she posed no burden to anyone. She felt very good.

Men had to follow their fate calmly. Sometimes they wound a long way, only to return to their starting point at last. What difference it would make if they followed fate at the very beginning.

Kazan got off the car. Xinhe could not bear to part with her. She got off too and walked over to give her daughter a big hug. She said, Kazan, if you meet with any difficulty, I'll be right there to help you. She paused and swallowed the rest of the words. She looked up at this daughter who was no blood relation to her. They gazed at each other for a moment, but Xinhe could not bear to face Kazan and diverted her eyes at last.

Xinhe's hair was tossed in the wind and twined around her temples, which added to the desolation on her face. Having been sleepless for several nights, she turned pallid with bloodshot eyes. Her bony figure was wrapped up in a black coat, the drape of which fluttered and rattled in the freezing wind. This kind, gentle woman who sacrificed for love ended up empty-handed and alone. This was truly deplorable. Kazan did not know what to say to console her. In the face of her mother, she could hardly retain her composure, and peace and tears came to her eyes.

She said only, Mom, may you be free from mishaps all your life. Please take good care of yourself.

She turned away and disappeared.

Jiansheng witnessed the parting scene in the car. He placed his elbow on the edge of the window and leaned his face against his fist when he clenched the teeth.

He chose to remain silent. He closed his eyes and darkness surged and enveloped him.

Chapter VI

Vows are void bonds for restless hearts and bond only with the void. The forest never vows to the seasons and blooms and withers with the time. The sea never vows to the shore and ebbs and surges as it pleases.

Even words are void. Between you and me there shall only be silence and being.

Jian Zhen, "Vows of the Sea"

1

The year closed in as winter advanced. The first snow came that November. The narrow, dilapidated dorm door and windows were closed. She fell asleep quickly every night when she lay upon the pillow and heard the whistling wind outside. The water in the heating pipes rumbled slightly in the darkness. In the early morning, the windowpane was coated with misty frost.

The single bed of the dorm was narrow and hard and shook noisily when she tossed about. Before dawn every morning, the matron turned the electric switch on and the fluorescent lamps lighted up the dark, still dorm in a ghastly whiteness. Then her roommates began muttering and tossing. Some lingered on the bed, and others got up with smoky eyes and began their morning routines: dressing, face-washing, bed-tidying, and cabinet-cleaning, etc. Noises took possession of the narrow space and the clanking and rattling gave Kazan headache.

She had caught a fever the night before. When she woke up, she found herself sore and stiff all over with a splitting headache. Her eyes were so dry that she could hardly open them, and her body was assailed in fits of heat and cold. She did not want to get up, so she went on sleeping wrapped up in the quilt.

After sleeping for she did not know how long, the banging of the doors woke her up again. The dorms gradually quieted down. One by one her roommates left the room, and the last roommate turned the lamp off with a click. The room immediately sank into stifling darkness again.

The day broke, but the wind was still whistling and rattling fiercely.

Excessive sleep aggravated her pains and languor. In her fever she could not even get out of bed when she woke up, so she turned around and slept away. In her many dreams the kaleidoscope of images and people flashed before her eyes in a chaotic order like a dysfunctional film, and the sounds were distorted beyond recognition.

In her last dream she saw herself standing still on the snow-covered land in the boundless moonlight. There was nothing on the horizon but the boundless whiteness that sprawled endlessly in ennui like a dull, long-winded narrative. The dark blue sky was empty except for the bright moon. The heaven and earth were as still as the end of the world. Everything could be forgiven and forgotten. Having washed away every blotch and stamp, humans freed themselves from sin or love and set off for reincarnation in the unknown world.

Standing alone in the icy universe, she felt utterly relieved and cleansed, like the dead.

The image was the contour of her homeland. It stood in her memory like a long lost friend. It stood still for many years and some day it would collapse abruptly. She found nothing but hollowness and regret when she looked back. It was too late.

She startled from the nightmare with cold sweat all over. She felt cold the instant she woke up. Her throat was burning and she could not utter a sound. Her vision was blurred when she opened her dry eyes.

She wanted to get hold of a pair of warm hands by her side. She hungered for the temperature of the palms and the dry, solid touch when they stroked her forehead. What a great comfort and relief they would give her!

But she found no one by her bed side.

Kazan got up and poured herself a cup of water. She found pills from her pack and went back to sleep after having them. She slept for a whole day and did not get up until her roommates came back in the afternoon. The fever was over, but she could barely stand on her own after too much sleep. A roommate offered to fetch her some food for dinner, but she refused the offer, put on her clothes, and walked out by herself.

She called Jianan downstairs. She heard the strange man's voice and could not help feeling her brusque blindness. She was not clear why she did that. She said to him curtly, come take me away, Jianan.

Jianan sighed with relief over the phone and said, I'm busy now and can't come over. You can take a bus to Zizhuyuan on the west section of the third ring road. There's a parking lot under the Zizhuqiao Bridge. Wait there for me.

Be sure to come, Jianan.

He promised, I'll pick you up there, but you'll have to come first. Call me when you are there.

She was disappointed and hung up the phone without another word. She wrapped herself up tightly in the coat and walked into the snow.

She ordered hot boiled dumplings. She had been hungry for too long and the food turned sour in her stomach. It was a small restaurant at the school gate. Its signboard was dilapidated and its floor was smirched with footprints as guests had to tread over puddles of snow water at the door. Students gathered here in twos and threes, eating, drinking beer, and laughing merrily. She sat down alone at a table in the corner and gulped down the hot dumplings. It had been a long time since she'd had such delicious food. The dumplings warmed her up and her frozen hands were heated by the hot bowl.

Fine snowflakes were still falling. Night had settled in and the air became chilly. She waited at the bus stop. Everyone on the street was curled up in cold. Some were waiting for buses, and others scurried by her in small steps. Everyone was silent and kept a distance from each other. The air that they exhaled, however, melted together and turned into white steam.

She finally hopped onto a bus and was seated close to the window. Outside the window the street lamps lit up the night sky. The light boxes offered splendid illustrations of the city's most desolate grandeur. Snow was piling by the street and the highway was damp and dirty. The bus crawled along languidly, stopping here and there.

She took a taxi after she got off the bus and finally got to the Zizhuqiao Bridge.

The traffic was lighter at night in the west section of the third ring road. The cars hurtled forward and whistled by each other at a relentless speed. Every object in the city seemed to have the same proud relentlessness. Every man and even every car were rushing after something blindly and paid no attention to anything except their targets. They dashed at a dizzying pace, made a wind in passing, and quickly vanished out of sight, casting a lonely blank behind.

She waited at the bridge and watched the cars speeding by. The whistling was all the more clear and bleak at night. Shaken to the core in coldness, she walked to and fro along the gloomy roadside and felt her hands and feet freezing. The cars parked in the dilapidated lot were as gloomy and still as corpses in tombs. They were the only things beside her that remained still in this bustling world.

She thought she waited forever before she saw Jianan's Porsche driving in.

She got into the car and was immediately greeted in the face by the heat and smell of cigarette.

2

The room was on the fourth floor. The lift was old and the light kept flashing as the result of unsteady voltage. The lift went upward slowly and drearily, creating a hollow, horrifying noise in the well. She felt as if the ropes would snap at any time and the lift would plummet and smash on the ground.

Jianan leaned against the wall of the lift in exhaustion. A faint, somewhat reluctant smile emerged around the corners of his lips. He asked, what wind brought you here?

Kazan paused before she said, I caught a fever and slept all day. I don't want to stay in the dorm and I have nowhere else to go.

The man lowered his head to light the cigarette. He said, I haven't slept in the past three days.

The room was minimally decorated with wooden flooring and white walls and nothing classy. It was not Jianan's own apartment in Beijing. He had his house refurnished, so he rented this one for a time.

The room was very messy and cigarettes were scattered about. He said casually, get yourself whatever drink you like and sit wherever you like. You can watch TV or use the computer if you want.

Jianan was so tired that he had difficulty in even saying these words.

Then he walked into the bathroom and soon she heard the shower.

Kazan sat awkwardly on the couch in the sitting room. In ennui she browsed a magazine by her hand. For a moment she wanted to leave. She was not clear why she ended up at the man's apartment and what she would do here. She had come here on an impulse.

But before she could flee Jianan had emerged out of the bathroom dripping with water, in loose, navy blue pajamas. He looked refreshed. Several drops of water slowly slid down along the handsome contour of his face. He walked over to Kazan, picked up the cigarette and lighter, and began smoking again.

The two of them confronted each other in the dim room. No words were exchanged. Not even a change of expression.

After the short pause, Jianan bent down, held her head up and kissed and caressed her. Their bodies rubbed against each other, and their gasping breaths and the rustling of their clothes resonated in the empty room. At last he raised his head and said, follow me, Kazan.

He picked her up and walked into the bedroom.

She'd had the same experience in her childhood, but it had happened so abruptly that it was tinted with an illusory color with the passage of time. Sometimes she thought it was because she moved to a totally different place afterwards that she could forgive and forget such a grave mishap.

She was not facing an awkward boy who would feel curious, nervous or embarrassed for the lack of experience. To Jianan sex was nothing new and exciting. It was just a simple, hollow process in which he sought for short-lived bodily comfort.

Lust was a door to the adult world. No matter how youthful they were, bodies would age rapidly once they were engulfed in lust. No matter how splendidly or bleakly men depicted lust, and whether they sought for pleasure or torture in yielding to it, it was but a behavior that best embodied our animal instinct. Anything that tore our masks and brought us close to the base instinct was hollow and yet forthright.

During intercourse she was never so close to his body and yet so far away from his soul.

Like a child who indulged himself in an exciting game, Jianan was numbed in the ecstasy and his mind went blank. Kazan, however, felt as desolate as ever when she embraced Jianan's naked body, which was as strange to her as if the man never existed. She said, take me away, Jianan. I don't want to stay here any more.

He gave no answer, but turned around and fell asleep.

3

Early in the morning she got up from the strange bed. The day did not break yet, but the horizon had betrayed pale streaks of sun rays. The windows were covered with a thick coat of mist and she could see nothing clearly outside. The silence and depression in the room chilled the air into ice.

Soft and silent, she put on her clothes and went to the bathroom to wash her face and rinse her mouth with cold water. The tap water in the winter was chilling to the marrow and her hands were frozen by it. She deliberately left some water on her face to keep sober.

In the bedroom Jianan had been sleeping. Kazan walked to the door of the room after washing and leaned against the wall. There she stood gazing at his sleeping face, which looked like an innocent child's without the fatigue and the indifferent, masculine smile. Dreams seemed to be perching on his long eyelashes.

She was touched by the beauty of this moment, so she walked up, bent over him at the bedside, and scratched at his hair naughtily to catch his attention. Slightly annoyed, Jianan clapped his hands on the quilt and looked up wearily at her. She said, I'm going back, Jianan. He mumbled something in a vague, low voice and went to sleep again with his eyes shut.

Kazan quietly stroked his head and turned away.

The city was still enveloped in mist in the early morning. The first bus on which she hopped was empty and slow like an icebreaker that pierced slowly and determinedly through the city while it was still asleep. She grew weary of the long boring trip. Leaning her head against the window, she felt that she was so small and lonely that she would vanish utterly.

The flow of time paused and the image of her memory emerged clearly. Born with the lively, brave blood of the highland, Kazan had been independent since her birth and had been accustomed to the nomadic life. Her light lay in the moonlit snow-covered highland that was deeply imprinted in her childhood memory. The antediluvian expanses of pure whiteness turned out to be an ominous prophecy for her. She was guided by the prophecy and chased after pleasure on the road. Since she was hurled into this gigantic, imposing capital by a sudden twist of fate, she felt as if she had not seen a road for a long time. She felt as if standing at the bottom of a deep well. Aside from the bare walls and darkness, all she could see was a bright sun streak overhead that shone down into the depths of fate. She was curious about the light, but never took it to be her sole hope.

That year Ye Lan came back at Christmas and went to visit her at the university. She made a call to Kazan first. Kazan answered the phone not without hesitation when she saw the strange number. Kazan, it's me. Ye Lan. I've just got off the plane. I'm coming to you. Let's meet at the school gate.

Ye Lan's long-parted voice beat merry tunes on Kazan's eardrums. In her excitement, Kazan dashed to the gate of the university and waited for her there, the same way she had rushed downstairs as a little girl when she heard Ye Lan calling her name.

The cold wintry wind cut through her face and the entire city looked weary and bleak. One or two figures passed in and out. It turned dark gradually and all of a sudden the street lamps lighted up. She did not mind waiting, so she sat on the edge of a flowerbed casually, swinging her frozen legs and rubbing her cold face with both hands. From time to time she gazed at the passers-by with a look of blank ennui.

Ye Lan's car drew close. The instant Ye Lan got out Kazan jumped up and almost bumped into her embrace. Ye Lan opened her arms and was hurled backward in Kazan's momentum. Pinching her face against Kazan's, Ye Lan felt she was as cold as ice. She said, I told you I just got off the plane, you silly girl! Why didn't you wait a while before coming out?

Kazan buried her face in Ye Lan's coat and deeply inhaled. Her voice was muffled: I missed you, Ye Lan!

I know. I missed you too, said Ye Lan. Let's go to my home, Kazan. Okay.

Traffic was heavy and they had to stop from time to time. The two girls sat on the back seat. Ye Lan asked the chauffeur to turn the heat up. Come, Kazan, you're frozen. She said.

I've terminated the adoption with my parents, Ye Lan. Now I'm living alone. Kazan told Ye Lan everything when the car stopped again.

Ye Lan was shocked. She reached out and stroked Kazan's head from time to time. She held up the disheveled ends of Kazan's hair and straightened them out bit by bit. She asked, why did you do that?

My dad decided to divorce my mom and move back to the city where he lived. There is a woman there he loved very much. She is sick and he wants to take care of her. He said he would accompany her until she dies or recovers. Who knows?

Kazan's voice faded away. She turned around and glanced at the window with a look of disdain.

She said, I can't stay in that family and wait for the court to decide who will get my custody. My dad won't want me of course, and it's cruel and unfair for my mom to raise me. I was not kin to them and I've already owed to them a lot for taking care of me for so many years. I'd despise myself if I clung on them.

Kazan paused here. Ye Lan quietly reached out and hugged her understandingly. Kazan crouched down on Ye Lan's legs and gazed at the rapidly deepening darkness outside the window. The full-lit city was as luxuriant and desolate as ever.

She lay there, held up Ye Lan's hand and placed it on her forehead. She murmured, Ye Lan, I'm always thinking that no matter how far we wander astray, we're destined to return to the point where we're destined to start. I was an orphan and lived by myself from the start. I thought the track of my life would be changed when I was taken away by kind people and hurled into the city. But now you see, I'm grown-up and by myself again.

Ye Lan stroked her face and said, you're wrong, Kazan. Everyone is alone. One may be confused at times when he has many companions, but when he becomes alone again he feels deserted by the world. In fact he just wakes up from the illusion to the true face of life.

Forget it, Kazan. At least now we are together.

Kazan dined at Ye Lan's house. Ye Lan had the dishes moved from the table to her own room and the two girls enjoyed the dinner together sitting on the floor. They took the liberty to open bottles of rum and deliberately lurched back and forth, making a mess of the room.

Ye Lan leaned forward to sit beside Kazan, put down the cup, and began to nibble her in the head naughtily and intimately as if playing with a toy ball. The two girls screamed, threw themselves in bed, and had a pillow fight. For a long time they indulged in the playing and fighting like two little kids and lay in bed when they were tired out.

They suddenly became quiet. The two girls lay face to face and gazed at each other. Ye Lan's hand perched casually on Kazan's hair and played with it gently.

I'll go with Jianan. I want to marry him, whispered Kazan suddenly, with a faint, self-mocking smile on her face.

Ye Lan said, you're crazy!

No, I love him. But most importantly, I want a real life. I don't want to stay here and muddle away my days.

You think by following him so blindly you're not muddling away your days?

That's different, Ye Lan. You know it.

They went to bed together that night and chatted in a low voice. They talked about the remote past and future, the people in their lives, their first kisses, the warmth and pains of their first nights, and their despair when a relationship turned hollow and compulsive . . . memories and oblivion alternated in their broken exchanges and words flew as smoothly and softly as water. They were not wont to talk about their private lives and never wasted their words on superfluities. They were only interested in talking with an exclusive number of companions. After all, talking could be very boring.

They finally fell asleep in the early morning.

Kazan remembered Ye Lan's last words: look, we've been chatting in the same bed since we were twelve or thirteen. It's so good we can remain like this after all these years.

The day is breaking. Good night, Kazan.

4

Winter vacation was approaching and the students began scurrying for exams again. The same old days of intensive cramming came back and they sat in the library studying night and day.

Jianan was energetic that day and picked her up at the university. She was reading at the library when he called, but she immediately put the book down to meet him.

She felt as if she had not seen him for a long time. She pranced forward into his arms when she saw him standing by his car at the gate. The man was amused by her and bantered with her merrily.

There had always been a free-wheeling aspect to her nature, but most of the time it lurked beneath her docility. Sometimes she could be exceptionally calm, but sometimes she was as lively as an innocent child. It was in such a free, casual manner that she approached Jianan after they met each other. She did this because she was despairing at heart.

During those days when she stayed with Jianan, she was picked up by him, went to bed with him at the rented apartment, and went out for dinner with him. Except for the dinner part they differed from most common young couples in that they did not go shopping, watch films, play computer games, hang out at bars, or sit and watch TV together.

But he took Kazan along when he visited the auction house, examined antiques at the expo, or had antiques identified at a clients' request. At that time Kazan learned much more from such experience than what was taught at the university. They caught the eye easily when they both walked on the street; Kazan inherited the tall, slender figure from her Tibetan ancestors and looked very thin yet curvy and energetic. The sunshine in her childhood left a natural shade of rouge on her face, and her clear, regular features looked as keen and brave as the wind-chasing steeds. Her beautiful suntan and long, pitch-black plaits attracted eyes of admiration. Jianan matched her perfectly with his distinctly half-breed face, clear-cut, handsome features, a tall, brawny figure, and a beautiful suntan. The two of them strolled together and attracted many eyes. They did not like such attention, though, so they seldom went out together in Beijing.

She either went out to work with Jianan or stayed at home with him.

One day, they were naked and cuddling together in bed. They kissed and caressed each other and exchanged vague, amorous words. Jianan held up her face and said, I'll leave Beijing in less than thirty days. I'll purchase some antiques from Tibet and have them sold out in Hong Kong and then go back to Nepal. It'll be a long time before I come back.

I want to take you along to Tibet, Kazan.

Not unless you propose.

I have two wives back at home and many children. They were arranged by my father. It's our tradition.

Kazan was slightly startled. But she said at last, well, it's no big deal for you to have another wife then. I'll go with you in the winter vacation.

Sure, he said lightly with a faint, weary smile. I'll help you with the passport and visa, he said.

When Spring Festival drew close, it snowed again. The streets were covered in the big snow, which was tramped into dirty potholes. Only the roofs and the treetops were clad in white snow. In some old, dilapidated lanes, dirty snow water formed black puddles around the corners. The closed doors were still flanked by couplets and barbolas of the previous year, which faded away and looked rather old and bleak. The snow-covered boughs were barren and one or two broken nests were perched amidst them. The wires sagged under the weight of the snow and trembled with the remains of kites on them in the freezing wind like lonely ghosts. Rusted freight tricycles were parked by the mouth of the lane. Poverty added to the frozen desolation in the grand festival in cold winter.

The streets, however, were joyous and bustling. It was a big occasion for family reunions and the stores were decorated with red lanterns and colored banners. Customers swarmed in and out of the shopping malls with large and small packs in their hands. Everyone was radiant with joy. Many children on holiday wandered in the streets clad in thick coats and long scarves.

Over the world of disparity domed the same blue and still sky. The pale white wintry sunshine sprayed impartially into every lane and street of the city, rich or poor. Another year of separation and reunion was drawing to a close.

Some schoolmates from other parts of China had bought tickets for home and told their families the dates of their return in sweet, urgent voices. Other ticket-less students were worriedly asking around. But Kazan did not even care about such things. This was not her life; this was not her life at present.

She wanted to visit Xinhe before leaving to see if everything was okay with her. But Kazan did not want to make Xinhe feel that she came by because she could not find anywhere else to stay for the holiday. Such a misunderstanding would be embarrassing. So she did not go back and was determined not to linger on the past.

Before the winter vacation, Kazan applied for a two-year suspension of schooling. Now that she was by herself, she did whatever she wanted without the slightest hesitancy. She dragged her luggage and followed the man without any idea. Like someone in snow blindness, she could see nothing on her horizon. She felt herself drifting aloof and the man beside her was but a flower on the other bank of the river, no matter how close he came to her when both of them were consumed in desire. As long as the man did not reject her and wanted to offer a plane ticket to take her along, she would set off.

She felt dizzy when she trod on the world, as if it were toppling down. Perhaps such dangerous beauty was meant for roads. She strode ahead in this world and with every step she took the road collapsed and vanished at her heel. The path that she took left no trace and she could never draw back. All she had to do was walk and walk without any stop. She had no choice but to advance.

5

She returned to Lhasa in the winter. Every step upon her homeland drew her into deeper confusion. This was a return she had been longing for, but she was hesitant when the wish came true. She wrapped herself tight in the coat and still felt chilly. The man put his hand on Kazan's shoulder reassuringly; the touch was solid but distant. She was dizzied by the bright sunshine and could not open her eyes.

Jianan's assistant met them at the airport and drove them to a five-star hotel.

She never thought she would revisit her homeland like this.

Jianan pulled aside the thick curtains of the hotel room and streaks of sun rays immediately thronged through the window.

The dim space seemed to open up suddenly and the man's shadow looked like a tall paper puppet against the light. Kazan found the scene somewhat familiar, but it acquired a mirage-like quality with the shift of time and space.

The man asked her, are you not well? She shook her head quietly.

I'll do business this afternoon and you can stay here to watch TV and have a rest.

Jianan, she called him, I . . . I want to go back to the highland where I grew up.

The man frowned and said, I'm not taking you here for sightseeing.

I know. I can go by myself if you like.

Don't be a child, Kazan. Let's wait till I finish my business.

Then I'll go with you this afternoon.

After lunch, Jianan's assistant picked them up and took them to an old house downtown to examine the goods. They walked into the cellar, which was gloomy like a tomb chamber with only one narrow exit. On the wooden shelf some dozen antiques were placed, most of which were golden and bronze Buddha statues, with a small number of jade ware and rock paintings. Jianan walked aside and whispered for a long time with his assistant.

Kazan examined the antiques closely. She told Jianan when he came over, Jianan, some of these are fakes. That set of jade memorabilia is especially suspicious.

Jianan said, yes I know. Set your mind at rest. Let's go over to the other place.

They went to a young man's house in town. The house owner took them to his collection. It turned out to be bronze, something like a square *lei*, a wine vessel.

Jianan smiled bitterly at the man and said, I heard you had some good stuff that no one dared to buy and had my man bring me over. Now that I see it, I understand why it finds no buyer. There are many treasures in Tibet, but everyone knows bronze casting is backward here. How can such an obviously Han wine vessel show up in this place? You must have been cheated and bought a fake.

The young man frowned and shook his head: don't speak absurdly if you can't identify the treasure.

Kazan found it odd and walked up to have a close look at the vessel.

She asked the man, where did you get it?

He answered, from a Han tomb.

You dug it out from a tomb?

Yes. This is my share of the treasures and the rest were taken away by my fellows.

Where did you find the tomb and what was the date of the tomb?

He sighed deeply and said, to tell you the truth, I was a new hand and didn't know what tomb it was. The tomb was discovered by an old hand and I simply dug it with him. He just told me it was a Han tomb so we did not feel guilty in digging it. That old hand was a playmate of mine. He returned from the central plains and invited me to plunder tombs to make quick money. He said the trade had existed for thousands of years in the central plains and it was harder and harder for him to carry on with fewer tombs, more sophisticated competitors, and stricter governmental control. In Tibet, however, tomb raiding was less prevalent and the burial objects were easy to obtain. But my dad was a devout believer and tried to persuade me many times to abstain from such offenses to Buddha and reason. I never heeded his advice and went along with my mate. My dad was extremely sad and upset and fell sick when he saw the burial objects I stole for the first time.

This must have been karma. I regretted it very much and decided to give up. My mate flew into anger and took away all our loot except this piece. I want to sell it to cure my dad's disease and donate the rest of it to the temple. I'll never do such offense again.

Kazan asked, the story is certainly impressive, but where is that tomb after all?

The man answered, it's close to Lhasa, but I can't go into details.

Kazan asked, if you really changed your mind and wanted to be a devout believer, wouldn't you feel guilty when you sold the loot for money?

The man was embarrassed. He said, my dad is very sick and I don't have the time to care about guilt.

Kazan examined the object for a long time and asked, how much do you want?

He answered, the doctor said it would cost some hundred thousand to cure my father, so I want 600,000.

Jianan sneered. He knew but too well that those who spun bizarre, winding tales in the antique trade were mostly cheaters who fished for profit with fakes.

He was tired of the man's trick and was too impatient to hear more of his tale. He took Kazan out of the house. Kazan was hesitant, but she followed him out without any comment.

When they were back at the hotel, Kazan said, Jianan, if I'm not wrong, the vessel is a treasure of treasures. It's a nice bargain.

As far as I know, she continued, bronzeware faking was not prevalent until the rise of epigraphy in the Song Dynasty, but Tibet had been besieged in four hundred years of tangled warfare since the ninth century towards the end of the Tang Dynasty. Since then the land had no longer been as close to the Han regimes as it used to in the prime of the Tang Dynasty and few Hans had visited Tibet. As the tomb owner was buried in Tibet, he must have lived in Luoxie for many years and could not have been someone after the Tang Dynasty.

And you know bronze casting techniques were never highly developed in Tibet. Besides, not every tomb owner can have so many pieces of bronzeware as burial objects. So I think the owner is probably an official who came to Tibet when Tang-Tibetan exchanges were blossoming. He must have been a great lover of bronzeware, so he brought the many pieces of bronzeware to Tibet and had them accompany him to his tomb. Gold and silver-inlaid cloisonné was very popular in the Tang Dynasty and the casting and imitation of bronze ware were extremely rare. The vessel must have been a real treasure since he chose it as his burial object.

Besides, I saw faint traces on the surface of the vessel and bronze pieces at the bottom that are different in quality from the original cast. It must have been cast in the oldest method of pottery modeling instead of the lost wax modeling method which became prevalent later. It might have undergone a reverse process from the ripe pit to the unripe pit, so its surface is dark and the patterns and inscriptions on it are no longer distinguishable. However, judging from the clear resonance of the vessel and the two layers of narrow, protruding patterns that are possibly mingled kui and hui patterns, I'm pretty sure it is a typical piece of bronzeware of the Shang and Zhou Dynasties.

Jianan interrupted her, don't be silly, Kazan. If it were a Shang vessel, how could it end up in the hand of a Tang official? Did he drink with a wine vessel excavated from an ancient tomb? Was he an antique collector in the ancient times? Does it make any sense for him to take the vessel all the way to Luoxie? Isn't all this ridiculous? That tomb plunderer must have been lying! He didn't even dare to take us to the tomb!

Kazan answered, that I don't know. But you know Tibet has no lack of legends. I think it is reasonable for him not to take us to the tomb. Don't you know that one major trick of those cheaters is to bury fakes in the ancient tombs that have been plundered before, and then lead you to the tombs and make you believe the fakes were real? Skilled plunderers would be very cautious either in tomb plundering or disguising. It would be a real bargain if the vessel were true. It's worth a shot.

Jianan said, how can you identify it as real without any equipment? I don't want to spend 600,000 on a fake.

She said, I'll buy it if you don't. Lend me the money and I'll pay you back if it's fake. If it's real, you'll get 20% of the profit besides the cost.

Jianan paused a while and smiled. He said, okay, I'll try my luck with the 600,000. But I'd rather buy it myself than lend you the money. Whether it's a fake or not will be none of your business.

Kazan realized something instantly. She said after a pause, Jianan, don't presume that I don't know a bronze vessel of the West Zhou Dynasty was auctioned at 9 million dollars in New York. After all, you've never seen such an antique and it's under my advice that you decided to buy it. Isn't it unfair that you make millions of dollars without even sharing part of the profit with me?

Jianan smiled quietly. He said, Kazan, even if I lend you the 600,000, will you be able to export it to New York? Can you pass the customs office with the prohibited antique? After all, you are not sure about its authenticity and date. You're only guessing. I won't charge you the 600,000 even if you are mistaken. Isn't it good enough for you?

Kazan, the man walked over to stroke her, don't come into the circle. It's not as simple as you thought. You're not up to certain jobs.

She smiled. Are you beginning to worry about me? Jianan, I won't meddle with your business, but I discovered today that you don't actually know your business very well. I'm not here as a competitor. I just wanted to visit my hometown.

6

How long have you been away from home, Jianan? Kazan asked him in the land cruiser they rented on their way to the North Tibetan Highland.

They were clad in thick coats and cuddled in the back seats on the bumpy road. Not many travelers dared to drive on the North Tibetan Highland in winter. The land was desolate and uninhabited. They hired a driver and drove four or five days on end from Lhasa. The unbearably long journey gave them swollen feet and they felt as if driving was all the journey was about. They dined at motels, temples or the local Tibetan residents' homes and slept in remote inns and even in the car when they could not find anywhere to stay over. From morning to night they headed towards the heart of the land mile by mile. The land was bleak, expansive, and rocky. At dusk the cold air loomed over the dome gloomily and the sky and earth was enveloped in a sorrowful stillness. It was a familiar sight to Kazan.

Certain things fade away in memory. You know they exist, but unwittingly or deliberately forget how. It is like an old friend whom you used to hug and caress; you used to be familiar with them from soul to body, but you grew tired or were forced to leave. Every friend leaves certain stamps on you when you part with him and the stamps serve as good excuses for your forgetfulness. When you turn back long afterwards, you only find an illusory reflection of yourself from the traces, while the original self remains forever hidden.

Look, we only remember we used to stay here, but forgot how.

The window was blurred with splashes of mud. She sat in the car and looked out curiously with her cheek pressed to the glass like a child who was less enlightened by experience. Jianan was tired out and showed no interest in the scenery outside. He did not want to take the trip, but he owed her a big favor because of the antique deal and had to go with her. He was discontented with the danger and desolation of the trip, so he had been sleeping all the way. What a distant lover.

They finally arrived at the upper part of Qinglunzhuo Grassland and had the car parked on the roadside. There used to be no path on the grassland, but after the many years a roadbed was paved. She shook his hand gently and said, Jianan, look, here we are.

She jumped out of the car and stepped in the snow. The snow was thin and watery but extremely cold. The gale immediately forced its way into her coat and made it flutter. She stood there and looked out into the distance, but she could see nothing except the sprawling insipid wilderness with grass here and there and the undulating hills to the end of the horizon.

There was no snow on her homeland in the winter, not to mention the yaks and the scattering black tents. She headed to the depth of the grassland in the hope of finding her grandpa's celestial burial platform. Perhaps that was the only image that survived in her memory of home.

She always felt as if she were still standing on the celestial burial platform in her childhood and looking over at the snow-capped peaks and wilderness in deep autumn. The boundless whiteness that undulated with the ground looked like a white pulu that shrouded the corpse of the land before the celestial burial. It sprawled in her deep memory. In the distance one could hardly tell the scattering black tents from herds of yaks.

She always felt as if she could hear clearly the fluttering of the vultures' wings in the sky and see the fleeting traces they left. At those old times her grandpa used to host celestial burials under the dome in the old, dark red cassock. The smoke of the juniper incense curled its way up like a sad home-going soul. The cassock was blackened after long exposure to smoke. Grandpa's profound, solemn face was half hidden behind the juniper incense and the vultures gathered and hovered over his head. People surrounded him in twos and threes in the same solemnity. They squinted a little and fixed a quiet, devout gaze at Grandpa. Their purple faces sparkled like lamps under the rampant sunshine.

She reached out both her hands impulsively to grasp the sunshine in her nostalgic dreams.

Kazan did not go far before Jianan called her back from the car. He got out of the car sullenly when he got no response from her and dragged her from behind to prevent her from going farther. He said, now that you've seen your hometown, go back with me.

She was torn away by Jianan. It was a brief, disappointing visit after the long trip. Kazan was grieved to leave after the brief stay on her homeland. She wondered if the ruins of the celestial burial platform about which she dreamt were still standing there after so many years. After all, what could she do if she found it there? She was no longer the child who, unenlightened by experience, lifted up the curtain of the black tent and peeped at the boundless horizon in the distance.

On their way back Jianan said impatiently, ten days of driving for an odd idea! How capable you are of messing about!

Kazan turned a deaf ear to him. He would never understand that this was no "odd idea", but a wrong obsession.

7

As soon as they returned to Lhasa Jianan booked plane tickets for Chengdu and transferred to Hong Kong. His partner had carried the antiques abroad, so Jianan was in a hurry to check them before delivery and prepare for the auction in Hong Kong.

She was seated next to Jianan in the airplane and found him quietly browsing magazines without taking anything. For a moment she felt she was about to be devoured by the loneliness in her heart. She laid her head on the pillow of the seat and closed her eyes.

She drowsed during the flight, dozing off and waking from time to time. When they were about to land, she felt Jianan's hand on her forehead. Do you have a fever? he asked her. Kazan opened her eyes and found the man's eyes became milder and affectionate. Kazan shook her head and said, no, I'm all right.

It was night when they arrived. The engine stopped when the plane came to a standstill and she could hear it was raining outside. Fine raindrops tapped on the window and made a slight, muffled noise. She followed Jianan out of the place, got the luggage, and went out of the airport through the bustling, spacious hall. Jianan's striding figure was half hidden among the crowd and she hastened her steps to catch up with him. For an instant she felt as if she returned to the year of her grandpa's death when Gibu took her to the Rilans. She stumbled blindly after a stranger all by herself, without any idea where she was going or what she would face in the future. She was panicked and confused.

He hailed a cab and called Kazan to come over in the crowd. She sped up in the rain and got into the car. The car crossed the streets in the dark night. Within a short day she left the desolate highland and came into another city. It was as bustling and brightly lit as any other city and reminded Kazan of a gigantic tomb.

Jianan took her to his house in a residential area in the central ring. On both sides of the street the restaurants that served late supper cast down beams of light and sweet smells. Jianan's apartment was located in an old building. The rooms were small and the interior decoration was old-fashioned but exquisite. It must have been uninhabited for a long time, as the furniture and the balcony were evenly covered with fine dust. The room was stuffy after being closed for a long time. Jianan opened the window and a cold draught immediately forced its way into the room, together with the bustling noises on the street and the pitter-patter of raindrops. Jianan stood by the window and ordered take-away food over the phone. He spoke Cantonese.

She knew this was to be another stop on her journey, so she sat down, opened her suitcase, and put away the clothes. The rice with barbecued pork was delivered and they began eating on the couch.

Are you hungry, Kazan? Jianan asked her after he finished his meal and put down the box. He reached out to stroke her face as if she were still a child. He looked at her while she was eating with mixed feelings.

She was wolfing down the food and met with Jianan's eyes when she looked up.

Come over, let me hug you. The man drew her close. Jianan wore so little that Kazan could even feel his temperature when she pressed herself into his body. He kissed and caressed her. After a while he said, I'll have a shower. Go ahead with your meal. He let her free and walked into the bathroom.

He had only a towel on him when he emerged out of the bathroom and fled into the bedroom in coldness. He shouted in the next room, are you finished with your meal? Clean up the table and have a shower.

Kazan put away the paper boxes quietly and dumped them in the trash can. She took up her towel and walked into the narrow bathroom. When she pushed the door open she saw gray drops of dampened dust dripping along the wall. She washed her body under the showerhead and suddenly felt everything disappointing and strange. She always felt herself cut off from the rest of the world. The confusing, pointless relationship precipitated her into hollowness.

She walked into the man's bedroom dripping wet in pajamas. Jianan lay in bed and gazed at her. Come over, Kazan. I didn't feel well in Tibet and didn't even hug you. Now I'm fine.

He dragged her into the quilt, pressed himself against her body, and took her pajamas off impatiently. Kazan felt herself devoured in a big, warm hole. She closed her eyes. A cold draught rushed through the window into the bedroom and blew over her like another cold pair of hands. Jianan turned the lamp off with a click.

Darkness enveloped everything again.

She spent two months with Jianan in Hong Kong. As soon as they arrived he had the rust on the square vessel erased with laser. He invited senior experts to identify the vessel repeatedly and it turned out to be a real square *lei* that dated from the West Zhou Dynasty. It was intact with an exquisite form and refined patterns. Its only defect was that there were few inscriptions on it and the antique was illegally exported. He entrusted it to the auction house and set the reserve price at 900,000 dollars.

At that auction all the antiques were sold well and the square lei was sold at the price of 2.95 million dollars. He cleared a huge profit and gave Kazan only a praise in return: you are very smart.

At that time he was in high spirits as the result of the profit and put on a relieved smile that Kazan had never seen before. His staleness and insipidity dawned on her. Those who could only derive true pleasure from business were as old as those who could no longer do it.

She chose a time when he was in a good mood and told him about her pregnancy.

Jianan asked her what she was going to do. Kazan told him, I want to marry you.

Jianan frowned slightly. He said, you don't have to get pregnant to marry me. It'll take quite some time to go through the formalities if you want to immigrate to Nepal. There's not enough time.

Then help me.

There was a cunning yet childish look on her face. She was attached to him, so she wanted to be with him. Such an attachment was a token of despair and redemption to her. Sometimes when she reflected over the places where she used to drift—from the highland where she was born, to the northern capital, and to the southern seaport now—she was amazed by the distance and the experience. She had been drifting from one place to another without a real home or relative. Her benefactors used to treat her as family, but in time they vanished from her life. She did not know how long such a life would last. She wanted stubbornly to be part of the man's life while she was still deeply in love with him, to see if she could find somewhere to perch, where she would live with him and go on with her unrequited love. After all, she had nowhere else to go.

8

She followed Jianan to Nepal with the baby inside her body and confusion and uncertainties in her mind. The first instant when she stepped on the land she was greeted by the mist at dusk in Katmandu. The city was traversed by a quiet, muddy river. The old town was cramped, noisy, poverty-stricken and restless. Narrow lanes ran through the town like needles that stitched up a broken fabric. Towering temples were built at every corner, which were the only higher buildings in the town. There was no open space except the square in front of the sacred temple and the royal palace. The thick, brown roof and the carved wooden window lattice lay in lethargy at dusk and looked distant and unreal. Shrines were everywhere along the streets.

She was in a totally strange world again and all she could hear was a foreign language. She saw some Nepalese sitting on the ground along the narrow street with grave, indifferent eyes.

For the first time she held Jianan's hand in the taxi. She looked at the man beside her shyly in her excitement and uncertainty. Jianan turned around and gazed at her quietly. There was a faint, ambiguous smile on his face. He was reticent.

He helped her with the luggage when they got out. The two of them walked through a lane and came to a carved stone door that faced a narrow street. The door was very old with an exquisite carving. Jianan stepped inside, but he found Kazan lingering behind in hesitation.

He said, this is my home. Come in, Kazan.

She followed him into the door. A large, old square courtyard popped out with a patio in the middle. The buildings varied in height; the west wing had two floors while the east wing had three. All of the buildings were made half of wood and half of red bricks. The moss along the walls was enclosed in a gloomy, decadent circle. The rotted, blackened woodcarving lattices upstairs were like pairs of black eyes.

Jianan turned around and said, let's go upstairs and put down the luggage.

Their feet thudded on the narrow wooden staircase. Jianan's room was on the east side of the second floor close to a hall. The door was open in the big room, where an old lady was sitting busy with handiwork. The wrinkles on her face had turned brownish and she was old and sunken like a shrunk walnut.

Jianan walked through the door, Mom, he called her in Nepalese. The old lady looked up wearily and said something quietly.

He turned around and dragged Kazan from behind him. He said, this is my mother. Say hello to her.

Kazan lowered her head and greeted her with her palms together.

The old lady did not look her straight in the eye. She said to Jianan, so you brought another woman back?

Jianan did not answer, but turned away in ill humor.

Kazan asked him, is this your own mother?

Jianan answered indifferently, no, she is one of the wives of my father.

She sat in Jianan's room and looked around the bare walls. The wooden building gave out a damp, moldy smell. She heard footsteps at the door. Then she caught a glimpse of a woman who passed by with her head bent and a basin in her hands.

I'll go see my father, Kazan. Sit right here. Don't go anywhere, he said.

She sat there stiffly after Jianan left. The gloomy courtyard made her feel the same old isolation from her childhood.

After many years, she could still remember her first dinner with Jianan's family. Jianan told her before the dinner, you have to sit on the corridor with the other women and wait. Don't come into the room until we are finished. Make sure you sit at the farthest end.

Hence she saw the women entering the dining hall with bowls and dishes and walking out after they had the table ready. They sat on the benches in the corridor, waiting. After a while, the men of the family entered the spacious dining hall on the second floor.

She sat at the back of the women at a loss. No one spoke to her or even turned to look at her. Even if they did see her they ignored her. The men did not finish their meal and emerge out of the room one by one until it was completely dark.

She followed the women into the dining hall. After she was seated she found on the table a big plate of rice, a pot of soup of mingled vegetables and beans, a plate of potatoes with curry, several bowls of pickled vegetables, and several glasses of water. The women silently picked up some pickled vegetables and potatoes and mingled them with soup with their hands. These young and old plump women were wrapped up in long skirts. They used to be pretty, but they were worn out by labor and humility. No one was curious about her or bothered to speak to her. Of course she would not have understood even if they had. She sat in the corner deeply embarrassed. She had not eaten with her hands for over ten years and had no appetite for the leftovers, although she was very hungry.

He did not take her to his father and mother, but led her to a small side room on the second floor. He said, tonight I'll sleep with my wife according to the custom. This room is yours from now on. The women's bathroom is in the corner on the first floor on the west wing, but you'd better not have a shower today.

Before he turned away he said, you'll attend my second wife's cremation tomorrow. She was sick for a long time and I didn't make it to see the last of her. She died a couple of days ago.

Kazan stood there dumbfounded while he finished these words indifferently and turned away.

Jianan never told her that he came back because his wife was sick and his mother urged him to see the last of her. It was not until that moment that she saw the selfishness and cruelty of Nepalese men in the special social context.

She took her clothes out of her boxes, only to find no cabinet in the room. It was empty except for a bed and a long narrow table in the corner. She had to fold the clothes up again and put them back in the boxes.

A strange smell in the bed assailed her nostrils when she lay down. The intense loneliness and isolation indicated to her this was not her home after all. Her memories of home still lingered at her childhood. Her definition and imagination of warmth were confined to the dim fire in the black tent where butter tea was boiled, the slight crackle of the wood in the fire, and the mumbling voice of her grandpa on the padding. A home could be dilapidated or poor, but could never be strange. She used to stand inside the black tent and peep at the outside world from behind the curtain. She never hastened to step into the outside world. She calmly hid herself in the fortress called home when one after another from her family left her, as if she were waiting there for them to return.

She began drifting about after she left that home. She was taken away to the big tent of the Rilans, to Jiansheng and Xinhe's home, to Ye Lan's home, to the dormitory at school, to Jianan's apartment in Beijing, in Hong Kong, and finally here.

These homes meant nothing to her but stops on her way before she set off again.

Some say that experience tempers maturity and strength. But men do not become mature or strong with experience, but obtuse and resilient. Under the hardened surface they become more and more feeble and long more and more for a resting place and a comfort. After all, there is no turning back after they step onto this grand stage.

There is no way of escape, so they have to forge ahead.

That night she was exhausted and fell asleep on the bedside without even taking her clothes off. She woke up early in the morning feeling cold, so she dragged the quilt over and went on sleeping.

The next morning a lady advanced in years came to her door and called her in Tibetan, please get up, girl.

Kazan opened her eyes and saw a Tibetan face. The purple color was the unique stamp of the sunshine on the highland and a birthmark of the Tibetan lineage. She must be Jianan's own mother.

The woman stared at her in deep sympathy and walked in with a bowl of porridge. She put the bowl on the table without any word and stayed by the door watching silently while Kazan got up from the bed and folded the quilt.

Jianan's wife passed away and the cremation is today. Please come with us. Her voice was surprisingly calm, as if they were only bidding farewell to a family member who would go on a long journey.

The old town was enveloped in the mist of the early morning. The country gradually woke up after a night's sleep over the shoulders of the Himalayas. One after another, shops were opened along the streets and the owners cleaned and sprayed water on the floor in a slow, leisurely manner. The Brahman monks of the sacred temples pulled open the doors to the courtyards and lighted up the faces of the sacred statues with bright lamps.

The mist cleared off. She trailed along behind the crowd. The men carried a stretcher up, on which lay a body shrouded in a yellow fabric. It looked as if the body were drifting over the heads of the crowd and moved forward along the Bagmati River. Kazan did not remember how long she had been walking. There was more coming-and-going on the street and motorcycles and tricycles slid past her dangerously. Some seemed to shift their sleeping places from their beds to the streets and sprawled on the stone staircases with the stray dogs. In the shops idle men were sitting and chatting over wine. Boys frolicked in the lanes wearing fake sports shoes made in China with earth bags in their hands. Old women sat on the corridors preparing vegetables with their legs crossed as solemnly as if they were chanting the holy scriptures.

The crowd finally stopped at an open space in front of a sacred temple. Kazan peeped through the crowd and saw Jianan put the stretcher down with the other men of the family and immersed the dead woman's feet in the river. The passers-by paid no attention to the funeral. Sadness was absent even among the family. After they remained by the riverside for a long time, they drew the body out of the river and put it on a square stone platform with heaps of firewood. A man in white washed the face of the dead with the water from the river and heaped the firewood around the corpse.

The man in white kindled the firewood and the flames were burning fast. A white smoke rose up in the indifferent gaze of the crowd and the man in white took up a long stick in his hand and kept poking at the firewood with it. The flames wrapped up the body and burned for a long time as if they were simply boiling a pot of water.

The funeral lasted an entire morning. After the fire went out, white ash was seen scattered around the black charcoal. The man in white put the ash in a container, wrapped it with a piece of white cloth, and buried it in the mud on the bank. He then poured a ladle of water on the stone platform and the wood ash was quickly washed away. No trace was left of the burial.

This was a traditional Nepalese cremation ceremony. Corpses were burnt on the riverside near a bustling block.

The funeral drew no crowd other than the family. Some tourists on the other side of the river were recording the ceremony with photographs and videotapes. Judging from the sophisticated outdoor equipment on their backs, their various skin colors, and the different languages they spoke, they were from a different world from the local people.

They came all the way here with backpacks, visas and plane tickets. As they never experienced poverty and backwardness, they sang praise to every exotic thing here.

Everyone said this was a clean land of Buddhism, a treasure bowl of world cultural heritage on the Subcontinent, a sacred haven closest to heaven, a red lotus at the foot of the Himalayas, a ferry of the solution to all riddles, and a country blessed with all kinds of charms and pristine beauty. Tourists came from all corners of the world to kneel down in the temples, take photographs, salivate before the pretty, toiling Nepalese women, watch the local people across the bank washing themselves with the polluted water in the sacred river, eat Italian food at restaurants, buy souvenirs at stores, and videotape the funeral. They would post articles at tourist forums about the dirty, crowded streets in Katmandu, the personal hygiene problem when eating with hands, the shop owners who never offered change, and bargaining tips when buying souvenirs, blah, blah. Then they would prepare another visa and ticket and fly to another haven on earth.

This was the curiosity of the rich towards the poor. When they grew tired of the affluence of the cityscape, they discovered the new tourist horizon in poverty and mishaps and took them up only for sightseeing and amusement. They took the people of the Buddhist country as apprehenders of the truth, while describing the indifference and awkwardness of most of the unhappy, poverty-stricken people as the spiritual transcendence on their way towards religious redemption. They took the pains as supreme stoicism—which they were indeed, as the people could not but accept their fate meekly and endure the flow of life. Only in this way could they survive in the world of poverty and confusion.

Hence they had to remain calm and indifferent in the face of death. They were like the holy river that carried on quietly with the myth of its clean holiness while turning a blind eye to the ashes, the microbes and the sewage.

The streets were still as bustling as ever and the sun was high above the sky.

This morning brought her back to her hometown in her memory. That quiet land was standing on the other side of the Himalayas. She could almost smell the mingled scent of mud, cow droppings, and weeds.

She could not believe that the illness and death of this wife, whom she never had the chance to see, made no impact at all on Jianan's life and business. This was clearly out of cruelty and indifference instead of the religious insight into life and death.

After the funeral the crowd dispersed and she followed them back to the courtyard. Hardly had she entered her room by herself and sat down before Jianan stepped in and said, pack up your stuff and follow me.

Jianan piloted her through the crowd, passed several streets and numerous temples, and arrived at another district of Katmandu. The cement street was flanked with old wooden houses and cement low-rises. Row upon row of stores lined the road with large quantities of similar goods.

He took her to the door of a restaurant and said, this is a Western-style restaurant run by my brother. The second floor is an inn. From now on you'll live and work here.

What do you want me to do?

My late wife used to work here. You have to replace her.

Jianan, I'm not here to find part-time jobs. I'm pregnant with your baby. I'm here to marry you.

Kazan, you have to understand in Nepal, no woman can live without working.

A woman dressed in red sari came up from his side. She threw some words briskly to Kazan and dragged her upstairs.

She heard Jianan's words from behind her: this is my brother's wife. Listen to her from now on.

She remembered that for a long time afterwards she had not heard any Chinese. Jianan seemed to have vaporized and did not show up until many days later. She was left to the hotel as the lowest maid without any salary; the baby inside her became the only thing that Jianan gave to her.

She lived in a narrow room around the corner in the small inn on the second floor. It was less than two square meters with a very narrow bed and a small table on the side. The entire restaurant and the inn were run by only four staff including Kazan, so she was rushed off her feet without even time to complain. She was in charge of the keys, room-tidying, sheet washing, and floor sweeping. Sometimes when there were not enough hands in the kitchen, she was also called in to help.

She felt those days much busier and more difficult than her stay at the Rilans' in her childhood. Sometimes she could not but wonder why she would end up a free laborer of Jianan's family. In her fourth month of pregnancy she was still busy preparing vegetables, slicing onions, peeling potatoes, and making curry. When there was no water in the kitchen, she was called to fetch it from the river; when there were not enough clean bowls and plates, she was called to wash bowls. There were too few hands here and Nepalese men were habitually tardy, so sometimes impatient customers would come directly to the kitchen to give them a good scolding.

She had no income. The only money she had was the allowance that Jiansheng and Xinhe gave her, which she kept to herself carefully. She could not have her dinner in the kitchen until there were fewer guests long after the meal time, but she could not eat anything due to sickness and too much toil. She felt nauseated and dizzy with hunger. Sometimes when she finally got some sleep at midnight, guests who forgot to carry the keys would tap on her window and she had to drag herself out of bed to open the door for them.

She asked Jianan's brother where her husband had gone, but he said he did not know anything and cared nothing about his business. She wanted her salary, but the brother told her self-contradictorily that this was between the family members and the reason he hired relatives was that he could make money without paying the salary.

When she asked him more questions, the man grew impatient and pretended that he did not understand her English.

Kazan was at her wits' end. She returned to Jianan's home and asked his mother about Jianan's whereabouts. The woman was sympathetic with her and said, Jianan never stayed at home for more than a month. Sometimes he would be away from home for years when he went on business trips. Women born outside Nepal are not accustomed to the poor conditions here at first, but they will accommodate themselves in time. This is the long-standing tradition, to which you and I must submit.

He has **not** married me yet. Kazan said sobbingly.

The **mother** said, then you'll have to wait, girl. He will come back to marry you. Maybe he is just too busy. But you have to know, girl, even if the **man** marries you, your subordination and your life will not change. For hundreds of years women here have been doing housework, breeding children, farming crops and vegetables, and taking care of their husbands. Don't you understand, girl? You are in Nepal, nowhere else.

Summer was approaching and the rainy season had come. The country was seething with political unrest and there were more and more armed soldiers patrolling on the street. Dengue fever and flood swept the land.

The hot, damp air filled every corner. She wanted to have a good rest after sweating and toiling all day, but she could not get any sleep in the stifling heat until late at night. Sweat rained on her forehead.

When she tossed about exhaustedly in bed, she felt she had never met with such hardships before. She had lost her parents and lived under others' houses, but she had never felt herself a miserable girl. She believed she was destined to be lonely and faced the mishaps with equilibrium.

For the first time in her life she felt hopeless when confronted with the crushing toil. She wondered if she would live here, give birth to the child here, and tug all year round until she was burnt into ashes and thrown into the river before seeing Jianan again.

In the sixth month of her pregnancy, Jianan came back suddenly. When he arrived at the inn he saw Kazan busy working at the dim, sweltering kitchen. She was big with child and shuttled awkwardly in the kitchen with plates, her face greasy with sweat, her hair messed up sloppily, her clothes dripping wet, with crumbs of vegetables on the temples. She was too weary to even raise her eyelids and looked like a countrywoman that came to the town to make a living. Her swollen body and the sloppiness and fatigue on her face after the several months of toil formed a cruel contrast to the beautiful university student he had met in Beijing.

He was in a bad mood and felt no pity but disgust for her when he saw her sallow face. He stood aside silently smoking without even calling her. Kazan did not discover him until she turned around inadvertently.

Jianan. She mumbled.

But the man's face was sullen and upset as if frosted with ice. She was indescribably grieved.

She did not know that Jianan had back luck on the business trip. The antiques that his partner tried to export were confiscated by the customs office. He lost a large amount of money and narrowly escaped from police arrest. To make bad worse, he was blackmailed by a former mistress when he sought for her help to escape. He returned home after these setbacks with a gloomy, irritable look on his face. He had been drinking and messing about for a week at home before he went to see Kazan at the inn.

She said, why did it take you so long to come back . . .

Jianan pulled his face and did not answer her. He smoked for a while and said, you're big with child and there are gossips. I'll marry you in a couple of days. Don't you want to marry me?

9

She was despised by the family for not being a Nepalese and coming to the family pregnant without any go-between arrangements or dowry. The wedding was somewhat different from the traditional Nepalese wedding, as the procedures of picking the bride up from her home were skipped.

At the wedding, she was wrapped up in a thick red dress and painted very thick. She sat by the feast in the hot sun and was irrepressibly sick with sweat all over.

Her eyes were filled with the merry faces of those who dropped by for food and their singing and dancing, and her ears were resonant with the strange language. When the guests toasted each other, torrents of the loud noise rushed into her ears and thundered on her eardrums, creating a splitting headache. The heat assaulted her; the bright red and yellow colors swaggered before her eyes ironically like a frivolous, confused drunkard. For a moment she felt she was about to collapse and blacked out. She closed her eyes for a moment and when she reopened them, she saw Jianan still quaffing wine and frolicking in the crowd although he was slurring with drunkenness already. She did not know why, but she heard fretful cries behind his voice that almost amounted to weeps. Perhaps it was the setbacks these days.

She witnessed the festive scene and suffered agonies in her illusion. She felt so lonely as if she was hopelessly stuck in a marsh.

She married this man.

That night Jianan was still drunk. He totally forgot Kazan's pregnancy and crawled to bed to make love with her. Reeking of wine, he took his clothes off while mumbling something and fondled her with his hands rudely.

Kazan was overwhelmed in shame and shoved and pushed out of her instinct. Jianan flew into anger and cursed and beat her as harshly as if abusing a prostitute. Kazan was deeply grieved and vexed. Born not without a temper herself, she kicked him off the bed.

Nepalese women were always obedient. Jianan's anger was kindled by Kazan's unruly behavior and, fueled by the alcohol in his blood, he got up immediately and started cursing her, slapping her face and kicking her back. He was carried away in such anger that he did not even control his violence.

She ducked with both hands on her belly with thick blood running from her nose. She felt she would be beaten to death by this man and screeched desperately like someone in a nightmare. Her screams startled some family members who rushed to their room to drag Jianan away. The drunken husband was still not sober yet and kept spitting out curses.

She crawled there, crying bitterly, but hardly anyone came up to comfort her. The family simply frowned on her, as it seemed ominous to them that the newlywed couple put on such a fight at the night of their wedding. Jianan's mother walked over alone to hug her, appeased her with a slightly harsh tone, and covered her mouth to stop her crying.

After that the crowd dispersed and Jianan was taken away too. The last who left the room turned the lamp off and closed the door. Darkness sheltered her again like a flannel blanket. Outside the window the old town was still enveloped in darkness; while the new town glimmered with neon light, it was not as clear as the still, starlit sky.

She lay down exhausted with scorching pains all over. Pains could etch a deep mark on memory, but they could also give rise to numbness and in time people would become so obtuse that they felt no more pains.

She fell asleep in fatigue after the savage abuse.

She was beaten by her drunk husband on her wedding night and stayed alone in that strange room. The next day she had to return to the inn and go on with her work. It was three days later when she saw Jianan again.

Jianan visited her at the inn and their faces were both frozen. Jianan said, I'll leave. You stay here and work. He said these words calmly with no expression on his face. There was no apology.

Kazan was expressionless too. She simply said, give me some

money. I worked for you for so long; at least give me some pocket money.

What do you need money for?

I'm an adult and I can't be penniless, right? I just want a thousand rubi.

Jianan slanted his face aside with an impatient look. He clasped his teeth with the cigarette in between and counted the money fretfully. He gave the money to her and immediately turned away without any word.

Intentionally or unintentionally, Jianan never took Kazan to the immigration bureau to register for marriage. The fact was covered up in the grand feast.

She fixed her eyes on Jianan's back with the little money she begged from him. She knew her marriage was hopeless. She was determined to wait until her child was born and leave the place with it. This was the only way out.

10

During those hard days she stayed in the inn and continued her work. She was gradually used to, or rather numbed by, the toil and became more and more silent. She hardly opened her mouth all day long except for short exchanges with the guests. She was busy working quietly with sweat all over. Her mind was hollow and her body was heavy with fatigue.

She would work hard to give birth to the child alone and extend her life and the life inside her.

The rainy season was extraordinarily long that year. Flood and plague wreaked havoc on the country and there were fewer guests. In the slack season she gradually found some time to sit down quietly. It often rained all night long, and the sounds of thunder and rain were clear deep at night. She could see through the water mist the temples towering in the rain in such solemnity as if they could not tear themselves away from the dream of history. When she woke up in the morning the eaves were still dripping with water and the old black wood carving gave out a rotten, damp smell. The roof looked sad like tearful eyelashes and eyes.

When she was off, she would sit on the bench at the door and looked at the streets. She could see part of the contour of the sacred temple above the rows of old buildings. Maybe it was the royal palace.

She never got to know the names of the temples, or the Buddha, or the street and the block. She never knew anything about Katmandu or went out of Katmandu. The more backward and poverty-stricken the country was, the more it relied on religion for an escape from reality. She would sink into rambling fantasies and memories when she pondered over the deceptive belief in happiness based on pains, and her heavy body would draw her back into reality again.

The passersby on the narrow street would hardly notice the pregnant woman sitting idly on the bench at the door. She was thinner with toil and fatigue and her figure was reduced except for the enormous bump on her belly. She was obviously bent down in fatigue and exhaustion, judging from the way she sat. Her hair was tied up in a mess and her features were rapidly eroded with aging and circumstances. Toil left a clear mark on her wan and sallow face and her heart became obtuse and heavy.

She began to call Ye Lan with the money that Jianan had given her. She called her mobile and her home alternately but she either could not get through or got no answer. She kept calling for half a month and finally reached Ye Lan.

She heard Ye Lan's voice over the phone. She was speaking English and her voice was sleepy and tired. It was midnight at her place because of the time difference.

Kazan said, is that Ye Lan? It's me. I'm in Nepal. I don't have enough money now. Can you call me back? This is the number . . .

. . . I need money, Ye Lan—she told her—I need money to leave with my child. She told Ye Lan everything and asked for her help. She sounded earnest and helpless, but she retained her composure. She knew Ye Lan was the only hope for her. She did not have any choice.

Ye Lan was shocked speechless for a moment at her experience. Kazan became nervous at her silence and her heart came to her throat.

Kazan, I can give you a check, but I think you may not get away easily after the birth of the child. At least you'll have to apply for an extra visa. I'll come to Katmandu as soon as possible to take you away. Tell me your exact address, Kazan. Wait for me, she said.

Kazan heard her words and clasped the receiver. She held the receiver more and more tightly as if about to crush it to pieces.

Her heart was back in its place. She knew how cold people could be in this world and, after all the mishaps and toil, she was rimming with grateful tears at the deep love she enjoyed.

11

October came and the long rainy season had just passed. Katmandu was like a lady who, having emerged from water in a wet sari, felt cool and smooth and blossomed like a red lotus.

That day she tidied up a room, changed the sheets, and walked back to the reception desk. She did not sit long before a woman came in.

I'm here to check in, Kazan.

Kazan looked up and found Ye Lan standing right in front of her with a backpack. Her eyes shone with a complicated expression.

Within a week during Ye Lan's stay at the inn, she took Kazan to the embassy to go through the formalities to return to China. As Kazan was not registered for marriage, the formalities were not complicated. But to make sure they got away safely and secretly, she bribed the Nepalese officials heavily. After all, Jianan was a local personage and Kazan was his wife, at least at the grand wedding.

They got the tickets as soon as the application was through.

Hence Kazan vaporized in Katmandu. Her departure was so secret that no one noticed her absence. She put the room keys back to place and kept everything the way before she came. She did her job and left with a clear conscience.

She caught a glimpse of the ancient city when her plane was taking off: the dilapidated low-rises, the innumerable temples, the dark red brick walls, gray cement buildings, the black wood carving and the brown roofs. When the plane flew higher, all she could see was large patches of green hills that covered most of the undulating land. The innumerable peaks were snow-capped all year long and formed a gorgeous sight. But her vision was soon blocked by thick clouds.

Ye Lan sat beside her and looked at her. Kazan, are you uncomfortable? she asked.

No I'm fine. I just want to have a nap.

She drew back from the window, lay on the seat in relief and closed her eyes.

When she reflected over the days in Katmandu a long time later, she wondered if it ever occurred to her that she would stay there for the rest of her life, grunting under the heat and humility, bearing children, and subjecting herself to endless toil until she was dead and burnt into ashes on the riverside, like a worshiper who took up torture as mortification of the flesh.

We either end up here or there; can we take another path and avoid the hardships that life must undergo?

She felt relaxed when she had been able to have a break after the hard work, sitting on the bench at the door and watching the old town in the rainy season. At that time she would feel as if all the toil and hardships were gone. Her heart was lightened up by a spark of happiness. It was negligible and fleeting and yet it surpassed any other pleasure in the world.

It had been a sense of belonging. She had been watching the world from her own place. She had felt the same when she'd sat in the black tent and peeped at the outside world. It was the sense of the home.

But maybe it was not her home. After all, she had wanted to leave.

She felt utterly relieved and slept for over five hours. Ye Lan woke her up when the plane landed at Beijing Airport.

We're home now, Kazan, she said.

At this time last year she had still been a common university student and had lived in the dorm. But her adoptive father had left and she'd chosen to leave the family so as not to pose any burden to her adoptive mother. She had dated a stranger and left with him.

She had been obsessed with his looks without even knowing him. After two dinners she'd found herself waiting at the bridge of the third ring road for him, having sex with him in the dim apartment, and living together with him. He'd held himself aloof but she had been determined and anxious to follow him. It was in such blindness that she'd been taken to Nepal and ended up working as a free laborer at a family inn.

After all this time she still did not believe that she did all these things out of love and could not describe herself as a woman who lived for love.

A woman who lived for love. What a humble, pathetic label. As if it were an ominous door to endless disappointment and a bleak life.

She knew she was not like that. She was a lonely woman who felt keenly the breach in her heart. Life was a huge funnel to her. She tried to fill it with her moods, love, and journeys in the hope of seeing it full and perfect, but found the funnel disappointingly empty as everything was turned into time and kept leaking from the bottom. It was never full and perfect as she wanted.

Insecurity led to more danger. It was a vicious circle. Now she came to the starting point and returned to the city where she had lived for ten years.

That night, Ye Lan took her back home. Kazan could finally have a comfortable shower after the long hard time. She stood in front of the huge mirror of the bathroom and for the first time was confronted with her pregnant self clearly. She saw her big belly and felt helpless. She never expected she would be like that and was not prepared to be a mother. But the Nepalese religion made it impossible to have a child abortion. Even if she could have, she'd been penniless. So she really had not had any other choice.

She washed for a long time and the water kept gushing out in the bathroom. When she was about to go out, she heard Ye Lan's knocks at the door. She was asking, are you okay washing by yourself, Kazan?

Kazan wrapped herself in a towel and walked out. She opened the door and found Ye Lan standing right before her. Ye Lan looked at her worriedly and reached out for her wet face.

I don't know how to take care of you, Kazan. I'm scared when you had a long bath. I brought you back but I don't know how to comfort you.

Ye Lan's voice thinned out. She said earnestly, Kazan, I can't say I know you well, but I can see your loneliness and desperation. You can't deny that you were trying to escape from the isolation, or rather were guided by it. You allowed yourself to be taken away again and again, to be discarded to different places, to grope for an exit in strangeness and darkness. Then you followed the isolation back to the starting point and there was nothing but blank snow awaiting you there.

I don't know if you'll waste your whole life on such a circle. You know every circle engraved a stamp on you, be it fortunate or not. This time the stamp is your child.

My case is different. I never wanted to put myself under the spell of isolation so I've been waiting here for my destiny to find me. It was out of the same hope that you departed again and again. I wouldn't say your efforts were vain, but I'm sympathetic with you.

We can only offer that much to others throughout our lives. I'm afraid I can't even manage to offer it well, Kazan.

She said, this is pretty much all I can do to help. You need to go to the hospital by yourself soon. You can live here as long as you want and hire a nurse to take care of you. But I'll have to go back to the U.K. now. I'm on my leave after all. I'll come back to see you at Christmas.

I know you've been taught to be independent by the isolation. You left your family for the fear of posing a burden to others when your adopted father left. Now I tried my best to help you. However little my help is, I know you will appreciate it.

She looked at Ye Lan and said calmly, yes. This is a huge favor and I don't know how I can ever repay you.

Chapter VII

Time coincided in a tree.

The old boughs and leaves huddle together like a lid and the new boughs are growing on the top of them. Time inscribes history on the tree and the eons are extended to the present before they fade away.

The old and the new and the past and the present are not foes. They recognize each other in the journey of time and head for the same destination of beauty.

Jian Zhen, "The One in the Eye"

1

When he had lived with his mother during those early years, summer always meant to him the sweltering air, the scorching sun, the damp and hot wind and the wet clothes with sticky sweat.

His mother's world had remained an ambiguous, unhappy riddle to him. As a woman of obscurity she'd undergone many hardships and had been disappointed at the fickleness of the world. She'd suffered from hyperthyroidism and had flown into an uncontrollable rage easily. As some say, it is hard to determine whether mishaps lead to complaints or complaints lead to more mishaps.

Since he was a little boy Jiansheng had known that into a shut mouth flies flied not. He had been so frightened by his mother's capricious temper that he had been depressed even at the thought of her. Silent avoidance had been his only resort.

He would hide himself in the corner where his mother could not see and observe her with melancholic eyes. When he'd seen his mother's face frozen he would withdraw to his own room in the fear of getting beaten by her.

When he'd returned from school in the summer and thudded over the staircase upstairs in sweat, he would bump into a familiar man on the corridor who swaggered down, seething with contempt. They would glance at each other in passing.

He might have seen the men more than once or never. Perhaps they had not been his mother's lovers at all. But he could not help associating them with his mother and found the liaison sickening. Of course he hadn't known at that time his mother had been forced to trade her body with these men in power.

He would slide into the room before his mother noticed and never emerged out again. He'd done his schoolwork, painted, and read. He'd had a quiet world all to himself.

He and his mother had been strangers for too long a time to feel comfortable in intimacy and affection.

He remembered how, one day after he got back, his mother had been in high spirits for some reason and smiled faintly. He had not known why and had entered his room as usual. After a while, his mother had knocked at his door when he was doing his schoolwork. She'd entered with a bowl of melon pudding. The pudding had looked lucent and smooth in the delicate glass bowl, and small chops of watermelon were mingled with it. The snack had just been taken out of the frige and looked cold and refreshing.

His mother had stood by him and said, I know you like melon and pudding. I was free today and found some melon in the frige, so I mixed them together. Try it.

Jiansheng had been overwhelmed by the unexpected favor. In his excitement he'd taken a large bite at once. But he'd found that melon had gone bad. His mother might not have known it. She had been so busy that she often bought things and did not remember to take them out of the frige until a long time later.

She'd looked at her son with expectant eyes. She'd kept asking him, is it good? I'll do it for you in the future if you like it.

Jiansheng had never seen his mother smiling so gently and pleasantly. He'd been too happy to tell her that the melon had gone bad, so he'd beamed with a smile and said, it's really good.

His mother had lit up and sat down by him. He'd known she would see him eat the pudding up. So he'd buried his nose in the bowl and looked up into her eyes, smiling after he finished it.

His mouth had been sour. The sourness had gone all the way to his heart.

His mother had been kept in the dark and had smiled and left with the bowl. She'd said, now go ahead with your homework, sweetie.

His mother had closed the door and left while Jiansheng sat still at the desk. As a sensitive boy, he'd been grieved when he thought how hard he'd tried to beg for his mother's love, however little it was. He'd wanted to bend over the desk and cry, but he could not shed a tear. It had been his simple but earnest wish that he would see more of such affection and happiness on his mother's face.

His wish never came true. His mother never treated him as gently until the last dinner he'd had with her, the night of his eighteenth birthday. That day she'd bought him a sweet cake that gave the same sour taste in his mouth.

He knew that in his painful adolescent years he'd pinched his only hope on Huai. Huai had given him more attention and care than his mother or anyone else. His attachment to Huai had hence become profound and complicated. He was always ready to do anything to prolong such attention and care.

So he did not regret giving up his family, forsaking his wife, leaving Kazan, quitting his job and possibly ruining his career. This was not a choice of reason. It was deplorable to observe his obsession with memories and his inability to tear away from the shadows and regrets of his adolescent years. He could not do away with his past, just as he could not erase the scar on his chest.

After all, not everyone would stab himself in such desperation.

Jiansheng took nothing with him except his clothes and some paintings he did as a boy. Having been rubbed for a long time, the pencil traces on the rough paper had faded away like water ink and the clear and even strokes had been obscured.

On the plane, he browsed the sketch book with the broken sentences and felt sorry for the past.

Memory was always beautiful. There were those who, when retelling the past, would rescue a memory from imperfection by polishing it with illusion and vanity, no matter how awkward and disgraceful the experience was. But such temporary relief could never take them far in this rapidly changing world.

Well, in this world where turning back was despised as weak and shameful, one would never arrive at the eternity he set out for, no matter how long he walked and how close he might get to his dreams. Men were creatures enslaved by regrets and aspirations. They could neither go far nor turn back on the one-way street of life.

Jiansheng returned to his home.

Huai was surprised to find him at the door. She never expected him to be back. She was used to being pessimistic about whatever promises others made to her.

Welcome back, Jiansheng.

She let Jiansheng in, but the latter looked at her with a blushing face like a happy boy. He put the small luggage down and asked her, are you better these days?

Huai smiled without saying yes or no. She shifted the topic naturally and asked how long he was going to stay here and if he was on a business trip.

Jiansheng was surprised at her questions. He stood still with the cup in his hand.

Don't you know I came back to take care of you? I've divorced my wife, quit my job and terminated the adoption with my daughter. I did everything to come back here. I meant to adhere to my promise. Why did you ask?

Huai smiled apologetically and awkwardly. She said, I'm sorry, Jiasheng. I never expected you would fulfill your promise. I really didn't expect you to do so much for me. You don't really have to do that.

Jiansheng was disappointed. Huai was still staying as aloof from him as he had been accustomed to before. He paused a while, put down the cup and said, after all, I've come and I can't go back, right?

Where can I put my luggage?

It was true that she never expected Jiansheng to be back, but once he was back, she was ready for the change. She had let her mother leave and had been living alone. Huai always took things as they came. She would have lit up if Jiansheng came back, but she could live alone if he did not.

What more could one do with others' promises?

The winter in South China was mild. The air was damp and warm like tears. There was no snow and green leaves were seen everywhere. It rained continuously. One could easily fall asleep at night with the sounds of rain by his pillow.

This must be the most peaceful state of life: returning to a childhood home in a warm winter, listening to the rain at night, and knowing that the beloved was sleeping in the next room.

His first night at Huai's was very peaceful. He had not enjoyed such deep, dreamless sleep in many years.

2

Huai, we can meet so many people throughout our life. We can spend a day, a month, or a year with them no matter whether we love them or not. When it is time to part we say goodbye to them without regret and find the next partner to spend a day, a month, or a year with.

It's pointless to say this man is lonely and that one is not. People differ from each other only in their attitude towards loneliness.

They fear loneliness because they fear the sublimity of the world. After all, human existence is so small and so transient compared with the universe. Such people like to accentuate their existence through excessive give and take of love. They want to bring themselves hope and comfort by overexerting themselves, but their vain efforts simply prove further the essential loneliness of their being. Sometimes they want to talk while no one is there to listen, and sometimes there is someone to listen when they do not care about talking. What an irony!

I know you are not one of those people, Huai. The give and take between us is so natural. I often feel that to you the course of life is but a stroll around a lake. You set off, go through a path interspersed with scenery, and return to the starting point at last. When you see a wrecked boat that floats towards the bank, you kindly stop for it, bail water out of it, fix it, and maybe walk along with it for a while. But when the wind is up and the boat is gone, you continue your journey peacefully.

You are that traveler and I am the boat you repaired. My sail is confined to the lake where you are and I long for you as the green waves long for the bank. I float only to meet you again at the next stop. If you can't move on, I'll take you along to the last wharf.

This is the best I can dream of as a boat confined to the lake of love. After all, the lake of our bond has presented us with beautiful scenery on our way.

This man who compared himself to a boat had a rugged face that bore clear traces of his adolescent years. He had changed little since he was a boy.

What a special, "unfinished" man he was. An average, mature man at his age would have learned to be forgetful and selfish. He would have known to take up responsibilities and let them go with the equal ease. They would have grown obtuse and solid with the passage of time and gradually decayed and faded away. They would have learned to expect nothing from the fixed grooves of life or groaned over his wasted talent. But Jiansheng believed in other things.

He was searching for the memory and light of his heart.

3

Before the winter vacation, Jiansheng began to offer painting courses for young students at a private atelier with the help of his acquaintances.

As a talented and diligent painter, he was a rising star in the circle and had just held a tour exhibition in several cities. Many people could not understand why such a professor from the top academy of fine arts would quit his job and offer painting lessons for kids in South China. But he never regretted his choice; he found it the only path to a rich and fulfilling life.

Huai was tired out after teaching the students of the affiliated high school for a whole day. She suffered from occasional spasm and the pains were spread to her limbs. Jiansheng tried to persuade her not to work any more, but she rejected his advice with a smile.

I may not be able to work any longer before long, but not now. She said, I need to work. I don't want to stay at home sick in bed day in and day out. Insipidity would make me lose hope in life.

Jiansheng only taught lessons on weekends and had a lot of spare time. He did household chores, tidied the rooms, and bought many potted plants and placed them on the balcony and the windowsill of every room. They were plain, regular plants: jasmines, gardenias, violets, cornflowers, and roses. He liked the way their faint scents floated about the air like the silhouettes of the memory.

He planted four morning glories on the balcony and made a trellis of poles for them to climb up.

An iron racket was fixed at both ends of the balcony to hold up the clothesline. So he found two baskets of maize-yellow cane, grew draping bracket plants in them, and hanged them up on both

sides of the rope. He believed that in the next spring or summer
the balcony would be covered with green foliage.

It took extraordinary patience and internal peace for a man to
enjoy growing plants, if he did not do it for a living. Jiansheng not
only loved tending flowers but also took great pleasure in decorating the rooms creatively. He removed the old lampshades and
replaced them with new ones made with delicately folded waste
blotchy Xuan paper and bamboo braces he collected. They took
various shapes: pyramid, taper cone, and irregular tube, etc. The
shades gave off an elegant light when the lamps were turned on
and looked like ink and wash drawings. What creativity!

He measured the waste splints at home and painted many small
sketches of flowers and plants. Most of them were bright watercolor
paintings, but there were gouache drawings and oil paintings as
well. He then framed the sketches with the splints and hanged
them up on the walls to cleverly cover up the pits and blotches.
Not all of the frames were complete. Sometimes there was only
one long flint left, so he would only fix the wood on one end of
the sketch, make two holes in the flint, and hang the sketch up
with a thick rope through the holes. The decoration was plain and
minimal, but with taste and originality.

Flowers were grown in plain glass vases everywhere on the tables
and cabinets. The green stems were deflected in the clean water
and presented a peaceful sight.

On her way back from work Huai would always guess what
new changes Jiansheng had brought to their home. The guesses
always filled her heart with sweet pleasure and made her all the
more impatient to get back. She would look around when she
entered and discover the unexpected little improvements like a
child ferreting for gifts in the corner. She was always able to spot
them in the first minute and rejoiced at them with smiles beaming on her face.

He would stand behind her and put his hands on her shoulders.
Do you like them? he would ask.

Jiansheng, you are my Santa. She would say with a big smile.

They dined in the kitchen. On the small walnut table a vase of white calla was placed close to the wall. There was a quiet elegance about the flower. On the table the thick plaid tablecloth was spread and several dishes were placed with inverted bowls over them to keep them warm. The chopsticks were ready too. He was not a good cook yet and served simple dishes and soup. But the dishes tasted fine.

Jiansheng always believed that careful management of life served as better therapy than medicine. A good mood, a regular schedule, clean and nourishing food, refreshing air, green, fragrant plants, and beautiful music were all good for Huai. He tried his best to offer her all of these.

The southern regions were never lacking in fruits and vegetables. On their dinner table there were always big plates of triangular slices of watermelon, peeled grapes, or chopped peeled peach. The fruits had bright colors and looked very appetizing. Sometimes he gave her a glass of fresh juice with a little sugar, which was mellow and enticing too. In the sitting room records were played on the gramophone; they were often slow cello solos and sometimes Russian folk songs by bass soloists. The elegant music flew nostalgically like a river. The two of them would sit face to face, chatting and laughing. Jiansheng spoke the gentle Northern dialect and his rhythmical voice was very comforting.

This man had been in love with her since he was a boy and was now by her side, looking after her and decorating her home.

Huai was so happy that she often feared sentimentally that such peace would end some day.

They retained the habit of strolling after dinner in the evening.

The air was chilly in the winter when they stepped out. The night sky was clear. On their way, Jiansheng told Huai about his experience as an overseas student in St. Petersburg. He said, I often came across plainly dressed couples who whispered to each other on the Neva. Once I was sitting on the bank working on a sketch. It cleared up after the snow and the sky was lucent and clean. The setting sun shone over the snow and the icy-cold air was very refreshing. In the distance were the spires of the Eastern Orthodox Church, which were covered with snow like what you see in fairy tales.

When I was drawing, a middle-aged couple was standing not far away from me. They were graying and looked rather stout in their black coats. They remained silent while following the flow of the river to the distance with their eyes. I was about to leave after drawing a long time when I heard the man saying in English, darling, are you cold? The woman said, no, dear. But it's time to go home.

Then the two of them quietly left the bank hand in hand as usual. They were like two doves who guarded the church when they stood there. They exchanged no hugs or kisses, not even a word. Between them there was only silence, and being.

They must have been an ordinary happy couple from Europe who went to Russia for holiday. I relished their brief exchange; their relationship must have been steady and close like the way they walked together. Words could not do justice to the beauty of such peace.

But now that I reflect over it after the many years, I realize how stupid and greedy I was then. Xinhe was right beside me at that time and we had been living in peace like that couple. But I turned a blind eye to the precious peaceful life we shared together and envied the happiness of others as if I were not as happy as they were.

Perhaps I could only make up for all the misery I brought to her in the next life.

Huai was silent. She could see his struggle and doubts. But all she could do was take things when they came. If he turned around at last and went back to pick up the happiness he cast away, she could do nothing about it. She only hoped to prolong this beautiful dream.

4

Jiansheng spent nearly a year with Huai from winter to autumn. The life was extremely quiet and he felt as if he were sinking slowly into the bottom of the sea. When he sank further and further the sounds on the shore faded away and light went out at last.

Light was still lingering outside the window. It lingered in time, memories, experience, illusions, and dreams. It lingered in Debussy's piano compositions. She was still sitting in the room facing the window with her back to him. Light waltzed through the lush leaves on the balcony and danced about her body into a lustrous halo around her. She was glistening to every single hair. Her body was wrapped in white pajamas that turned almost translucent in the sun. She was so thin that the pajamas draped like a hollow cicada casing. She always turned her back to him so that he would never get to see her pains.

It's fine today. Jiansheng. I've never seen a sunny day like this.

Huai had stopped working. She was no longer able to work, for her hand would be seized in a spasm at any minute and unable to hold the brush. Her feet were numb, painful, and unsteady. She could only stay home, sleeping long hours and stretching her body according to the doctor's advice. He looked at her from the back and said, Huai, we'll go to the hospital tomorrow for examination.

Huai said, I'd rather not go there any more, Jiansheng. It's pointless. I'm all right.

Once they fell ill, people did not have many choices and had to be confined to bed and subject themselves to the manipulation of others. There were different therapies for different diseases. Injection, fluid infusion, traction, drainage, puncture, blood purification, transplant, and chemotherapy . . . once they were in the sickbeds shame and self control became luxuries. What they could control were family and friends sitting beside them, if there were any. So they began to moan, to demand this and that, to rattle away their misery and pains to the visitors, and to murmur in such a feeble voice that the visitors had to bend down to hear them. They did all these to make up for their weakness and powerlessness. They asked in panic, Doctor, am I going to die?

All men die sooner or later. But men were always greedy and could not resign to fate when faced with the deadline.

She did not want to find herself confined to bed and subject to others' manipulation, or manipulating others with her illness. She chose to stay at home and die slowly with a smile, as if nothing had happened. Actually, when you truly believe that nothing has happened, that something will become invisible from your consciousness. This was a positive self deception; or in a more eulogizing way, everything was a product of the mind.

She struggled to live on with such mentalist beliefs, so he decided to satisfy her practical needs. He took care of her, bought medicine, cooked, washed, and tidied and decorated the rooms. They strolled together and painted together.

As they slept in separate rooms, Jiansheng became a light sleeper and would wake up at the slightest noise. Sometimes he would get startled when a car passed outside and cast a light through the window on his eyes. When he woke up, he would get up to see if Huai was okay. He would stand at the door and pull the door backward an inch. If he found it dark and quiet inside he would return to his room in relief. He visited her room so often that it almost became a compulsion.

Every time when he was at the door peeping at Huai's blurred shadow, he would feel as if he were still that boy who had just lost his mother and fallen inextricably in love with the woman who took care of him. When he lay in bed, he would be obsessed with the thought that his beloved was sleeping in the next room and toss about uneasily for a long time without any sleep. He wanted to get up and have a look at her, but he was afraid to disturb her and returned to his room quietly. He went to bed and tossed about again and the day broke in a while.

He was still under the spell of the adolescent hunger for love and, fueled by the Oedipus Complex, had been loving this woman obstinately. He was so attached to her that he found himself unable to love or face others' love with equilibrium.

What a lucky and gratifying thing it is, now that he reflected, to live with her day and night, see her beloved face, and share pains and happiness with her.

She knew it every time when he peeped in her room. Sensitive people always sleep lightly. No matter how gently he pulled the door, she could hear it and feel his gaze in the darkness. The door would be closed after a while and the room would be quiet again.

She was in pain indeed. Her forehead and limbs were aching badly and her entire body was numb. But she endured it quietly in bed. Pains always kept her alert. She knew her pains would never go away when she groaned and asked for help, so she taught herself to endure them.

During those sleepless bright nights in pain, she would look up and watch how the chilly silver moonlight poured onto the floor and how the carving in the lattice and the potted plants cast down shadows on the bedside. It was so beautiful.

5

One morning in November, she woke up and saw everything in doubled, blurred images. It took her only a second to accept the fact. She knew she was visited by diplopia again, which was worse than last time.

Jiansheng walked over and bent down with a smile, did you sleep well, Huai?

Huai pondered if she should tell him. After some hesitation, she decided not to worry him as she thought the symptoms would be gone after a while. After all, she'd had a fit or two six months before and recovered for no apparent reason. So she said calmly, yes. I'll get up right now.

She knew she would need time to get used to the vision. She narrowed her eyes and sat for a long time on the balcony. The flowers that Jiansheng planted were growing robustly. She felt peaceful when she saw a blurred vision of greenness. For an entire morning she did nothing but sit there and feel herself warmed up inch by inch in the sunshine. She could not do anything anyway. It was noon before she noticed. She heard Jiansheng calling from the kitchen, Huai, lunch is ready.

She sat down at the table. With her blurred and overlapping vision she had to take caution at every move now for the fear of breaking any bowl and alerting him.

He did not know Huai was as sick as that.

He took Huai out to stroll that evening and found that she put her arm in his and walked at a slow, hesitant pace. Jiansheng asked her, Huai, are you aching again?

No. I just want to walk slowly, she said.

That was the first time they walked with linked arms like a couple.

She was clear about Jiansheng's love for her from the very beginning. She used to bear no hope for love, but after all these years she never expected that the boy in love with her would come back to her and take care of her with such resolution and patience. She was so deeply touched by the depth and profundity of his love that she felt that speech amounted to nothing at all.

Jiansheng was whispering in her ear, are you tired, Huai? We can go back and watch a film if you don't want to go further. It's a rare film and I bought the disk.

He did not know her eyesight was failing. And she did not want him to know it.

What's its name?

Blue. Derek Jarman directed it. I've been looking for it for a long time and found it at a stand on my way back from the supermarket this afternoon. So I bought it.

Is he the English painter Jarman?

Yes, but he is not only a painter. I saw his *The Garden* and *War Requiem.*

So she sat next to him and saw a blue screen. From the beginning to the end, blue was the only color she saw of the film. She could see nothing else.

The noises at the corridor of a hospital, the roll call in the waiting room, footsteps, a sharp, brief noise as if some machine was burning, the waves, and so on. The narrator told every detail of his memory and life through the voiceover: his broken shoes, his friends, the last days when he was sick with AIDS, the ennui in the waiting room, the nurse's intravenous injection on his right arm, and the news he read on the newspaper about the refugees. His voice was calm and clear and interspersed in the many noises of life. He murmured in a low voice: Blue, blue.

As if calling a lover by the seaside.

Such a film might not be loved by everyone, but it always left a deep impression. She asked Jiansheng to find more information about Jarman and read it to her.

This blue British man was a director, and also a poet, painter, botanist, and social activist for the rights of homosexuals. Born in Italy, he had loved painting since childhood and used to hold exhibitions in Japan and other countries. Later he dabbled into film making. The films he shot were guided by his painter's instinct and cared nothing about the story. He was an avant-courier director who sought for a subversive expression. He died of AIDS in 1994 and *Blue* was his last film. He was completely blind when he shot it.

He said, I want to shoot a film and let people know what death is about and what living with AIDS patients is about. So he left the world with this film of sounds and memories and passed away.

Some said he was a prodigy, a hero of the homosexuals at that time, and an avant-courier in subverting the cinematic expression. He left in curses and worship. He wrote in his last journal, I sit on the canvas chair and gaze at the direction where the sun sets, and the full moon rises behind the lighthouse in the evening glow. The pebbles in the garden glisten in the moonlight. They can hear me humming tunes in the kitchen.

Later people read in his epitaph: I lived in love.

"The pearl fish in the Aegean . . . the deep sea water scored the deadly island . . . in the gentle breeze . . . slept the lost boy eternally . . . the hugs and the salty kisses we exchanged . . . our names will be forgotten and no one will remember us . . . I put down on your tomb a blue glade of delphinium . . ."

The director refused to offer images in this film. He was blind and his film was blind too. There was no character, no story, no scene. It was blue, the color of the shroud, the color of silent distress. It was also the color of the sky, the sea, and the delphinium.

Humans perceived their existence by sight and hearing. If a healthy man woke up one day and found himself blind, deaf and deprived of every means to believe in the illusions of the world, would that be an approximation of death to him?

At the end of the film, Huai felt uneasy, as if she was facing her own reflection in a clear mirror.

6

One night in December she went to have a shower in the bathroom. Jiansheng prepared a tub of hot water in case she caught cold.

Do you need my help, Huai?

She shook her head.

Call me if you feel uncomfortable.

Okay.

She took off her clothes and immersed herself in the tub. The water was very hot and the excessive heat quickly overwhelmed her. She tried to bear it, but she soon felt very uncomfortable with chest tightness. When she sat up to reach for the tap she found herself unable to move. Panic-stricken, she struggled again and again, but was frustrated to find that her legs were stiff and powerless, and her fingers and arms refused to budge as if fastened to a plaster board.

Huai lay in the hot water gnawing in fear and anxiety. She would not reconcile to the fact and tried to move herself. But her body was beyond her control and splashed the water loudly. She called him, Jiansheng, Jiansheng, and found her voice feeble as if her throat were choked with something.

Jiansheng heard the noise in the bathroom and came to knock at the door. Are you okay, Huai?

The noise of the bathroom quieted down into a frightening silence.

Can I come in, Huai? What happened to you?

He heard no answer and was more frightened. He pushed the door open with a bit hesitation.

Huai was lying in the bathtub. Her face was pale in the steam and her body was stiff. She explained, I was trying to turn the cold water on when I found myself unable to move, Jiansheng. She sobbed while she finished these words feebly.

Jiansheng walked over and held Huai up. He felt her entire body stiffened.

This was the first time that Jiansheng saw her naked body, but he never expected the occasion to be so cruel and heartbreaking. The body before him was broken, stiff and pale like an old plastic puppet. The sight slung such pangs in his heart that he could not bear to look at her. Jiansheng helped her sit on the edge of the tub, wrapped her up with two big towels, and helped her up into the bed with both hands.

He sat on the bedside, dried her with the towel, and helped her lie down under the quilt.

The drastic change of heat and coldness plunged Huai into bad spasms in the limbs. Jiansheng sat on the bedside and watched her. Her pains, her spasms, her loss of control, her misery . . .

His tears were rolling down in threads. He bent down and held her head to his chest. Huai, Huai, he murmured her name.

The woman in his arms burst into an uncontrollable convulsion. He found the Baclofen tablets, poured a glass of water with trembling hands and tried to feed them to her.

Open your mouth, Huai . . . he pleaded her in sobs.

He finally put the pills in her mouth, but he was not able to deliver the water amidst her spasms. His own hand was shaking involuntarily and spilled half a glass of water on the quilt after helping her with a sip.

He hugged her carefully and tightly like a pot of tears that was as thin as paper and fragile as ceramic. He stroked her back again and again to comfort her and alleviate her pains.

Huai, Huai, he murmured, overwhelmed in surges of black sorrow.

Deep at night she gradually quieted down in Jiansheng's arms. He could feel her fatigue and pains. After the endless struggle she closed her eyes in exhaustion and fell asleep quietly. He sat on the bedside and lay her down slowly.

Darkness and silence gradually immersed her.

After the attack Jiansheng was very worried and took her to the hospital. The doctor scolded him severely when he heard that she got the spasm for bathing in hot water. You almost killed her, you know? This is very dangerous.

She was examined and required to stay at the hospital for observation.

During her stay at the hospital the doctor changed his prescription and Huai was not attacked by the spasm again. She kept walking slowly for an hour every day and gradually increased the amount of exercise.

Jiansheng always stood by her side and supported her considerately every time when she walked out of the ward. She, however, was overwhelmed by his patience and love and always hesitated to accept his help. This man was too perfect for her to even dream for.

When they strolled in the recuperation area of the hospital she said, I know you will never rest assured until you see me treated here. But you know therapy is futile. The disease is complicated and there is no effective way to cure it. Meanwhile I'll have to lie in bed and undergo all those expensive, pointless examinations every day. I've been sick for years since my divorce and am used to it. I can take medicine and exercise anywhere. I don't really need to stay in the hospital, Jiansheng.

People in good health often forget what a blessing it is to be healthy and take it for granted. But I have no grudge against my illness when I think it over, however painful it may sometimes be. After all, I lived most of my life healthily and now I'm simply returning the health when it's due.

Jiansheng, I don't want to spend the rest of my life at the hospital.

But what do you want, Huai?

Let's go to Lingxi, Jiansheng. I want to visit there. It's been a long time since our last trip there.

7

Jiansheng, do you remember when we first came to Lingxi?

Yes. It was a summer vacation. You took the five kids of the painting class on a bus trip and stopped to paint sketches when you saw good scenery. I remember we climbed a hill and rested and painted at the top. We were all tired out and complained but you were very nice and patient. The wind was up on the peak and I could still feel the goose bumps on my skin at that time. The air was very refreshing and pierced through our chests. It was evening when we got to Lingxi. The town was flanked by the lake in the front and the hills in the back and traversed by a brook. We had dinner together and I took a walk alone. I was mesmerized by the beautiful landscape and forgot to return on time. You came to look for me deep at night and we walked together along a small path.

The moon was bright and cool that night. We spent a couple of days in the town and you said you wanted to go up to see if there were more spots on the hills where we could sketch. I wanted very much to go with you and kept glancing at you. Later you agreed to take me along, but I stumbled on the way and made a mess . . .

You remember everything so clearly, Jiansheng. I have gradually forgotten the details, but I have the impression that the place is quiet and green. With these words she seemed to sink deep into memories and her voice seemed to flow up in the air.

On their way to Lingxi Jiansheng and Huai exchanged sporadic comments. The trip was long and Huai dozed off from time to time. Jiansheng watched her sleeping face calmly and soberly. But all of a sudden he felt as if that long-cherished dream of his came true.

In the dream he and Huai hopped onto an old, empty bus that drove slowly into a damp, lush forest. Green vines dangled outside the window and dripped with sweet dew. Even the sun beams turned green and pierced through the dim bus. The breeze that lifted up the hair on Huai's temples was as cool as a green jade.

Huai, I missed you so much.

That dream of his boyhood still lingered at the summer many years ago. Now winter had settled on the forest and gloomy clouds shrouded the hills. It was chilly. The windows were covered with a mist of water as if salivating for a grand breakfast they had long waited for. He held Huai's hand and fixed his quiet, sentimental eyes on the clouds and the forest.

It was evening when they arrived at Lingxi. The small town was shadowed by the hills and sank into an indigo-blue glow. Broken, bean-like lamps flickered from the depths of the narrow lanes and the light was reflected on the damp, lustrous flagstone walks like a galaxy of fallen stars.

The town was bleak. It was not a scenic spot in the first place and had fewer visitors in the winter. He and Huai decided to stay over at the same guest house. They walked across the tranquil courtyard amidst the fine rain and went upstairs. Their room was minimally furnished with two clean wooden single beds and white walls. The beams and lattice were made of old, precious brown sandalwood that gave out a mellow smell of time. The windows opened to a beautiful, tranquil view of the river and lamps of the Lingxi town.

They saw clearly how beautiful life was in such tranquility. One always has to trek through innumerable muddy and bumpy roads to savor the most profound sweetness at the heart of his fate. Conversely, it is in the expectation of such moments that one lingers on life. The world becomes expansive when everyone dwells in his dreams, but it is also because of the expansiveness of the world that we keep forgetting the first dreams we had on our way.

This is the paradox of paradoxes: the paradox of life.

Huai, if I had not loved you, I would never have been able to go so far in the world of art with so many beautiful memories. I did undergo anxiety and confusion, but I always remember the goodness and beauty of the love. I never forgot the impossible gap between us. We were never a perfect couple in others' eyes. We are hardly a couple. But you know we can only love once in this world and give that much to our beloved. We keep the rest to ourselves to improve and continue our being. I would not know how to survive without you, so I need you to be there for me. Don't reject me or doubt my love because you feel it too profound and unreasonable. After all, I love you so willingly and obstinately only to mend the gap in my being, so this is a well-meant, selfish act indeed. This is the true cause of every great love that remains hardly known to the world.

He said these words when he strolled with her that night.

That night in winter the sky and the earth were solemn and still. Thick patches of dark blue clouds drifted on the night curtain like faint songs. They walked through the desolate lanes of Lingxi with misty moonlight lavishing quietly behind them.

During their stay in Lingxi they strolled about and recollected their past. They would take food and drinks and hop on a bus to sit a whole day on the lakeside. Jiansheng took his drawing board and pigment along and spent all day painting plain watercolor or pen sketches. When he sat down and set pen to paper he was as focused as an innocent child. She would sit happily beside him and watch him painting. Sometimes she was touched so greatly by his concentration that she wanted to stroke him on the head. She felt as if he were still the lonely, quiet lad in the corner who learned painting at her summer class. She remembered how his handsome face was half hidden behind the easel while his eyes glimmered sorrowfully and affectionately like a lake.

He finished a sketch with several strokes and presented it to Huai in childish pride. Do you like it? he asked. Huai would hold the sketch up at an arm's distance to pretend she was observing it carefully.

Jiansheng did not know that Huai's diplopia was so serious that she could no longer see clearly what he drew.

That day she was in high spirits and invited him to climb the hill, like what she had done many years ago. As it had been a while since anyone visited the place, the path was slippery and some sections of it were covered by shrubs and reduced to inches. This time Jiansheng walked ahead of her. He reached out and said, come, Huai, come over.

Huai put her hand in his palm. Nostalgia filled her heart when she found the two of them in reversed places. Many years ago she walked ahead of Jiansheng and turned back to find the boy glancing at her with a blush after stumbling on the path. At that time she reached out and said, come, Jiansheng, come over.

How they had altered! She followed the man up the hill in deep nostalgia. Jiansheng kept turning around and asking her, do you need a rest? Do you want to go back? She shook her head with a smile.

She was tired and in pain. But she said nothing; she lowered her head and struggled ahead. The tall trees all over the hill hid the gloomy sky over their heads. The forest was very damp and cold. A mist of water rose up and the lonely, melancholy song of a bird was resonating in the woods.

They watched over the familiar town from the hilltop. The green trees looked gloomy and chilly in the winter and were not as luxuriant and bright as in the summer. A mist enveloped the woods and the cold blast whistled by and pierced their lungs. All she could see was blurred, overlapping images like misplaced film. She had become used to the double vision after so many days and never revealed it to anyone. But she felt it such a pity at that moment that she could not see clearly the scenery in her memory. The sorrow slung such a pang on her heart that she could not remain still, as if a vibrating bell in resonance.

They stood shoulder to shoulder for a while quietly, deeply immersed in their respective memories. As they had done many years ago.

Let's go back. She said.

Deep that night her feet began aching acutely after climbing hills all day. She felt clasped tightly by an invisible hand and her body was burning as if pricked by a needle. She could not get any sleep and tossed about in pain. But she remained quiet until her body was tired out and gradually stiffened.

Outside the sandalwood window it was pitch-dark night. No light pierced through the darkness. She struggled with the pains for a long time and fell asleep in fatigue. That night was exceptionally long. She woke up again and again and it was as dark as ever. As if weighed down by the darkness, she could not even lift a finger. So she fell asleep again and again.

Jiansheng's voice was beside her. She heard him calling her name, Huai, Huai.

What?

Are you aching again?

I'm okay. I had a fit at night but I slept it off.

Do you need more sleep, Huai?

What time is it?

Ten.

Ten . . . ?

She opened her eyes wide. It was ten in the morning but all she see was darkness.

At that instant tremendous fear surged in her heart. She tried to reach out for something to hold, but she could neither raise her arms nor lift a finger.

She could no longer hold back her fear and tears gushed out of her eyes. Jiansheng saw the convulsion of her arms and bent down fearfully: What happened to you, Huai?

After a long while, she said in a feeble voice, Jiansheng, I think . . . perhaps I'm blind.

8

An icy rain began to fall when he left Lingxi with her in a hurry. It was dark and gloomy. Huai could no longer walk now. Jiansheng held her up with his hands, fought his way through the crowd, and hopped on a bus awkwardly at the bus stop of the town. As soon as they were in the city, he took her directly into the hospital.

He always remembered how he fled the town. When he fought through the noisy crowd he felt as if he were in a dream and could hear nothing at all, as if the noises were muted by an invisible hand. All he could see was the people who struggled miserably and groped blindly, crying for help at the bottom of the wheel of fortune.

He was stuck and lost in this absurd, indifferent world, holding his beloved woman in his arms in despair and anxiety.

Huai was blind already. When she was sent to the hospital all her muscles were stiffened and she could not speak or move her limbs. At the hospital the rude, impatient nurse pushed a cold wheelchair over to them and said to Jiansheng, help her sit in the chair. Come with me and pay the bill.

The corridors at hospitals were always cold, gloomy, endless, and smelt of peroxide. Jiansheng sat on the bench in the corridor and quietly gazed at the wheelchair by his feet. It glistened coldly and clanked against the iron frame of the chair when it was rudely pushed over. The clanking sound resonated with hollowness and indifference along the corridor.

For two consecutive days Huai was continuously attacked by fits. When her mother and her sister hurried over to the hospital from their hometown in North China they jolted into the most horrible scene:

Huai was lying in bed in continuous convulsions. She muttered unintelligibly like a patient with cerebral palsy, with the water of her mouth dribbling along her chin and her blind eyes staring in a dark, hollow direction.

Jiansheng was holding her head up and trembling involuntarily in sorrow.

This was Huai, the girl who used to be as pretty and sweet as a violet camellia. She was his first and last love for whom he waited early at the atelier on those lush summer days and by whose apartment he lingered all night long. She was the woman who took him home without hesitation and took care of him carefully when he was desperate and suicidal. She was the woman who accompanied his adolescent years after his mother's death. She was the one whom he could not forget from his childhood. His beloved.

With her virtue and beauty she deserved a long, healthy life, a faithful lover, and a peaceful, painless death at the velvet bed of beautiful memories.

But now she was stuck alone in this dark, blind world and struggling in pains. Her ghastly pains stabbed his eyes like a sharp dagger.

Jiansheng was in tears at last.

In the days that followed she was attacked by convulsions more and more frequently. The convulsions gave rise to respiratory failure and cardiac arrest and she was sent to the emergency room twice.

During her last days in that winter the only ways for her to get out of bed and move about were sitting in the wheelchair or lying in Jiansheng's arms.

She lost control of her body and needed to be taken care of twenty-four hours a day. She would fall silent on the balcony of the ward and was seized by a spasm all of a sudden. Her neural system was quickly breaking down and no medicine could help it.

It was very cold that night. The wind kept whistling outside and the windowpanes were shaking. The lamp in the ward cast down a ghastly white light. The night deepened and it was time for her to go to bed. Jiansheng held her up as usual and put her in bed. Her bony body felt light in his arms like a handful of dry grass.

When he held her up close to his chest, Jiansheng heard her mumbling something.

She was blind already, but she seemed determined to say something. Jiansheng put her in bed and bent over again and again and pressed his ears on her lips to hear what she said. But he could hear nothing except indistinct guttural sounds.

Hot tears rolled out of Huai's dim eyes. Her voice thinned out until it perished totally. Jiansheng knelt by her bedside and held her cold hands.

What do you want to say, Huai? What?

His chest was slowly weighed down under an enormous, silent power. It was so enormous that he bent down his body and buried his head in his lap. He was blind and deaf at that moment as well.

He saw her again.

In the first instant when his life began, in the lush summer of his adolescence, he visited her for the first time.

He came to her door nervously and knocked at it politely. She was casually dressed in dark draping pajamas and opened the door with her empty hand while holding a paperboard with the other hand and a charcoal in her mouth. Her hair was tied up, her slender neck was bare, and her collarbones were as obtrusive as those of a skinny boy. She had clear, regular features and her skin was as white as the magnolia downstairs. She smelt of plants.

She stared at this nervous boy in surprise.

The boy asked uneasily, may I attend your painting class?

She paused and said with a smile, of course you may.

The boy was so excited that he floundered, thank you. Thank you.

9

Have you witnessed someone dying?

You saw through the glass she was lying there in another drastic convulsion. She gave a last lonely, hoarse groan when the splitting headache began. She had been mute for a long time. Blindness. Dribbling, incontinence of urine, loss of self control, involuntary exposure of her body, endotracheal intubation. She was inserted with tubes all over and wired to various equipment. Continuous cardio-pulmonary resuscitation. This was the third time she was sent to the emergency room.

The white matter in cornus ventriculi lateralis changed pathologically and the lesions stiffened and turned white in the medullary sheath. She lost her consciousness and the damage was irrecoverable. She could only inhale and exhale with the support machine. The nurse came out with the à la morte notice and slipped a pen in the old woman's hand to sign her signature.

The old lady trembled and collapsed with the pen in her hand. You went over to help her stand.

In the next twenty minutes, her heart beat for the last time. She respired autonomously several times, then her pupils dilated and her breath stopped. She quieted down and stopped struggling in pain, lying there with closed eyes, as if she was in a peaceful sleep.

Ten minutes later, the doctors gave up. They tore away the equipment, took out the tubes, and drew the white sheet up to cover her body. Then they walked towards you.

But why? Why would you see her face as soon as you shut your eyes that night?

You saw the stamps she engraved on your life and those moments. They were the memories and slight touches that she gave you when she was alive. They were the sobs of guilty conscience and regret over the unspoken words. They were the deep inscriptions of a family. However, that once lively face and the hands that used to touch your face had sunk into coldness. They were utterly deprived of life.

She was unable to leave any word before she left. Her departure was as clean and aloof as her life.

Jiansheng was informed of her death at the hospital and was nailed to the ground. He did not even shed a tear.

He used to cry sadly when Huai was seriously sick, but he faced her utter departure with composure. He found everything taking place at such a rapid and unreal pace that he felt as if it were all leaky illusions that were fabricated in the haste and deserved nothing but laughter. He was also relieved to hear that she finally got rid of the pain.

He was not sad because he always felt she was right there. Or, sorrow turned mute when it rimmed over the limit. As the greatest love needed no expression and the greatest music had the faintest notes, greatest sorrow would only be silently savored for the many long years afterwards.

Huai was pushed by two nurses to the mortuary. They had witnessed too many deaths to be moved by them. Huai gradually disappeared in peace, as if she would arrive at a more beautiful world after she transcended the tunnel. Jiansheng did not walk up when she slowly passed by him. He stood still while fixing his eyes on her. His mind was as still and dark as the bottom of the sea.

Huai's mother and sister, however, were overwhelmed with sorrow. The old lady collapsed into the bench on the corridor and wept and wailed. It was a heart-rending sight. He could not bear it any more, so he squatted down after a long while and carried the lady on his back out of the hospital.

It was still and dark that night. There was no wind or moon. One or two stars were scattered on the night curtain and glimmered faintly. He stood by the street with Huai's mother on his back and hailed a taxi to take her and Huai's sister home for a rest.

It was early morning, but the world did not wake up yet from its fatigue.

10

November saw the first snow in Beijing. Ye Lan gave Kazan a call from the U.K. and told her she would come back to see her at Christmas. She said over the phone, go to the women's and children's hospital, Kazan. Go right away.

She answered, all right, all right. Don't worry.

She waited for the childbirth alone at the hospital. The young mothers-to-be beside her were mostly surrounded by families, but she did not envy them. She felt relived and comfortable, now that she did not have to slice onions at a small restaurant in Katmandu one hour before childbirth.

That day she was sleeping in bed when she felt someone touching her face. She opened her eyes and saw Ye Lan. She reached out to hold her hand in her excitement.

Welcome back, Ye Lan.

She had taken an international flight and come all the way again to see her from the other side of the earth. If she were a lover, such earnest concern could have been explained easily, but Kazan knew how precious Ye Lan's affection was for a childhood friend.

Ye Lan bent down to kiss her forehead with a smile beaming on her face. She was always so beautiful.

It snowed heavily the night the child was born. She was exhausted and felt little delight, especially when she saw the newborn was tiny and pitiful just like a mouse, with slime and blood all over itself, and its skin all wrinkled. Held in her hands, this bloody little thing, only as big as her two hands, was so stunning to the sight.

Yes, when he was washed clean and grew up a little, skin tightened, wrapped in the white and soft towel and brought to her, his lovely and tender baby face would arouse immense fondness. However, the unwelcome spectacle was the very debut of life. Human beings can choose deaths without pain, blood or wailing, but cannot avoid births with pain, blood and wailing.

She closed her eyes and felt the welling of an indescribable pain. She was crystal clear that this was a sin. She was not entitled to pass on all her wandering and resolution to this baby. He was doomed to face the absence of paternal love, while his mother was not at all prepared, not able to give him a satisfactory life, not even a home for his cradle. There was no idea how he was going to carry on.

She had an undulant mind and suddenly burst into tears.

In those three days and nights, she suffered from extreme fatigue and lapsed into sleep and woke up time and again. However, once she closed her eyes, she would see the landscape of her homeland. It was when her mother was still alive and carried her on her back when she went on a pilgrimage. On the broad back of her mother, she could feel the grand warmth at her bosom from the maternal body beneath. The alternation of her bending down and standing up made her dizzy and excited. The dazzling sunlight lifted the sky so high that the shiny rays splashing arrogantly from right over her head made her unable to open her eyes.

It turned sunny after the snow. The blazing light from outside the window shone the floor white and clear. Time stopped there. She could feel her mother's hand on her forehead, stroking gently.

She opened her eyes and saw Xinhe and Ye Lan by her side. Xinhe stroked her face with touching gentleness and tender love.

She asked, Kazan, are you alright? I've come to take you home.

Kazan fixed her eyes on her face, speechless. Being touched, her eyes were filled with tears.

I've come to take you home, Kazan.

11

How were you doing in the year away from home, Kazan? she asked.

She had no idea how to begin. It was her own choice to leave the school and follow that almost strange man to many a place, get pregnant and finally settle as a laborer in a small hotel in Katmandu. She went through hardship and endurance, but she got to leave.

The hunger of the soul and the fever to pursue that initiated this life of a flotsam would wear out after all, and left her in fluster. She didn't feel frustrated. The years did go by fast but would appear so dragging in a recounting. Kazan looked at her mother, not able to come up with an answer.

So she asked Xinhe back: How are you?

She of course could imagine. In the extremely lonely period after Jiansheng left, Xinhe lived all alone. It is common for women in love.

She had worked fanatically then, locking herself up in the dark-room all day long, processing reversely the black-and-white roll films, experimenting her innovative techniques time and time again. She had pursued the extraordinary effect to such an extreme but for countless times ruined her work with mere carelessness and had to start all over again. In the red room where the films were hung all over, she had used a timer to rigorously set the time for each process, three minutes, five minutes and thirty seconds, etc. Standing there, not knowing the time, she had dimly remembered something, or nothing. Sometimes between the silences, her tears would fall into the fixative. When she'd walked out of the darkroom, it was dark outside as well.

She would open the fridge in a search for fast food, sit on the sofa to eat it alone, feel the hunger, but not be able to swallow.

She would spend a very long time in a shower in the bathroom and fill the home with the hollow clamour of water.

She would walk into the bedroom and lie down at midnight. When the light went out, she only got the company of the silent night.

Darkness is the grounding of sleep, dreams and peace. Darkness is different from shadowiness. Darkness is the boundless tolerance, a warmth as sorrowful as tears, massive enough to house the inner world.

She felt herself a woman against light.

That day, Ye Lan came to her door and told her about Kazan's difficult situation. She asked her to go to the hospital and bring Kazan home. Hearing these things, Xinhe didn't hesitate at all. She went with Ye Lan to the hospital.

She took Kazan home and arranged her in her old room. She also bought a crib and put it by her bed. More baby things were brought home. The house was alive again with the baby's crying, the talking, the food, the towels, the clothes, the nursing bottle, the one-off diapers, the pots and pans and everything. It was completely a different scene from the former quiet and lonesome single life.

Her dark life order was broken and the light shed over it again. She treated her homeless daughter with patience, and the newborn boy, too. Xinhe didn't have her own child. Gazing at this strange and fragile life in her hands, she couldn't help feeling sad.

She loved the baby. In order to take care of the baby, she even gave up her work at the studio. The baby slept in daytime and at night, but would turn energetic during the small hours. At his cry, she had to wake up and check if he was hungry or thirsty, or troubled by a wet diaper. A few times later, he was finally put to sleep, but it was often twilight. A delicate uneasiness was turned to willing efforts by the fondness deep in her heart. This protected the little life from the worldly bitterness and let it grow up safe and sound, carefree.

Kazan got protection and peace again. She was back in this nest of goodwill and grace, like the lucky baby. She felt like she was back in the old good days. Those were the most peaceful and beautiful days she had spent. Sun rays from the seams in the curtain, blended with the scent of the warm bed sheet and the sweet newborn, created a dreamy peacefulness. That was a sudden bliss.

Was this a circle of life, back to its starting point?

It was in the small hours. The baby was asleep, but they were not any more. Sitting there, they talked on and off. Kazan asked about Jiansheng. Xinhe looked gray and low.

I was not immediately able to face the fact that both of you left. There was sorrow and the difficulty to control myself. After that, day and night, I thought it over and believed he deserved forgiveness. That poor thing. He was a weak man, too weak to shoulder the full responsibility of a complete man. He did not have the stoutness and broad mind to gain oblivion and to say goodbye, while he was so kind-hearted that he pushed himself into an awkward position. Or this was destined. It may have nothing to do with his character. Even when he was negotiating a divorce with me, his thinking logic was very simple and idealistic.

I have come to reconciliation with everything out of my love for him. I still miss him very much. I don't know if I've lost him forever. I don't know if he's really not coming back any more. But I hope he will. To some extent, I know he cherished me, and needed me, just as I needed him. The two needs were totally different, but this mutual need brought us together for such a long time.

Kazan, you know I loved him so much.

12

The plants on the windowsills had died for days of lack of water. Jiansheng cleaned them up one after another. These were the plants that he had grown for her. As the old saying went, men had feelings while plants did not. But after Huai passed away, these plants also followed her in death. The mysterious bond between her and the plants made him sigh with deep sentiments.

During the days when he waited for Huai's cremation, Jiansheng stayed at home taking care of Huai's mother and sister and cleaning up everything from albums and letters to electric appliances and furniture.

He took Huai's paintings out one by one from the old boxes and gently wiped off the soft dust on them. On the yellowing sketches the pencil traces were blurred indistinctly and the small unframed oil paintings with the rugged edges turned gray. He examined them one by one carefully and slowly as if exploring the crumbs of rocks on the fault of time.

He asked the old lady when he did not know how to dispose of the objects. She said, sell everything, please. When my daughter lived here this house was clean. Now that she is gone, I want it to be clean too.

Nostalgia was the most powerless and humble thing in life. When it was time to bid farewell, there was nothing that the living could do to hold back the dead. The living would die as well, which formed the transmigration of souls and the continuation of life.

Jiansheng used to regret that he had sent her back to the hospital in such a hurry. What a peaceful death it would have been for her if she could have slept in his arms amidst the flowing brooks and glimmering lights of Lingxi.

He knew he was about to leave for good, so he went to visit his mother's tomb.

It was a rainy morning. He stood there by himself and placed a bouquet of white violets as usual. The four-character epitaph was inscribed with bold strokes at the back of the tombstone and covered with green moss. No word could do justice to the stillness.

As the ancient said, one should take good care of his parents while they were alive instead of throwing grand funerals after their decease. One had to learn to forgive and love when his family was alive to end his life with a clean conscience and no regrets. Funerals, however grand they might be, would never make up for regret in life. He did not realize the profound meaning of this saying until he was in his middle age, after several decades. He never expected that he could have the opportunity to make up for what he did not do for his mother, with Huai.

He was kept in the dark about his mother's affection and love for him by the mishaps in his life. Therefore the relationship turned ugly and tempestuous. It was too late when he finally realized the truth, so he could only swallow his sobs with regret. Men were always like this.

He stared at his mother's tomb for a long time. He knelt down, bowed to her, and got up and turned away.

Spring Festival was coming. He disposed of the house and Huai's stuff, bid farewell to the city to which he was no longer bound, and took a train with Huai's family to carry her ashes to her hometown. He could not afford three plane tickets, so the three of them had to take the cramped train. It took them two days to get there. The wheels clanked on the railway and the sound resonated in his heart.

After the many peaceful yet profound incidents, he slowly sank in the drift sand of time on the wilderness of life. He sank further and further until he was stifled. He redeemed himself through self-cleansing. On the train Jiansheng fell asleep in fatigue amidst the noises. There were no nightmares or frustration. But he could no longer see the lush forest and the morning glow as reflected in the dew. He was finally able to reach the other side of pure equilibrium.

But I'm still missing you, Huai.

13

Jiansheng came back to the North. He felt at home as soon as he set his feet on the sublime northern land. Huai was buried in her hometown. The funeral had been simple, sad but peaceful. He only remembered in fits of sorrow as he saw the birds flying across the sky and the black cigarette powder fluttering in the air. The sky was cold and the wind was whimpering.

At the end of a year, people and things tend to settle down in perfection. He was relieved finally. After all, he finished a good deed with all his efforts, from the very beginning to the end, enough to put a period to this love. He felt broad and calm.

He had also given careful consideration to where he should go afterwards. He smiled at the thought that he would have boldly followed her to the other world if he were in his younger days. However, the worldly path he had taken put his heart at ease and made him understand that to live is harder than to die, and life is more to cherish because of this hardship. He had taken a burden of others' love. He owed them. It would be heartless to leave. Only those who are brave enough to endure the hardship and elegance of living are entitled a glorious death.

Without much hesitation, he thought of going home. If he had always been wrong for giving his heart to his bedside companions, it was time for him to become sober.

Xinhe. After all, she was the nice lady he had decided to spend his life with. It was all natural like the start. It was all out of his own will.

He returned to Beijing alone.

It was the Eve of the Lunar New Year with a flurry. Florid fireworks filled the city night with a jolly atmosphere of celebration and cameraderie. In a telephone booth by the street, he dialed Xinhe's number.

He heard her voice, so familiar. Sorrowful warmth surged and left him speechless for a long while.

He could only utter her name lightly, Xinhe.

The inquiring was put to a stop immediately. Both ends were silence.

There was a long silence. The noise in the surroundings died down as if at the ticking of remembrance. They could almost hear each other's breaths. Standing in the glass booth, he could feel the surging in his heart but could not utter a word.

A graceful golden firework rose in an instant and unfolded its petals with leisure in the depth of the night sky. It transformed into thousands of flowing splendors and shed beautifully down to earth from over his head. Jiansheng raised his head, his face lighted up by the bright firework.

He asked, Xinhe, may I come home?

I've been waiting for your return.

She said.

Quilt Is the Tomb of Youth
An Acting Afterword

When I wrote down the title—"Quilt Is the Tomb of Youth" once again after three or four years, I keenly and honestly felt the soft melancholy aroused by the remnants of the puffed-up sentiments in my mind.

Quite a few days have passed since I tried to do some serious writing for the first time. However, those vividly emotional hours, like thriving plants, still abounded with fresh juicy substance and grew robustly in my memory, which, I believe, will carry on in the future.

Let us recall what we said at the age of sixteen, which I took from your notebook:

There are things out there that are meant to be perfect and there are people out there who are meant for you beyond your imagination. I have made the best of whatever God endowed me with and composed a seventeen-year story of joy and sorrow with clear marks left by the people and things on my way. Now I've learnt internal peace, lies, composure, silence and resilience. Therefore, when the happiness I gleaned on the way broke into a floorful of glaze pieces, I managed to stand firm in the wind and sweep them into the darkest corner of my heart. It did not matter any more. I learned to smile brightly to others while my soul was bursting in sorrow or hesitating in the silhouette of melancholy. I learned to be strong at all times.

These are the sentimental passages that we chanted at the age of sixteen.

Now that I reflected over my first essay, "Quilt Is the Tomb of Youth", I burst into laughter from time to time. I cannot but sigh with gratitude for those tolerant and patient senior writers who bit their tongues and clenched their teeth when evaluating and awarding such childish, sentimental scribbles. Their kindness and understanding gave us the earliest encouragement and momentum on the outset of our writing career.

On the other hand, our self mockery and understanding laughter in the review of the past writings also show that we did not spend the past years in vain. We did grow up after all.

This is a summary of my thoughts when I reflect over the previous nineteen years.

In fact, I started the conception of this novel early on but encountered great difficulties soon after I started. There was also a large blank interval in the course of my writing during which I did not touch it at all. Later I proceeded and altered it beyond recognition. I did not know why I tortured myself in writing it out day in and day out. As soon as I was seated before my computer, I suffered from a stomachache. Sometimes the stomachache grew so acute that I had to curl up in pain. But once the monitor was out of my sight, the ache would disappear. This has remained a mystery to me till now.

I poured my nineteen years of life into these characters, words, sentences and passages and now gladly present to you all of them, their beauty and flaws alike. I did not realize how hard it was to face her past and express it with ease until I completed the writing.

Although I have to apologize for my naïveté in the words above I do not regret saying them. For perhaps the past nineteen years is just a beginning.

Qu He said to me after reading the earliest part of the draft:

. . . . . .

. . . . . .

You were the first who popped out of my memory when I thought of those who traveled a long distance. The night before you went to college, I asked about your past jokingly. Your past was certain to contain many hardships besides the part you revealed to me. You were afraid to give me the impression that you were complaining all the time, but you might not know I always understand how difficult it was for you to accomplish so much. I always fancied that you would conceal all your past some day and only reopen it on real, pressing occasions. This is what I required myself to do all these years. So I have to say sorry, for I had just realized in my unconsciousness I was always imposing on others those things which I took as good. I used to believe I could keep aloof from others in my observation; this is easier said than done, as I used to dream of handling complicated matters in a simple way, or at least expressing them simply.

I said you always looked back, but the comment had nothing to do with your writing. I never thought the work was a failure. But if it were composed by another person, I would be pleasantly surprised. However, it was by you. I could tell at first sight that you were still caught up in the memory and seemed to dwell there forever. I used to think that writing is a gesture for us to say goodbyes: we leave heavy thoughts to our writing and lightness to our life.

. . . . . .

By no means can writing empty our past. Language takes the place of thought and memory is deepened and reconstructed in our writing and narration. In time we will forget the original look of a thing and remember only its representation in literature and the unreal but keenly-felt pains.

I was told that Chinese are implicit because they would rather keep the wonderful things to themselves than spell them out. It is true, but it is only one side of the coin. Expression is a boundary that one has to take caution to cross over.

. . . . . .

Your neurotic sense of responsibility resembles the preponderant style of your work. Or maybe it was the style that enlightened your thoughts? However, I must admit a cliché that while any utilitarian composition will go astray from the writer's true nature, there is no such writing that is absolutely free from a purpose. However, the more ambitious we are, the further away our writings will run from our true nature. If you base the deviations on lies it is certainly admirable, but if they spring up from reality, what we miss most in the records will leave an inerasable stamp.

. . . . . .

. . . . . .

Although she wrote me this letter for some other reason, my tears began to drop when I read the fifth sentence; when I finished reading it, I could not control myself and covered my face with both hands.

I do not know how many years it has been since I was so deeply touched.

What I tried to hide with an elaborate scheme and relatively awkward means was eventually found out by others.

Yes, we are grown up. Words cannot do justice to what we feel about many things. I used to seek redemption from language but more often than not found it became fetters to me, as I was not strong and courageous enough to face language earnestly, writing and memory alike.

I am still not sure how I shall face language, but the one thing I do know for sure is that I will try my best to handle it in my own way and never give in. When it comes to writing and speaking one has to be respectful. The two things are worth our awe, respect and efforts.

To be frank, I will spare no effort in such a cause. After all, humans have limitations.

I dreamt an unexplainable dream from time to time:

My heart is like a vast plain on which lamps are sparsely erected. The travelers can only see the sparks they give off, but they never know the darkness in between.

I thought about this dream many times. It may be a metaphor of my inner world. To a certain extent, I deliberately avoided and despised the so-called symptoms of adolescence such as melancholy, puffed-up feelings, pessimism and tears and have not seriously and honestly reflected on those dark silhouettes in my mind for a long time. However, darkness does not vanish because I avoid it. On the contrary, as I never faced them squarely and solved them, the darkness festered like stubborn diseases and rotted away behind the disguise of light pleasure. Someday the wound would ulcerate beyond cure and I would be torn apart by the dark internal urges and the bright surface. It is like the heart-land: the bright sparks are for others to savor, but one has to solve the darkness in between.

We all know most people are not like what they appear.

Perhaps sentimentalism is not a shame. But we, or rather, I, need to consider it earnestly and glean more significance from those thoughts that survived the passage of time. I will keep what I gleaned in mind and forget or forgive the rest. I will grow up and learn to appreciate in this process.

I am always slow and awkward in such evolution of the self. But I know I have been striving from the very beginning.

There are many friends whose generous help I want to acknowledge. They helped me with my growth and filled my way with precious and beautiful memories. Perhaps they would never read my novel and would never recognize it was me who wrote the novel they are reading.

But you know it. I will always remember you.

This book is just a beginning. In the course of the writing I tried my best in conceiving its structure, but regrets and defects are unavoidable. All in all, I still believe that this was the best I could offer by now. I know it is difficult, but I still hope that the novel will become a farewell on my way. As I said just now:

What a good thing it would be, if we could really handle complicated matters in a simple way, at least render them simply.

LaVergne, TN USA
25 February 2010
174200LV00003B/42/P